THAT FIRST
Night

JENN MCMAHON

BOOK ONE OF THE

Firsts in the City

SERIES

Cover Design: Emily Wittig

Editing: Caroline Palmier

Proofreading, Formatting: Cathryn Carter

———

For Gigi,
I wish you were here to read this. Thank you for always pushing me to believe in myself and chase after all my dreams. This one's for you, my angel.

For Kelse & Briel,
This one's also for you girls. If it wasn't for both of you saying my
crazy idea to write a book wasn't so crazy, I would have never written
the first words and this book wouldn't be in the hands of readers. You
inspired these friends. I'll forever be grateful for your friendship.
Powerpuff girls for life.

CHAPTER ONE
Peyton

"I'm not cut out for this shit," I mutter to myself as I slip into a fancy ass dress.

It's way outside of my comfort zone from what I'm used to wearing. I'm the one you'll usually find wearing a black pair of yoga pants, an oversized tee, and my hair up in a messy bun. Certainly not this elegant black gown and dressed to the nines.

"Would you just relax, Pey?" Avery says to me from the couch. "You look fucking hot."

I'm wearing a slim fit floor length black gown. It's strapless and shows every curve I have, leaving little to the imagination as far as my shape goes. And trust me, I have shape.

"Kali, are you *sure* you don't want to take Avery tonight instead? You know how I get in social situations," I say with a baby-faced pout.

"No Pey." She raises her finger and points it to my chest. "You're not getting out of this tonight. You promised me you would be my plus one to this charity gala." Now she's poking me in the chest.

"Ugh Kali...fine," I huff as I retreat away to her bathroom to finish getting ready.

I don't understand why she asked me to go in the first place.

We are going to a charity gala tonight for her job. Kali is an editor of a popular fashion magazine in New York City and her boss contributes to many different organizations that support children in all different circumstances. Tonight's event is to raise money for children with pediatric cancers.

If it wasn't for the children, I would be doing everything I could to get out of going. I am not the friend you want to take to a social event, because I am quiet and have social anxiety. Even tequila doesn't loosen me up enough to be comfortable at a social event.

And Kali knows this about me.

She was there when I embarrassed the shit out of myself our first year of college.

All my life I had wanted to be a teacher. I love kids and I love being around them, which is why I've worked in a daycare center for the last two years. Part of the curriculum for first year students was taking a public speaking course. Our very first assignment was a *"How to"* presentation where we had to pick a topic to show the class. Kali crushed her presentation, of course. She has always loved fashion, so she did a full presentation on how to accessorize sweaters in the fall. The class loved it!

My presentation was a total fail. I mean, I ended up passing by the skin of my teeth. I did a presentation on how to make my signature vegan chocolate chip cookies. When I walked up to the podium, I tripped over my own chair because I was so nervous and that caused some students in the class to chuckle at me. My face became hot, and I probably looked like a tomato by the time I got to the front of the class. When I finally got myself together, I realized that all my cards were out of order.

While I stood there, the giggles from the class kept coming. I was already so embarrassed, so the last thing I wanted to do was make eye contact with my classmates. I knew that if I kept my focus on Kali, I would find enough comfort to continue the presentation.

Only when I looked up to find her face, she had a straight look of horror plastered on her face, almost like she was embarrassed for me. Giving her a little *'what is it'* look, her eyes trailed down to my chest and then back up to my eyes. Her eyes got wider as if to tell me, *'Look down, sis.'*

When I looked down, I noticed the top three buttons of my blouse were completely opened, exposing my thin white lace bralette.

I had basically flashed my entire COMM 110 class.

I ran out of the class so fast with tears streaming down my face.

I am forever grateful that my professor let me restart the presentation after I had collected myself and I got a C+ on it. I took that as a major win, because you know, C's get degrees. And I'm not talking about my tits.

So yeah, the anxiety is real.

I have no idea how I managed to have two best friends who are total extroverts. They would prefer to go out on Friday nights, while I would much rather stay in and rewatch episodes of *Friends*, drink wine, and eat cookies.

But I promised Kali I would be there for her.

So here I am, in this tiny New York City bathroom in Kali's apartment, finishing the last curl of my long, blonde hair. Shuffling through my bag, I find some bobby pins to style my hair half up to keep it away from my face and slightly off my shoulders.

I'm not the type of girl who should be wearing this dress. I wouldn't consider myself to be a bigger girl, but I certainly don't have a model type body. I am self-conscious of my shoulders and chest area. I have a little extra fluff around the armpit and it's the exact reason why I hate strapless dresses, but Kali gifted this one to me and I found that it covered up my insecurities beautifully. Kali tells me that I'm nuts for being insecure about things like this, but as my best friend of 15 years, she's required to say these reassuring things. But wearing this dress, I actually believe her.

As I step out of the bathroom, fully ready to go, Avery lets out a low whistle from the couch.

"God. DAMN. Pey," she says with wide eyes. "You're a fucking knockout."

Avery has no filter on her what-so-ever. We welcomed her into our friend group 5 years ago when she moved here from Vermont and was hired as an assistant to one of Kali's bosses. We fell in love with her no bullshit attitude. Out of the three of us, she's the wild child. She was the missing piece of our best friend puzzle and ever since, the three of us have been inseparable.

"I would literally fuck you right now if I had a dick," she says as she walks into the kitchen to refill her glass of wine. "Maybe tonight is the night you find one to fulfill those *needs* of yours."

"Avery," I say as I send her a pointed glare. "You know I swore off any form of dating after the last failed attempts."

She tips her head back and lets out a loud laugh, "Did I say fuck about dating?"

"Avery—"

"Pey, she's got a point," Kali chimes in as she walks down the hall to join us in the kitchen.

Changing the subject, I say, "Kali, you look absolutely stunning."

Kali smiles and gives us a little *look at me* twirl.

She is wearing a deep maroon floor length gown. It has a halter top that dips low enough to show some cleavage. She has a rack that is perfect for this dress too. Her long, dark hair is pinned into a top knot bun, exposing her entire back. She makes a top knot look so elegant. I would give anything to have even an ounce of the confidence that she has.

Kali finishes twirling as she says, "Don't try to change the subject. Back to you, Pey. You have needs. You don't need to have a dating label," she says making air quotes, "with someone to have the most epic orgasm of your life."

How am I friends with these two, I swear.

I have a history of failed relationships. I don't even know any more if it's a me problem or a *them* problem, but they always end terribly. I even had myself convinced that I had a sign on my head that said, '*You should totally cheat on me.*' Because that's how my last relationship ended. The sex was mediocre at best too.

And my problem? I think I get too attached too easily.

When I fall, I fall fast.

This has caused me to develop a whole bucket of insecurities when it comes to dating.

"You guys know how I am. I can't let myself get into a situation where I become attached," I say pouring a drink of tequila and lime. "One epic orgasm and I would spiral right into the needy girl wanting more."

"That was 3 years ago. You have come so far since then, Peyton," Avery says, taking a seat at the counter bar stool. "And besides, not every guy out there is like Dick."

"His name was Richard."

"Po-tay-to, Po-tah-to." Avery laughs.

Kali touches my wrist so delicately as she says, "Listen Pey, I understand your hesitation because of your dating history. Ave is right-"

"Damn fucking rights, I'm right," Avery says, punching her fist in the air.

"Bitch, would you shut up for two seconds and let me finish?" Kali says to her.

Avery lets out a small laugh while sarcastically rolling her eyes and takes a sip of her wine.

"Anyway, you can't let the hurt that Richard caused stop you from going out there and being open to something coming into your life. You're still a young spring chicken at a ripe 22 years old." She puts her arm around me. "Not that you will find Prince

Charming tonight, but you just need to go there with an open mind."

"And open eyes," Avery cuts in, fanning her face. "So many rich men in suits."

"You're such a horndog, Ave." Kali laughs.

"I just don't think I'm ready," I say, looking down at my wrist, twirling my bracelet around.

"Let's just see what happens, okay?" Kali says coming in for a hug.

"Yeah," I say, wrapping my arms around my best friend to return her hug. "I'll try my best."

"You two get the fuck out of here," Avery says, throwing herself on the couch. " I have a date with *Friends* and the rest of this bottle of wine. I need to figure out if Ross and Rachel were really on a break or not."

"I'm so jealous," I whine. "That's my favorite show. Why can't I stay home?"

"Because you have hotties to meet," Avery says. "By the way, Pey. Did I tell you about my coworker who hates that show?"

"She does not!"

"She does, girl. Like how the fuck is that even possible?" She throws her hand in the air. "Someone said the word seven and my mind went right to *that* scene." She laughs and throws her hands around in the air to prove a point. "You know, the scene! And no one understood what I meant. I felt so out of place."

"Trust me, I know, Ave." I laugh at her. "True *Friends* fans know what you mean when you throw your head back, close your eyes, lift seven fingers and repeat *seven, seven, seven,* over and over again."

Avery throws her head back and laughs. "You get me, babe. You get me."

"The Uber should be here any minute," Kali interrupts, typing away on her phone.

Looking in the hallway mirror, I apply the bold red lipstick Avery gave me that is so not me, but I trust my two friends.

Taking a step back, I look at the full-length mirror giving myself a once over. I run my hands down the dress to smooth it out to perfection before I fluff out the loose curls cascading down my back.

I can't believe I am doing this tonight.

"Alright, let's get this night over with."

CHAPTER TWO
Thomas

"I can't get enough of this shit," I say to my brothers and best friend. "Free whiskey, gorgeous women, and appetizers being passed around all night? Sign me up!"

I'm sitting at the bar of the Edison Ballroom in New York City with my brothers for a charity gala that supports children with pediatric cancers. Being born into money has given us the luxury of being able to give back to so many charities like this one. Our father founded Ford Investments, and as I am the oldest child, I took it over at the age of 22, when he passed away suddenly, four years ago.

Dad was in great health when he developed pneumonia that took a turn for the worse. He was always a stubborn mule who hated doctors and believed he was fine even when he was the sickest in his last days, but his respiratory system failed, and we ultimately lost him.

My father always donated to these events, and I always said I would continue to donate on his behalf when I took over.

Everything I do in this business, I think, '*What would Tom do?*' I looked up to Dad so much and the loss hit me hard. Every day, I strive to make him proud of the man I am today.

Proud of the multi-billion-dollar business owner I am at the age of 26.

Proud of the older brother I am to Marc and Oliver and my little sister, Emiline.

Proud of the son I am to Ann Marie and being there for her. My mom is just as stubborn as he was, though. She coped with his loss by traveling the globe with her friends to keep her mind off losing the love of her life. I used to try to call and check in on her often, but finally I just let her be the one to check in because she lives a busy life. I hear from her every couple of months which works for our busy schedules.

"Dude, the women at these events are always unreal," my best friend, Logan, says next to me, taking a sip of whiskey.

Logan comes to these events with me strictly for the whiskey and women. Typical fucking playboy if I have ever seen one. Come to think of it, I have never seen him in a relationship in all the years I have known him. We are basically the same person, which is probably why we are such good friends. He's a police officer in the city and always makes sure to book time off for these events so he's not stuck working them. From the stories he tells us though, I think he picks up more chicks when he's working. Women seem to love a man in uniform, but I don't get it.

"These fucking dresses," my brother, Oliver, pants like a dog in heat as a blonde passes by him in a bright red dress that looks like it was painted on her. "Be right back, " he says, getting up as quickly as possible to go after her.

"Fucking Oliver," I scoff and shake my head at his antics before turning my gaze to Logan, "Bro, how did last night go with that blonde?"

"Dude, you have no idea. She rode me like I was a fucking porn star. I was all about her spending the night for round two, but she had to get home to her kids." He takes a sip of his whiskey. "Moms are fucking hot, dude."

"She was a mom?" my brother, Marc says, almost spitting out his drink that he was sipping.

"You would never know with that tight ass body," I comment.

"Don't talk about my MILF like that," Logan spits back.

"Woah, *your* MILF?" Marc laughs. "Have you heard from her today?"

"Well, no. We didn't exchange numbers." He shrugs.

"Fucking dumbass," I mutter, as I throw my head back and laugh.

My brothers and I are some of the most eligible bachelors in New York City. I love women and I love fucking them. But I am not a relationship man and have no interest in being tied down to one woman for the rest of my life. I don't see kids in my future, and I don't see a house in the suburbs with a stupid white fucking picket fence.

Listen, I know that I'm far from Prince Charming. We fuck and then I never see them again. It just works for me. My younger brother Marc; he's looking for all of that. He wants a wife and kids. I've seen him in plenty of relationships and he's the Prince Charming type. But he gets attached too easily and I think the girls run when they realize that. Can you imagine being tied to the same woman all your life? Sex with the same woman all your life? No thanks. I like a little variety.

My youngest brother, Oliver, won't ever get married or even date for that matter. He's the free bird of the family and a total wanderlust. He wants to have sex around the globe, backpack through Europe and doesn't seem to stay in one place for more than a month.

Then there's our baby sister, Emiline, who is only 16. And as her older brother, I can't allow her to ever date or have a boyfriend. Fuck. That! I am very protective of her to avoid slime balls like her brothers who are only after one thing.

We're typical guys. What the hell do you expect?

"What about you, Marc? Anything on your radar here?" I say as I scan the room.

"No one here is doing it for me," Marc says, scanning the room.

"Stop looking for a wife for five fucking seconds, Marc." Logan laughs, slapping him on the back of the head. "You do realize you have to date someone first before you marry them?"

"Stop being a dick." He laughs, slapping Logan back on the arm. "You think I don't know that?"

"I'm just saying, bro," Logan says, opening his arms as if to showcase the entire room. "We're surrounded by some of the most beautiful women in New York City. Relax on the wife shit for a minute and open your eyes."

"Logan," Marc hisses. "I know how to do relationships, unlike you fuckers. I actually want to sweep a woman off her feet."

"I know how to sweep a woman off her feet," Logan snaps back. "All I have to do is roll up my sleeves, because you know women love some arm porn. Then pick her up, throw her over my shoulder and toss her on the bed. See? Swept off her fucking feet."

"You're the biggest dumbass I have ever met." Marc shakes his head and takes a sip of his whiskey.

"You two keep bickering," I interrupt, rising from my bar stool. "I'm hitting the can before this show starts."

"Logan, shut up." I hear Marc snap to whatever Logan says as I walk away, shaking my head at my brother and best friend arguing back and forth.

As I start walking towards the bathroom, someone causes me to do a double take at the big double doors that enter the ballroom. Call it a weird buzz in my body, but I'm drawn to who's standing at that door like a moth to a flame, causing me to stop dead in my tracks.

I can't see her face, but it's the long golden blonde hair pulled back that hangs down her back that catches my eye. It's so long that it almost reaches her ass. Her perfectly round ass, might I

11

add. I can tell it's a perfect ass, because her floor length black gown leaves nothing to the imagination. I can picture myself with both hands gripping that ass from around her waist as I hold her flesh with my body.

Holy. Fuckkkkkkk.

I continue to stare and it's as if she can sense me, she turns around in slow motion. When I say slow motion, I feel like I'm watching a film and the clip speed was turned down just for me. Right now, it feels like the entire room just emptied of everyone attending the event.

Like she feels the same buzz as me, she turns, and her eyes meet my stare across the ballroom. Her sky-blue eyes catch mine, and I feel my jaw fall to the floor.

She's not smiling, but she's without a doubt, the most beautiful woman I have ever laid eyes on. I can only imagine the beauty I will find when those lips finally curve up. She's got blue eyes and the hottest red lips that I can picture wrapped around my cock. She has the most banging body with curves in all the right places, and that dress molds to her body like it was made for her.

After what feels like minutes, I see the corner of her lip turn up the slightest bit as she tucks a small strand of hair behind her ear and sets her gaze to the ground, as if she's shying away from my stare.

A dark-haired woman grabs the crook of her elbow, smiles at her and pulls her towards the table they are going to be seated at. My eyes try to peek around the guests, but there are so many people huddled by the doors that I lose sight of her when she gets pulled away.

My eyes scan the room quickly to see if I can catch a glimpse of her again, but she's gone. Just like that.

I know that I need to find her again tonight.

Returning to the bar where Marc and Logan sit, my mind is still reeling about this mystery woman. Who is she? What's her story? Logan slaps my chest with the back of his hand, snapping me out of my trance, and says, "You alright, bro?"

I let out a sigh and pause before I speak, because I'm not about to take the risk of sounding like Marc looking for a damn wife.

"Yeah, I'm good, bro. I just need another whiskey. Stat."

CHAPTER THREE
Peyton

"Tequila and lime please," I say to the bartender trying to calm my nerves.

"You got it, ma'am."

"Oh gosh." I chuckle. "Don't call me ma'am. I feel like a senior citizen."

"You got it, sweetheart," he replies with a smile and a wink before walking away to make my drink.

A small smile crosses my face while nerves dance in my stomach. I just caught the hottest guy here staring at me from across the room, not even five minutes after arriving.

I scan the room while waiting for my drink and realize I don't know anyone in this room, or who that man is. He is dressed in the sharpest navy-blue suit, and I can tell from afar that he's built like he lives at the gym. You know the saying, *that guy doesn't skip leg day*—well, this guy doesn't skip *any* gym day. He could squish me like a damn bug if given the chance.

Yes, he could destroy me.

And don't get me started on those eyes. Dammit those eyes. Even from across the room, I could tell they are a deep blue. I was able to get a good look when he was staring straight through me. His mouth slightly parted as if he was shocked to see me.

I wonder if he thinks I'm someone else.

Someone he knows.

The way he was staring at me was burning through me, right to my core. I felt a fire in my belly that I can't even explain.

Is it a fire? Or is it nerves from his stare?

I can't do this tonight. I am not ready to meet someone or have anyone stare at me the way he was looking at me. Which is why I found myself hightailing it right to the bar to order my signature drink, a tequila and lime.

"Thank you," I say, as the bartender slides my drink to me before moving to the next person.

"Whiskey neat, please." I hear a deep voice to my right.

I turn my head to see the face behind that deep voice. I'm forced to do a double take when I'm met with those deep blue eyes again.

The corners of his lips turn up as he meets my stare. I can feel the heat rise to my cheeks and I find myself tucking a strand of hair behind my ear before moving my gaze back to my drink and preparing to walk away.

What I'm not prepared for, is his large muscular hand to grip my wrist in the most delicate manner causing this weird energy to shoot through me. It feels like a goddamn electric shock is jolting through every part of my body, and now my stomach is rumbling with nervous butterflies.

I stand still as I look down at my wrist and then slowly drag my gaze from his hand up his body to meet those gorgeous eyes again.

"Don't go yet," the deep voice pleads.

"E-excuse me?" I stutter.

"I'm sorry." He lets out a small laugh. "My name is Thomas, and I would love to buy you a drink."

"Y-you want to buy me a drink?" I ask as my eyes search the

surroundings, as if I am looking for someone to save me from this adonis standing in front of me.

Where the fuck is Kali?

He lets out another small laugh and casually sits down on the bar stool, nodding at the stool next to him, gesturing that I should have a seat.

I take the seat that he offered next to him, and when I do, the scent of him takes over every inch of me. He smells fresh, like soap and aftershave. I love when a man smells as crisp as he does right now. Men don't need to smell like the forest and pine needles to turn me on. This scent on him, it fits him.

"I saw you when you first came in tonight," he says with a smirk.

There's the answer to my question from a few minutes ago. I'm not someone he thinks he knows, and I am not someone he expected to be here. His stare from earlier was meant for me, which makes me even more nervous to sit next to him.

For the first time since I saw him, I allow myself to really get a good look at the man. He is incredibly handsome, tall with dark brown hair that is styled with a sophisticated, but sexy comb over. He has a sharp jawline that looks strong, like he could eat me alive. And that navy-blue suit, don't even get me started. It's painted on him and tailored exactly for his body. It's basically suit porn if I have ever seen it.

The height difference between us is what romance books are made of. You know, where the girl has to lift her head up to look at him and when he hugs her, her face is squished into his strong chest. This man looks like he stepped out of one of my romance books. Which causes me to think about what his body would feel like on top of me.

Fuck, it's been too long since I've thought about a guy like that.

"I could let you buy me a drink," I say with a small smirk and just a touch of confidence. "But you know this is an open bar, right?"

He tips his head back in a full body laugh and my cheeks heat up once again.

"I need to work on my pick-up lines then, huh?" he says through his laugh.

That line causes me to let out the smallest chuckle with him.

Is he trying to use pick up lines on *me*?

"You've never been to one of these events before," he says it as a statement, not a question. Pausing his thoughts as his eyes trail from my legs all the way back up to meet my eyes. "I would have remembered you if you had."

Nervously swirling the ice in my drink with my straw, I reply, "No, this is my first event."

Licking his lips, he stares at me for a pause. I feel a throbbing sensation right to my center, and instinctively find myself rubbing my thighs together in my seat.

What is this man doing to me?

"What's your name?" he asks.

"P-Peyton." I extend my hand awkwardly for a handshake.

He looks at my hand like he's offended by my gesture of an introductory handshake. His eyes move from my hand, back up to my eyes, before they land on my lips. As soon as they do, I see his tongue swipe across his bottom lip.

I swear, this man would devour me if I let him.

He finally reaches for my hand to shake it and that weird buzz courses through me again. "Peyton," he says with the corner of his lips pulled up the slightest bit. "A beautiful name, for the most beautiful woman in the room."

I blush at the compliment.

"So, Peyton, what's your story?"

What's my story? I'm not sure how to take that. Does he want to know where I'm from? Who I've dated? What brings me here today? My astrology sign? I tend to word vomit in situations like this. I'll spill my entire life to a stranger, and it causes them to run quicker than that guy who broke all those crazy records in the *Olympics*.

"What do you mean?" I finally ask, swirling the ice in my drink with my straw.

"Tell me a little about yourself, Peyton."

A smile forms on my face and my eyes lock with his.

The way he's looking at me has me forgetting who I am. I'm glad I told him my name already because right now, I don't remember it. He's already having this wild effect on me. "I've never been to an event like this before. This is all new to me. I'm here with my friend as her plus one."

"You look like you fit right in," he says as his eyes scan me from head to toe.

"T-thank you," I stutter. "Do you come to these events often?" I immediately regret the words after I said them because that can double as a cheesy pick-up line.

"I do. My father used to donate a lot to these organizations and after he passed, I made sure I would continue his legacy."

"I'm sorry for your loss," I say sympathetically. "That's really amazing of you to do this for him and for the kids."

His eyes are locked on mine again as he takes a sip of whiskey and contemplates what he wants to say next. "This might be very forward of me, Peyton, but I have to ask. Are you seeing anyone? I would love to get your number and take you out sometime. You know," he pauses and lets out a soft laugh, "and actually buy you a drink."

"I-I'm—" I'm cut off when I hear the stool pull out to the other side of me.

"Hey, girl," Kali says as she digs into her small purse, looking for something. "I'm so glad you found the bar. I need a fucking drink stat."

I don't reply to her and when Kali senses that, her eyes shoot up to mine and then bounce between me and Thomas. I give her a wide eye look that only the two of us understand as friends and a grin forms on her face.

"Kali, this is Thomas," I introduce him.

"Pleasure to meet you, Kali." He extends his hand across my waist and the two of them shake hands in front of me.

"Same to you, Thomas." She smiles up at him. But her smile isn't a normal *'nice to meet you'* smile. It's a smile that only I know. It's one that says *'please, fuck my best friend.'*

"I have to use the ladies' room," I cut them off from their handshake. I don't really need to use the restroom, but I need a second to compose myself. The air around Thomas is thick and I am struggling to breathe.

"I'll come with you." Kali jumps off her stool. "We will be right back, Thomas." She winks at him as we hurry off to the restroom.

She practically throws me into the restroom, locks the door before she turns to me and says, "What. Is. Happening?"

"Kali," I whisper, setting my gaze to the ground, leaning my back against the door and finding my shoulders slouched down. "I can't do this. Did you see that man? He's already asked for my number. He's so hot that I can't even form words and I don't even know my own name. And, oh my god." I groan. "He smells so fucking good. Are you ready to go home?" I fire back with a pleading tone.

"Oh, no you don't, Pey. You don't get to do that tonight."

I'm back to that moment where I wish I had even an ounce of confidence that Kali has. I have watched her with guys before. She can pick up any guy, at any bar and she radiates confidence when doing so. Me, on the other hand? I clearly struggle to form words. For once in my life, I just want to feel okay talking to a man.

The problem right now? The one man that has shown any interest in me for the first time in three years is a fucking walking gift from God. Honestly, it should be illegal to look as hot as he does. I actually should ask him if he has a permit to be walking around with those looks, because they are destructive. No, stop. Obviously I can't ask him that. See? This is my problem. That would be so fucking awkward.

"Peyton," she sighs. "Listen to me. I need you to understand this as your best fucking friend in the whole wide world. You have got to stop letting the *boys* from your past determine your future. Yes! I SAID BOYS! Because what you dated in the past was just that, a bunch of twat waffles who didn't know a dick from an eggplant."

"That makes no sense." I raise a brow at her.

"Shut up." She swats my arm. "I mean it, Pey. You're truly the most beautiful person I know. That man was looking at you with stars in his eyes before we came to the bathroom. I'm glad you said you had to go because I needed to tell you this so you didn't get all *'what's your zodiac sign and ring size'* on him before even knowing who he is."

I laugh at that. "Okay, Kali. I get it."

"Great. Let's go." She claps her hands together and bolts towards the door.

"You go, I am going to just freshen up and take a few deep breaths in here. I will be out in a minute."

She nods, and with one parting glance in my direction, she looks me in the eyes and says softly, "You're a fucking ray of sunshine, Peyton. Please know that."

I nod, twisting my bracelet around my wrist, feeling a deep pit in my stomach at the words she chose. "Thank you, Kali."

As she exits the bathroom, I walk over to give it a quick lock before I let out the biggest exhale and walk over to the bathroom sink.

I allow myself to think about my past for a moment as I stare at myself in the mirror. In college, I landed myself the captain of the basketball team. He was the typical star athlete who could have dated any girl in that school. In fact, half of the cheer squad was gunning for a chance to jump into his bed. They weren't missing out on much in the bedroom department, if you're picking up what I'm putting down. One of those cheerleaders was able to weasel her way into his bed and that was when he cheated on me. She made sure the entire school knew about it too.

Then there was Richard. Fresh out of college. He was a successful businessman. He was older by a couple of years, and I thought that this was it. He's responsible, he's got a good head on his shoulders, that he might want to settle down, the whole nine; but I was so wrong and naive to think that he wanted all that. Despite him telling me that he wanted to spend his life with me eventually, he also wanted to spend his time with his secretary spread out on top of his desk so he could get dessert before he came home for dinner. Yup, that's what I walked in on one afternoon when I went to the office to drop off cookies for him and his partners.

Then a realization dawns on me; it's been three years since anyone has shown me any interest, and it's been just as many years since I received an orgasm from a man. I hate to even admit that. Lately, I have been getting by just fine with *buzz buzz*, my battery-operated boyfriend. What if just for one night, I allow myself to be ravaged by a man who would give me the most epic orgasm of my life?

"Fuuuuccckk," I murmur to myself in the mirror.

How long have I been in this bathroom? Shit, it's time to face the walking masterpiece back at the bar.

I retouch my lipstick and toss my curls around to fluff them up before I give myself one more once over before I leave.

I'm about five steps out of the bathroom when a large hand circles my wrist, gently tugging me in the opposite direction. Snapping my head around, I am met with the back of his head as he's gently dragging me down another side hall, past the bathroom I just left.

"What are you doing?" I whisper shout.

Before I can process what's happening, he has me spun around and pressed to the wall in the darkened part of the hallway. I inhale, fully prepared to speak, but no words come out when I try. Both of his arms are now caging me in, large hands frame each side of my head, and his body hovering only inches from mine. The same electricity shoots through my body and I can't help but lose my breath at the feeling of him being this close. He's a complete stranger but my body reacts like I have known this man much longer than just tonight.

He's a little bit more disheveled than he was before. His suit jacket is now unbuttoned exposing his white button up dress shirt that also looks like it was tailor made for him. My body betrays me when my hands find their way to his suit jacket, fisting it tightly as if I never want this man to let me go.

His eyes are locked with mine and I can feel his breath on me. It smells like whiskey. I don't even fucking like whiskey, but on him, it works. I will happily get drunk right here, right now.

Inching his body closer, his lips now hover over my ear and his slightly scruffy, perfectly cut beard gently brushes my cheek sending shivers down my spine.

He whispers, "I need you."

CHAPTER FOUR
Thomas

Fuck. Being so close to her has me wound up tighter than a rubber band ball. I've been with my fair share of women in my life, but something about this one has me wanting to take her right here, right now, in this dimly lit hallway that I dragged her down.

What if she's not that kind of girl? I know nothing about her other than I need her.

We're at a fucking gala and all I can think about is sliding up this sleek black gown and feeling if she's as hot for me as I am for her right now.

The way her breath hitches and the fact that she can't even respond to me, tells me that if I bunch this gown up and slide my fingers into her panties, I will find her soaked for me. Just the idea of her being wet with arousal, has my dick ready to stand at full attention.

"Tell me you don't have a boyfriend, Peyton." I lean in to whisper in her ear, taking a moment to inhale her scent. She smells like fucking roses. My hands aren't even touching her yet and I can feel the heat radiating off of her. I have her head caged between my hands, but I have this need to touch her.

"I-I'm single," she whispers back as her eyes close and her head presses back against the wall.

It isn't until I pull away from her ear, that she opens her eyes to look right at me. All my restraint is out the window when those light blue eyes with thick full lashes stare directly into mine. I waste no time placing my hand directly on the back of her neck, letting my fingers find their place in her hair while my other hand grabs her hips with a tight squeeze.

Not another second passes before I crash my lips to hers like I have waited my whole life to kiss her. The jolt of electricity that shoots between us, is something I have never felt with another woman. I don't ever kiss women, I fuck. Kissing is too intimate, and women think I want a relationship when I kiss them. That's why I have always avoided it with the women I bring home. But Peyton has this pull over me and I have this *need* to kiss her that's driving me insane.

For a moment, I think she is going to pull away, but then her hands find the back of my head and she pulls me closer to deepen the kiss. She has to raise slightly on her toes to reach me, forcing us together. Right here, in this dimly lit hallway, the fronts of our bodies are fused together like glue. Her body melts into mine and feels like it was made for me. My hands fight the urge to learn and explore every part of her body.

The feel of her curves against me have me pinning her to the wall. She lets out an audible gasp between kisses, when she feels how fucking hard she has made me.

My tongue slips past her lips and she opens up for me, allowing our tongues to dance. She tastes like tequila and even though I am not a tequila man, fuck if I don't love the taste of it now.

I gently give her bottom lip a bite as I pull away from the kiss, wanting more than anything to taste the rest of her. When I pull away, she tips her head back against the wall to look up at me. I take that moment to dive right into the hollow of her neck, inhaling that scent of roses. God. Damn. Fucking. Roses.

"From the moment you walked in tonight," I say as she melts further into me the second my lips touch the pounding pulse on her neck, and I start trailing kisses from her ear to her collar bone. "I've had a raging hard on, picturing what's underneath this dress of yours and wondering how you feel." She lets out the faintest moan and I swear if I wasn't paying attention to every little thing she's doing, I would have missed it.

Yup. That does it for me and confirms that if I lift this dress, she will be soaked for me.

Removing my hand from her waist, I continue peppering her with kisses, while I slowly bunch up her dress to slip my hands between her thighs.

"Thomas," she moans, as her hands find my shoulders.

"Tell me, Sunshine," I whisper between kisses. My hand skimming her upper thigh. "If I slip my hands between your pretty little legs, are you going to be wet for me?"

Without hesitation, she says, "God, yes."

My hand slips under her dress to cup the outside of her panties and fuck, she didn't lie. "Fuck," I groan. "You're soaked." My dick is going to burst through the seams of my pants any second.

My hand finds the hem of her panties and with one swift motion, I tear them off. I don't think I have ever ripped panties off a woman before, but she has the inner animal in me coming out full force.

She lets out a gasp as her eyes trail to my hand where I am holding her bright red panties and she watches me stuff them in my suit pocket. "You can have them back later." I smirk knowing that she will, in fact, not be getting them back later. They just have to be bright fucking red? It's the sexiest thing I have seen in my life.

My hand finds its way back to the warmth between her legs and without hesitation, my thumb finds her clit. As soon as I do, she lets out a faint moan and her lower back arches off the wall to press into my hand. Her hips slowly start to grind into my hand, telling me she wants more.

"That's it," I say into the nape of her neck. "Ride my hand. Take what you need from me."

"Thomas," she moans into my ear.

I let out a growl as I move my finger from her clit to dip inside of her and I can already tell how tight she is. She has the softest pussy I have ever felt in my life. I continue working my finger in and out of her, her body wiggles around me, telling me she wants more.

"More," she whispers, as if she thinks I can't tell from the way her body responds to me.

"Do you like this, Peyton? Do you like the feel of me playing with your tight little pussy while we are out here in the open where anyone can see us?" I whisper into her ear.

Her body shivers at my words but doesn't hesitate when she responds with, 'Yes. Thomas, yes."

I slide my finger out and immediately dive back into her tight pussy with two fingers, working her G-spot and continuing to rub my thumb over her bundle of nerves until I feel her convulse around me.

"Yes, Thomas," she says with a loud moan. "That's the spot."

The thought of someone hearing her sweet fucking moans has me acting primal. I want to keep her moans bottled up for me and only me. "Let go, Peyton. Let me feel you go over the edge." As soon as the words leave my mouth, I can feel that she's there. "That's it, Sunshine. I can feel your pussy pulsing around my fingers."

"*Thomas. Thomas,*" she screams as her orgasm courses through her body, and I feel her cum soak my fingers and drip down my wrist.

Holy fuck. She is the hottest fucking woman I have ever seen in my life.

She's coming back down from her orgasm, but I refuse to remove my fingers from her soaking wet pussy when I crash my lips to hers. Immediately, her arms wrap around my neck to deepen our kiss as if she doesn't want this moment to end.

I pull away from her kiss at the same time I remove my fingers from her heat because I need to fucking taste her.

I focus my eyes on her bright blue eyes with fluttering lashes as she stares back at me, catching her breath. She watches as my fingers soaked with her cum dive into my mouth, sucking her arousal off of them.

Her mouth opens slightly as if she can't believe what she's seeing right now.

"You taste so fucking sweet, Sunshine."

"I-I," she stutters, completely speechless. "Wow."

I need more of her. I want her bright red lips wrapped around my dick. I want to be inside of her and feel her pussy squeeze my cock with her cum dripping down my balls. I want to give her ten more orgasms and another few in the morning. I have never wanted a woman to spend the night, but I know just one will never be enough.

"Come home with me tonight," I whisper.

She pauses, as if she wants to say no. But a look falls over her face and I can feel how much she wants to say yes to my question. I can't let this night end with just that.

"Let me go get washed up," is all she says back as she pulls herself off the wall to walk towards the bathroom.

I'm left standing where she left me, staring at her backside as she adjusts her dress as she walks away. My dick still hard and my mind reeling over what just happened in this hallway. I feel like my feet are cemented here and if I move or even blink, then it would all be just a dream. She pauses slowly and turns over her shoulder to tell me, "Oh and Thomas?" My gaze meets hers. "I'll go home with you tonight." With one small smirk on her lips and a wink, she turns and walks toward the restroom.

I give her a tight nod because apparently, I have forgotten how to speak around her. The way she moves her body, the way her body responds to mine and the cutest fucking little facial expression she gave me, has me wanting to know everything there is to know about her. Like I said, I don't do this relationship shit, but two fucking hours in the presence of this woman has me wanting more of her. I want to know all about her. What her favorite breakfast food is, what movies make her laugh and what makes her cry. I want to know what she likes to do in her spare time. I want to know *why the fuck* I sound like Marc.

I smile to myself as I start to walk back out of the hallway and into the ballroom, deciding I'll meet her back at the bar where we were before this.

As soon as I sit down, the loudest noise fills the room. The fire alarm is blaring in our ears and the entire ballroom erupts in pure chaos. My eyes scan the room and I see people grabbing their belongings, screaming, and running in all different directions. No one knows where to go or what is happening. Is this a real fire? Did someone accidentally trip the alarm? As soon as the thought hits my head, I smell smoke.

Peyton.

I have to find her through this chaos.

"Please exit through the east wing doors. There is a kitchen fire close to the west wing doors. This is not a drill," comes blaring through the DJ speakers.

I find myself running towards the hallway I just came from, where the bathrooms are, to see if I can find Peyton. It's impossible to move in that direction because hundreds of people are trying to exit the ballroom at the same time. I can't get there. I feel like I am a sheep being corralled in a farm towards the east wing exit. My eyes never stop scanning the room to look for her, though.

Next thing I know, I'm outside the entrance. My eyes continue to scan the crowd to see if I can find even a glimpse of golden blonde hair in this crowd.

"Thomas!" I hear my best friend, Logan scream. My head snapping in his direction. "This way! We have to get out of here, the fire is spreading fast."

"I have to find her," I scream at him.

"Who?" he's screaming back. It's so fucking loud out here with everyone running around in a state of panic. "Forget it, bro. We have to get out of here."

His hand grabs my elbow to drag me away and my body follows reluctantly as my eyes continue to scan the crowd outside for any sign of her around. Did she get out? Was she still in the bathroom? I can't find her in the sea of people filling the streets of New York City. Fire engines blare in the distance and smoke fills the streets. After what feels like hours of looking through the crowd as we're running through the streets, I don't find her.

She's gone.

CHAPTER FIVE
Peyton

Five Years Later

"Peyton, where do you want this last box?" Avery screams from the hallway.

I'm unboxing the little bit of my life into this small New York City apartment that I'm sharing with Avery and Kali. I don't own much because what I did have was only enough to fill a small bedroom in my home in South Jersey. When I lost my parents about a year ago tragically in a car accident, I tried to stay because I loved that home and the memories from my entire life were there, but I just couldn't afford it. I couldn't afford much since I only worked as a substitute teacher for kindergarteners. I begged for more hours, but they couldn't offer anything more. I even looked for a permanent kindergarten or preschool position, but nothing ever opened up.

The city life has never been for me, if I'm being honest. I loved living in the suburbs and having a yard, a driveway, and not having to share an entire building with strangers.

I was forced to sell the house, the furniture and most of my own belongings just to be able to give myself enough cushion to get my life started here in New York City. I'm quickly learning that shit ain't cheap in this neck of the woods.

My Gigi, Esther, who lives right outside the city, offered me a room to move in with her. I thought about it for a hot minute, because I would still be close to my best friends, and if I landed myself a job in the city it wouldn't be a difficult commute. But I didn't want to disrupt her life and routine. She always has her best friends over for card night. Yes, they call it card night. Because those little bitties loved to play *CARDS AGAINST HUMANITY* together. Gigi and her friends are some dirty old birds, that's for sure.

That's how I landed myself in this small apartment, splitting the rent with Kali and Avery. They begged me to let them take over my first three months because they knew I didn't have much, but I couldn't find it in me to accept that offer. I have never been one to let someone else take care of me like that. I consider myself an *'independent bitch'*.

"Thanks Avery," I say as she enters my room. "I would have gotten it. That box is heavy. You didn't need to do that for me."

"When are you going to learn, that that's what friends are for?" she says with a smirk on her face, placing the box on my bed. "Besides, it was blocking the front door. Who has this many fucking books?"

I shrug my shoulders. "I like having my smut trophies on display."

She shakes her head at me throwing herself on my bed. "Pey, I am so pumped you're here in the city with us!"

"Me too, Ave. I have to admit though, I'm a little nervous about city life."

"You're in good hands with us. Just remember my biggest tips," she says very matter of factly.

"Refresh my memory."

"Just remember to adjust your pace when you walk because you don't want to be *that* guy. Definitely master the art of jaywalking. It's what we do." She shrugs. "Oh and pizza is a way of life. Duh. Lastly, Battery Park is not a place to charge your phone or your vibrator," she says with a pointed finger in the air.

"Noted."

"You will be fine as long as you stick with Kali and me," she says and moves to pull some books from the boxes and put them on the shelf for me. "Oh hey, have you gotten any hits on your flaming hot nanny for hire ad?"

"Avery," I say, giving her side eyes. "That is not the ad I put out there and you know it."

She lets out the smallest giggle, "You might as well have. Let's face it. You are a flaming. Hot. Nanny. For hire. It's what your ad should have said."

Kali talked me into putting an ad out letting people know that I am looking for work as a nanny. I have never been a nanny before, but I have worked with kids for years now. I love working with kids, especially toddlers. I know it's probably the hardest age for parents and people who work with children. The toddler age is when children are focused on developing a greater sense of self-control. They are just finding themselves and their own personalities at this age.

That's why this seems like the perfect job for me as I take on the adventure of moving to a new city and finding a leg to stand on.

"Avery—" I'm interrupted by my phone ringing in my hand.

"It's Gigi," I tell her before answering it. "Hey Gigi."

"Hi sweetheart. How are you? Are you all settled in?"

"I'm getting there," I say with a small laugh. "How are you feeling? How did your appointment go?"

"Oh, you know them." She laughs. "They want me to start a new treatment within the next two months. I feel just fine, though and I'm in no pain."

Gigi is the most resilient person I know. She also will never let me know if she really is in any pain, so I take everything she tells me with a grain of salt. Two years ago, she was diagnosed with Non-Hodgkin's Lymphoma, and she has been a true warrior through the process. There is no one in the world stronger than her and if I could become half the woman she is in life, I would be happy with that.

When my parents passed away, she became my rock and backbone in life. She is my go-to person when I need someone to talk to and that woman sure can cook up a storm. When I visit her, I am guaranteed a good meal and some wild stories. She drives me up the wall most of the time, but I know I can't take my time with her for granted.

"That's good to hear, Gigi," I sigh. "You know I'm a lot closer now. If you need anything, I am only a phone call away."

"Oh, I know, sweetheart." I can hear her smile through the phone and it's my favorite thing in the world. "How's the job search going?"

"You mean the nanny ad?"

"Yeah, the hot nanny for hire."

"You've been texting with Avery, haven't you?" I laugh, giving Avery a side eye glare. Her hand shoots over her mouth to hide her laughter.

"You know her and Kali are like second granddaughters to me."

"Esther, you're my favorite person in the whole world." Avery screams from my bed so that Gigi can hear her. "I'm going to come over this week for some pepperoni bread," she adds.

Now all three of us are laughing. Gigi has a way about her that all my friends have adopted her as their grandma. I think strangers in the grocery store have even started calling her Gigi. She's sort of a social butterfly, so she knows a lot about a lot of people. She knows the butcher's favorite football team. It's the Jets if you're wondering. She even cooks for the pharmacy technicians and her dentist. Pepperoni bread is her specialty. It's a little weird that she does it but that's what makes her happy and gives her something to do.

"You know I will make it for you anytime, dear."

"Once I get all settled here, I will come by and see you this week," I tell her.

"I would love that," she sounds delighted through the phone. "I miss you, sweetheart."

"I miss you too, Gigi."

"But back to the question you're avoiding. Have you gotten any hits on your hot nanny ad?" She laughs.

"No hits just yet." I shake my head as if she can see me through the phone. "But I am hopeful because I have experience with kids and I'm sure someone is in desperate need for some help."

"You're so good with kids. Anyone would be stupid not to hire you for the job."

"Thank you, Gigi. You don't have to tell me all those things."

"I do. And I always will. I am always so proud of you and whatever you choose to do," she says. "Your parents would be so proud of you."

I don't respond because it's hard to hear that. I want them to be proud of me. I hope they are looking down on me and knowing I made the right decisions in life.

"Listen, sweetheart," she says, knowing that I can't respond to that. She knows me better than anyone else. "I have to go because Lee is coming over and we're going to go to the farmers' market."

"No flirting with the men, Gigi." I burst into laughter.

"Don't tell her what to do," Avery cuts in. "You go get 'em, Esther!"

"I make no promises, sweetheart." She chuckles with us.

"I will call you later tonight, okay?"

"Okay, Peyton. I love you to the moon, stars, Jupiter and back."

"I love you too." I smile into the phone before I hang up.

"God, I love that woman. She's like my spirit animal," Avery says. She and Gigi really are so much alike. If I knew my grandma when she was Avery's age, I would bet that she was just as wild as Avery is now.

I move to open up the box of picture frames and place them on my little end table next to my bed. I put the photo of Gigi and I down first. It's from New Year's Eve one year; she's double fisting with a beer and a bottle of champagne and she has the cheesiest smile on her face. I reach for the second photo, a picture of me and the girls. It was a trip to New York City a few years back and we're standing on a balcony. Our hair was blowing wildly in the wind, and we were laughing so hard. It was truly one of the best nights of our lives. The last picture I pull out is a picture of my Mom and Dad one summer on the beach. I miss them so much.

Pictures are a funny thing. Sometimes when we're caught up in the moment, we forget to take the pictures to remember the memories. But when we do, we're so happy to have that memory to look back on.

We're sitting in silence right now because Avery can tell my mood after unpacking this box. It holds a lot of weight in memories for me, both happy and sad. But our silence is broken when my phone starts ringing from across the room. I assume that it's Gigi calling me back because she does that. We hang up the phone and she calls me back to tell me about something good she made for lunch.

I get to my phone and notice that it's an unknown number. I look up to Avery sitting next to me who also takes note of the unknown number.

"Answer it! Maybe it's someone calling about your flaming hot nanny for hire ad!"

I shoot her a quick *shut up* glare before answering the phone.

"Hello?"

"Hi, is this Peyton Kelly?" the voice on the other end says. She sounds young, so I don't think this is regarding the ad.

"Y-Yes." My voice breaks and I swallow the lump in my throat. "Yes, it is. May I ask who's calling?"

"Oh yes!" I can hear her voice perk up with excitement. "This is Emiline Ford! I am calling regarding your nanny for hire ad."

Placing my hand over the speaker, I whisper to Avery, "It's for the ad."

Avery throws herself on the bed, letting out a small squeal of excitement and starts kicking her legs up and down like a dead bug stuck on its back trying to flip around.

"Hello? Are you still there?" the girl says.

"Yes. I'm so sorry." I chuckle at my friends' antics. "Are you looking for a nanny?" I reply back to her.

"Yes. Well no," she corrects herself. "It's for my brother. He's so busy with work that he put me in charge of finding the nanny for him. I have been watching little James for the last three years since he was born, but I finished my pre-requisites for my nursing school program. I am going to be starting the actual program and I won't be able to commit to watching James as much as I have been anymore."

"I understand." I nod.

"And since I am the one who can't watch him anymore, he asked me to look for someone to replace me."

"Of course," I say, a little more excited that I intended it to come out. "I love children, especially the little ones. So that makes James three, right?"

"Yes, he's a little more than three and a half, to be exact."

"Well, I would love to get together to meet with him and see if we would be a good match for each other."

I hear a squeal come from the other end of the phone. "Oh my gosh, YES!" she shrieks. "I would love to get together so you can meet him. He's the greatest kid."

I find myself smiling at the phone even though she can't even see me.

"Are you available tomorrow morning around 9am?" she asks. "I know it's super short notice, but I usually take James to the park on Tuesday mornings and then we get donuts for breakfast. But don't tell his dad that when you meet him." She chuckles.

"My lips are sealed." I laugh with her. "I can definitely meet at 9am tomorrow."

"This is so great!" she shrieks again. "This is my cell I called you from. I will text you in the morning when we are on our way. It's the orange and green playground in Central Park. James' favorite spot because of the colors."

"Of course, I will see you there. I look forward to meeting you both."

"See you then. Thanks again, Peyton," she says before she hangs up.

I look down at my phone in disbelief. There's no way I landed a nanny job this quickly after only moving here less than 24 hours ago. It took me months to find a job in New Jersey that could afford me to stay at my childhood home and now, I have a possible job lined up in less than a day.

"This is too good to be true," I mutter out loud.

"PEYTON!" Avery screams. "I THINK YOU HAVE A JOB!"

"I-I think I have a job," I stutter, still staring at my phone. "Providing little James actually likes me."

"Shut up, bitch." She smacks my arms. "He's going to love you. We already know this, you're so good with kids. You're a ray of sunshine, remember?"

I swallow the lump in my throat. The girls have always reminded me that I'm a ray of sunshine when I need a confidence boost. Whenever I want to stick my turtle head back into its shell, they both are there to remind me that I am a ray of sunshine. That I shine brighter than any fear or obstacle that I may face.

I don't have the heart to tell them to stop calling me that, because it reminds me of a man named Thomas. He blew my mind with the most epic orgasm of my life with just his hands. I lost him that night, never to find him again. When I hear that word though, the flood of memories comes rushing back.

"She said that she helps her brother out by watching his son," I say, ignoring her term of endearment. "I wonder if the mom is in the picture... I have so many questions to ask Emiline when I see them tomorrow."

"Oh shit, you're gonna be working with a daddy."

"Well, yeah. He is a dad." I roll my eyes at the obvious.

"No Pey, a D-A-D-D-Y. Daddies are fucking hot, girl. And from the sounds of it, he's a single fucking daddy. You *know* that's my favorite trope in your collection of smut!"

"How am I friends with you?" I shake my head at her, moving back to the boxes to unpack some more.

She's out the door and halfway down the hall when she screams, "You wouldn't be able to do jack shit without me, bitch."

She's right. Between her and Kali, I wouldn't be able to do much without them. It was Avery that convinced me to move in with them and it was Kali who convinced me to put that ad out there for this job. They both rushed to me the night my parents died. It was them who checked on Gigi for me when I wasn't always able to make the trek north. And it has been both of them that have kept me sane all these years. They are like the sisters I never had, and I wouldn't be able to do jack shit without them.

CHAPTER SIX
Thomas

"Daddy, what's a dingleberry?"

I'm taken aback and find myself in silence trying to figure out how to answer his question. Where in the world does this kid hear this shit?

If it wasn't for my little sister, Emiline, he would be fully corrupted at such a young age. All he's known his whole life are me, Emiline and my two brothers, Marc, and Oliver. Oliver alone is enough to corrupt any kid, at any age. I am willing to bet all the money to my name, that Oliver is who he heard about dingleberries from. And I have a lot of money to my name.

"It's not something you have to worry about right now, James."

"But Daddy, Uncle Ollie said I have to watch out for them dingleberries anytime I make a deposit in the golden throne."

Just wait until I talk to Oliver next. I swear to God… I don't care what country he's in right now, I am going to wring his neck.

I shake my head. "First of all, the term is porcelain throne. And second of all, you need to stop talking to Uncle Ollie. Lastly, this conversation is over."

James, or JJ, as we like to call him because his full name is James Jacob, is only three and a half years old but he is a sponge of knowledge. He is the type of kid who will ask questions about anything you say and do because he wants to know it all. It's one of the reasons we have to watch what we say around him, because he's sure to repeat it at some point. He has Ford blood in him, after all. I know I am biased when I say this, but he's the smartest kid I have ever met, and he certainly didn't get that from his mother.

God, his mother. Sheila is a fucking joke.

James is the product of a one-night stand. A one night stand I wish I could erase from my brain, but I can't, and I won't because it brought me James. He is the greatest thing that has ever happened to me. I never wanted to be a dad, it wasn't part of my plan or something that I thought would fit into my life. I am a businessman, first and foremost. I am ruthless in the board-room and always set out to win, but then James happened. Looking back, I never knew what I would be missing out on because he is my greatest adventure in life.

It hasn't been easy since his mom walked out on us. She was young and had a life to live. Well, at least that's what she told us. Sheila had these major goals in life to be a model or an actress or some shit. Fuck if I know. She resented James for changing her body. She knew before even giving birth that she wasn't going to stick around. I wasn't a relationship kind of guy, but one look at James the day he was born, I knew I wanted to give him the world and so, I tried. I really did. I wanted her to stay and be a mom for him. Who knew my biggest mistake would turn into my greatest gift in life?

I'm not happy she left, but in a way, I am thankful she did it when he was so young, because now he doesn't know the differ-ence. He just thinks he's got a daddy superhero. His words, not mine. Again, smartest kid in the world.

"JJ, are you ready to go? Auntie Em is going to be here soon to pick you up for the park," I shout, from the bottom of the stairs, after he ran off like a dinosaur on a warpath.

"Heck yeah, Daddy!!"

"We don't say heck, buddy," I shout back.

"Sorry Daddy, I love going to the park with Aunt Em and getting circle pasties with holes," he says running down the stairs.

"Circle pasties?"

"Donuts, Daddy. Get with the program."

I shake my head. "No donuts today, Monkey."

"Okay, but—" he's interrupted when Emiline comes running through the elevator doors.

"Where's my favorite nephew?" Emiline screams.

"I'm your only nephew, Auntie Em!" He giggles, running straight into her arms for a barrel hug.

Emiline loves him as if he is her own. I hit the jackpot with my family, that's for sure. When shit hit the fan and Sheila walked out on us, they stepped up to be extra parents for him. Every day, I am beyond thankful for that. James deserves it. I know deep down, someone will come into our lives and become a mother figure to him. But for now, he's got all of us.

"You ready to go, buttercup. We're going to the park to meet a friend of mine."

"A friend?" I question her and what she's up to. "You don't have friends."

"Yes. A friend," she scoffs. "Who might just become James' new nanny by the end of the day."

A nanny. For fucks' sake. "I don't need a nanny. I just need some help with James here and there, and we have that covered."

"We don't have it covered, Tommy," she says sympathetically. "We *need* a nanny. You are working more with the new investment in the high rise being built across town. Marc has been inundated with new real estate business since his partner walked out on him. Oliver," she pauses, noticing James still standing right next to her. "Well, Oliver is busy sticking his eggplant in holes around the globe."

"Daddy, why is Uncle Ollie sticking eggplants in holes?" he questions me.

I shake my head, and say, "He's a gardener." It was the quickest thing I could come up with. Fuck.

"And you know I am starting the nursing program soon. My life is going to be over for the next 18 months. It's an accelerated program and it's the hardest program in the tristate area."

I am so damn proud to be her big brother. Emiline has worked so hard since she graduated high school. She's always wanted to be a nurse like our mom. She never let boys get in the way of anything either. She still hasn't been in a relationship, or even kissed a boy for all I know, and I would like to keep it that way. I will never stop being protective of her.

"Okay. Okay." I rub my hands down my face. "I guess I do need a nanny." I pause for a second thinking about this. "Let me at least come with you to the park to meet your friend. If she's going to be spending time with my kid and possibly moving in, I think I should approve. Don't you agree?"

James jumps up and down like a little kid on Christmas morning, "Yes, Daddy!! Come to the park with us." He pulls Emiline's arm down so he can whisper in her ear, "Does this mean we don't get pasties with holes?"

She laughs at him. "Maybe we can talk your dad into donuts for once in his life. He needs to understand that one donut treat isn't going to destroy his 8-pack that he's got going on." Turning her gaze to me she asks, "What about work? Don't you have to get to the office?"

"I'm going to call and work from the home office today." I reach for my phone in the back pocket of my pants and click it open,."I just have to call into a conference call in about a half hour. It will be quick."

"What *ever* will the office do without you, Mr. Ford?" She sighs, throwing the back of her hand over her forehead in a very dramatic fashion.

I growl at her in frustration, "Let's just go and get this over with."

CHAPTER SEVEN
Peyton

Sitting here on this bench in Central Park, all I can think about is the fact that I should have worn a tank top or a sundress. I can't believe how hot it is right now and it's the first week of September. I am so ready for fall.

I feel the sweat dripping down my back as I sit here waiting for Emiline so I can meet James. That's when my phone starts vibrating in my purse and I just hope it isn't her canceling on me. I need this job so much.

Fetching it out of my wristlet, I see Kali's name flash across the screen with a video call.

"Hey Kali, I am still waiting. Looks like they are running a little late."

"Ahh ok. I was calling to make sure you're ok and ready for the interview. As in, I'm just making sure you're not running off to bake a batch of fucking cookies."

I bake when I'm stressed, and it seems that's been happening a lot lately. Some people cope with stress by working out, cleaning, drinking, or whatever their vice is. My vice is baking cookies. Kali and Avery always know when it's been a day for me when they come home from work and I'm standing over the oven waiting for the timer to ding. Trust me, they aren't mad that there is always a chocolate treat waiting for them, but I can tell they get concerned.

"Kali, it's barely an interview." I laugh. "I'm just meeting the kid and seeing if we would be a good fit." I shrug, fanning my face because this heat is insane right now.

"Like I said, an interview." She throws her head back and laughs at me.

"Whatever," I say, giving her an eye roll. "I can't tell if this New York heat today is making me sweat or if it's my nerves. I should have just gone with the sundress."

"I wasn't going to be the one to tell you, but yeah, that shirt does nothing to show your—" she pauses as her eyes trail my upper body in the frame of the phone. "Assets."

In the last year, I've lost about 15 lbs, but my tits stayed nice and plump. I am not mad about that, and I feel so much better about myself. I was going down a slippery slope with weight gain. I wasn't eating right. I eat strictly vegan, but it wasn't the healthy vegan options I kept reaching for. I still like to indulge in my famous vegan chocolate chip cookies once a week, though.

A text notification pops up at the top of my screen from Emiline telling me she is walking up now.

"Kali, I have to go. She's going to be here in a minute."

"Okay sister, you got this! Remember, you are a ray of fucking sunshine," she shouts.

I laugh at her giving her a nod. "Thank you, girl." And quickly hang up the phone when I see a girl walking up with a little boy. This must be them.

She is simply stunning. She looks to be about 21 years old, dressed in the most beautiful baby blue sundress. She has long, light blonde hair and from the looks of it, it seems like she doesn't even break a sweat in this heat. Shit, I should have worn the damn sundress.

"Hi, Emiline?"

"Yes! I am so sorry we are late. James was playing dinosaurs at home." She giggles. "Then we had to wait for his dad because he decided he was going to come and join us to meet you too."

"Oh, of course," I mutter in a voice lower than I intend it to be.

Shit. Now my sweat is definitely from nerves. I was not ready to meet a daddy today. I need to brush that thought out of my head. Avery has put it in my head too much that daddies are all hot. For all I know, this could just be your average Joe. Either way, I am not here to meet a guy, I am here for a job. A job I need more than anything right now. So if *daddy* is fine as fuck, I need to push that down immediately.

"W-where is he?" I ask.

"He's parking the car and then he had to take a conference call quickly. Those meetings can be such a bit-biscuit," she quickly corrects herself and winks at me.

"Aunt Em, why are meetings such a biscuit?" the little boy wonders.

Looking at him and then looking back to me, she says, "This here is James. And he is too smart for his age and will pick up on everything that comes out of your mouth." She laughs.

This little boy is the most adorable child I have ever seen. He looks to be a little short for his age, but the way he speaks, you would think he's much older than a 3-year-old. He's got the perfect little blonde hair brushed over to the side and deep blue eyes, like he could actually be a model for a toddler magazine. His smile hasn't left his face either since he got here, and those little dimples, I swear, I could just eat them up and pinch them.

Crouching down to meet his eye level, I introduce myself, "Hi there James, my name is Peyton."

"Are you related to the football player?" he asks.

I can't help but chuckle at his cuteness. "No buddy, his last name is Manning. My last name is Kelly."

"You have two first names?" he asks me with a questioning head tilt.

Emiline is right. This kid is too smart for his own good.

Laughing at him, I proceed to sit cross-legged on the grass in front of him to continue the conversation. "I guess you could say that. Some people have a last name that can also be someone's first name. I happen to be one of those people."

He pauses for a moment to process what I just said and takes a seat right next to me in the grass. "There's a girl in my class named Kelly. She's A-NNOY-ING," he emphasizes. "You're not annoying, are you?"

"I'd like to think I'm not annoying, little guy."

"Hey, I'm not a little guy. I'm this many years old." He puts up his thumb, pointer finger and middle finger to emphasize that he's three years old and not a *little guy*.

"My mistake. You certainly are the biggest boy," I laugh.

"I am. My daddy is a superhero daddy. He says I am going to be a superhero too. But I want to be a dinosaur when I grow up." He jumps up from his seat and assumes the position of a T-rex. "RAWRRRRR"

Emiline and I start laughing at him.

For the next half hour, I chase James around on the playground and learn that his favorite color is green. He wishes he could have breakfast food for every meal but loves broccoli, which is a new one for me when it comes to children his age. Christmas is his favorite holiday and it's not because of the gifts. He says it's because of the *'super awesome movies they have.'* Oh, and he wants a puppy, but not just any puppy, he wants a fluffy one that he can snuggle with and dress as a dinosaur.

James and I make our way back to the bench where Emiline is typing away on her phone. I sit next to her and notice that his dad isn't here yet. "Did you say his dad was coming?" I ask her as James continues to run circles around us, screaming dinosaur screams.

"Yes, he should be here any second," she says checking her phone. "I should warn you before he gets here, though."

Oh God. I don't like that I need a warning before meeting James' dad. Is he an asshole? Does he not want a nanny? Is he going to ask me 900 questions? I can feel myself starting to sweat again with nerves.

I didn't realize I was sitting there in silence until she interrupts my thoughts with a light shoulder nudge.

"It's nothing like that. Take a deep breath," she laughs as if she can hear my thoughts. "Tommy is very protective of James. He is hesitant on getting a nanny because James has only ever had Tommy, myself and my two other brothers. He's also been a little grumpy over the last 5 years," she says with sad eyes. "Yes, even before James. But before that, he was the happiest guy. I don't know what happened to him since, but he's just gotten… how do I put it… angry? I don't know how to even explain it. Not to James though, that boy is the only thing that can light up his life."

I nod. "I understand."

The more she talks, the more I am curious about who I am about to meet and his story. James is only 3 years old, so his dad's grumpiness can't be related to the fact that his mom is not in the picture.

I turn my gaze to see James still playing on the playground and find myself staring at him for a moment. Whoever his dad is, he must really be a superhero daddy because I can tell from the small interaction with him that he's such a great kid. Kids are a direct reflection on the parenting they receive. So, whatever he's doing, he's doing it right and I applaud him for that.

"Oh, perfect timing, he's walking up now," she says.

I remove my gaze from James on the playground to turn around the direction Emiline is looking, to get a look at James' dad.

I swear, my world stops at that moment and I'm pretty sure my jaw is sitting on the grass.

It's… him, I say to myself.

My one-night stand, if you want to even call it that. More like the most epic fucking orgasm from the hottest man I have ever met in my entire life. No joke. Since that night, I haven't had an orgasm of that magnitude or even a relationship for that matter.

Please don't tell me this is happening right now.

He's wearing a pair of dark wash jeans and a solid black t-shirt. It's a simple outfit, yet he still looks like he belongs on the cover of GQ Magazine. He's got the faintest amount of scruff on his jawline that's perfectly cut and shaped. His hair is longer and a little more rugged looking than the last time I saw him, but he's still the finest specimen I have seen. I can tell he still hasn't missed a day at the gym since becoming a dad.

Then a realization hits me.

Since becoming a dad.

What are the chances that he recognizes me? I'm sure he has given half the women of New York City epic orgasms. There is no way in hell he will remember our little finger bang session in the dark hallway. Right? There's no way. *Fuuucckkkk.*

"DADDDDYYY!!" I hear James scream, breaking me out of my trance. How long was I staring at him, exactly?

James jumps off the monkey bars and runs full speed to where his dad is walking towards us. He has yet to lift his head to notice us standing here. He shifts his eyes up from the ground to James and opens his arms wide for a big bear hug.

"Monkey!" he says to his son. *That voice.* That damn, deep raspy voice I remember so vividly like it was yesterday. Hearing it again sends chills down my spine.

"Come meet me new friend, Daddy! She's not related to a football player and she's so cool that she has two first names!" He jumps up and down. "Two first names, Daddy!!"

It's at that moment, he turns his gaze to look in the direction of his sister and me. Finding my eyes, he stops dead in his tracks while James tries to pull him towards us. His mouth slightly spreads apart like he just saw a ghost. If looks could start a fire, consider me completely engulfed in flames.

The last time I saw this man, we were in the hallway of a fucking venue where he gave me the most mind-blowing orgasm of my life with just his fingers. I was in the bathroom getting washed up from that… *experience,* when the fire alarms started blaring overhead. A fire broke out in the kitchen and spread like crazy. I managed to find Kali as soon as I walked out of the bathroom, and she pulled me to the closest open door without looking back. We knew we had to get out of there before the mob of people all tried getting out of one door at the same time. If I could picture it, it was probably worse than Walmart on Black Friday when the doors open at 5am.

He breaks out of his trance from where he was standing and continues walking towards us. His deep blue eyes, that match James', never leave my eyes.

When he reaches us, he stops directly in front of me, hand in hand with his son, but doesn't even acknowledge Emiline standing right next to me.

We both stare at each other silently.

"What the hell took you so long?" Emiline's voice breaks our spell.

"I got stuck on the call," he answers Emiline's question, but his eyes are locked on mine. "I'm sorry it took me so long to find you guys."

I don't see it, but I can feel Emiline's eyes bouncing between Thomas and me, questioning the fact that we are staring at each other with such intensity. His gaze is burning a hole through me the longer we stand here. I can't even find the breath to say hello. He beats me to it, breaking our silence, and the word that comes out of him is the last thing I expected.

"Sunshine."

CHAPTER EIGHT
Thomas

I feel like I'm in an alternate universe.

It's been five years. Five years since I last saw Peyton. I lost her that night when the fire alarm went off. She was gone and I couldn't find her after we all evacuated into the streets. I spent a year trying to find her again. I've never felt a connection with another woman, like I felt with her that night. There was so much electricity between us. Yes, I use electricity because chemistry doesn't seem to cover it.

That night, I never got her last name, where she was from, where she worked or anything about her, but the feel of her body on my hands is a feeling I haven't forgotten, *ever*. And the smell of her forever lingers on me.

Roses. I will never forget the roses.

She looks almost the same as she did that night. Her gorgeous long golden blonde hair is tied up in a hair clip. She's wearing a pair of jean shorts and an oversized t-shirt that's tucked into the front of her shorts. I'm a good foot taller than her. She has to tip her head back just slightly to look me in the eyes when I'm standing this close to her, but her legs seem like they go for days.

Now here she fucking is. Standing in front of me and she might be James' new nanny?

"Wait... Sunshine?" Emiline questions, eyes bouncing between us. "Tommy, do you know Peyton?"

"Yes," Peyton answers for me. "We met a few years ago at a charity gala here in the city."

"This is amazing!" my sister shrieks. "Peyton is looking for a job as a nanny, and from what I've seen of her interactions with James while we waited for you, she's your best bet. Plus, I can tell James is comfortable with her already."

Peyton as my son's nanny? I can't wrap my head around this. I am struggling enough to be in such close proximity to her again without wanting to wrap her up in my arms, inhale her scent, and put my lips on hers. How this woman has this effect on me all these years later, I don't understand.

There's a brief moment of hesitation from Peyton as she looks at me with worried eyes.

"I-I don't know if this is going to work out," she whispers, stealing her gaze from mine to look at Emiline. "I'm so sorry to waste your time this morning. I'm going to get going."

Before she can finish the sentence, she's taking off in a speed walk down the path of the park. She's almost in a run as if she can't get away from me fast enough.

"What the fuck just happened, Tommy?" Emiline scoffs, throwing her hands in the air.

I turn around to see if Peyton is still there and quickly look back over to my sister.

"Watch James for a second, let me go talk to her."

"Don't let her get away, Tommy," she yells as I take off in a sprint to get to her.

I'm running down the path to catch up to her. She's already made it around the path to the wooded area of the park covered with trees. I spot her and immediately pick up my pace.

When I catch up to her, my hand finds the crook of her elbow to stop her and spin her around. The momentum from my pull causes her body to crash into mine with more force than I intend. Her hands are on my chest as if she's ready to push me away and tell me to fuck off. But she closes her eyes as she attempts to regulate her breathing, not moving her hands from my chest. My hands move up to find her wrist and I can feel her rapid pulse under my delicate touch.

"Sunshine," I whisper. "Look at me."

She opens her eyes to look directly into mine. "I-it's you," she whispers. She has the same effect on me that she had five years ago, lighting a fire in my soul with just one look.

"It's you," I whisper back.

Ever so gently, she removes her hands from my chest and takes a step backwards, putting space between us that I don't fucking care for. After all this time, she's standing right in front of me. I need her to take that step back into me. What the fuck has happened to me? I am never ever like this with women. But her? I can't let her go again.

"I'm so sorry for wasting your time here. I had no idea that it was your son when I got the phone call. I just moved here and really need a job."

"Peyton, stop saying you're sorry," I snap but offer her a soft smile. "The past is the past. I need some help with James, and you need a job. Maybe we can help each other out here."

Her eyes widened like she didn't expect me to still ask her to help me out with James. Like she didn't expect me to offer her the job.

I can do this right? Keep this strictly professional?

"But that night—"

"Was one of the best nights of my entire life," I cut her off, not wanting to hear what she has to say about that night and make it any less than what it was.

"I'm not sure this is going to work, Thomas. We have history. If I were to agree to this, it has to be strictly professional. I can't risk anything because I need this job," she says.

"Well lucky for you," I say with a smirk. "I would be your

boss. And from what Emiline told me about you before I ran to catch up to you, I can't let you go. Not again."

"Again?" she repeats, tilting her head just a little bit to question what I just said to her.

"Again, Sunshine," I repeat. "I lost you once. Now, my son needs you. He's the most important thing in my life. He needs a stable person in his life to guide him for the times that I can't be there."

"What exactly are you looking for as far as this job goes?"

"Well, you have to be at the penthouse before he goes off to school and when he gets home. He does half days of preschool right now and with my work schedule, I can't be there to get him to school or get him after school. I work until 6pm, five days a week." I pause to read her expression before I say the next sentence. She shows no expression other than to listen to what the job entails. "I would need you to move into the spare room of my penthouse."

I watch as she sucks in a breath, not expecting to hear that.

I can't have this woman in such close proximity to me. I can barely stand here without touching her as it is, but I need her to be there for James. She wouldn't be moving in for me, she would be moving in for James. Our paths would barely cross. I try to keep my hours regular so James and I can have dinner together every night but sometimes that's not possible. It's likely that we would barely see each other.

I hate this part of being a parent and a businessman, but I know that everything I do and all the work I put in, is helping James have the most stable future to chase whatever dreams he has. Even though right now, he wants to be a fucking dinosaur. I'm sure that phase won't last forever. No matter how much I work, he still looks at me like I hung the moon and fuck if it isn't the best damn feeling in the world.

Before I let her speak again, I continue, "You would have your own space in the apartment. You'd have your own bedroom, bathroom and living space. The kitchen is yours for free range to do whatever you need. When you're off the clock, you don't even have to see us."

"When would I be off the clock?" she asks.

"You would have evenings off as soon as I walk in the door as well as weekends."

"I-I don't even know what to say," she whispers. "Can I think about this?"

"Absolutely, Peyton, but I hope you say yes. James is a very special kid." My hand finds her shoulder. Fuck, my body just needs to touch her.

"He seems like a great kid."

"And I think you would be amazing with him."

"You don't know anything about me, Thomas," she cuts back.

"I would like to know more, Sunshine."

CHAPTER NINE
Peyton

I'm baking a batch of chocolate chip cookies when Kali and Avery get home from work. I wanted to be finished with this batch and hide the evidence that I have been baking since before they got home, but I was unsuccessful in my attempt. I blast some music and immerse myself in the baking process of cookies from scratch. Unfortunately, the girls know.

"Oh fuck, here we go." I hear Avery mutter as she walks into the small apartment. I'm assuming she smells the freshly baked goods through the apartment.

"Don't even start, Avery," I cut her off, my voice louder than I intended it to be. "I have a pounding headache and had the afternoon from hell. I can't even get my brain to work properly right now."

Taking a seat on the barstool at the counter, Kali notices I have opened the tequila and sliced up some limes. Something I don't reach for too often anymore. It's only for emergencies. Today was an emergency that called for baking, tequila, and throwing myself on the couch to watch reruns of *Friends*.

"Dear lord, she's got the tequila out, Avery!" Kali screams over her shoulder before Avery struts into the kitchen.

"Fuck," Avery groans taking a seat next to Kali.

"It's taco Tuesday, Pey," Kali says. "Put the oven mitts down and get dressed. We're going for tacos and drinks at Old Jose. Right fucking now."

Fuck, is it Tuesday? I forgot that before I moved here, we decided that Tuesdays would be our day for getting together at Old Jose for tacos and drinks. It's one of the few places in the city that makes the best buffalo cauliflower tacos. They have a whole vegan section and ever since we found the hole in the wall restaurant, we decided it will be our spot every Tuesday.

Tonight though, I am not in the mood.

"You're going to shut this cookie operation down right now, Pey. And when we get to the restaurant, you're going to spill about whatever the fuck happened that caused this mess here and how your interview went," Avery says, swinging her purse over her shoulder.

I let out an audible groan and before I know it, they are dragging me out the door.

The restaurant is busy tonight, but we're seated quickly in a corner booth in the back, close to the bar. It's like they knew we were going to need more than one round tonight. I order my usual mango margarita. Because tequila; enough said. And then order my buffalo cauliflower tacos.

The girls waste no time getting to the point of dragging me here.

"Spill," Avery says.

I let out a deep breath. "Do you guys remember the charity gala that Kali dragged me to 5 years ago here in the city?"

"Yes," Kali cuts in, laughing. "The night you had the most epic orgasm of your life."

"I'm not laughing, this is serious, you guys."

"Okay, okay, don't get your panties in a twist," Avery says, still fucking laughing. "What about that night?"

"He is the little boy's dad," I let out with a long-drawn-out sigh.

"SHUT THE FUCK UP," Avery screams.

"Would you keep it down?" I shush her, glancing around to make sure she hasn't drawn attention to us. "*This is serious!* I need this job like I need air to breathe."

I don't think they really understand the magnitude of me needing this job. Selling my parents' house and all the belongings that went with it gave me just enough cushion to get started here in the city. And of course, the first job offer I get happens to be with the one guy I thought I would never see again in my life.

"Pey, I don't understand why you're freaking out so much," Avery says. "This job is perfect for you. You are amazing with kids. And honestly, it's not like he's going to be around if you're there to watch his kid. You leave when he gets there. Minimal interaction."

"Well, about that," I whisper, looking down at my drink and immediately taking a sip of my margarita. "He wants me to move into his apartment."

"Woah, woah, daddy wants you to MOVE IN??" Kali lifts a brow at me. "This sounds…. messy."

"I am the messiest person in the world," Avery cuts in. "But this might top anything I've done."

"He said I would have my own space in the apartment. He would be out of my hair. Oh, and I get weekends off."

"Your own space? In an apartment? Where the fuck does he live?" she says.

"That's not important. The problem at hand is how can I work with him and take care of his son when we have *history*."

"I would hardly classify a finger banging orgasm as history," Kali scoffs.

She has a valid point. What history is there between us? It was one night, if you even want to call it that. I'm internally laughing at myself right now for overreacting. There is no history. There's nothing. It was one night that I had forgotten about up until today.

Okay, that is a lie. It took me months to get over that night. I had to get under two different guys to get the memory of him out of my head, but neither of those guys erased that memory because that one orgasm destroyed me for all future men in my life. I gave up trying to chase an orgasm. I am still riding my anti-relationship train that showed no signs of stopping for any man anytime soon either.

"It wasn't just an epic finger banging orgasm," I groan. "When I saw him again, when he was in my personal space again, I felt that same weird buzz in my body from all those years ago," I sigh. "It's still there."

The girls remain silent as they stare at me and then at each other.

"What should I do, guys? I just moved into your apartment. Do I take the job and move out when I just moved in with you?" I ask them both, my gaze bouncing back and forth between them, looking for answers.

"No," Kali answers. "You said you get weekends off? So, you can come and spend the weekends with us. You do your job, keep to yourself and we decompress over the weekend together."

"And don't worry about paying us," Avery interjects. "You're going to be spending most of your time there. It will be like weekend slumber parties." She's now bouncing up and down in her seat, clapping like a little girl who just got told she can finally get the puppy she wanted for so long.

"Are we completely sure about this, you guys?"

"Yes," they both answer simultaneously.

After meeting James at the park, I knew my answer would be yes. In my short interaction with him, I could only imagine how much fun we would have together. I can tell he's such a smart and funny little boy. My only hesitation was when I found out who his dad is, but the girls are right, it's not like I'm going to be spending a lot of time with him. Once he's home, I can clock out and head into my space.

"I think you need to look at this from a different perspective, Pey," Avery adds.

"What do you mean?"

"For one, you get to live in, what I assume, is a massive penthouse. Live that shit up, girl." She dances in her seat. "And two, you can have someone to take care of your *needs* with no strings attached."

"Do you ever pull your mind out of the gutter?"

"Never. My brain lives in the dirtiest of the gutters," she laughs.

"Well, my brain doesn't," I snap back. "And right now, the only thing my brain is focused on is finding my bearings here in the city."

"Pey, out of curiosity, how long has it been?"

"How long has it been since what?"

"Since you got off from something other than *buzz buzz*," she laughs.

Buzz buzz. My trusty vibrator that hasn't failed me yet. I have to think about this for a minute because *how long has it been*? It has to have been three years now since I've been with another man.

"Too long," I finally respond, straightening my back to exude confidence. "And I'm not ashamed of it. You know, I've never had an overactive sex drive like *you*, you freak machine."

"She totally is a freak machine." Kali laughs to my side.

"You're just as much a freak too, Kali. Stop trying to hide that shit," Avery cuts in. "It's not that you're not a freak machine, it's just that you haven't found the right man for the job. The man that *makes* you want it. Once you find him, trust me, you'll turn into a freak machine too."

I scoff at her comment because I think she's wrong. A good orgasm isn't going to make me crave it. I've had some decent orgasms before, and not one has made me run back begging for more. However, there is an exception to that, because my orgasm with Thomas had me wanting to feel his hands all over me for months after that. In fact, I still want to feel his hands all over me.

He's about to be my boss when I accept this job though.

"Okay, I'm gonna do this, guys," I admit.

"Are you going to let daddy bang you into next week, as well?" Avery questions.

"I'm not going to actively pursue him, Avery. But I'm also not going to stop anything if he decides to pursue *something* down the road."

"That's my fucking girl," she screams.

My mind is all over the place right now and I can't help but think of the consequences of giving into him if he did try something.

I need this job. I need this job. I repeat to myself, and I think the decision is finally made.

Who knew the answers to life's questions could be found over tacos and tequila.

CHAPTER TEN
Thomas

"What the fuck is up your ass this week, shit bag?" Oliver mutters.

He's home after spending the last month in Egypt. Doing fuck knows what. I don't ask questions because his answer is always the same, "*I was getting my dick wet.*" It's always the same song and dance with my brother. So, I just stopped asking him about his 'adventures'.

"Nothing, butt fuck," I snap back, taking a long swig of whiskey. "And get your feet off my desk. This isn't your home."

"He's got a point, Tommy," Marc cuts in, "You're grumpier than usual this week."

He's not wrong. I can't seem to get the thought of the new nanny out of my head. Although she's not even my nanny yet, since she hasn't given me an answer. What is there to think about? I am offering her a job that she says she desperately needs, and a place to live at no cost. Fuck, did I tell her that it's no cost? Maybe that will convince her.

What the hell is her story? That's what has me so wound up. Where did she come from? Did she not live here before? Is she not accepting the position because she's in a relationship now? Fuck, that thought didn't even cross my mind.

"It's about the possible new nanny. She hasn't accepted the position yet." I run my hands down my face. "With James starting preschool again next week for the school year, I need her to start as soon as possible. Emiline starts nursing school the same day and I'm basically fucked if she says no."

"You know—" Marc starts to say but is interrupted by my office phone ringing.

"Mr. Ford, I have your sister, Emiline on line one," my assistant says over the intercom.

"Thank you, Ruth," I say, picking up the phone to answer the call. "Emiline, what's up? Is everything okay?"

"Hi, big brother. I'm doing well. How about you?" she mutters sarcastically on the other end of the phone. I let out an audible groan. "Of course everything is okay. I'm calling regarding your nanny!" I can feel her gleaming over the phone.

I pause because... SHIT. My stomach twists and an uneasy feeling surfaces in my gut. Please, for the love of God, be calling to tell me that she said yes.

"What's the verdict, Em?"

"It looks like you have a new nanny, big bro," she shrieks, and I find myself taking a breath of relief. "She wants to meet with you today if you're available. I told her you're working, but she was pretty persistent and would like to see you as soon as possible."

"Yes, of course. I need her to start next week, so today will work. Can you send her to my office?" I open my planner to check to see when I am available today. "I am free for the next 3 hours. Have her come into the office as soon as she can. I will give the desk her name."

"Great, I will relay the message. She—"

I don't even let her finish before hanging up the phone. My head is reeling over the fact that she said yes. James is going to be so happy. After they met a couple days ago, James hasn't stopped talking about her, and is so fascinated by the fact that she has two first names. I am still trying to get him to understand that the last name sounds like a first name, but it's really a last name. I gave up, and just started letting him think what he wants to think in that magical little brain of his.

"So?" Marc cuts me off from my thoughts.

"Sounds like she agreed to be the nanny." I rub my hands down my face, letting out a frustrated breath.

"Why are you still all fucked up over it, then?" Oliver laughs, helping himself to my office whiskey stash.

"Dude, this isn't your fucking house. Hands off the whiskey," I snap at him, returning my gaze back to Marc. "We have *history*. I don't know how to maneuver this whole situation."

"History?" Marc repeats, "You knew her before you met the other day?"

"Yes. Remember that charity gala five years ago? The one that got cut short when the fire started in the kitchen?"

"How could I forget." Oliver clutches his stomach, laughing so hard. "You went nuts for hours when we evacuated, trying to locate the girl you finger fucked into orgasm land. It was like she didn't exist, though."

And then, Oliver abruptly stops laughing and his gaze turns to Marc who is already looking at him with his jaw on the floor. It's written all over their face, that they figured out the fucking problem I am having about the new nanny.

"So, you two fuck twits understand my situation now?" I say, louder than intended with my arms spread out in the air to make a goddamn point.

Looking back at that night with Peyton, I think maybe I did go a tad bit psycho over losing her. I mean, she didn't get a chance to tell me that it was an epic orgasm, but I witnessed the way her body reacted to me. The way she moaned my name over and over, as her orgasm rippled through her body. Great, now I'm rocking a fucking semi. I need to get my brothers out of here before she shows up.

"You two need to go," I say when the two of them don't respond. "I don't want you here when she shows up."

Oliver throws himself back on the couch, kicking his feet up on the coffee table and crossing both legs. Both hands are behind his head signifying that he doesn't plan on moving from his spot. "I'm good right here, big bro."

"Get out, both of you." I snap my arm out, pointing my finger at the open door.

"Fine, we're going." Marc throws his hands up in a surrender. "But we want updates tonight. Don't forget about drinks tonight at Moores."

"Fuck, is it Wednesday already? Shit, yeah I'll be there," I confirm, running my hands through my hair.

When we all turned 21, we started meeting every Wednesday for 'hump day' drinks at Moores, a quiet bar in the city. We chose this day of the week because the bar isn't too packed, and we always left with a chick that we can hump into Thursdays. Since we started that, a lot has changed. It's about every other Wednesday now, give or take, and now it's just Logan or Oliver bringing girls home. I mean if he's even in town. Since James was born, it's been more of just getting together with Marc or Logan and decompressing from the work week.

"I'll call you guys as I'm heading out," I say to them as they walk out the door.

As much as I don't feel like going out tonight, I think I am going to really need that whiskey after meeting with Peyton. I'm doing my damn hardest to get that night out of my brain and function like a normal human being when she's around. She's going to be my son's nanny, so I have to reign it in and do my part to keep this professional.

I have to keep it this way because my son needs someone. Emiline told me all about their interaction before I walked up at the park yesterday and she was adamant that I needed to hire her because of how she interacted with him and not let her go. This is what he needs right now. More than that, that's what he *deserves* when I can't be there for him.

I close the door behind my brothers, fall onto the loveseat in my office and call the front desk to let them know about Peyton coming. Now, I can have some quiet time to really focus on my thoughts. *I can do this, you know, be in her presence after all these years. I know I can.* I can't do relationships anyway because I swore them off after Sheila burned me. I didn't do them before her, but I tried to make one work for James. Epic fail. That alone is enough reason to control myself around Peyton and make sure no part of me even thinks about pursuing her. After an hour of internally battling with my own brain and attempting to get some emails answered, I hear a soft knock on the door.

"Yes, come in," I call out.

Everything I just talked myself out of has gone out the fucking window as Peyton slowly walks into my office. She looks even more stunning than yesterday when I saw her at the park. Her long hair is let down with soft curls hanging over her almost bare shoulder. She is wearing a light blue sundress that matches her blue eyes and flows just above her knee.

"Peyton." I can feel my voice crack when I say her name. "Please come in."

"Thank you for meeting me on such short notice," she says, staring at the ground as she takes a seat at the farthest seat across the room from me. "I just want to discuss some details of the job before I get started."

"Of course, of course." I cross the room, unbuttoning my suit jacket and lean against my desk. I cross my arms in front of my chest and continue, "James will be very excited to hear that the two first name nanny will be taking care of him."

I think I have successfully broken the tension in the room when I hear her let out a light laugh. "I am very excited to be his nanny," she says, looking up from the ground. "It seems like you have done a very good job raising him."

Hit me right in the chest with that compliment, why don't you?

"T-thank you for that. I do the best I can with the schedule I have," I say, crossing the room to sit in the chair near her. I don't feel like I am as close to her as I want to be, but it's just enough space for this moment. Taking a seat, I lean back and cross my leg over the other resting my ankle on my thigh.

I can visibly see her swallow from her seat as she shuffles to cross her legs.

"What do you do here for work?" she asks, as she scans the room to take in the large office.

"I own Ford Enterprises," I say confidently. "We invest in properties around the city. It's mostly high-rise businesses and apartments."

"But isn't most of the city built full of high rises and large apartment buildings?" she asks.

I smirk a little at her question. "It is. And my name is on all of them."

Her mouth falls open when the realization hits her. "Thomas Ford?"

"In the flesh," I say, spreading my arms out wide.

She pauses as she fiddles with the hem of her dress. She's sitting so close, yet so far away from me.

"The other day at the park, you said you just moved here. Where did you move from?" I take that moment to ask her. I want to dig into her life and get to know her the way I didn't get to know her the first night.

Tucking a strand of loose hair behind her ear, she looks up and says, "I moved here from South Jersey. I grew up in a small town outside of the shore and it's where I lived my whole life, up until a couple of days before I met you in the park."

That explains why I was never able to find her again. For a while after the charity gala, I would find myself walking the streets of the city and keeping my eyes open and waiting for a golden blonde-haired beauty to walk the crosswalk. You know, like the movies where they find the girl they have been dreaming about for so long and it's all in slow motion? Yeah, I was waiting for that moment with her, but it never came.

"That explains it." I nod.

"That explains what?" She tilts her head, questioning me.

"Why I couldn't find you again."

"Y-you looked for me?" She gasps.

"Every day for almost a year, Peyton." *I didn't want to admit this to her right now*, thinking to myself, after the words came out. I should have kept my mouth shut because I don't want to scare her away. She's here to discuss the job. Fuck, I hope she hasn't changed her mind at my confession.

Her eyes go wide and she's completely still and silent, as if she doesn't know what to say in response to me. "Let's get back to why you're here, Peyton."

"Of course, yes. Why I'm here," she repeats nervously, giggling and playing with the delicate strand of her hair.

God, her fucking laugh is the cutest sound I have ever heard.

Rein it in, boss! Fuck.

I let out a light laugh with her. "I know it's very short notice to get things moving, but James starts school on Monday and Emiline also starts nursing school the same day. So I am going to need you to move into the penthouse within the next couple days," I pause, looking her directly in the eyes. "No later than this weekend. Does that work for you?"

"A penthouse." There was no sense of question in the words that just came out of her mouth.

"Yes, you would have your own space. We would be completely out of your hair and vice versa when you're off shift." I let out a breath before I continue, "But I just have one important rule."

"What's that?"

Looking her directly in the eyes, I say, "Let me know ahead of time if you are going to have any male guests in the apartment. James is a very curious kid and questions a lot and I don't want him to start questioning you."

She blushes at my request.

"You have nothing to worry about in that department."

I breathe a fucking sigh of relief. I hope that means what I think it means and that she's single. My request was more for me to find out because I don't plan to pursue her since she will be my employee. But fuck, I don't like the idea of seeing her with another guy in my own living space.

After what feels like minutes of silence, I feel a strange hesitation radiating off of her as she sits there spinning her curls in her hair as if she's nervous to say the next words that come out of her mouth.

"H-how much is the pay?" she finally stutters.

Returning my gaze back to her, I let out, "Six thousand a week and that includes your housing."

Her eyes go wide, and you would think her eyeballs were about to pop out of her head. She clearly was not expecting me to offer her that amount of money to live in my house and take care of my son. She should know by now that I have more money than I know what to do with and James is worth it to have the best nanny.

"I-I don't even know what to say," she says as her gaze turns to the floor. "That's a lot more than I expected."

I stand up from the chair as she continues her rambling and nervous thoughts.

"This is my first nanny job, and my only experience is working in a daycare and substitute teaching. I-I don't have the experience for that kind of pay. I—"

I interrupt her thoughts, moving over her small frame, putting my finger delicately under her chin to guide her gaze up to look me in the eyes.

"You're worth it, Sunshine."

CHAPTER ELEVEN
Peyton

I'm left speechless as I look up at him from my seat while his fingers delicately touch my chin.

There is no way this man is seriously about to pay me *six thousand dollars* a week to live in his home and watch his son during the week. I don't have any experience being a nanny and the experience I do have with kids, it's from working part-time in a daycare center. I wonder if he's on some sort of drugs today, or has he been drinking? It's eleven o'clock in the morning. I think maybe he's just crazy.

Part of me could really use that money while I try to make something of myself in the city. I have spent most of my life dependent on my parents. This nanny job wouldn't be a forever thing and this amount of money would definitely get me out of the hole I'm currently in. I want to be able to help my grandma out with medical bills and living expenses, so she isn't living check to check with social security. I would be able to save enough that I can move back to the suburbs and buy my own house with a yard closed in by a white picket fence and a long driveway.

How long have I been sitting here staring at him? Shit.

I break the silence by asking, "What would the week look like as far as working with James?"

"James wakes up around 7am every morning to get ready for school. I am out the door by 7:30 and then a car comes to get him around 9am," he states.

"Okay, great."

"He only does a half day at preschool, so the car drops him back off around 1pm. Once he is home, you're free to do whatever you'd like with him," he says. "James loves going to the park or just staying home and playing with his never-ending pile of toys."

"How far is the park from where you live?" I ask, forgetting that I haven't told him that I don't own a car anymore. It was one of the things I had to part with to be able to afford moving to the city. Kali assured me that I wouldn't need one because everyone gets everywhere on bike or by foot.

"It's not far, about 3 miles away," he says. Sensing my newfound nervousness, he asks, "Is that okay?"

"I-I..." shit, how am I going to tell him I'm a broke bitch without telling him I'm a broke bitch? "I don't have a car," I say, frowning at him. "I had to sell it in order to afford moving here. Plus, I assumed I would just use the subway or walk anywhere I have to go."

He stops for a moment to take me in. He's not looking at me in disgust or pity, he's looking at me like he wants to know more. I want to tell him all about me and I want to get to know him more, but these lines can't be crossed anymore. We have our history and it's just that. History. From here on out, it's going to be about James and keeping my relationship with Thomas as professional as possible.

Reaching into his desk, he digs for a moment and pulls out a set of keys and tosses them to me. Looking down in my lap, I see the symbol of what I think is a foreign car brand. I don't know jack shit about cars, but I can tell from this thing-a-ma-jig, that this is probably the key to something expensive as shit. It doesn't even have a key to insert into an ignition.

"Take that one," he says without hesitation as if he's got a plethora of cars at his disposal. "It's an SUV, so it's safe for you to drive around with James. The backseat already has a car seat installed for him. It's yours while you're working for me."

"I can't accept this."

"You can," he abruptly replies. "The safety of James is a priority for me, and I want you to be able to take him where he wants to go, without question."

"I don't know what to say."

"Just tell me you'll accept the job, Peyton."

I came here to his office already knowing I was accepting the job. He might have thrown me a couple curve balls with the car, crazy pay and talk of living in my own space of a penthouse but I am one hundred and ten percent sold on the job because it's more than I have ever dreamed that would happen for me.

"I just have one last question," I say to him, trying to find confidence in my words, "When can we expect you home each night?"

I can tell that I have offended him with that question when I see a shift in his body language and the look he points in my direction. It's a valid question on my part, though. I need to know if he's going to be home at normal working hours. Does he have a girlfriend who he stops by to see after work? Does he like to go out for drinks at the bar if he has a long day? I don't know enough about him to know for sure.

"I'm always home right after work, Peyton," he pauses. "You can expect me home anywhere around 6pm, but sometimes as late as 7pm. It just depends on how late my meetings run."

"I don't mind staying with James longer if you go out." I shrug.

He stalks across the room to stand directly in front of me, closing in on my personal space. The temperature in my body begins to rise with him being this close to me and I feel myself sucking in a breath, waiting for what he's going to say.

"I don't go out," he says as he looks me in the eyes. "I don't live that life anymore, Peyton."

What does he mean by that?

I want to ask him more, but at the risk of sounding too clingy and blurring the lines between us, I just say what I came here to officially say.

"I-I would like to officially accept the job, Mr. Ford."

The corners of his lips slightly curve up. "Please, call me Thomas."

He starts to move away from my personal space. The air suddenly feels colder now that he's no longer in such close proximity. *Come back,* I want to say, but it would come out hoarse like Rose laying on that stupid door in the cold ocean after the Titanic sank. There was plenty of room on that fucking door for Jack to live.

Thomas walks behind his desk and removes his suit jacket to place it on the back of his chair, then rolls up the sleeves of his white dress shirt. His thick, corded muscles on his forearms are covered in tattoos, something I hadn't seen before today. Seeing the veins protruding from every exposed part of his arms, just proves to me how strong this man is. I am such a hoe for a man's forearms.

With him standing behind his desk, I use this moment to take him in and watch him as he moves. I can only imagine how he dominates the boardroom and I bet he owns the shit out of it. He's wearing a dark navy-blue suit, the same as the first night I met him, and I wouldn't be surprised if his entire closet was lined with navy blue suits. He starts shuffling through his desk to pull out a piece of paper.

"Here is the address to the penthouse," he says, handing me the paper. "When you get to the building, just give your name to Jim at the front desk. He will get you a personal key card and guide you to the private elevator at the back of the building that goes directly to my floor." He pauses, to take me in one more time. "And here's my cell phone number, program it into your phone. Send me a text later today and let me know what day you plan to move in. I will get the housekeeper to have your room ready for you."

Looking between him and the piece of paper in my hand, I return my gaze back to him. I have words lodged in my throat, but I can't seem to find anything to say.

"T-thank you," is the only thing I can muster up to say.

He crosses his desk to walk towards me and as he gets closer, I feel air trapped in my lungs, finding it hard to breathe. He stops directly in front of me and my head tilts up slightly to meet his gaze. His hand tucks a small strand of hair behind my ear and electricity shoots through my body. I let out a breath of air and lean into his hand. My fucking body has a mind of its own when he's this close to me.

"No. Thank *you*, Peyton." The corner of his lip tilts up. "You're going to be really helping me out a lot with James."

I nod and when he takes a small step away from me, I grab my bag and walk towards the door. I pause at the door and give one more glance over my shoulder to find Thomas standing in the middle of his office with both of his hands tucked into his pockets and a smile on his face.

"I'll text you later today," I say and raise my hand to give an awkward wave.

"I look forward to it, Sunshine."

I'm out the door with his nickname for me ringing in my ears and I can't decide if taking this job is the best or worst decision I've made since moving to the city.

CHAPTER TWELVE
Peyton

I texted Thomas a few hours after leaving his office yesterday, letting him know that I would be over today to start moving my stuff in. My thoughts were all over the place before I gave him a definite time because part of myself wanted to move in at the last possible minute and the other part of me wanted some time to get to know James and make him comfortable with me living in his space.

Now, I'm packing up the last of my stuff at Kali and Avery's before I spend the rest of the day unpacking into the new space.

"Okay, you're all packed up here," Avery says, pulling me from my thoughts as she steps into the room.

"Thank you, Ave," I say quietly. "I appreciate your help."

"That's what friends are for, bitch," she laughs. "Besides, I want to see what daddy's apartment looks like."

"Please stop calling him that," I laugh back at her.

"What?" She throws her hands in the air. "I'm just calling it like I see it and he's a daddy."

I roll my eyes at her as I brush past her to bring the last box into the hallway.

"Are you ready to go?" I ask her.

"You're not bringing your smut trophies with you?" She smirks.

"No, Avery. What if James gets his hands on them?"

"He's three! He can't read them." She picks one up and opens it up to a page I have tabbed and annotated to read a line out loud, "*Fuck, baby, do you feel how hard my cock is for you? Do you feel what you're doing to me*?" She mocks as I swipe it from her hand.

"Hey!" I chuckle. "Lulu Moore writes about some hot hockey players. Those boys are some of my favorites and you can't blame a girl for wanting a little smut in her life. Hockey players are a superior trope."

"That's not even a trope!" She laughs at me. "Besides, single dad is the superior trope. Try and fight me on it."

"You be quiet, I'm making it a trope." I laugh back as I place *Felix* back on the shelf with the rest of the New York Players collection from Lulu Moore. "Besides you haven't even read Maren Moore's *Totally Pucked* series. If you did like I told you to forever ago, you would understand that hockey is the superior trope." Her body rumbles with a full belly laugh and she rolls her eyes at me. "Now let's go, Avery. I want to get settled before he gets home from work."

We hustle out of the apartment and load the boxes into her car. Pulling out the paper he gave me yesterday with his address on it, I plug it into my phone's GPS and we're on our way.

Before I know it, we're pulling up to the largest building in the city. I mean, close to the largest; it's certainly not the empire state building but it might as well be. Standing next to the vehicle, I look up at the building in front of me. It must be a hundred stories tall. I glance down at the paper to make sure we're at the right address.

Before we unload the car, I want to confirm it's the right place. We enter the lobby and find an elderly man sitting at the front desk, typing away on the computer. Glancing at his name tag, I see the name 'Jim' and I know I'm in the right place.

"Hi," I greet him. "My name is Peyton Kelly, I'm here-"

"For Mr. Ford," he interrupts.

"Yes, that's me."

"Welcome to Sunset Square, ma'am. I have already made you a key card for the private elevator that takes you to Mr. Ford's penthouse."

I look over to Avery standing next to me with her jaw on the floor.

Girl, I can't believe this myself.

"Thank you, that's very kind of you."

"It's my pleasure, ma'am. Allow me to show you where the elevator is."

He opens his arms to guide me down a hall that has a sign that says, 'staff only beyond this point.' When he said private elevator, I was expecting a separate one just off to the side of the main elevators that needs a special key card to access it. I was not expecting it to be so private that it's in the staff quarters.

He swipes my key card to make sure it works before he hands it to me and the three of us load into the elevator. I look down at the card and notice a photo of the New York City skyline at sunset. When I flip the card over, I see that it says, *'Private Access to the Thomas Ford Penthouse,'* and I suck in a breath as I stare down at it, completely unsure what I am about to walk into.

Jim breaks the silence for us. "This elevator only goes to Mr. Ford's penthouse. You just need to tap your card and press the arrow up."

"Thank you," is all I can muster up the courage to say.

The elevator dings, the doors open, and my mouth falls to the ground. My feet are cemented in place as I take in the sight in front of me.

The elevators open up to the largest living space I have ever seen. There is a large tv mounted on the most gorgeous gray marbled wall that hangs right above an electric fireplace. There's a plush gray sectional sofa in the middle of the space packed with pillows, right in front of the floor to ceiling windows that open up to a balcony overlooking the New York skyline.

Finally, I allow myself to walk into the open space to take in the rest of the apartment. There's a staircase just behind the sectional, which I am assuming is where James and Thomas' rooms are, and multiple hallways leading off of this living space. I don't know which hallway is where I should be heading.

"Right this way." I hear Jim say, as if he can hear my thoughts.

He leads me down the hallway that's in the opposite direction of the staircase. It's a long hallway and I notice that there aren't many pictures on the walls. We pass by a door that's open, and I can see that it's set up like an office. That must be where he works when he's home.

Continuing down the hall, I'm led to another living space that has a couch, tv and a bedroom off to one corner. Pausing to take it all in, I notice this space is about as big as my apartment with the girls.

The bedroom is small, but it's the perfect size for me. Like the other living space, it has floor to ceiling windows and the views are beyond incredible. I make my way into the bathroom and I'm pretty sure my jaw is on the floor when I take in the view before me. There's a shower that can easily fit four people in it with two different shower heads and a massive Victorian style bathtub that sits in front of floor to ceiling windows that overlook Central Park. The first thing I will be doing is soaking in that bathtub and enjoying the view. My eyes travel to the double sinks on the opposite wall and take note of the basket put together for me filled with lavender soaps and body scrubs.

I can't help but pinch myself because this must be a dream. I'm being paid six grand a week to live here.

"Peyton," Avery interrupts my thoughts as she steps into the bathroom. She's spinning around and taking it all in with me. "This place is unreal! You are such a lucky bitch."

I don't respond back but give a tight nod still staring at the bathtub and the view.

"Pey, come check out this balcony!" Avery bellows from outside, now.

Stepping onto the balcony that connects to my room, I am blown away by the view. I can see the entire skyline of the city including Central Park. I hadn't noticed before but there are only windows on one side of the building. Every window faces West, which is where the sun sets. That must be why this place is called Sunset Square.

I nudge her shoulder as we both take in the sight. "Hey, I should have brought my books. This would be the reading spot for some smut, huh?"

We look at each other and burst out laughing because I think neither of us can believe that this is really happening right now. I know I can't.

"Come on, Ave. Let's get my stuff unpacked before he gets home."

CHAPTER THIRTEEN

Thomas

"Daddy, what does frick mean?" James asks from the backseat.

"Who said that, JJ?"

"Uncle Marky said, 'What the frick are you doing?' today to one of the peoples at his work. What does it mean?"

Shaking my head, I respond with, "You're too intuitive for your own good, James."

"What's int-intuative mean?"

"Okay, that's enough for the day." I laugh at him. "We're almost home, James. Remember I told you that Ms. Peyton would be moving in today? She's going to be helping daddy out and watching you when Aunt Em starts school."

"I can't wait!" he shrieks from the back seat. "She's going to love my dinosaur collection. I'm going to teach her how to sound like one too! I have the best RAWR, Daddy!"

"That you do, bud."

The drive home after getting James from Marc's apartment has me more nervous than normal. I am not a person who usually feels these types of things, but I haven't had anyone live here since James was born. That side of the penthouse has been practically untouched.

I lived in a total bachelor pad before this. It was the perfect spot, close to all the bars and clubs so I could go out with the guys and come home for a happy ending. I bought this place because I knew James needed a solid foundation of a home to live in. There were supposed to be three of us here, but Sheila wanted no part in any of it.

With Peyton being here, it's going to feel all sorts of weird as fuck because we aren't used to having a female around us all the time. And another part is her history with me, but James obviously doesn't know this. When she showed up in my office, I almost lost all my restraint around her. My hands craved to touch her, and I wanted to spread her out on my desk to eat like it was my last meal. I'm damn proud of myself for keeping it as professional as I did.

I park the car and James and I walk hand in hand into the lobby.

"Good evening, Mr. Ford," Jim greets me with a smile. "And good evening to you too, Mr. James," he says to James.

"Hiya, Jimbo!" James greets. "How's Dooky-west doing?"

Jim and I both let out a full belly laugh. Every day, James asks how 'Dooky-west' is doing. Yes, dooky... like one you drop in the toilet. When James was two, Jim asked him what he should name his goldfish and James chose Dooky-west. Jim didn't have the heart to tell James to pick another name when he saw how excited he was. So here we are, asking how Dooky-west, the goldfish, is doing today.

"He's doing great, James," he continues to laugh. "Have a good night, Mr. Ford."

"Thanks, you too, Jim."

"Oh and Mr. Ford?" He stops me as I walk away. "Your new guest has settled in nicely."

I give him a tight nod as James and I enter the elevator. I can feel my stomach sinking with nerves and I hope he's right that she is settled in and feels comfortable here.

The elevator doors ding open and it's dark and quiet in the living space. James immediately runs upstairs to his room to get ready for his bath. He's so good with his routine when we get home in the evenings, and I am so lucky that he never tries to fight me on it. While he makes himself busy, I find myself walking down the hallway to greet Peyton and see if she needs anything.

I pause outside the door of her space when I hear music coming from the other side. I give three hard knocks on the door. When she doesn't answer after a few moments, I turn the doorknob to see if it's unlocked and sure as shit, it is.

Slowly pushing the door open, I scan the room, but I don't see her anywhere.

"Peyton?" I call out to the room.

She still doesn't answer, so I walk over to the bathroom door where the music is coming from. I knock three times on that door, calling her name but there is still no answer.

Panic takes over me that something might have happened to her. I don't know why my mind always goes to the worst-case scenario. Maybe it's the dad instinct in me, but I don't hear movement on the other side of the door, just the music. Turning the knob, I fling the door open, and Peyton lets out a shriek.

She's naked.

She's fucking naked, soaking in the oversized bathtub in the ensuite bathroom directly next to the floor to ceiling windows that overlook the city.

"Thomas!" she screams.

I can't find it in me to look away and for some reason, she hasn't moved her hands out from under the water to cover herself up either.

Her hair is pulled up in a messy bun and her breasts are beautiful, rounded mounds that would fit my hands perfectly. I can't see anything below them because of those stupid bubbles that are covering her slim waist and tight pussy I remember so vividly.

"THOMAS!" she bellows again, and I'm snapped out of my trance.

My hand finally snaps to cover my eyes, to respect her privacy and you know, keep the lines of professionalism drawn, blah blah. *Fuck the lines.* That's what I think.

"Peyton, oh my God, I am so sorry!" I yell back at her, with my hand still over my eyes. "I knocked multiple times, and you didn't answer so I wanted to make sure you were okay."

"I'm okay—"

"I *know* you're okay," I interrupt her as I adjust the semi growing in my pants so she can't see it.

"We can talk when I get out," she replies in a much softer tone from our bathroom yelling match. Even though I can barely hear her over Taylor Swift singing about how she's the problem.

"I'll be in the kitchen."

And then, I'm walking out the door before I even let her respond.

If Peyton was comfortable before I got home from work, she sure as fuck is uncomfortable now.

———

I was trying to avoid an awkward conversation with Peyton before James went to bed, so I didn't wait for her in the kitchen. Having a kid who asks too many questions shouldn't be listening to this conversation about how I barged into her bathroom and saw her naked as fuck, taking a bubble bath.

After putting James to bed, I make my way downstairs to the kitchen and find Peyton shuffling through the cabinets, like she's looking for something.

Her long hair is still wet from her bath and hangs down to her lower back. She's wearing a pair of tight black leggings and a gray oversized sweatshirt that says 'DiLaurentis' on the back with the numbers '66' written underneath it. My heart begins to pound at the thought that she's wearing her boyfriend's sweatshirt. She told me in my office that I had nothing to worry about when it came to men coming to visit her at the apartment. Did I read her response wrong?

She doesn't hear me approach, so she's startled when she hears me pull the bar stool away from the counter as I take a seat.

"You scared the shit out of me, Thomas," she shrieks.

I let out a chuckle. "I'm sorry, I thought you heard me come in. Are you looking for something in particular?"

"I was going to make something for dinner because I haven't eaten yet, but I can't find anything I can eat here," she says in such a soft tone, I can barely hear the end of the sentence.

"What do you mean? Rosie stocked the pantry before you came."

"Rosie?"

"Rosie is my housekeeper. She also does the grocery shopping for me. Occasionally she makes some meals for us and puts them in the fridge for easy grab and go lunches."

"Oh," is all she says back, feeling defeated.

I tilt my head to the side to question her without pushing it. I want her to tell me what the big deal is. I know for a fact that Rosie stocked the fridge and the pantry with more than what we usually get because she knew a guest would be moving in here.

"I-I can't eat a lot of this stuff," she answers my silent question.

"I don't understand."

"I'm a vegan. I don't eat meat, fish, eggs, cheese, or milk. You know? All the good stuff everyone wants for snacks that comes from animals." She laughs at herself.

"I am so sorry, Peyton. I had no idea," I rise from my stool to take a pad out of the junk drawer. "Here. Write down what you need or would like to have in the house, and I will make sure Rosie gets it for you. If I had known…" I run my hand through my hair and scratch the back of my head. "I would have made sure it was here."

"It's not your fault, Thomas. You didn't know," she replies

softly. "But I really appreciate you doing that for me. I can always walk to the store in the morning."

I start to think about what else I don't know about her as I move to sit back at the bar stool. I know she's amazing with James and has a history of working in a daycare center where she worked for many years. Her dedication to one place tells me she's a committed employee. But it seems like she sold her life to move here, but why?

I really want to avoid awkward conversation about the incident earlier, so I start with, "Tell me more about yourself, Peyton."

At the same time, she says, "About what happened before…"

We both look at each other and laugh.

She's standing on the other side of the large white marble island in the kitchen, leaning on her elbows facing me and I'm planted on my bar stool. I make a move to pull out the bar stool next to me, encouraging her to take a seat by patting it with my hand.

Moving to take a seat, she speaks first, "I'm sorry for screaming at you earlier in my bathroom."

Is this girl serious right now? Why is she apologizing for *me* barging in on *her*?

"What in the world are you sorry for, Peyton?"

"I shouldn't have screamed at you like that. This is your home."

Without thinking, my hand lands on top of hers resting on the counter. The same buzz I felt all those years ago races through my body.

"Peyton." I let out a sigh. "This is your house now too. I invaded your personal space. You had every right to yell at me the way you did. I'm the one who needs to apologize for not being able to take my eyes off you."

She blushes at my statement but makes no move to remove my hand from the top of hers. "Y-you avoided me tonight." It's a statement, not a question.

"Admittedly, yes and I'm sorry for that. I just felt really bad about barging in on you like that when you've only been here for a few hours."

"Apology accepted." She turns her head to give me a faint smile.

God, she's so fucking cute.

My eyes scan the front of her sweatshirt and it's as if she can sense me wondering about the university logo on the front. Her eyes shoot down to scan the shirt she's wearing, and I can see her cheeks turning red when her gaze returns to mine.

"I didn't go here," she admits with a smile. "It's not even a real school."

I tilt my head to the side to give her a questioning eye.

"D-Dean DiLaurentis," she stutters. "He's a character in one of my favorite hockey romance books. I won it in a bookstagram giveaway and it's the coziest sweatshirt I own."

I am not even going to attempt to understand what a bookstagram is.

I breathe out a sigh of relief and I feel my mouth curve into a smile at the realization that the sweatshirt doesn't actually belong to a boyfriend.

"So, you said you were hungry?" I move to get up from the stool and shuffle through the junk drawer full of take-out menus. "What's your pick for dinner?"

"Are you in the mood for tacos?" she says enthusiastically, like she's praying I say yes.

"I could totally go for some tacos," I laugh back at her cuteness.

"Old Jose has the best tacos," she says. "And they make an awesome buffalo cauliflower taco dish!"

"Old Jose it is. I'll order and have Eddy grab it for us."

"Eddy?"

"He's my driver. He runs any errands for me, drives me to work and brings James to and from school."

"Wow." Her eyes widen. "Here you are with a whole driver, and I don't even have a car."

"Correction." I lean in close. Her scent taking over the space between. "You have a car now."

She nods. "I guess I do."

"I'm going to shower, and I'll meet you in the living room."

We both make our way in that direction, and I watch her as I make my way up the stairs slowly. She makes herself comfortable on the corner spot of the couch. She's surrounded by pillows and pulls the blanket down from the back to cover herself up.

I peek in on James to see he is sound asleep before I head into the shower. The thoughts of her covered in soap from earlier and her perfect tits hovering just about the water line take over my brain and I find my hand reaching for my cock in the shower. One hand lays on the tile shower wall and the other is fisted tightly around my dick, stroking it to every thought of her I have had since she returned back into my life. Her tight pussy convulsing around my fingers years ago, her cum dripping down my wrists, and the sundress she wore to my office. Cum spills out of my dick, harder than I have ever come before and I find it hard to move out from under the hot water flowing down my back.

I allow myself this one last time to think these thoughts about her.

She's my son's nanny.

She's here for my son.

She can never be anything more than that.

CHAPTER FOURTEEN
Peyton

I wake up to light pouring into my room and I realize I'm in a strange place. I'm not in the apartment with Kali and Avery, nor am I in the new room I was supposed to be in. I am sprawled out on the softest couch I have ever been on, surrounded by pillows.

I'm still half asleep when I feel a tiny hand tug on my arm.

"Ms. Peyton, are you awake?" he whispers.

"Good morning, James," I whisper back. "Please just call me Peyton."

"My daddy told me I have to be respectability to you."

I laugh in my half-asleep state, because he's the cutest kid trying to use big adult words.

I haven't seen James since I moved in yesterday and while my shifts don't start until Monday morning, I want to take the morning to get to know him a little bit more, I want him to be comfortable with me. I take a minute to take him in. He looks so much like his father with his blue eyes and little combed over hairstyle. His hair is lighter than Thomas', but it's the same style. James is wearing dinosaur pajamas and I wonder what time it is and where Thomas is this morning.

"Where's your daddy, bud?"

"He's still sleeping," he whispers. "He told me last night he wasn't going to work today and was going to work from home."

Shit, I wasn't expecting that today, nor was I expecting to wake up on the couch. Last night, Thomas ordered us dinner and said he was going to take a shower before it arrived. I must have fallen asleep while he was upstairs. I was starving after having that weird conversation with him because sometimes people look at me different when they find out I'm vegan. The fact that Thomas didn't, caused my belly some weird fluttery feelings. Instead of judging me and questioning my choices, he just asked me to write down what I like so Rosie can stock the kitchen for me. Talk about swoon.

I have been eating vegan since I was about 18 years old. It's mostly for my love of animals but it's also just a personal preference. I noticed when I switched to a plant-based diet, I started to feel better in general. I started sleeping better and had less stomach issues. Contrary to what people believe, I actually enjoy my vegan food choices.

To add to the conversation about my food preferences, we had to tackle the elephant in the room. He walked in on me soaking in the luxurious bathtub.

Last night I learned two things: first is the reason why they call this building Sunset Square, because when I stepped into the bathroom and looked out the window, there was the most beautiful cotton candy sunset I have ever seen in my life. I have seen some beautiful sunsets living by the beach on the Jersey Shore, but the one last night was the most beautiful one I've ever seen.

The second thing I learned was that Thomas can hide no emotions from his face. What do I mean by that? The look on his face when he barged in on me in the bathtub is a look that made me thankful that I was sitting in a bathtub full of water and bubbles to hide the fact that my hands were deep in my own pussy getting off to the thought of him. That fucking suit and seeing those strong forearms got me. I made no motion to remove my fingers or stop rubbing my clit when he was standing there in that fucking blue suit. His mouth dropped open and his eyes went wide when he trailed his look from my face down to my exposed breast and then to the bubbles that covered everything below my chest. *Thankfully*. After I screamed his name in a mix of shock and pleasure, my eyes trailed down his body and I didn't miss the bulge that was starting to grow in his pants. Thankfully he was in such a state of shock, that the way I screamed his name made no difference to him. His body language told me that he wished he saw more, and I won't lie when I say that I wish he had seen more too.

After I screamed at him to get out, I finished myself off with his name rolling off my tongue and wishing it was his fingers touching me in my most sensitive spot. He apologized profusely last night in an effort to keep this professional, but the last thing I wanted him to do was apologize for it. He should be sorry for not stripping his clothes and climbing in with me.

BE PROFESSIONAL, PEYTON.

"I'm hangry," James says, breaking through my thoughts of last night.

I chuckle and get up off the couch because I am too, bud.

"Do you like waffles, James?"

"I LOVE WAFFLES!" he shrieks. "Will you make me some, Ms. Peyton?"

"Absolutely, buddy. But let's keep it down and let Daddy sleep in a little bit."

James doesn't respond but skips into the kitchen, taking a seat on the barstool on the counter.

"Let's make you some waffles, buddy!" I say enthusiastically.

"Can you make them with sprinkles in them, Peyton? Like the funtetti."

"Funfetti?" I laugh with him.

"Yeah, that's it!"

I walk to the oversized pantry, and I stop dead in my tracks. Since last night, everything here is different. Many snacks were removed while a lot of different things have been added. I don't grab anything because I am in such a state of shock. I make my way to the refrigerator to see if anything in there has changed and opening the door, I see that everything has changed in here too.

Vegan options. *For me.*

My stomach crumbles and my mouth falls open. Did Thomas have all of this done last night after I fell asleep on the couch? He had snacks replaced and he stocked the pantry with some of my favorite ingredients I use to cook. The refrigerator is packed with fruits, vegetables and I even noticed my favorite brand of tofu sitting in one of the pull-out drawers.

He did all of this for me when I didn't even write a single thing down on the notepad that he gave me last night.

"Is that all okay for you?" Thomas asks from somewhere behind me pulling me from the trance I'm in.

I don't have it in me to turn around and look at him. I have the refrigerator doors open and I am staring through teary eyes, trying to blink them away. I don't think anyone has ever done something like this for me before.

"Y-yes," I say back in a hoarse whisper, still refusing to turn around. "It's more than okay."

"I wanted to make sure you had something for today so I had Rosie get whatever she could find."

I allow myself to pause at his words for a minute and then I slowly turn to face Thomas. When I do, I can't help but check him out from across the kitchen. He's casually leaning against the archway that leads into the kitchen with both his arms and legs crossed. His dark hair is scruffy from bed head and he's wearing a plain black t-shirt that allows me to really get a glimpse of his tattooed forearm porn and gray sweatpants. Gray. Fucking. Sweatpants. Do guys not understand what gray sweatpants do to women? This man is standing here with not only forearm porn but gray fucking sweatpants. *I am so fucked.*

He pushes himself off the wall and walks into the kitchen. I still haven't said anything because I'm rendered speechless from the sight in front of me. He's a navy-blue suit guy without a doubt, but seeing him like this, in his most relaxed state, is my new favorite thing in the world.

"Good morning, JJ." He kisses the top of James' head and messes his hair. "What are we making?"

"Waffles, Daddy!" James screams. "The funtetti ones!"

We laugh at how excited James gets over the waffles and Thomas moves to grab the waffle maker. "Sit," he orders. "I've got this."

Thomas moves around the kitchen with ease as he whips up some waffles for James. After he serves them to James, he begins to mix another batch of waffles with different ingredients. I realize quickly that this batch is for me. He's making vegan waffles and my mind can't stop spinning at the events that have taken place this morning.

Did he look up this recipe so he could make me breakfast?

He throws a few sprinkles in it as well and serves them to me with sliced strawberries on top. As he slides the plate across the island, he gives me a wink and moves to clean up the kitchen.

"T-thank you," is all I can find the words to say. I take a bite, "Wow, these are the most delicious waffles I have ever had."

"You're welcome." He smiles at me. "Glad you like them. It was my first time trying the recipe. I looked it up last night after you fell asleep on the couch because I wanted to make sure you had something good for your first meal here."

I pause mid-bite to give him a smile, but I can feel the heat rising in my cheeks and I know that I am blushing at his statement.

"I was supposed to take the day off, but a meeting has come up and I have to go into the office for an hour or two," he says as his smile falls from his face. "I hate to ask you this when you don't officially start until Monday, but do you think you could hang out with James until I get back?"

"Of course," I reply, without hesitation. "I don't mind

spending the day with him and getting to know him a little bit better."

"It would only be for an hour or two."

"Take all the time you need," I say, shaking my head at him and then moving my hand to mess up James' hair. "We'll be fine."

"I really appreciate it, Peyton. I'm going to get ready." He nods, turning to look at James, "James, be good for Ms. Peyton today, okay?"

"Of course, Daddy," he says through a mouthful of waffles. "I'm going to show her all my dinosaurs upstairs and teach her how to RAWR like me."

"I can't wait to see them, buddy," I say to James.

Thomas leaves to get ready for work while James continues to eat his waffles. I try to finish mine, but my stomach feels all sorts of weird feelings about everything that has happened this morning… Shit, I've only been awake an hour and I haven't even started the job yet.

I have an uncomfortable feeling in my chest as my heart begins to pound wildly.

These two are going to make me fall in love with them, aren't they?

The last thing I want is to fall for my boss.

CHAPTER FIFTEEN
Thomas

My meeting went longer than expected. I sent Peyton a text to let her know that I would be longer than planned and she assured me that all was well at home and sent a video of James dressed up in last year's Halloween costume. Which, of course, was a dinosaur. James was running around his playroom doing his signature RAWR and in the background, I could hear Peyton laughing.

I was already smiling at the antics of James, but her laugh made me break into the biggest shit-eating grin on my face. She just has that effect on me.

She also said that she's perfectly okay at the house with James if I have to spend more time at the office. She's extremely understanding, which is a trait I am not used to, especially from a female.

Since taking over this business, my job has always come first because it has allowed me to afford things for James and give him the best life possible. But lately, I have been wanting to slow down my work hours and spend more time with James since he's at an age that he's going to start noticing my absence a lot more. I'm also trying to tell myself that it has nothing to do with the new nanny living in my house.

Snapping my head to the office door when I hear it open, I see Marc and Oliver walk in. Marc takes his usual seat directly across from my desk while Oliver takes his seat on the sofa with his legs propped up on the coffee table.

"How many times do I have to tell you, get your fucking feet off my table, Ollie."

"Relax, shit head." He laughs. "Your table looks like trash anyway."

"Don't you have a flight to catch?"

"Not today, big bro." He laughs. "Today my mission is to piss you off."

I shake my head at him because I just don't have it in me to deal with him today. My two brothers are total opposites of each other. You can always find Oliver dressed in a pair of faded wash jeans and a plain cotton t-shirt. It's usually some obnoxiously bright color, which matches his personality. Marc always has a relaxed, business casual look. He wears dress pants with a button-down shirt to work but skips the jacket and the tie unless he has a meeting to attend.

"How's it going, Tommy?" Marc says.

"It's going."

"Is your new nanny getting settled in nicely?" he asks.

"Yes, she is." I nod. "We had a bit of an interesting first night."

"I need to hear this," Oliver cuts in.

"Well to start, I walked in on her taking a bubble bath and couldn't peel my eyes away from her tits."

"Were they hot, bro?" Oliver sits up, full attention now on the conversation. *Of course he is, I just mentioned tits.*

Giving him a side eye, I reply, "Hottest tits I've ever seen in my life."

"OH YEAH, BABY!" Oliver screams, throwing his fist in the air, "She single? Is she home now? Can I stop by?"

"I think she is," I reply to the first question, and quickly shoot back, "Yes and no."

"Yes, I can stop by?" He stands up, ready to bolt out the door.

"Sit the fuck down. No, you're not going over there right now or *ever*, if I have anything to do with it."

"Ohhh, possessive." Oliver wiggles his brows.

"Ollie, shut up. Let Tommy finish talking," Marc cuts in, and turns his direction back to me. "Was that all that happened?"

"Well, no." I scrub my hands down my face. "I had Rosie stock the house with snacks and food so that we had food to eat. I didn't even think to ask her what she eats or if she has any preferences. Turns out, she's a vegan and I had absolutely nothing she could eat."

"No shit, dude!" Oliver beams. "Vegans are hot."

Marc and I both give him a pointed look.

"She's a vegan but she's still trying to eat ya boy," he says with a sing song and a little dance in the spot he's sitting in.

"Did you just quote *Jack Harlow*?" I ask him with a raised brow.

"That's my homeboy," he laughs, still doing his little dance. "Young Harleezy is my anthem. And that's for us, big A-listers."

"Okay, that's enough with the Jack quotes." Marc deadpans.

"Agreed," I say. "There will be no *eating ya boy* over here. Yes, I have history with her, but I can't allow it to go anywhere because she works for me. There is no mixing business with pleasure."

"So, what's your plan then?" Marc asks.

"I don't really have one," I say, shrugging my shoulders. "I am just keeping my distance to give her some space. When I get home from work, she will be off the clock and is free to leave the apartment or do whatever she pleases."

"Do you want her to leave you alone?" Oliver asks.

"I do, but I don't," I admit. "I like having her around already. She's so great with James and it's nice having someone comforting in the house for him. But the more I get to know her, the more drawn to her I am."

"You are sort of a hardass," Marc laughs.

I don't get a chance to respond because a text from Peyton comes through on my phone.

Is James allowed to have donuts for dinner?

Absolutely not.

That's what I told him. Apparently, it's National Donut Day?

This kid, I swear. He knows I am not the biggest fan of sugary snacks so anytime he is with his Aunt or Uncles, he tries to trick them into getting donuts. He tells them *'Every day is National Donut Day,'* and because they love to spoil him, they give him the damn donuts.

No, tell him that's June 2nd.

The fact that you know that…

What can I say, I love me some donuts, too.

You don't look like you love donuts…

I'm smiling down at my phone because… *Is she… flirting with me?*

That's an interesting observation, Ms. Peyton.

What can I say, Mr. Ford?

I am very observant.

Fuck, this woman is making it so damn hard to not cross the line with her. She's totally flirting and telling me that she's checked me out before. Reading *Mr. Ford* through her text, just does something to me that I can't even explain. I can picture her wearing next to nothing, a pair of hot heels and her walking over to me, saying my name just like that in her most seductive voice.

"Everything okay?" Marc says, cutting off my thoughts.

"Yeah." I nod. "James is pulling his National Donut Day shit with Peyton."

"That kid gets me every single time, Tommy." Oliver tips his head back into a full-blown laughing fit.

"He is very persuasive, Tommy." Marc joins in on the laughter. "You're going to be in big trouble when he becomes a teenager. Kid is too smart for his own good."

"That he is." I nod.

———

I'm leaving the office way later than planned and I hope that Peyton isn't furious with me. I plan to fully compensate her for her time today.

Walking into the penthouse, the lights are off and the only thing that lights up the room is the TV playing a cartoon. My eyes move to the couch to see something that makes my heartbeat faster than it has in a long time.

Peyton is laying on her back at the corner of the couch and James is snuggled up next to her. His little head is resting in the crook of her arm, and she has her arm placed around his shoulders. The two of them are sleeping soundly.

Seeing James with her just hits me right in the chest. I have never seen him with a female like this before. His mom left when he was a baby and Emiline is just not the snuggly type. If she ever took that *Five Love Languages* test, she would not rank high on physical touch. He's never had anyone in his life that would snuggle with him.

Heat rises in my chest, and I can't control the pounding in my rib cage.

Moving across the room, I stand over them to make a mental memory of this moment. As I am about to scoop James into my arms to take him to bed, Peyton stirs and tightens a protective grip around his shoulder.

"It's just me, Peyton," I whisper.

Her eyes fling open, and she looks startled to see me.

"I-I'm sorry," she whispers. "We must have fallen asleep."

"Don't be sorry." I shake my head. "I'm sorry for breaking the snuggle-fest."

She blushes at my comment, and I scoop James up and take him up to his room. He must be tired because he doesn't wake when I place him in bed. Giving him a kiss on the head, I leave his room, close the door behind me and make my way back downstairs and find Peyton in the kitchen.

"Hey." That's what I decide to say, because I can't think of anything else.

"Hey, you," she smiles at me. "I made dinner earlier. I'll heat some up for you."

She what? Did she just say she made me dinner?

The pain inside my chest is back and I feel my heart rate start to spike again.

"Peyton," I say, as I let out a sigh. "You know you don't have to cook for me."

"I know. I didn't." She glances in my direction, and I think she can sense what's happening when she says, "Relax, will ya? It's just spaghetti. Here, come try the sauce I made. James loved it."

I hesitantly walk over to her where she holds out a small spoon with some tomato sauce on it. Stepping into her space, I can feel the heat of her body from our close proximity. Or maybe, it's the heat of the oven? Regardless, I feel that weird buzz like I do every time she's close. She moves the spoon from over the saucepan and towards my mouth. My eyes stay locked with hers as she puts the spoon into my mouth so I can taste the sauce.

Just like I expect, it tastes amazing. My hand is about to move up to my face to wipe the corner of my lips when a small hand reaches for my lips first. Her eyes still haven't left mine and as she wipes the corner of my lip, her thumb lingers for a second longer than it should. My head instinctively leans towards her touch and the hand that was moving towards my face now encircles her wrist so that she keeps her hand there just a second longer.

"Thomas," she hoarsely whispers, as if she's struggling to speak.

"T-that is amazing, Peyton," I say and take a step close to her, which forces her to tilt her head up to maintain eye contact with me.

She doesn't make a move to back away from me and her lips are right there for the taking. I'm terrified, for the first time in my life, to move, in fear that I will lose this moment.

"Thomas," she whispers again.

"Dance with me, Peyton," is what comes out of my mouth. It's the most random request I have, but I want to feel her close to me for just a little longer.

"What?" She gasps, with wide eyes and a slightly open mouth.

"Dance with me."

"There's no music."

"Echo, play songs by *Nate Smith*," I say loud enough so the speaker can hear me.

She turns from the direction the speaker is, to look me in the eyes with a small smirk forming on her lips.

"You listen to country music, Mr. Ford?"

And there it is, the way she draws out Mr. Ford with the cutest fucking smirk plastered on her face. *I don't stand a chance with her.*

"I do, Ms. Peyton." I give her a smirk back. "It's my favorite genre."

The music starts playing over the kitchen speakers. She hesitates, but I grab her hand in mine and drag her to the middle of the kitchen. Using my other hand to pull her flush with my body, I hear a gasp come from her as our bodies collide. I keep my hand on the small of her back and bring her other hand with mine where they rest together on my chest.

We start swaying to the music playing over the speakers and I wonder if she can feel how fast my heart is beating right now. Country music has a way of hitting your soul and the lyrics of the songs can be so relatable. This song that is playing has every lyric hitting me deep in my chest.

She's branded my soul with a touch that's here to stay.

As the song continues, I start to feel like this is a bad idea because I can't find it in me to pull away from her. I want to hoist her up, wrap her legs around me and walk us to my room, throw her on my bed and have my way with her like I wanted to do, all those years ago.

Things are different now though because she works for me. I can't be dancing with my son's nanny in the kitchen. Hell, I shouldn't even be touching her.

"Peyton." I lean in to whisper in her ear, and feel a shiver run through her body. "I need you to walk away before I do something I'm going to regret."

She pulls away from me and I immediately wish I had worded that differently because her face is plastered with a look of disappointment. Fuck, I don't do this shit, I don't act like this. I can't seem to function or find words when she's around.

She continues to take a few more steps back to create some distance from me. Without saying a single word, she turns her body so her back is facing me and darts out of the kitchen.

"Peyton, wait," I call out to her.

She doesn't stop, she just keeps going.

So does the music playing over the speakers.

Baby, you got under my skin.

CHAPTER SIXTEEN
Peyton

"How was your first week with James?" Kali asks.

It's the weekend after my first full week with James and it's been an interesting week. I did my best to make little conversation with Thomas since our weird dance in the kitchen the week before. I had made homemade tomato sauce and spaghetti for James and made sure to make a little extra in case Thomas was hungry when he got home. He certainly was hungry, but it definitely wasn't for the spaghetti.

"Earth to Peyton," Avery says and slices through my thoughts.

"Oh, I'm sorry, guys." I turn to face them. "I'm having an off week."

"Talk to us," Kali says.

Letting out a long sigh, I begin, "Do you guys remember that first day when Thomas worked late, and I had James before I was even supposed to be working?"

"Yeah?" Kali questions.

"Well, that night when he got home, he got really close in the kitchen. Out of nowhere, he asked me to dance with him. My body was basically reacting for me at that point, and we danced to my favorite slow song." I throw my face into my hands where I'm sitting at the counter. "I thought he was going to kiss me."

"What did you do, Pey?" Avery shrieks.

"Avery," I growl. "What makes you think I did anything?"

"Because you avoid any form of closeness with the male species like the fucking plague," Avery raises her voice. "I don't get it because if I looked as hot as you and I lived in THAT penthouse with a daddy, I would be chasing an orgasm from him any chance I get."

"Avery!" I cut her off, allowing myself this moment to be mad. "He stopped me!"

Her eyes go wide, and her mouth drops open.

"I didn't make a move to push him away," I say, bringing my voice back down. "He said *'I need you to walk away before I do something I'm going to regret'*, so I did that. I walked away, without saying a single word."

"Oh, Peyton," Kali says sympathetically.

"No, it's okay," I say, shaking my head. "I swore up and down that I wasn't going to actively pursue him. That day we had exchanged a few text messages that felt flirty and then when he came home and got so close to me, I was led to believe that something was about to happen."

I have been fighting myself with this battle all week, constantly reminding myself that *'he's my boss'* and that was why he wanted me to walk away. *He* was trying to keep it professional more than I was. Clearly.

Monday morning, he tried to talk to me over coffee and I was saved by his phone ringing and him having to leave for the office. Thursday night, I put James to bed before he even got home. I locked myself in my room and when I heard a knock on the door, I pretended to be asleep to avoid him. It's probably childish, but my heart just can't let that happen and when he's around, that thing in my chest pounds and has a mind of its own.

Besides, we have James to think about.

"What did you want to happen, Pey?" Avery asks.

"I wanted him to kiss me," I admit out loud with a groan and move to get up from my seat. "It's so hard to deny the way my body reacts around him."

"Would it be so bad if something blossomed from this?"

"Yes," I say without hesitation. "You two know how bad I need this job. The pay is out of this world, and I get to stay in the most epic penthouse."

"I still don't get the problem here."

I shoot Avery a side eye but don't reply.

"I'm serious, Pey. He's paying you an ungodly amount to watch his son and isn't charging you to live like a fucking queen." She throws her hands in the air. "It doesn't matter what you do, he's not going to let you go or fire you if you decide to ride his dick like a porn star."

I can't help but shake my head at the shit that comes out of her mouth.

"What?!" She throws her hands in the air. "From what you said, it sounds like he's trying to have some restraint. I think it's your job to try and break that restraint. He fucking wants you, Pey. Make Mr. Daddy work for it a little bit."

"I don't know, Ave."

"I'm not fucking saying commit to a relationship with the guy, but a woman has needs, Peyton. You literally live with a man who has the tools below the belt to fuck you six ways to Tuesday."

"Do you only ever think about sex, Avery?" I laugh.

"Just on every day that ends in Y," she says with a shrug.

"Anyway," I draw out. "What do you guys think I should do?"

"Break him," Avery says at the same time Kali says, "talk to him."

"I think you need to talk to him and just see where it goes," Kali says, "and if he makes a move, let it happen, Pey."

"And if he fucking tells you to walk away again, you stay

planted right where you are like you have cement blocks tied around your ankles." Avery laughs.

"And then," Kali adds. "You fuck him six ways to Sunday."

I sigh and run my hands down my face, staying silent because I have nothing to say to that. I want to feel him close to me again and have his hands all over me. The way my body reacts to him when he's around feels like nothing I have ever felt around anyone else.

I push the thought out of my head and glance down at my phone to look at the time and see a text message from Thomas.

> Hey, Peyton. I just wanted to let you know I won't be home until late tonight.

This is weird. Why is he texting me when I'm off to tell me when he's going to be home? Instantly I feel nerves swarm my belly and the worst thought crosses my mind, *is he going out with a lady friend tonight?* It is Saturday night after all.

"What is it?" Kali says, as she notices my reaction as I stare at my phone.

"Thomas just texted me he won't be home until late tonight…" I pause. "He's never done that before."

"Oh OH!" Avery beams. "This is your chance to really break that tension between you."

"What do I say back? What if he's telling me this because he's going out with a woman tonight?"

"Tell him you're having a girls' night at the penthouse," Kali insists.

"But I'm not having a girls' night."

"You are now," Avery chuckles. "Guys get so hot when they think about girls' nights and what we do."

I give her a side eye because I don't understand that.

"Listen, I don't understand it either," Avery says. "I think they think we get naked, talk about sex and have pillow fights or some shit."

105

The three of us burst out laughing because that is exactly what Avery does. I swear she would be a nudist if it was socially acceptable.

Picking up my phone, I decide to write him back instead of avoiding him. I am done with this awkward bullshit between us.

> Okay, no problem.

> Do you mind if Kali and Avery come over for a girls' night?

Ok.

"All he said was '*Okay*,'" I sigh.

"Perfect!" Avery lets out an excited cheer, "Girls' night at the penthouse, it is!"

I don't even respond to her because there is no telling Avery anything less than the word '*yes*'. We spend the next couple minutes cleaning up the kitchen in their apartment when I feel my phone vibrate on the counter. Picking it up, I see Thomas has texted me again.

What exactly does girls' night consist of?

I can't help the smile on my face and think that maybe he's also trying his best to talk to me too. I mean, I put up this wall between us the past week and I want it broken because I have to coexist with him in the penthouse. Then again, he might also be thinking exactly what Avery says guys think about when it comes to girls' nights.

Feeling bold hiding behind my phone, I decide I want to be friendly with him to show him that I'm smashing down the wall. There's something about Thomas that has me feeling a sense of confidence I have never felt before. It's a strange fucking feeling but here I am.

> You know. Girl talk and things...

Interesting.

> I'll see you when you get home tonight.

I like the sound of that.

My mouth falls open. *He likes the sound of what?*

Nerves take over my stomach and I decide not to respond to the message. I don't even know what to say to that.

"Alright, let's go. I guess it's girls' night at the penthouse."

"Yes!" Avery shrieks. "I'm totally not leaving until I meet daddy."

"You have to promise me you won't call him that to his face."

"I make no promises."

I shake my head. "Let's go, you two."

Kali grabs the car keys and Avery grabs a bottle of tequila. As she does, I give her a questioning look.

"Hey, tequila and cookies do wonders for calming nerves before adult conversations take place," she says, laughing.

She's got a point because I need to calm my nerves before he comes home later tonight. I'll need liquid courage before I have an adult conversation with a man who makes my body buzz and my pussy wet with a simple look from across the room.

Tonight, should be an interesting night.

CHAPTER SEVENTEEN
Thomas

Peyton has been avoiding me for the last week. Which is leaving me on edge more than usual.

First, I had to go and text her that I would be home late. Part of me was happy I did because I felt like our conversation was actually friendly and maybe she was done avoiding me. But then I had to go and say *'I like the sound of that'* in response to her message and she never wrote me back. She said she would see me at home. *Home.* As if it was *our* home. That left the other part of me wishing I kept my damn mouth shut.

That's why I'm now at Moores with the boys for drinks because I could use a whiskey or two before I get home. I was forced to go into the office on a Saturday to get shit done because we are so busy with the high-rises across town. The back-to-back meetings I had all week, put me behind on paperwork.

When I finally walk into the bar after I leave the office, Marc and my best friend, Logan, are seated at our usual table. I unbutton my suit jacket and take a seat next to Logan. Thank God they had a whiskey ready for me at the table.

"Bro, does it hurt you to smile every once in a while?" Marc smirks behind his glass of whiskey before he takes a sip.

"Don't start with me tonight." I growl back. "I'm not in the mood."

"What's going on, Tommy?" Logan asks.

"It's my fucking nanny." I run my hands down my face. "She's consuming my thoughts when she shouldn't be. She was avoiding me like the plague and now she's sending me texts like everything is fine."

"How the fuck can she avoid you if she lives with you?"

"Simple." I take a sip of the whiskey. "I come home, and she's gone off to her room. When she texts me about James, it's just pictures and she avoids any other conversation."

Both Marc and Logan pause to look at each other and take a sip of their whiskey.

"Okay, hear me out," Marc is the first to speak. "Isn't this what you wanted?"

It is what I wanted.

I wanted space from her because the closer I get, the more I can't control what my heart and body wants. The problem is, whenever she's around, a buzz shoots through my body like it's something I can't deny.

The other night I came home from work, James was already in bed and Peyton was eating dinner on the kitchen island. I ran upstairs to get changed as fast as I could and shot back downstairs so I could talk to her so there isn't so much tension between us. By the time I got back downstairs, she was gone to her room and the lights were out. After I knocked and there was no answer, I peeked my head in and saw her sound asleep.

"I know," I sigh.

"Bro," Logan cuts in. "Do you want her? Like, do you want her in your life as more than a nanny?"

"It's complicated."

"You fucking sound like Marc." Logan laughs. "You just need some pussy. That will fix all your problems."

"How long has it been anyway?" Marc asks as he deflects his comment.

I can't admit it to these two, but it's been almost two years. After James turned one, I turned all my energy into raising him and working as hard as I can. Trust me, it's not that women aren't throwing themselves at me. If I tried hard enough, I could leave with one tonight, but I don't want to bring them back to my place because of James. And I'm not about to fuck in the backseat of a car when it's been this long.

"It's been two years," I whisper.

"Could you fucking repeat that louder?" Logan snaps.

"Shut up, you heard me."

"No. No. No," Logan is shaking his head. "There's no fucking way you just said two years."

"You have a fucking kid and tell me how easy it is to get your dick sucked, asshole," I snap.

"Dude, chicks dig dads." Logan shrugs, "Something about a guy with a kid turns them on. I think it's like a theme in those romance books that they read or some shit. What do they call it?"

"A trope?" Marc asks.

"Yeah, that." Logan snaps his fingers to Marc, like his point is made. "They read those porno books about single dads all the time. It's a thing apparently."

"You're out of your fucking mind, Logan." I laugh.

"You think I'm kidding?" Logan laughs. "When you're done being on the outs with your hot nanny, ask her what kind of books she reads."

"I am not asking her what kind of books she reads."

"Text her right now," Logan begs.

"I can't text her and ask her that."

Logan grabs my phone from my hands, and I don't move to stop him because a small part of me is actually curious.

> What kind of books do you like to read?

I read a little bit of everything.

> But romance books are my number one
> favorite.

Logan scoffs before showing me her response on my phone.

"Hot nanny definitely reads porn." Marc laughs after reading the message.

"Okay, we're done here." I grab my phone from his hand and make a move to stand up. "I want to get home in time to see James before he gets to bed. I'm outta here."

I throw a couple twenties on the table to cover my drinks and some of theirs and I'm out the door. I lied when I said I wanted to see James before he went to bed because he's not even home tonight. Emiline wanted to spend some time with him, so they are having a sleepover. I need to talk to Peyton so we can put this shit behind us.

When I get home and walk through the elevators into the foyer, the house is dark, and I hear faint giggles coming from the kitchen. *What is that smell?* It smells like chocolate chip cookies.

I don't bother going upstairs to get changed and I can feel my heart rate picking up as I make my way to the kitchen. Turning the corner, I spot Peyton sitting on the island countertop, a blonde woman sitting on the opposite countertop and a dark-haired woman sitting at the barstool. I've seen the dark-haired woman before and if I'm not mistaken, she's the same girl from that first night I met Peyton.

They still haven't noticed me as I stand in the archway to the kitchen. I take a moment to take Peyton in, my eyes skimming her body from top to bottom. She's wearing black sleep shorts that expose her long lean legs and a matching black top. It's a silky material and the top is much larger than her body, so it hangs slightly over her shoulder when she moves. Her golden blonde hair sits at the top of her head, in a messy bun.

They have tequila out on the table with a couple of lime slices chopped up on the cutting board. Her two friends are doing some perfectly choreographed dance to *Salt and Pepper - Push it*, while Peyton laughs uncontrollably at them.

I lean against the archway as I cross my arms over my chest, and I feel my mouth curve into a smile instinctively as I take these girls in. I notice she hasn't stopped smiling since I've been standing here. You can tell that these must be her close friends because they bring out the best in her.

The selfish bastard in me wants her friends out of my house, though.

I clear my throat and all three of them startle from where they are sitting.

"Thomas," Peyton gasps, "I'm so sorry, I didn't know you would be home this early." She moves through the kitchen to turn off the music and clean up, as if she's a kid who just got caught eating snacks when they shouldn't be.

"Peyton." I feel a faint smile pull at my lips when her name comes out of my mouth, "It's fine, you're allowed to have your friends over. You live here, too."

The blonde hops off the counter and does what looks like a little skip over to me. I don't know what that move was, but it was something that I would see my three-year-old do.

"Hey there, Daddy, I'm Avery." She holds her hand out to shake mine.

"Avery—" Peyton growls at her.

I can't help but laugh at how she just called me 'Daddy'. Reaching my hand out to hers, I reply, "Hello, Avery. I'm Thomas, but my friends call me Tommy." I turn my gaze to Peyton and give her a wink.

Avery's mouth falls open and her eyes dart back and forth between the two of us.

The dark-haired woman that I recognize from the gala when I first met Peyton, chimes in, "Alright, Avery. It's time to get you home." She hooks her arm into Avery's elbow. "Hi, Thomas, my name is Kali. It's so nice to finally meet you. I'm sorry about her."

"Likewise," I reply with a small laugh. "However, we've briefly met before."

She nods and smiles, "We have, haven't we?"

Avery's mouth falls open again, she's definitely drunk. "How do I miss all the meetings with the hot daddies? This is fucking ridiculous," she shrieks, throwing her hands up in the air.

"On that note, we're out," Kali says, pulling Avery towards the front door. "Peyton, call us in the morning" she calls from over her shoulder as the two of them walk out of the kitchen.

I watch and wait as the elevator doors close behind them before I turn my gaze back to Peyton. She's standing over the oven pulling out a tray of chocolate chip cookies. When she places the tray on the top of the oven, she removes the oven mitts and turns her body to face me. I take a moment to scan her from her legs to her face. When my gaze reaches her face, our eyes meet, and I see a gorgeous smile on her face.

"Where's James?" she asks.

"He's having a sleepover with Emiline. She misses him." I shrug. My eyes scan the bottle of liquor and baked goods and I smirk. "Tequila and cookies, Ms. Kelly?"

"Of course, would you like some?" she replies with a smile. With just that one simple question and the tone of her voice, I know that the tension from this week has gone out the window.

I cross the kitchen to meet her at the oven. When I do, the buzz from being in her presence comes back full force and my hand finds the small of her back as I lean in and reach for a cookie with the other hand. Facing her, I take a bite of it and just as I suspect, it's amazing.

"Mmm," I groan, "This is delicious, Peyton."

She blushes at my compliment. "Thank you."

She steps away from my personal space to go to the sink and clean some dishes. As she's walking to the sink, she begins to talk with her back facing me, "I wanted to talk to you about something."

I feel my stomach drop into my balls.

I lean back against the kitchen counter and cross my arms across my chest while an uneasy feeling takes over me because I'm not sure what she's about to say. I hope this isn't about the last two weeks of being uncomfortable around here and she's decided to quit.

She pauses at my silence and turns to face me, leaning herself against the kitchen sink and says, "I just want to say I'm sorry for how I've acted the past week."

Oh, thank fuck.

"I shouldn't have been avoiding you like that and acting the way I did," she continues. "It was very childish of me, and I'm embarrassed about it."

"You don't have to apologize, Peyton."

"But I do," she cuts me off. "I guess I thought…" she pauses as if she's trying to avoid saying the wrong thing.

While she's trying to find the words to say, I push off the counter and walk towards her to bring myself closer to her. She sucks in a breath and her mouth pops open as she takes in the fact that I am inches from her body. My hands move to my pockets to avoid touching her, despite every bone in my fucking body wanting to.

"What did you think?"

"I-I thought," she stutters and then her voice drops to a whisper, "I thought you wanted to kiss me that night."

If I wasn't paying the closest attention to everything coming out of her mouth, I would have missed the whisper of words that she just said.

Removing my hands from my pockets, I lean down to bring myself eye level with her. Caging her in with my body as my hands find space on the counter behind her. Staring into her eyes, I take a moment to inhale the addictive scent of roses. The combination of her closeness, the aroma of *her*, and the way her eyes are filled with desire causes my dick to twitch.

"You thought I wanted to kiss you, Sunshine?" I ask, as my lips hover dangerously close to hers.

"Yes," she breathes out.

"I've wanted to kiss you since you walked back into my life that day in the park," I admit, without missing a beat.

Her mouth falls open as she asks, "Y-you what?"

"You consume my thoughts, and I can't think about anything else but my lips on yours."

"So kiss me," she blurts out.

"Say it again," I inch closer, my lips grazing hers.

"Kiss me, Thomas."

There is no hesitation when my lips crash to hers. My hands move from the counter to her hips and her hands fly to my hair to pull my head in to deepen the kiss. She wants this as much as I want it. She tilts her head up the slightest bit and opens her mouth for my tongue to graze hers. I can feel her body melt into mine and she lets out a moan. Instinctively my arm wraps around the small of her back to press her into me so she can feel how hard she makes me.

I start to pull away from her kiss and as I do, I feel a slight bite on my bottom lip from her before she whimpers, "Thomas."

"I'm sorry, I got carried away." I press my forehead against hers and I smirk. I feel her erratic breath on my lips.

"You should be sorry you stopped."

I feel a growl vibrate in my chest as my hands reach to cup her ass and hoist her so she's now sitting on the counter. Her legs open for me to step into her and my hardening cock presses into her. My mouth goes right to the most delicate part of her neck where I can feel her pulse on my mouth, and she lets out the softest moan.

"Peyton, tell me to stop."

"Don't stop."

My lips skim down her neck to her collar bone, pulling the shoulder of her already loose button-down pajama shirt down when I realize she isn't wearing a bra. This turns me into a complete animal. I fist the shirt on both sides where the buttons meet and I rip it open, causing buttons to go flying in every direction of the kitchen. She's left sitting there completely exposed to me.

"Thomas," she groans my name. Fuck I love the way she says my name.

"I'll buy you a new one." I feel the corner of my lips turn up before my mouth finds its place back on her collarbone and she lets out a ragged breath.

My hand moves to one breast as my mouth makes its way to the other. As soon as I start to suck on her nipple, she throws her head back again and my name comes out of her mouth as a moan. Her nipples harden under my tongue, and I can feel her hips start to grind into me as she wiggles on the counter. Her body craving more contact from me. I remove my mouth and take a small step back as my eyes scan her up and down.

"You are without a doubt, the sexiest thing I have ever seen," I say as my eyes find hers again.

She smiles and her hands grip my hips to pull me back into her, forcing my raging hard on to crash into her center and her hips roll into me, telling me she wants it. "Right back at ya, Mr. Ford."

"Oh, are we playing that game?" I grin, "Tell me Ms. Kelly, if I dip my hand into these sexy little silk shorts, am I going to find your pussy soaked for my cock?"

"Yes," she moans.

I slide my hands down her sides, gently brushing her skin, and let my fingers dip into her waistband of her panties. She sucks in a sharp breath as my fingers graze her clit before I push a finger inside of her. "Fuck," I say through gritted teeth. "You are soaked."

I withdraw my finger and grip the waistband of her silk shorts and rip them down like the fucking animal she turns me into. As soon as I do, I step back once more to drink her in. She's now completely naked, perched on top of my kitchen counter, her legs spread wide and her perfect pussy on display for me. I can see the glistening of her arousal in this position and the corner of my lip turns up as I rub my bottom lip with my thumb like I'm starved for her.

She yanks the collar of my white dress shirt and crashes her lips to mine, sliding her tongue into my mouth. She knows how to fucking kiss, that's for sure. The way she angles her head and teases me with her tongue makes me completely lose my mind. I feel her hands move to untuck my shirt from my pants at the same time I'm unbuttoning it and pulling it off my arms.

She runs her hands down my bare chest before pulling away from our kiss to move her gaze to my stomach. "Holy. Fuck." She gasps as her eyes explore the tattoos that she probably didn't know I had, covering my chest and left arm, completely.

I waste no time sliding my finger back into her pussy while I press my thumb to her clit. Her eyes close and her head falls back. "Peyton," I hiss. "Eyes on me. I want your eyes on me while I make you come."

She lets out a moan with my name on her lips as she leans back on her elbows and focuses her eyes on me. This angle allows me to press my finger deep inside of her. I withdraw my finger to add a second. "You're so fucking tight, baby," I say, as I continue to pump my fingers in and out of her while my thumb circles her clit.

"Thomas," she screams. "I'm already so close."

I pump my fingers harder and harder as her hips buck into my hand and her pussy pulses around my fingers. She moves her body so that she's propped up on one elbow and her other hand moves to her nipple as she pinches it into her hands. I swear my dick is as hard as steel right now at the sight in front of me.

"You like this, don't you?" I say in a deep raspy voice close to her ear. "Me fucking you with my hand while you're spread out on the kitchen counter?"

"Yes," she moans. "Fuck yes."

Just as she's on the brink of her orgasm, I remove my hand

and I can see her face morph into disappointment as she falls back to both elbows. "W-what?"

"For weeks I have been desperate to know how you taste on my tongue." I cut her off with a smirk as I lower my head between her open legs. I tap on her leg, letting her know I want her to spread them wider. "And right now, I'm starving."

My mouth grazes her inner thighs, and I can feel the goose-bumps form on her legs as she brings them to rest on my shoulders. I waste no time bringing my mouth to her pussy and lapping her arousal with my tongue. She moans my name as soon as I do, and I see her head fall back.

"Eyes. On. Me."

Her head shoots up, her mouth slightly parted with pleasure and her eyes are on me like daggers. I can feel how turned on she is just by the way she looks at me. I keep my eyes on her as my mouth goes back to her pussy and my tongue flicks her clit. My eyes roll back the slightest so she can see how much I love the taste of her.

"Don't stop, Thomas."

My tongue plunges into her just before I bring two fingers to her pussy and push them in with force, causing her back to arch and a moan comes out of her mouth. "Oh God," she screams out. "That feels so good."

"God is not the one worshiping this pussy right now."

"Thomas," she corrects herself through a moan. I can tell she's close because she's practically riding my face. "I'm going to come."

"Come, Peyton. Come on my fucking tongue. I want to taste every last drop."

With just a couple more swipes of my tongue over her clit, she is sent over the edge. She comes so hard, with my name rolling off her lips. Her body shakes as her orgasm ripples through her body, and I can feel her pulsing around my fingers. Watching her orgasm, and hearing the moans she makes, solidifies the fact that I don't think I will ever get enough of her. I already can't get enough of her, and I haven't even had my dick inside that tight pussy yet either.

She falls from her elbows and straight to her back as she tries to catch her breath. My body leans over hers because I have the strongest desire to kiss her. My mouth is on hers with a hard crash, allowing her to taste her own arousal on my tongue. As soon as her arms wrap around my neck, I use the moment to pull her up so she's back to sitting on the counter.

"Thomas," she says as she pulls away, "That was—"

"The hottest fucking thing ever," I cut her off.

She tucks a strand of loose hair behind her ear that fell out of her bun, and I can see her cheeks heating up at my comment. Then she does what I least expect, and her hand finds the hem of my pants and she begins to unbutton them. "My turn," she giggles, and my head falls back because this must be a dream. I have literally jacked off to the thought of her lips wrapped around my cock for years. Yes, I said years. Images of her with that red lipstick from that night have been ingrained in my brain ever since.

She pushes off the counter to stand in front of me, and just as she's about to unzip my pants, my phone rings from the other side of the kitchen. Peyton gives me a questioning head tilt and I say, "Let it go to voicemail."

But as soon as it stops ringing, it's ringing again.

"Fuck," I yell "let me get it." I walk over to the counter where my phone sits, and I see that it's Emiline calling. Panic courses through my body that something is wrong with James. "Emiline, what's wrong."

"Thomas," she says, and I can hear the worry in her voice. "It's James. He hasn't stopped throwing up and he's got a pretty high fever. He said he wants to come home."

I groan into the phone at the inconvenience of him getting sick but also wanting to get him home as soon as possible because I'm worried about him since he rarely gets sick or spikes fevers. "Of course. Okay," I say, pacing the kitchen. "Uh, I'll send

Eddy to grab him while I get his stuff together for him to relax here at home."

"Okay, sounds good. I'm sorry, Thomas."

"No, don't be, Em. It's fine," I say as I hang up the phone with her and move my gaze back to Peyton who's getting dressed, and her back is to me.

"I-I'm sorry," I stutter, running my hands through my hair. "James is pretty sick. He's on his way home."

"It's okay. You don't have to be sorry for James being sick," she says with her back still to me like she can't even look me in the eye.

"But…" I pause, not sure how to approach what just fucking happened here in the kitchen. "We need to talk about what just happened."

"I-I think we both got a little carried away. I'm sorry I let it get that far."

Does she… Does she fucking regret it?

"I'm going to head in for the night," she says crossing the kitchen. "Please let me know if you need any help with James. I'm here if you need me." And without a glance back or allowing me any time to respond, she's out of the kitchen and I hear the door to her room close.

What the fuck just happened?

CHAPTER EIGHTEEN
Peyton

I wake up to the smell of waffles engulfing my senses and a throbbing soreness at my center which brings me back to the memories of last night. My plan was to have a talk with Thomas and apologize for how I've acted the last two weeks. I had no fucking plans of letting him spread me open on his kitchen counter and devour me like I'm his last meal, but clearly, my body doesn't know how to control itself in his presence.

I have never, *in my life*, climaxed that hard before. Unlike the night he finger fucked me into oblivion in a dark hallway, last night was slow and calculated. That man fucking knows his way around a woman's body, and he sure knows how to work his fingers with the right moves to send me over the edge.

This morning, my body aches from being touched for the first time in so long and it's craving his touch again. I'm starting to understand what Avery is talking about when she says the right orgasm will leave you wanting more.

On top of that, something about Thomas just makes me feel comfortable. I know that doesn't make sense but I'm the type of person who prefers to have sex with the lights off because I'm self-conscious about my body. There was something about the way he looked at me last night, though. He made me feel so sexy, and that's a very foreign feeling to me. I mean, I rubbed my own nipples in front of him, which I have never been bold enough to do before.

I have no clue where last night would have gone if Emiline hadn't phoned about James being sick. Not that I would have regretted going further with him, but I feared that *he* might regret it, since he's my boss.

That thought causes my heart rate to pick up because I wonder if he *does* regret last night. Thomas doesn't seem to be the type to do relationships or call after a one-night stand.

The smell of waffles continues to consume me as I lay there with my thoughts frantically running through my brain. I swing my legs off the bed and get up to get dressed. I decide to go for black leggings and a casual buttoned down knit blouse that I like to wear when I'm just kickin' it around the house.

Just as I am about to leave, my phone buzzes and I notice Gigi is calling. Quickly, I answer because I get nervous when she calls me this early. "Hey, Gigi."

"Hi, sweetheart." Her voice sounds tired.

"Are you okay?"

"I'm fine, honey. I'm just tired today," she sighs. "I was calling to see how things are going with you over there?"

Relief takes over, even though I know she could be lying to me. She doesn't ever want to show her pain because she always wants to be the strong one. I admire her for that.

"Things are going okay," I pause to gather my thoughts and think about what I can tell her. "James is pretty sick though. I was just about to check on him."

"Oh no, poor thing."

"I think he's got the stomach bug."

"That's the worst. I hope he's okay." I can hear the worry in her voice for a small child she's never met before. She loves kids. "Do you need me to bring you anything for him?"

Just like her, to worry about others before herself.

"No, Gigi. Thank you, though." I smile through the phone.
"Is there anything I can get for you?"

"No, sweetheart. I'm just fine." I can feel her smile through
the phone too. "Lee is bringing me over some bagels."

Lee is her best friend. They have been inseparable for years.
They travel the world together and do just about everything
together. She keeps Gigi grounded and is always looking out for
her like a sister would.

"Make sure you get that boy some old-fashioned chicken
noodle soup. That shit is good for the soul."

I laugh; I love this woman. "You got it, Gigi. I will call you
later today to check in on you, okay?"

"Okay, I love you."

"I love you more."

———

As I enter the living room, I find James laying on the couch with
a small garbage pail next to him with his head resting on a
pillow. His face looks pale, and his body looks weak as he lays
there in nothing but a pair of shorts.

"Oh, buddy," I say sympathetically as I walk over to him and
press my hand to his forehead. He must still have a fever
because he feels warm. "How are you feeling, James?"

"I don't feel so good, Ms. Peyton." He begins to cry.

I crouch down beside him and bring him into my embrace
and let him curl in a ball on my lap as he continues to sob into
my shirt. I hate it when children are sick because they are so
small and there isn't much you can do for them at such a young
age. I feel tears forming in my eyes because I know he feels so
crummy if he's crying like this.

"It's okay, buddy. I got you."

I'm rocking James in my lap when I hear a throat clear
behind me. I turn my head to see Thomas standing with a plate
of waffles.

I swallow and my throat feels like it's about to close up at the man standing there with no fucking shirt and a pair of gray sweatpants barely covering his hips. Doesn't this man have any other color sweatpants or is he purposely torturing me? He has the most perfectly cut abdomen that has the sharpest V shape. Avery calls them *fuck muscles* and on Thomas, they look more like *fuck me* muscles.

"Good morning." I barely manage to get the words out while my eyes skim over his body once more. "I, uh, I don't think James will be able to eat that."

"These aren't for James." He runs his hands through his hair. "These are for you."

My mouth falls open and I can't help but stare at him.

He made me breakfast?

I grab the plate from him with my free hand and place it on the coffee table in front of me. "T-thank you," I stutter, looking at the plate of perfectly placed waffles. "You didn't have to do that."

"I know I didn't, but I wanted to," he says before walking back into the kitchen, not even allowing me a chance to respond.

I lay James gently back on the couch and bring the light throw blanket up over his shoulders so that he's cuddled under it. "I'll be right back, bud. Call out if you need anything, okay?"

He nods his head, and his eyes begin to drift shut. Instinctively, I bend down to give him a kiss on the forehead. Not even thinking about what I'm doing, just that I've grown to care for this kid a whole lot the last couple weeks. I felt a weird twitch in my chest from my move, but I stand up anyway and make my way to the kitchen with my plate of waffles.

The minute I step foot in the kitchen, I see Thomas cleaning the dishes. I don't hesitate when I walk right up to the counter across from him and take a seat at the stool and ask him, "Do you want me to stay and help with James today?"

"That's not necessary." He moves his gaze from the sink full of dishes to me. "But I have a lot of work to do so I'm going to try to get some work done from home while he rests."

"Thomas," I say, but it comes out more like a whisper, "I'm here. Why don't you head into the office and get your work done? This way you have quiet. I'll take care of James."

A look of confusion crosses his face, and I can tell he's trying to figure out what to reply.

"Peyton, I can't ask—"

"It's really no big deal," I cut him off. "We can have a movie marathon on the couch together. I used to love doing that with my grandma when I was sick as a kid."

He pauses, clearly trying to think it over. "You really don't mind?"

"Not at all."

He moves quickly when he rounds the kitchen island and pulls me in for a hug. His arms circle my head while my arms wrap around his waist and my cheek is pressed into his bare chest. I suck in a breath, and he rests his chin on my head and whispers, "thank you, Peyton. I really owe you one," before he pulls away. It was a quick embrace but the way he pulls away feels like he didn't mean to do that.

"I'm going to jump in the shower and get ready for work," he says as he walks out of the kitchen, leaving me with the thought of him naked and water dripping from his tattoo covered chest down his chiseled abs and then down to his... *Get it together, Peyton.*

I cut through my own thoughts and move to finish the dishes that are left. It's the least I can do since he made me the most amazing waffles. He's really become a pro at those vegan waffles.

I'm not sure how long I've been in the kitchen cleaning when I feel Thomas' presence. My gaze travels to the entrance and I pause what I'm doing when I see him standing there looking like the boss he is. My mouth falls slightly open because he's wearing his signature look. I swear this man only owns navy blue suits to get me hot and bothered. Does he know this color compliments his ocean blue eyes perfectly? He *has* to know.

"I'm heading out," he says as he's looking down and adjusting the cufflinks on his white dress shirt. "Please call or text if you need anything. I have medicine and a thermometer in the bathroom cabinet upstairs. I'm going to try to get home early today." He lifts his gaze to meet mine. "Are you sure you're okay staying home with him on your day off?"

"Of course. Get out of here." I playfully slap his arm. "I'll text you updates."

"Thank you," is all he says in a very flat tone. He moves towards the refrigerator to grab a bottle of water and a grab and go meal that Rosie had made. Then he pours himself a to-go cup of coffee not saying another word or acknowledging I'm still here. Next thing I know, he's out the door and is gone without even a glance back.

Hmm, that was weird.

When I enter the living room, I find James still sleeping on the couch. As soon as I sit down, he wiggles in his sleep and wakes up to see me sitting next to him. He moves quickly to curl up next to me. His head falls onto my chest and his arm lays over my stomach.

"How are you feeling, James?

"My belly really hurts."

"I'm sorry you're sick, bud." I tighten my arm that wraps around him. "Do you want to have a movie day with me?"

"Oh, yes," he says with a little excitement in his voice. "Can we pull all the shades down and act like we're in the movie theaters?"

I giggle at him. "I wouldn't have it any other way."

Over the next three hours, we have successfully watched two movies and neither of us has moved from the couch since we started. I haven't updated Thomas, so I pull my phone out to shoot him a quick text and I see five missed calls from Avery and

Kali. Deciding to call them back in a little bit, I pull up the text thread I have going with Thomas to text him.

> Hi. I just wanted to update you that James hasn't thrown up in three hours and I think his fever is coming down.

Ok.

Woah.

What the fuck happened between last night and this morning?

Is he… regretting last night?

Maybe I'm looking too much into a one-word response.

Looking back at the events that took place this morning, I begin to overthink everything and the more I do, the more I think he is regretting it. He didn't so much as smile when he found me with James and offered me waffles. But he hugged me? When he came down after his shower, he was much colder towards me. He was barely able to look me in the eyes when he left and now, I'm getting one word text messages back.

Deciding to not respond, I look over to see James sleeping again so I make my way into the kitchen and decide to call Kali back out of all the missed calls. The video chat rings, and her face pops up on the screen and I prop my phone against the candle sitting on the counter.

"Hey, babe." Kali beams.

I sigh. "Hey. What's with the multiple missed calls from you and Avery. You two okay?"

"We can't call you because we missed you?"

"I literally just saw you both yesterday."

"How was last night?" she asks.

I pause and check the living room quickly to make sure James is still asleep and then look back at the phone. "It was… interesting."

"Oh, no you don't," she snaps. "I saw that look around to make sure no one's listening. Spill."

I groan in frustration at her knowing my every move. "Last night we, uh, did things. But it was cut short when—"

"Stop right there." She holds up her hand. "I need all the details on the *things* before you move on."

"I am not giving you details on my sex life."

"YOU HAD SEX?" she screams. "SHUT UP!"

"Would you stop screaming?! I did not have sex," I say in a stern tone but whisper the word sex just in case James wakes up. "But he kissed me."

"That hardly counts as *things*."

"Well, it led to other things," I say.

"Ohh, spicy," she rolls her eyes.

"He finger fucked me on the kitchen counter and ate me like I was his last meal," I snap. "Happy now?"

"I am so happy!" She laughs. "But why don't you sound happy about it?"

"Because I wonder if he's regretting it." I drop my head into my hands. I proceeded to tell her about how he made me waffles and when he left for work his demeanor was very cold. I add about the brief exchange of text messages where he gave me one-word answers and how that's not normally like him to be so short with me. "What should I do?" I ask.

"Why don't you just ask him if everything is okay?" she says as she gives me a little shoulder shrug. She's always the logical friend with the right answers. "He's clearly battling some weird shit in his head. How did things end last night?"

"He got a phone call that James was sick and coming home." I prop my chin on my hand. "So I got dressed and went to bed."

"Wait, you just got dressed and left?" She gasps.

"I mean," I pause. "Yeah, I guess I did."

"That's your problem right there. He probably thinks *you* regret it."

The thought of that stuns me for a second and I think back to last night and how we left things. When he got the phone call, I knew by the tone of his voice that something was wrong. James will always be number one and I will never try to interfere with that. I proceeded to get dressed and head in for the night so he could take care of whatever was wrong with James. I didn't *mean to* run out of the kitchen.

"Fuck," I mutter, running my hands down my face.

"Take a deep breath." She sighs. "Just talk to him. I'm sure he will understand that you just wanted to give him space to figure out what to do about James being sick."

"Yeah, you're right. Thanks, Kali." I hear tiny moans coming from the living room. "Listen, I gotta go. James is waking up. I'll call you later." I hang up the phone quickly and pocket it to head to see if James is okay.

"Hey, buddy. You alright?"

"No," he moans, "My belly hurts so bad, Ms. Peyton." As soon as the words leave his mouth, he throws up all over me and the couch. Thank God this type of stuff doesn't bother me. I have sort of become immune to it after working with kids for so long.

"Oh, buddy," I sigh sympathetically. "Let's get you all cleaned up."

"I want my mommy," he cries.

Woah. His mom? I don't know how involved she is in this situation, but since being here I haven't heard him speak about her or go spend any time with her. My thoughts immediately go to what the history is between his mom and Thomas. I do know that there is something about being sick and having your mom there to comfort you. Moms always know exactly how to comfort a child in their time of need. I'm not his mom, but I am a female figure in his life that can comfort him in his time of need.

"I know I'm not your mom, James, but I can help you get cleaned up and snuggle with you, if you want," I tell him as I remove his pajamas covered in vomit.

"I would like that a lot, Ms. Peyton."

"James, can you do me a favor?"

"Yes?"

129

"Stop calling me Ms. Peyton." I giggle. "Call me Peyton or Pey. That's what my friends call me."

"Do you want to be my friend?" he asks with a small head tilt and a frown on his face.

"I already am your friend, silly goose." I laugh and ruffle my hands through his hair.

His face lights up like he just heard that Santa was about to walk through the door with an entire store full of toys for him. It makes my heart all fluttery at the thought of me being his friend making him so happy right now. Before I know it, James is crashing into me and wrapping his hands around my legs for the biggest hug and if I wasn't paying attention, I would have missed the faint whisper of his voice into my legs when he says, *"You're my best friend."*

After getting James washed up in the tub with lavender and eucalyptus scented bubbles and into a fresh pair of pajamas, I can tell that it has helped soothe him a lot because he's a little bit perkier. He was even able to eat some crackers and keep them down so I'm hoping he's on the mend from whatever bug he has. After he was settled watching his cartoons, I noticed that he fell asleep on the couch again, so I took the opportunity to take the best shower of my life, which was so necessary after being puked on. I straightened my hair, which I practically never do, so I can look decent when Thomas gets home later. I need to talk to him about last night and move past this awkward stage. I bake some more chocolate chip cookies because you know, I do that shit when I'm stressed. I also clean, so the apartment is fucking spotless right now. There is no smell of vomit or signs that anyone here has been sick all day.

I hear the elevator doors ding as I place the throw blanket that was in the dryer over the back of the couch. I wonder if Thomas is home much earlier than expected, but then I hear a female voice and peek around the corner to see Emiline walking in.

"Hey, girl," she says, putting her bags on the table. "How's James doing today?"

"He's doing much better now, thank God." I smile. "It was a rough morning and there was a lot of puke. He had a nice bath, though, and kept some crackers down."

"That's great!" She beams. "Thank you so much for being here for him today. I will say it on behalf of my brother, since he's such a fucking grouch and probably won't thank you himself."

I turn my gaze down to the floor and tuck a strand of hair behind my ear. "Can I ask you something, Emiline? You can tell me if it's too personal. But James said something today that made me curious."

"Of course."

"Where is James' mom?"

"Fuck if we know." She laughs. "She hasn't been in the picture since James was a month old. She was very set on pursuing her acting career or some shit. A child didn't fit in that career path for her. She signed all rights over to Tommy. Why? What did James say?"

"After he got sick all over me." I laugh. "He was asking for his mommy."

"Oh wow." Her eyes go wide. "Yeah, he's done that before, here and there. He doesn't remember her or know anything about her, but I think he sees other kids in school with their mom. A part of me thinks he craves that warm embrace of a mom. Does that make sense? I mean, have you met Tommy?" she scoffs, "he loves James so much, but he's the least affectionate person on the planet. I don't think he's ever told anyone in his life that he loves them, besides James. When it comes to my brothers and I, Thomas finds ways to *show us* he loves us. We learned growing up that he doesn't have to say it, we just know it."

I feel my heart rate speeding up as I stand there and listen to her. I don't understand how two people can have so much physical chemistry with each other and be totally opposite in every aspect of life. Was him pursuing me and kissing me, just about sex? Am I just someone in his life that he pays to watch his son but also there for a quick fuck in the kitchen when he needs it? My mouth is still on the floor, and I know I need to talk to Thomas.

I give Emiline a nod because I can't find any other words to say back to her. Crossing the room, I reach for my phone on the coffee table to shoot Thomas a quick text message.

> Your sister is here. She stopped by to see James.

Ok.

I guess we're still doing one word text message replies. I want to come right out and ask him if everything is okay, but I don't want to come across as clingy. Knowing my history with this sort of situation, it will lead to a disaster and in the end, I'm the one left with a broken heart. So, this is me working on my own personal relationship issues.

And the truth of the matter is, I'm not about to go there with my boss.

CHAPTER NINETEEN
Thomas

The last place I want to be right now is in the office and attending these mundane meetings on a fucking Sunday. I hate when James is sick because I know that he needs his dad there to make him feel better. It's the recipe for kids getting better by snuggling with mom or dad. The issue is that his mom isn't around, and she won't ever be. I have to do the job for both of us, and today, I can't be there for him.

Normally in this situation, I would have had to call Emiline or one of my brothers. None of them are comforting in the sense of being what he needs. I know my son and I know how he gets when he's sick. He turns into a total cuddle bug, and he's got this thing about making the house look like a movie theater with all the blinds drawn shut. James is lucky because I know without a doubt that Peyton will give him exactly what he needs today.

My thoughts drift to last night in the kitchen and how things ended so abruptly. I didn't get any sleep because I was over-analyzing everything we did and wondering if this is something she regretted. *Did I go too far?*

This morning when I left, I maintained a professional composure because I know that's what she's also trying to do. She hasn't said those words, but her body language says otherwise.

She's been sending me updates on James throughout the morning and I just keep giving her one-word answers because I apparently act like a fucking high-school kid around her. I don't want to talk to her about jack shit until we can discuss last night, if I'm being honest. So yeah, I'm a highschooler today.

I'm disrupted from my thoughts when Marc comes flying into my office, the door rattling on the wall behind it. "Sorry I'm late," he says, clearly out of breath.

"You're not."

"Wait, what?" he says, looking confused.

"I told you that the meeting for the 108th Street lease signing was at noon so you would show up on time." I let out a chuckle. "We don't have to be there until 12:30."

"You bastard," he huffs as he sits down on the couch. "It's bad enough these guys want to do this signing on a Sunday. I don't understand why this can't wait until tomorrow."

"Trust me, I don't feel like doing this either. Especially with James being sick."

"How's he feeling?"

"I think he's on the mend," I say, pulling out my phone to show him the last text from Peyton. "This was the most recent update."

He reads the phone for a brief second and his eyes shoot back to me, and he starts laughing. "Alright, let's hear it."

"Hear what?"

"I just saw the last message and your one-word response back." He laughs. "And I didn't miss the other three responses back to her from you, either. All one word. You don't even send one-word texts to us when you're annoyed."

I run my hand through my hair and down my face out of frustration. Of course he saw that and that's what he chooses to point out. Marc will find any opportunity to call me out on being the asshole that I am.

"I'm trying to remain professional," I say as I straighten my tie.

"That's a fucking lie," he scoffs.

I sink down into my chair because I know he's right. "You're right. It's a lie. I am so beyond screwed with Peyton. I think I fucked up last night."

"What do you mean? You couldn't get it up?" He laughs out loud.

I pick up the stress ball sitting on my desk and chuck it at him like I'm a pitcher in the major leagues. Marc starts laughing harder at the fact that I threw a soft little stress ball at him like it would cause damage or something.

"It went up just fine. Thank you very much," I scoff. "In fact, it was so hard that I thought I was going to burst the seams of my pants."

"First of all, I don't need details on how hard your dick gets," he snaps. "Second of all, why was it still in your pants?"

"We never got far enough to remove my pants because our cock blocking sister had to call me."

"But you got somewhere?"

"Yes." I smirk. "I ate her on the kitchen counter like a starved bear who has been in hibernation for two years."

"Damn," was all that Marc could get out after being rendered speechless.

"Yeah." I shrug. "So, the dilemma is that Emiline called about James and then Peyton ran out of the kitchen. I am like 99.9% sure she regrets what happened."

"Did she say that to you?"

"Well... no, not exactly," I say, as I run my hands through my hair.

Marc stands up from the couch and crosses the office to stand in front of my desk. His face is painted with the most stoic and serious features. "Listen Tommy, I am going to be honest with you here for a second and I want you to listen closely. You are not the relationship type. You never have been."

"Gee thanks," I say, rolling my eyes at him.

"Are you going to tell me I'm wrong, Tommy?" He crosses his arms in front of his chest.

"Her sister was a witch. The wicked witch of the East, bro," I add because I can't not say it when someone says that. I love to piss him off and I will find any opportunity to do it.

"You're dumb as fuck," he laughs. "What I was getting at before you rudely interrupted me is that I see the way you get so flustered over Peyton. I don't know what she looks like or much about her other than the fact that she has you by the balls," he scoffs. "I understand both of you are trying to keep it professional, but what is so wrong about doing this with her and maybe trying to pursue a relationship?"

"You know I can't do that," I snap back. "I don't do relationships and the one time I tried, she left me and James."

"That doesn't solidify your point because you didn't love Sheila. That wasn't even a real relationship. You tolerated her because of James."

"I don't love Peyton either," I mutter back, as I start to get our things together for our meeting.

"But you could," he says as he stops me from moving around the office. "You could get to know her more and see where things go."

I still have nothing to say because part of me really does want that with Peyton, but the other part of me sees this type of thing as completely foreign. Not only did I lose her once, but I also tried a relationship and it ended with Sheila leaving me to raise my son alone. Two factors that scare the shit out of me.

"Tell me what to do, you big relationship guru."

"Text her." He shrugs.

"That's your best answer?"

"Yes," he says confidently. "Right now, looking at your conversation, you look like an asshole because all you're doing is giving her one-word answers."

Pulling my phone out from my pocket, I stare at it while trying to figure out what I can text her that isn't the word 'ok.' I scroll back for a second to see our previous conversations and I realize I am such an asshole. She's here doing her job and texting me updates about my son who's at home sick with her. I should have approached this so much differently because I truly am appreciative that she offered to help me with him today so I could work. And what did I do? I treated her like an ass because I can't get my own head right.

I keep scrolling back and land on a conversation in our text thread where I'm almost certain she was flirting with me. When it comes down to it, I want to be her friend, first and foremost. Like Marc said, I want to learn more about her. We have the physical chemistry down pat, that's for fucking sure. I want to explore beyond this though.

I want to break the tension between us. I need to see her to talk about this and get it off our chests. If she's regretting it, then we can discuss it and I can deal with being her friend.

> Is she hanging out for a little bit?

Yes.

Touché, Peyton.

I hold my phone up to show Marc that she hit me with a one-word text basically saying '*Fuck you too, Mr. Ford.*' We both laugh at that response.

"You are so screwed." Marc throws his head back and laughs. "Let's get this signing done and over with. I have a meeting with a new assistant across town."

"What is with these people wanting meetings on a Sunday? Is he any good?"

"He is actually a she," he says. "Apparently she is the best assistant this city has to offer."

CHAPTER TWENTY
Peyton

I was sitting on the couch with James and Emiline, still contemplating texting Thomas just to ask if things were ok. Before I could even figure out how to say what I want to ask him, my phone vibrates in my hand, and I see a text come through from him.

Is she hanging out for a little bit?

Yes.

Take that Mr. One-Word. I'm about to dust my shoulder off because well, that was pretty great giving him a taste of his own medicine, but I'm left gasping when I see the next text come in.

Come to the office in an hour.

Why?

Because I said so.

I'm with James.

No. Emiline is with James. You're coming to my office.

Nerves flutter in my stomach and I can't help but wonder if Emiline coming here was set up so that Thomas can bring me to his office and fire me. *There's no way, right?* Panic rises as I fire off another text message.

> If you're having me come to your office to fire me, just tell me now and I'll pack my things.

Is that what you think, Sunshine?

His term of endearment leaves me gasping, but I forget to release it. I remember when he used that nickname on me that first night and it left me just as speechless then as it does now.

I'm staring at my phone trying to find the words to reply when it pings again with another message.

Firing you isn't even on the list of things I want to do to you, Peyton.

Well. Fuck me then.

———

After asking Emiline to stay with James because Thomas wants to see me at the office, I can't help but wonder if she already knew. She was entirely too understanding. But she was happy to stay and watch a movie with James.

I stand at his office door with my hand raised to knock but allow myself a moment to gather my thoughts. The last forty minutes, I have been on the verge of breaking out into a full-blown fucking sweat. I took the time to fix up my hair and put on a bit of makeup to make myself look presentable. I'm wearing a deep blue sundress that hangs just below my knees with a pair of white sandals.

What did that text message mean?

What does he want to do to me?

My thoughts run rampant as I close my eyes one last time, take a deep breath and exhale, before I knock on the door.

"Come in." I can hear Thomas say.

I open the door where I find Thomas resting against the front of his desk. His one leg is crossed over the other and his arms are crossed over his chest. He's wearing a white dress shirt with his sleeves rolled up to his elbows. I feel my nipples harden as my eyes trail down his body to take it in. There is fucking something about tattooed forearms on a man. *This man.* I just fucking can't. I'm definitely sweating.

"Hey," is the only word I manage to form.

"Hi," he says with a stern tone. "How's James?"

"Good. He was a lot better when I left to come here."

"Okay." *Another fucking one-word response.*

"Listen, Thomas. About last night—" I cut right to the chase because I'm done with this awkwardness between us. I can't pinpoint exactly where I went wrong last night and it's driving me mad.

"What about last night?" I see a change in his demeanor as he straightens his spine.

"I'm sorry I let it get that far." I turn my gaze down to the floor. "I know it was very unprofessional of me. I know I am here for a job, and that I have to take it more seriously. I just wanted to—"

I'm cut off from my ramble when I see Thomas taking strides across the office to stand in front of me. Ever so slowly, his hand raises to my hair, where he tucks a strand of loose hair behind my ear. I close my eyes as heat spreads through my body because I can't help how my body responds to his touch. My hands find his chest as if I'm ready to set boundaries and push him away, but I feel the strong muscles in his chest and I can't seem to find the energy to do anything.

Both of his hands find the sides of my neck with his thumbs lightly brushing my cheeks and he delicately lifts my head so I'm looking directly at him. I find the courage to open my eyes, only to find him glaring into my soul. His deep blue irises turn a shade darker, and I notice his pupils dilate as his sultry eyes move from my eyes to my lips. He hovers over my lips with a sense of urgency, like he asked me to come here just to kiss me.

"We can't do this," I whisper against his lips.

"The way your body reacts to mine tells me another story, Sunshine," he whispers back, lightly stroking my cheek bone with his thumb.

A shiver runs down my spine and I remain silent. I feel myself in a constant battle between my brain and my body. He's not wrong, though. My body does react to him, and it drives me absolutely wild because it has never reacted this way to another man. Not Richard or any of my other past relationships. My brain is fighting its own battle that this might be just sex for him. It's convenient because I'm living in his home. Let's be real for a second, Thomas can have any woman he wants. I bet he's had models kneeling for him after one look of him in that fucking suit.

"I thought," Thomas whispers. His brief pause tells me he's battling his own thoughts. "I've spent all day thinking that you regret last night. I know I crossed a professional boundary with you. Something I don't ever do. But fuck." He runs his hands through his hair. "I couldn't stop worrying that maybe you regretted it."

My mouth parts and I suck in a breath. We both crossed major boundaries that should have been a clear line in the sand screaming at us to not blur it. There is absolutely no denying the fact that I want this man with every fiber of my being. But he's completely off limits. I don't do casual sex and Thomas doesn't do relationships. I'm asking for my heart to be broken if I keep this up.

My body betrays me in this moment, though, because the next thing I know, my hands are fisting his dress shirt and untucking it from his pants. Our eyes are locked on each other, both afraid that if either one of us blink, this moment will pass.

My body trembles at the intensity of his stare as my hands move to his buttons and I begin to unbutton them one at a time.

"Peyton," he whispers through gritted teeth, as he stands there unmoving with his shirt open and exposed to me. My eyes wander to his lips, and I see him roll his tongue over his bottom lip, causing my nipples to harden and a wetness to pool between my legs.

I shift my stance so I'm an inch closer to him and I feel his cock brush against my stomach. He swallows a lump in his throat when my hand moves to his belt to undo it. I feel a strong hand clasp around my wrist to stop me from going any further.

"You don't have to do this."

"I know," I whisper as I shake his hand from my grip and lock the door behind me. Undoing his zipper with our eyes still locked on each other, I reach my hand inside of his boxer briefs and grip his girth. *Holy fuck.* I say it in my head but there's a small chance I said it out loud by the way the corner of his lip turns up. "I want to show you how much I did *not* regret last night, Mr. Ford."

He throws his head back and mutters a '*fuck me*' under his breath.

I'm telling you, there is just something about Thomas that brings out the confidence in me. I don't know what it is but when he's around, I turn into this vocal, and bold, bad ass sex vixen. Staring at this man in front of me with my hand wrapped around his cock, in his office, being as vocal as I am?! Like who even am I?

I pull my hand from his cock and move it up to his chest. With one swift move, I push him back until he falls onto the couch behind him so he can fully enjoy this pleasure. I move to the waistband of his pants to pull them down to free him from his boxer briefs, but I don't get that far when his hands move up to my breasts to cup them through my dress.

"Nope," I say, swatting his hand away and smiling. "It's your turn."

"If I can't touch them, at least let me see them."

Without hesitation, I reach for the hem of my dress and pull the whole thing off, exposing myself in the bright office lights, wearing nothing but a white thong and a lacy black bra. Reaching behind me, I unclip my bra, and in the most seductive manner I can, I remove the bra and dangle it off to the side of me with a grin on my face. I watch his eyes widen as his eyes travel to my exposed breasts. His tongue sweeps along his bottom lip and my panties become even more drenched just watching him react to me.

"Holy fuck," he draws out. "You have the most perfect tits."

I shy at his words for a brief pause before my hands move back to his briefs to pull them down and expose his cock. The minute it springs free, my eyes widen. I felt it and I knew it was huge, but *shit*. This is nothing like I have ever seen before.

Thomas must sense my shock when he says, "You like what you see, Sunshine?"

"I-I," I stutter as my eyes bounce from his cock to his eyes that are glistening with amusement.

"You can take it."

I swallow the lump in my throat and move my hand to grip the base as I begin to stroke his hard-as-steel cock up and down.

"Peyton," he moans in a low breath as his eyes close. "I need you to take your time. I don't want to come before that hot little mouth is on me."

I giggle at the fact that my body and touch have that effect on him. My mouth moves to the tip, and I lick the pre-cum that's dripping from it while I continue stroking up and down his length. Using my hand to steady him, I lick him from the base to the tip before I take him in my mouth. He lets out an audible moan and I feel myself rubbing my thighs together as my pussy is desperate for his touch.

I bob my head up and down, licking the tip as I come up each time. His hands find the back of my head and grip my hair. "Good girl," he praises. I move my gaze upward and notice his bottom lip in his mouth as he bites down on it. "Good fucking girl," he growls. "You take my cock so well, Sunshine."

I moan at the continued praise, and I know, without a doubt, that my panties are fucking destroyed. I sink his cock deeper into my mouth until I feel him at the back of my throat while my hand moves to gently squeeze his balls at the same time. He lets out a moan and I can tell he's already close.

"You're like a dream," he says through a strained voice. "Here in my office with your mouth wrapped around my cock while it stretches your throat." I take him even deeper, and I can feel tears leaking from my eyes. "Shit. You're going to fucking make me come, baby."

Baby.

I pick up the pace and suck harder with his dirty words as I move my head up and down. His hand never leaves the back of my head. My hand instinctively moves to my clit because it's craving the friction and release.

"Don't you dare make yourself come," he warns me. My hands leave my clit with a groan in frustration. I need to come. "That's my job."

That nearly sends me over the edge. I suck his length hard and bob my head faster when I feel his hand leave my head and cups my jaw so that I can release his cock from my mouth, and he says, "I'm going to come."

My eyes flicker between his in amusement as I choose not to release him from my mouth. Instead, I sink deeper until he's so deep that I gag. Within seconds I hear him whispering '*fuck*' over and over again as hot cum shoots down my throat. My mouth circles his length like a suction cup as he empties himself into my throat.

Allowing him to come down from his orgasm, I release him, and my finger moves to wipe the corner of my mouth. His intense stare burns into me as I take my finger and suck it clean with a small smirk on my face.

His hand comes to my face to move the hair away from my

eyes. Tension fills the room after what just happened but finally, he snaps. *"Fuck it,"* he whispers as he takes my body by the waist, lifting me up as if I weigh nothing, and my legs instinctively wrap around his waist. In one swift move, his desk is wiped clean as he lays me down on top of it.

"Thomas," I shriek.

He runs his fingers slowly from the hollow of my neck to the delicate part of my collarbone and down to my breasts, where he stops to cup them both. He takes one of them in his mouth with a moan. "Perfect," he whispers before he takes the next one in his mouth. My back arches into him. He doesn't even have to try and get me off. I'm already so close.

"Feet on the edge of the desk," he orders.

I do as he says, scooting my ass back just the slightest so I can rest my feet on the edge of the desk. It's no surprise that my legs spread easily for him. He steps back and his eyes trail me from top to bottom. "Fucking perfect," he repeats under his breath as his tongue swipes his bottom lip. "Such a pretty pussy. I can see how wet you are for my cock without even touching you."

"Yes," I moan, biting my bottom lip as I hold myself up with one elbow. My finger trails down to swipe myself, as he watches the arousal coat my fingers. "Soaked for you."

He moves closer as his hand grips my wrist, holding my hand in place as he takes the fingers wet with my arousal in his mouth and sucks it off me. It's the hottest thing I have ever seen.

"What do you want, Peyton?"

"You."

He growls as he steps towards me. His hands trail down my body as he spreads my legs more and his thumb finds my clit. He starts to rub slow circles, and I moan as pleasure runs down my spine. He doesn't hesitate when he inserts two fingers inside of me and begins to pump me hard with his hand. "I want you to come for me, Peyton. I want your cum dripping down my fucking desk," he says before pressing a gentle kiss to my collar bone causing a wild sensation to take over my body.

145

"Now," he demands. I fall apart at his demanding words. His dominance turns me on so much. I never imagined I would find that so incredibly sexy, but coming from him has me seeing stars in seconds. I shatter around him, and I swear I see stars. My pussy is pulsating around his fingers as he continues to press gentle kisses on my neck. "Fuck," he groans.

He allows me to come down from my orgasm the same way I let him come down from his, and I watch him closely as he pulls his fingers out of me. He brings them up to his lips and licks them clean. His eyes close as he sucks each finger completely clean. "You taste so sweet, Sunshine." He hovers over me and leans down to whisper in my ear, "So fucking sweet."

My mind starts spinning as both of us begin to get dressed. His gaze moves to look at me every so often, watching me with unspoken words about what just happened. Tension has snapped and we both want this. It's very clear that our chemistry could light the world on fire.

I know this can't ever be more than it is.

I know we are crossing so many boundaries.

I'm so fucked.

CHAPTER TWENTY-ONE
Thomas

Peyton has been driving me insane. The way she dropped down to her knees without hesitation when she showed up in my office two weeks ago and gave me the best blow job of my life. She looked like a goddess in that deep blue dress that complimented her eyes. I expected her to tell me how she regretted what happened in the kitchen the night before and how it shouldn't happen again. Next thing I know, I'm living out my wildest fantasy of having her spread out on my desk. I feel my dick twitch in my sweatpants at the vision of her perfect pussy on full display for me. *Fuck*.

She has not pursued me since then, but I swear she's on a mission to drive me insane. The next day, she woke up early to make James breakfast and she was wearing the new pair of silk pajamas I had bought her because I tore off the last pair being the animal that I am. When I approached the kitchen, she smiled at me and said, "*Good morning, Mr. Ford,*" and winked at me. She fucking winked at me.

A few days later I came home from work to her blasting my favorite country music station in the kitchen and making chocolate chip cookies. She didn't hear me get home but when I peeked into the kitchen, she was having a full-blown dance party by herself. Her hair was in a messy bun, and she was wearing black sweatpants with an oversized t-shirt that said something about a romance match up with the names Tristan and Remy on it. I assumed it had something to do with the books she reads. Seeing her in that state is the sexiest I have ever seen her. She was so carefree and happy dancing to *my* favorite music.

More and more she has been having this effect on me that I just can't describe. I want more of her, but can I picture her in my life as more than just a nanny? Can I picture myself in a relationship with her at all?

My thoughts are disrupted when the elevator to my apartment dings with the arrival of Marc and Logan. They took James for breakfast and are coming over for a boys' day to watch Sunday football.

"DADDY!" I hear James scream as he comes running into the kitchen to find me.

"Hey, JJ!" I open my arms and squat down to embrace the tackle hug he's about to give me. He leaps into my arms and wraps his arms around my neck. His hugs are the best thing in the world.

"Ready for some football?" Logan says as he enters the kitchen, carrying a case of beer and a tray of pretzels. I sure can fuck up some soft pretzels and cheese dip during a football game.

"You ready to watch your boys lose?" I say to Logan with a smirk.

"Dude, there is no way the Giants are beating the Cowboys today. Your quarterback isn't even playing," he snaps back. He's very defensive over his football team. It just so happens that today, both of our teams are playing each other in the league's biggest rivalry. Don't even get me started about how he's a Cowboys fan living in Giants territory.

"Relax," Marc chimes in. "It's just a game."

"Just a game?" Logan raises his voice. "It's the biggest game of the season!"

"The biggest game of the season!" James cuts in, trying to join the adult conversation. "Are you ready for some fooootballlllll," he shrieks, as he runs off with his hands in the air.

The three of us burst into laughter and shake our heads at the crazy kid.

"Is Peyton here?" Marc asks.

I stop laughing to give him a side eye. "No, it's her weekend off. She's with Avery and Kali."

"Are her friends hot?" Logan asks, still laughing.

"Don't even go there."

"What?" He throws his hands in the air. "Curious minds want to know."

"You are not fucking the nanny's friends."

"She's back to being just the nanny, huh?" Marc hits me with a sly smile.

"She's always been just the nanny."

"No, she was your meal on the kitchen counter a couple weeks ago when you got home from work," Logan scoffs.

The memories of how sweet she tasted rush through my body and my dick wants to salute to that flavor. *Down boy.* Now is not the time. I can't help but tip the corner of my lip up to the thought of that and I am pretty sure the two of them caught on to it.

"I was her meal at the office the next day." I shrug my shoulders.

"SHUT THE FUCK UP!" Logan snaps. "When were you going to tell us about this?"

"I wasn't."

"Are we ever going to get to meet this *nanny?*" Marc asks, using his fingers as air quotes when he says the word nanny.

"She will be home sometime today. It's Sunday and she usually comes home in the afternoon."

"She comes *home*." Marc mocks me, emphasizing the last word.

I'm becoming too attached to Peyton. I can't help the words that come out of my mouth sometimes. I should have worded that differently but things with her are just different. She makes life easy. Is this how relationships are? I wouldn't know.

The thought of her making this a permanent home creeps up and I feel a little overwhelmed over it. We've only had a few intimate moments and she hasn't tried to pursue me since then. I don't even know if she has feelings for me, honestly. I'm not sure if a relationship is something she would even want to pursue with me. But I'll be damned if I let her go before I find out for sure.

"I think I'm going to invite her to the shore house for my birthday weekend," I tell them but pause before continuing. I scan each of their faces to see what they might be thinking. Marc's lips part as if he's in shock and Logan gives me a shit eating grin. *Mother fucker*. "To help with James of course," I add.

"Right," Logan draws out. "It's definitely to help with James. There won't be enough people there to help him on *your* birthday weekend." He's so sarcastic, I could punch him in the face.

"I'm going to tell her she can invite Kali and Avery too. That way, when she's not helping with James, she can hang out with them and have something to do."

"I like the idea of that." Logan wiggles a brow.

"I'm telling you for the last time," I snap, raising my voice louder than I should. "You are not fucking my nanny's friends."

"Who's not fucking us?"

I can feel my face turn white as the three of us turn our attention to the entrance of the kitchen. Standing there are all three ladies. Peyton has a shy smile on her face while Avery wears a huge smile, and her hands are propped on her hips.

"I-I—" I start to mutter but can't find the words.

"Tommy boy," Avery says with a shit eating grin. "I don't think you should be deciding who I get to fuck."

My eyes move from Avery to Peyton, and I watch her cheeks flush with embarrassment. She covers her eyes with her hand and is shaking her head at her friends' antics. Avery is a ticking bomb ready to explode.

"What the fuck?" Logan asks her in a cop like tone.

"I'm Avery," she extends a handout to Logan. "I'm the friend who apparently, no one is fucking. Which is such a shame because that's my favorite sport." She laughs and throws in a wink for good measure.

"Avery—" Peyton growls at her and moves her gaze to me. "I'm sorry about her. We went to brunch. You know, mimosas and Avery are a lethal combination."

"Best combination," Avery giggles.

"I'm sorry, guys," Kali cuts in. "We just stopped by to drop off some of her bags from shopping this morning." She points her thumb to where Peyton stands.

"Don't be sorry." Logan waves a hand. "We're about to watch some football if you ladies would like to join us."

"Logan—" I scowl at him. Peyton has already been driving me crazy enough as it is. I don't need her driving me crazy in front of these two nitwits.

"Oh, where are my manners?" He extends a hand to Peyton with a smug look on his face. "I'm Logan. Nice to officially meet you. I'm this guy's best friend."

"Nice to meet you too." She accepts his hand to return the shake. "I'm Peyton."

"What are you doing here?" Marc interrupts the introductions. I turn in his direction, and I take note of the scowl on his face. *What the fuck?*

"Oh," Avery says, as she notices Marc standing there and shoots him a cheeky smile. "Nice to see you again."

"You two know each other?" Peyton and I ask at the same.

My eyes bounce between the two of them and Peyton's jaw falls to the floor.

Avery smirks. "Yes, Sir. I'm his new assistant."

"This was the new job you got?" Peyton asks. Shock is plastered on her face. "Wait. Marc Ford?" She shakes her head as realization hits her. "I should have put two and two together."

We're all cut off from the awkward conversation when James comes barreling into the kitchen screaming "Ms. Peyton!" He wraps his little arms around her legs. *Fuck, my heart.*

"Hey, buddy!" Peyton wraps her arm around his shoulders. "How was your weekend?"

"It was so good. But I missed you."

"I missed you too, bud." She moves so she can crouch down to his level and open up her arms for a real hug. James wraps his arms around her neck, and she wraps her arms around his tiny body. I swear my lungs have no oxygen in them. I don't get the opportunity to watch the two of them interact often and seeing this makes my heart feel weird shit that it's not used to feeling. My heart rate picks up and I can feel Marc's eyes on me as we all watch the display of affection between the two of them.

"I got you something at the store this morning," she tells him.

"You did?!"

"I did," she says before reaching inside a small bag. "Now you can't have these unless Daddy says it's okay." I love hearing the word daddy come out of her mouth. "They are dinosaur gummy snacks! I know how much you love dinosaurs."

"DINOSAURS!" he shrieks. "This is so cool! Thank you so much, Ms. Peyton."

"You are so welcome, big dude." She giggles.

"Are you home for good now? Are you staying for some football? Are you going to eat pizza with me? Are you going to play with my dinosaurs?" He rattles off question after question to her and all of us start laughing at his energy. He talks a mile a minute when he's excited.

Her eyes look up to Kali and Avery like she's silently asking them if they want to stay. *Please say yes. No, wait. Please say no.* My heart can't handle this shit today. I watch both of them look at each other and give Peyton a soft smile. The three of them just spoke to each other with no words. Female friendships are weird.

"Yes, bud." She looks back at James. "We'll stay and hang out with you. Have you met my best friends?"

"No, but I'm your best friend too," he says in the sweetest little voice but has a frown of disappointment on his face.

"You are," she chuckles. "You are my bestest friend."

"Hey, I take offense to that," Avery smiles with her hands on her hips. "Hey, James. I'm Avery, but you can call me Ave."

"That's so awesome that I can call you a cool nickname," James says. "Ms. Peyton says I can call her Pey. That's so cool."

"I think you're so cool." Avery laughs.

"And I'm Kali," she says, extending her hand to shake his hand. "You can call me Kali."

"Well, that's not a cool nickname."

"James—" I scowl. "Be respectful."

Kali lets out a soft laugh and says, "How about you give me my cool nickname, bud?"

I can see the wheels turning in James' head as he thinks about it for a second. My brain is on overload right now witnessing this conversation. How are these strangers to James so welcoming to my son? They must know how much Peyton cares about him. I didn't have to see her and James together to know that she cares about him. My heart won't chill the fuck out.

"I'm gonna think about it, Ms. Kali," James finally says.

"Come on." James starts tugging at all three of them. "I want to show you guys my dinosaur collection upstairs."

The three girls giggle but follow James out of the kitchen and I stare at the entrance of the kitchen for what feels like forever. The thoughts of my nanny are consuming my mind. I can't believe I have never noticed how the two of them interact together and how much James loves Peyton. Yes, I said love.

Because he is three and loves everyone he meets. The way he ran into the kitchen and wrapped his tiny arms around her legs showed me everything I needed to know about how he feels.

"You're so fucked," Logan cuts my thoughts.

"I am so fucked," I repeat back, still staring at the entrance of the kitchen.

———

The day goes surprisingly well, despite my nerves over all of it. I think it was the tequila and whiskey that I always keep in stock now. Once Peyton moved in, I made sure to always have tequila on hand. I learned early on that it's her favorite drink when she's happy, when she's stressed, or on Tuesdays with tacos. Tequila to Peyton is like whiskey to me.

Everyone has gone home, and Peyton is upstairs putting James to bed. He specifically requested she put him to bed because they are the *bestest friends*. Watching the two of them interact all day only solidifies the fact that she is the perfect nanny for him. She is so patient with him, which is what he needs.

Logan actually behaved himself today, which was shocking. Thankfully, he didn't seem too interested in her friends. *Thank fuck*. I don't need him getting tangled up with them or anyone close to Peyton because I don't know what is happening with us.

I could tell Avery is developing a *thing* for Marc though. That girl holds nothing back and I'm sure the tequila helped her loosen up. If I didn't know any better, I would think she was trying to flirt with Marc, and he was shutting it down every chance he could since she now works for him. The two are complete opposites of each other and she is *not* his type. Avery is a wrecking ball and Marc is looking for a wife to settle down with. I really don't see that blossoming into anything serious. Another, *thank fuck*.

I feel my chest tighten when I think about Peyton today. She moved through the apartment and interacted with my brother and Logan as if she's done it for years. As if she's not just a nanny in this house. As if she's something more. And *fuck me* watching her watch football. She's a Giants fan, which only gives her bonus points in my book. The highlight of the day was when she gave Logan shit about the Cowboys, even though we lost to them 40-6. She just has this natural carefree way about her where she fits into any situation and makes the most of it.

I must have been completely zoned out staring at the blank TV when I feel the couch dip to my left.

"He's all tucked in," Peyton says in a tone barely above a whisper. I turn my gaze from the blank screen to her. Her head is tipped down and she's tucking a strand of hair behind her ear. She is without a doubt the most beautiful woman I have ever seen. Why do I melt into a puddle of mush whenever she's around? I'm not a fucking mushy dude.

"I didn't get a chance to ask earlier, but how was your weekend off?"

"It was okay," she says with a frown. "I went to visit my Gigi. She's been sick, so I've been trying to visit her whenever I'm off."

Damn, I had no idea.

"You know, if you ever need to see her during the week, just let me know."

"I was actually going to ask you about that." She twirls her hair nervously.

"Anything you want, Peyton. Consider it done." I don't know what makes me say that but at this point, she could ask me to buy her the largest skyscraper in the city, and I would give it to her.

"Thank you." She smiles. "It's just about the car. I know it's for me to take James wherever he needs to go, but I wanted to know if it was okay if I take it to go see Gigi tomorrow while James is in school. The bus isn't the fastest mode of transportation," she huffs out a laugh. "I'm afraid I wouldn't be back in—"

"Peyton," I cut her off. "Of course you can take the car. Have you been taking the bus this whole time?"

"Well... sort of."

"Peyton." I pinch my eyebrows together to give her a stern look. "I told you to use it. I gave you the keys for a reason. I *do not* want you riding the bus again. Do you understand?"

She nods. "I really appreciate that, Thomas."

"One problem," I pause. "James is off school tomorrow. For what reason? I can't tell you because I don't know. I swear this school has the most random days off."

"Shit," she murmurs under her breath and a look of disappointment flashes across her face.

"But why don't you take him with you," I offer. "James can make anyone feel better and put a smile on their face."

"You're not wrong." She laughs. "James really can turn someone's day around. I wish his funny personality could cure cancer. But at least it can make her day a little brighter."

I had no clue about any of this and I feel a stab in my chest at her admission. I've heard her on the phone with her grandma often. I know she cares about her a lot and she's an important person in Peyton's life. I'm going to make a mental note to shoot Eddy a text later to drop a care package off to her first thing in the morning.

"I'm so sorry, Peyton."

"Don't be. She's the strongest fighter I know. She's going to beat this a second time," she says with a soft smile. "She's going to be really happy to finally meet James."

I nod. The thought of her talking to her about my son makes my heart skip a couple beats. I remain silent because I need to collect my thoughts. Finally, I ask, "D-do you want to watch a movie?" I don't know what makes me think to ask her that. It's late and I'm sure she's exhausted from a long day.

She pauses for a moment to lift her head and look me in the eyes. She's sitting with her legs tucked under her and her arm draped over the back of the couch. She's a good distance away from me. "What do you have in mind?" she asks.

"What kind of movies do you like?"

"I don't watch movies too often, but when I do, chick flicks are definitely my jam." She lets out a light giggle.

"Chick flick it is," I say as I raise the remote control to turn on the TV and flick through the movie guide.

"W-wait," she pauses and smirks. "You're willingly turning on a chick flick right now?"

If it's something you want to watch, then I'll watch it with you.

That's what I want to say. Instead, I clear my throat and turn back to clicking through the channels. My eyes are not on her anymore, but I feel her presence all around me and the smell of roses takes over my senses. I don't know if it's a lotion, a perfume or just her, but I can't seem to get enough of it.

I clear my throat and adjust myself in my seat to rest my ankle over my opposite leg. I need to hide the fact that her sitting next to me on the same couch is making my dick harden.

"We have *Legally Blonde*, *The Proposal* or *How to Lose a Guy in 10 Days*. What will it be, Sunshine?" I turn my gaze to her with a smile and I immediately regret the term of endearment I use because I can see shock grow in her facial features. Her mouth is slightly parted, and her cheeks are flushed pink.

The first time I ever called her Sunshine was that night we met. When she first caught my eye walking through the doors of that event, she looked like sunshine. It was dark outside, and the lights inside were not all that bright but for whatever reason, *something* shined down on her. The light mixed with her golden blonde hair flowing down her back, she was a ray of sunshine.

"Peyton, I just—" I want to redeem myself, but she cuts me off when she says, "Let's watch *How to Lose a Guy in 10 Days*."

I clear my throat. "Okay."

"Let me just get changed really quick." She moves to get up from the couch. "I'll be back in seven minutes."

"Seven minutes is very specific," I let out a chuckle.

157

I can see her cheeks turn rosy again as she lets out a soft laugh.

"What can I say, I'm quick," she says with a wink and she's off to her room.

This girl is trying to kill me. I swear.

I'm such a mother fucker that my mind immediately goes to dirty thoughts and how I bet I could have her cum dripping down my fingers in seven minutes if she let me. I stand up to adjust my now hardening cock in my sweatpants. I apparently have seven minutes to think of something that will bring this pony back to its stable.

Dog shit.

Grandpas in tighty whities.

Football.

Well, that one doesn't help because I can picture Peyton cheering on our team while wearing their jersey.

I get myself situated back on the couch with a small throw pillow on my lap to rest my arms on and hide my growing hard on. I flick through the guide to find *How to Lose a Guy in 10 Days*. It's not my first choice, but it's hers. I grab the second remote to turn on the electric fireplace for some light in the room and I turn off the big lamp that is too bright for a movie.

She comes back into the room *almost* seven minutes later wearing a plush robe. Is she wearing something under the robe? I sure fucking hope so because I am on the verge of losing all restraint I have held for this woman. She moves to sit in her spot on the couch. I call it her spot because whenever I find her on the couch, she's always perched in the corner the sectional surrounded by pillows.

"I'm ready," she says with a smile as she pats a few of the throw pillows and pulls a blanket to cover her lower half.

"Are you comfy?" I ask her with a chuckle.

"Very," she says as she settles down into the pillows with her feet stretched out almost touching me.

I press play on the movie, and we sit in silence watching it. It isn't until halfway through the movie that I realize I don't even know what we're watching because all I can think about is her. The woman next to me. The woman with the soft giggles at the funny parts of the movie. The woman that can't fucking sit still on the couch next to me.

Without saying a word, I scoot closer to her and bring her feet on top of the pillow that is resting on my lap.

"W-what are you doing?" she stutters. Her eyes are wide with shock as her gaze bounces back and forth between her feet and my eyes.

"I'm rubbing your feet," I tell her. "You seemed very restless in your little corner over there."

"I-I," she pauses, tipping her head down and tucking the strand of hair behind her ear again. "I am. Just a little." I've learned about Peyton that she does this often when she's nervous. Her head dips down ever so slightly and she tucks that small strand of hair behind her ear. It's always the same strand.

"You're nervous." It's a statement, not a question.

Her eyes shoot back up to me and the look on her face tells me she is shocked I have her all figured out. "H-how did you…" she pauses, releasing the hair from her hand. "How did you know?"

"I noticed." I clear my throat before I continue, "that when you get nervous, you look down at the ground and tuck that little strand of hair behind your ear."

"You noticed?"

Looking into her baby blue eyes, I respond to her statement, "I notice everything about you, Peyton."

She doesn't say anything back. Her eyes dance back and forth again between my eyes and her feet. After a brief moment, she relaxes even more into the couch, shifting her body closer to me and now, most of her legs are resting on my lap. I've never been more thankful that I put this pillow on my lap. Otherwise, she would be feeling how hard she's made me with just the slightest move.

My hand moves to rub her feet which is something I've never really done to a woman before. My hands round her foot, and my thumbs press firmly in the sole and moves in small circles. My eyes are back on the movie because I can't take a chance at what her face is telling me. I continue to move up and down her foot in small circles with my thumb. I move to the next foot and repeat the movement. I can feel her getting restless in her seat again at the same time I hear her breathing get more frantic. She keeps shifting her ass like she's got an itch that needs to be scratched.

I can itch it for you, baby.

STOP IT.

As soon as the thought is in my mind, I hear her let out a small moan. A fucking MOAN! From a foot rub. *Is she joking right now?*

Feeling overconfident in that moan she just let out, my hand moves to her ankles where I continue to massage. She's still wiggling that itch she can't scratch, and her eyes are closed with her head pressed into pillows around her. I continue to move up her leg to her calves. Rubbing the back muscles of her leg, I see her hand clutch the blanket as if she's about to orgasm. *There is no way.*

"Are you okay over there?" I smirk.

"Yes," she moans. Her eyes still closed, and head still pressed back. I swallow a lump in my throat as my hands travel higher on her legs.

"Does this feel good, Peyton?"

"Oh god. Yes."

I move the plush robe up the slightest bit to expose her thigh and continue my massage up her legs. My hands are right above her knees and as soon as my hand hits her mid-thigh, I hear another moan erupt from her mouth.

"Peyton," I growl. "Those noises you're making…"

"I can't help it," she cuts me off. She lifts her head to look me in the eyes as she bites her lower lip. "This feels so good."

"Do you want me to keep going?"

"If you don't keep going, I'm going to scream." She laughs as her head falls back into the pillows. My restraint is gone. I've learned that when it comes to this woman, I can't help myself. I need her. I want her more than I have ever wanted anyone. I don't know what to do or where to go from here, but I do know how to make a woman feel pleasure. And I plan to fully give her any pleasure she wants to take from me.

"The only thing I want you to scream is my name when I make you come in seven minutes." Her head shoots up at the same time her mouth falls open.

"What can I say? I'm quick," I say with a wink.

I continue to travel up her thighs with my hands to the hem of her shorts. Only... she isn't wearing any shorts. I inch my hands a little higher to find no panties either.

"Where the fuck are your panties?" I manage to say through gritted teeth.

She props herself up on both elbows as she looks me in the eyes, taking her bottom lip between her teeth. She has never struck me as the seductive type of girl, but right now, she has a look of 'fuck me' written all over her face. "I don't wear them to bed," she says, barely above a whisper.

"But you weren't going to bed. You were coming to watch a movie with me."

"Semantics," she says, rolling her eyes with a smile.

"Were you hoping something would happen, Sunshine?" I grin as I lift an eyebrow. My hands are massaging the highest point of her thigh.

"I mean," she pauses and shrugs her shoulders. "I wouldn't be mad."

I don't feel the air leave my lungs, because now I'm holding my breath as my hand moves to cup her center. My hand connects with her bare skin, and she arches her back as her head falls back. Her hand has moved to grip the back cushion of the couch and I swear my dick turns to steel at the way her body reacts to my touch.

My fingers trail through her slit and I feel wetness coat them as a growl comes from deep in my throat. "You're soaked, baby."

"Yes," she moans.

"You're always so ready for me." I can feel her hips start to rock in a rhythmic motion as I slide a finger inside her. I slowly move it in and out as my thumb continues to press firmly on her clit in slow circles.

"More," she says, barely above a whisper.

"More of what, Peyton?"

"More."

"I need you to be more specific. Tell me what you want more of."

I can hear her breath catch, but she whispers, "Your fingers. I need more."

I withdraw my fingers to throw the pillow away that was on me and pull her to straddle my lap. My hands grip her hips, and I'm sure she can feel the steel between my legs because sweatpants do nothing to hide my raging erection. She lifts up to allow my hand to dip between us and I don't waste any time before diving two fingers deep inside of her.

"Take what you need, baby." My mouth finds the hollow of her neck while her hands cage me in as she grips the back of the couch. "Ride my hand."

I can tell she's on the verge of tipping over the edge because her pussy is squeezing my fingers. At that moment, I press them in as deep as I can, and I know I've hit her G-spot when my name falls off her lips with a moan.

"Thomas, don't stop."

I don't plan on fucking stopping anytime soon, that's for sure. I slip a third finger in. Feeling her tight pussy stretch for me. "So fucking tight," I breathe into her neck.

"Thomas, Thomas," she repeats as her hips continue to rock back and forth on my fingers deep inside of her. I know that if she keeps this up, I am going to come in my sweatpants. I haven't done that since middle school.

"Come for me, baby."

Seconds later, her moans grow louder, and I feel the walls of her pussy contracting around my fingers. I will never get over how sexy she looks when she lets go for me. Her body is shaking, and her breathing is rapid and frantic as her head falls back, coming down from her high.

While I withdraw my hand from her, our eyes lock, and she attempts to regulate her breathing. I slowly bring my fingers up to my mouth where I insert them and suck them clean. "Mmm," I moan. "You taste so fucking sweet, Peyton."

"That's…" she brings her bottom lip into her mouth. "That's so hot."

"No, baby." I smirk. "Your orgasm is fucking hot."

She does that thing again when she's nervous and I'll be damned if it isn't the cutest, but also the most frustrating thing she does. She has no reason to be nervous around me. She tries to move off of my lap, but my hands grip her hips and press her down onto me so she can feel me. Her eyes meet mine and I can see her cheeks flush.

"Why are you nervous?" I ask her as I take my hand and cup the side of her face. My thumb delicately brushes the skin on her cheek bone.

"I guess," she pauses for a moment as if she is trying to figure out how to put words together. "I guess, I want—"

"What do you want, Peyton?"

"I want you to fuck me."

CHAPTER TWENTY-TWO
Peyton

I don't know who the hell I think I am.

When did I turn into the girl openly asking to be fucked six ways to Sunday by someone who looks like he belongs on the cover of a GQ magazine? Damn it, Avery. She was right about the right guy doing that for you. Me sitting on his lap like this is making it hard to catch my breath after the best orgasm of my life. I mean, was this the best one? Or was it the one where he had me sprawled out on the kitchen counter? Fuck if I know. But it seems to get better and better each time.

I want Thomas. There's no denying that.

Is asking him to have sex crossing so many lines? Yes.

Do I care about these stupid lines anymore? No. I mean, yes. Wait, no.

Relax brain. Let me have this moment, even if it's just this once.

Thomas interrupts my thoughts when he continues to gently brush my cheek with his thumb and says, "There's a lot of things I want to do to you, Peyton."

"Y-you do?"

"Yes, Peyton. I can't stop thinking about every one of them."

"Can…can you tell me?" I ask as I place my hand on his shoulders. I'm ready to drive him as crazy as he makes me. Again, who the hell do I think I am? Not only does Thomas light my body on fire, but he also brings out this confident and sexy version of myself. A side of me that I never really had the opportunity to tap into. Only he can make me feel this way, and I want more of it.

"You want me to tell you about the fantasies I have of you when I'm fucking my fist at night?" His hand gently glides down my arm, barely touching as it travels down to my wrist and back up my arm. "You want me to tell you all the ways I have made you come in those fantasies?"

I think my jaw is on the floor. Scratch that, I know it's on the floor. Did he just tell me that *I* am the object of his fantasies when he jerks off? No, I heard that wrong.

"You think about me." I meant for that to come out as a question, but it comes out more like a statement.

"More than I care to admit, Sunshine," he says with a grin.

I don't reply, but I let Thomas cup my face with both hands. His thumbs rest on my jawline as his eyes bounce between my eyes and lips. I can see his jaw clench as if he's fighting the same battle I've been fighting regarding professional boundaries. But the battle is lost when he leans into my ear, his five o'clock shadow tickling my cheek. "I'm going to show you," he whispers. "I'm going to live out each and every one of those fantasies with you."

He takes a nip at my ear right before he starts peppering kisses along my jawline until he reaches the corner of my lips. "You're so goddamn beautiful, Peyton," he says as he softly kisses the corner spot before pulling back to look me in the eyes. "And so fucking sexy when you come," he says right before his mouth crashes to mine. The kiss is not gentle. This kiss is fierce and full of hunger.

My hands travel to his hair, as he tilts his head just slightly to the side to deepen our kiss, his hands getting lost in my hair as he holds me there. It's like I'm drowning, and this kiss is the oxygen I need to breathe and survive.

We're fused together at the lips, and I feel my body move on its own as I sink down on top of him until I feel how hard he is between my legs. And if I were to move and get up right now, you would be able to see my arousal on his gray sweatpants.

His lips leave mine to trail down my jawline as he opens my robe the slightest bit to expose my breasts. His eyes bounce between my breasts as he licks his lips before he lets out a small moan of approval and starts frantically kissing my chest until his mouth is wrapped around my nipple sucking it into his mouth. My hips begin to rock to gain the friction I am craving. His hands move to my hips to still me, and he releases his mouth from my nipple. "Peyton," he groans. "If you keep moving like that, I am going to come before I'm even inside of you."

I feel my cheeks flush, but my body heats up at the thought of him inside of me. This man makes me feel wanted. He looks at me in such a way that if he closes his eyes or takes his eyes off me, I'm going to disappear. His touch lights me up like fireworks on the Fourth of July. At this moment right now, I have decided that I want this. I want him. Fuck the consequences of my actions.

"Then take them off, Mr. Ford."

I watch his eyes darken right in front of me. I can feel his grip tighten on my hips as if he's still trying to hold some sort of restraint. "Tell me you really want this."

"Yes, I do," I reply without an ounce of hesitation.

I feel a deep rumble in his chest as he moves to get up off the couch with me in his arms. My legs tighten around his waist and a small squeal escapes my lips as he tightens his hold around me. It's not a hold that he's afraid to drop me, it's a hold that tells me he wants this as much as I do.

"Thomas," I giggle. But he doesn't answer me as we head down the hallway towards my bedroom. We don't even make it halfway down the hall before he lowers me to my feet and presses me against the wall with force and his lips find mine again. His tongue dances with mine as his hands grope every part of me like he can't figure out where he wants them. He presses against me, and I can feel his cock against me, and a small moan escapes my mouth.

"Do you feel this, Peyton? You do this to me."

"Thomas," I whimper. "Take me to the bedroom."

He grips my ass to lift me against him again. This time, I am pressed directly on his hard length as he holds me and kisses a line along my collar bone. He releases one hand from my ass to open the door and slam it shut behind us. Before I know it, he has me thrown on the bed. I'm still wearing my robe with nothing underneath it. The tie to the robe has come undone, revealing a small part of my stomach and the top hangs off my shoulders. I lift myself to my elbows as I stare at his dark eyes drinking me in. The way he's staring at me burns a hole right through me and I can feel a throbbing sensation growing stronger at my core.

I watch as the corner of his lip lifts to form a small smirk on his face and his hand rubs along his sharp jaw as if he's contemplating what he's going to do to me first.

I don't wait for him to decide. I pull the strap of the robe, my eyes never leaving his. It falls open, completely exposing me to him. His eyes move from mine to my breasts and my nipples harden from the cool air hitting them mixed with the fire from his eyes. He moves to pull his t-shirt over his head in one swift motion. Instinctively, my jaw hangs open at the sight in front of me. His V-shaped sex lines are on full display while his sweatpants hang a little too low on his waist.

I swear to God, it's Niagara Falls between my legs as I drink his body in.

I pull my lower lip between my teeth as a grin forms on my lips and within seconds, Thomas is on top of me, caging my head in on both sides with his thick, corded forearms. The way he's staring at me sends goosebumps down my spine, while his close proximity heats up every other part of me.

"Kiss me," I tell him.

With a murmur of curse words under his breath, he lowers himself so that his lips are on mine. His body is pressed hard against mine as my hands begin to grip his back and my hips rock up to crave the feel of him between my legs. I want him so badly that my hands move to the waistband of his sweats to try and push them down the slightest. I want him to know that I want this. Why the fuck are they still on?

He swats my hand away and hisses, "No, Peyton." My hands fall from his waistband, and I am sure the look of disappointment washes over me. But it's not for long because he takes my chin with one hand to make sure I'm looking into his eyes when he tells me, "I want this. I want you," he pauses, and his eyes bounce back and forth between mine. "I have wanted you like this for so long. You naked and spread out for me. My lips kissing every part of your body. My hands learning your every curve. My cock stretching your tight pussy," he pauses to plant a quick kiss to the corner of my lips. "But I want to take my fucking time with you, Sunshine."

My hands grip each side of his face as I stare intently into his eyes. However, I can't find the words to say back to him so instead, I pull his face to mine to give him another kiss, silently telling him that I want him too.

As soon as he hits my collar bone with his lips, my fucking weak spot, my eyes close and my head falls back while a small moan comes out of my mouth. His one hand moves to grip my breast in his hand while his mouth travels to my other breast and he takes it into his mouth.

"Thomas," I breathe out. My back arches into him because the feeling is so strong, and he has me so worked up already. He sucks hard on my nipple and I'm almost at the point that the pleasure is too much. "I need more."

"I'm going to give you more, baby," he says, barely above a

whisper. As he speaks, his hand travels down my body to the area throbbing between my thighs. He squeezes my upper thigh and continues to speak, "I know what you need." His fingers dive into my wet pussy, and he presses firmly on my clit, causing an electric current to charge through my body. "This pussy was made for me." My eyes close and I can barely register Thomas speaking, "And I'm going to give you exactly what you need, Peyton."

His lips are not touching mine but are close enough that I can feel his heavy breathing on my lips. His eyes never leave my face as if he wants to watch me fall apart with his fingers deep inside of me. The second he slips another finger in and continues to pump me with his hand, I do just that. I fall apart as an intense orgasm crashes through me.

"Less than seven minutes, baby," he whispers into my ear before planting a kiss on my neck. I am still trying to regulate my breathing. My clit is still throbbing, despite my release. I want, no, I NEED more from him.

He peppers kisses in a trail down my chest, reaching my stomach and I feel myself suck in a sharp breath and my hand moves to cover the lower part of my stomach. Suddenly, all of the confidence that was buzzing through me vanished. I don't have the slimmest waist. I'm just an average girl so there's some fluff there, but I'm an expert at hiding it inside my high waisted leggings.

"Don't do that," he hisses.

"Do w-what?"

"Hide yourself," he says. "Don't hide yourself from me. You're fucking perfect, Peyton."

I don't say anything in response, but I move my hand away from my stomach and let out the breath I was holding.

"So fucking perfect," he says under a bated breath, as if he's telling himself that confession while he kisses every part of my stomach before his head is between my legs. My legs move on their own and open up for him. I can feel his breath before he turns his head to kiss the inside of my thigh. "I don't think I will ever get over how good you taste," he says, before I feel the stubble from his beard brush my skin as he scoops his arms under my thighs, and almost instantly his tongue slides through my wet pussy.

"More," I moan. I don't want him to stop doing what he's doing because it feels so fucking good. His tongue continues to work my clit before he sucks it so hard, I'm pretty sure I see stars. I am literally on the verge of a second orgasm already. This man is trying to kill me.

"First, I had you coming on my fingers," he growls against my clit. "Now I want you to come on my tongue, Peyton. I want to drink up every last drop from this sweet pussy."

"I can't." Because there is no way I can come again so soon.

"You can and you will," he hisses as my hips move on their own. "Ride my face, baby. Come for me."

His tongue continues to lap my clit for a few minutes before he suction cups himself on my clit and I'm sent over the edge again. Fucking again. How?

"Such a good girl," he murmurs as he lifts himself up from between my legs.

"Hands and knees," he orders.

What? No. It's my turn.

I sit up on the bed and cross my arms over my chest and he tips his head to the side with a questioning glare. "What's with the pout, Ms. Kelly?" he says playfully.

"You know," I say, with a seductive glare into his eyes. Moving off the bed to stand in front of him, my eyes remain on his as my hand moves to cup his hard length in his sweatpants. "You're not the only one who has fantasies." I slip my hand into the waistband of his sweatpants, gripping his cock from inside.

A moan erupts from his chest, and he hoarsely mumbles my name, "Peyton."

"Do you remember," I slide his sweatpants down just below his hips, my hand never leaving his cock, giving it slow strokes.

"That night you walked in on me in the bathtub?" The sweat-pants fall to the floor, and it allows me deeper access to grip his length up and down from base to tip. "You want to know what I was thinking about, Thomas?"

He swallows the lump in his throat as his dark eyes trail from mine to my hand stroking him slowly. "What?"

"You," I admit. My tongue slides across my bottom lip as I lower myself to my knees in front of him. "You couldn't see," I continue as I drop to my knees, eye level with his cock. His breath becomes rapid and uneven. "But my fingers were so deep in my pussy." I watch as he sucks in a sharp breath at my admission. "I couldn't stop thinking about this." My tongue licks the precum from his cock while my hand continues to stroke him. "Your cock. And how it would feel." I lick up his long length while keeping eye contact with him, before sucking the tip. "Deep inside my pussy instead of my fingers."

"Peyton," he growls. His eyes never leave my lips.

I smirk up at him one more time before I suck the tip of his cock and take the whole length in my mouth. I bob my head a few times and I hear him moan a string of curse words before his hands tangle themselves in my hair.

"Fuck, Peyton. You take my cock so well." My one hand grips his ass as his cock bobs in and out of my mouth. Alternating between licking and sucking, my other hand is stroking as I suck hard. I watch as the muscles in his stomach tighten. He's already close. "Is this what you thought about? My cock buried deep in your throat?" His deep voice cuts through me and my eyes lift the slightest to watch him as I suck harder. "Touch yourself, baby. Rub your pretty pussy for me while I fuck your face."

I gag with his cock deep in my throat and my hand that was gripping his ass for a deeper suck, is now rubbing my clit. I barely register the tears streaming out of my eyes uncontrollably as he fucks my face. I'm definitely going to fucking come again.

"Peyton." My name comes out in a strained voice at the same

171

time the hand that was stroking him cups his balls. "I'm going to fucking come."

"Mmm." The noise leaves me as his cock sinks deeper into my throat and I rub my clit harder.

"Fucckkk," he groans. "Fuck, baby. I'm coming. Now."

With that, hot cum pours down my throat and I drink him up like I've been dehydrated for months. A third orgasm courses through my body and I am stunned at the fact that this man has already made me come three times tonight and he hasn't even been inside of me yet.

When we both come down from our orgasms, I remove my mouth and wipe my bottom lip and suck the excess off the corner of my lips while I smirk up at him. Within seconds, he's pulling me off my knees and I wrap my legs around him.

"You on your knees for me is the sexiest thing I have ever seen," he says. I can feel his cock begin to harden again as my legs tighten around his waist. "But I'm not done with you."

He places me down and checks his pockets for a condom but doesn't seem to have one there.

"Bedside table," I tell him. The smirk he shoots me over his shoulder is the sexiest thing I have ever seen.

I stand there and watch closely as he pulls one from the drawer. Using his teeth, he tears the wrapper and rolls it on his long length before he begins to walk over to me. He sits on the edge of the bed, and I move to stand between his stretched out legs. His fingertips brush up the back of my legs before he reaches my ass.

"This fucking ass," he hisses before he smacks one cheek.

I giggle in his arms as my hands rake through his hair causing him to lift his head to look me in the eyes. His eyes bounce between mine. Something is shifting between us, and I can feel it. There is more here than him being my boss and me being just the nanny. I can see his thoughts running wild through his brain with the look he gives me.

"Peyton," he pleads.

I don't let him continue as I playfully push him back so he's lying flat on the bed. I crawl on top of him to straddle him. No words are spoken between us as I line my center up with his steel hard cock before I slowly lower myself onto him and that's the moment that everything between us changes for good.

"Fuckkkk," he says through gritted teeth. "Fuck."

"Oh my God," I scream out.

His hands grip my hips hard as I move as slow as possible to accommodate his size. Moving up and down on top of him until he has stretched me out just enough to take him in fully.

"I feel…" I pause. "I feel so full."

"You're so fucking tight," he growls.

With his words I begin to move my hips faster. Alternating between rocking back and forth and moving up and down. His hands move from my hips to cup my bare breasts. I lean forward just enough so my hands are resting on each side of his head. His stare burns deep through me and shoots right down to my core, only intensifying the pleasure of this first time with him.

I know I won't be able to come back from this. I have never, in my life, experienced sex of this intensity. The way he looks at me. The way that he touches me.

"Fuck. You feel so fucking good." His praise causes me to pick up the pace. "That's it, baby. Ride my fucking cock." He bucks his hips up the slightest bit, only intensifying the pleasure coursing through me. "Give me one more, Pey."

"Fuck," I moan, but it comes out as a scream. "I don't think I can."

"Yes, you can. Come for me," his grip tightens on my hips. He's hitting the deepest spots inside of me that I didn't know could ever be touched. "Your pussy is squeezing me so hard."

My pace quickens, the friction causing me to shatter on him once more. "Thomas," I scream over and over. The pleasure is the most intense thing I have ever felt.

"Let it out, baby." He bucks his hips harder and faster, pounding into me. My body stills on top of him and I'm unable to move in any direction. "Scream for me." He fucks me hard and possessively with each thrust of his hips. "Let the whole city hear who this pussy fucking belongs to."

"Fuck," I scream out. "Oh my God, Thomas!"

"This." *Thrust.* "Pussy." *Thrust.* "Is." *Thrust.* "Mine."

"It's yours," I scream as my orgasm crashes hard and fast. "It's fucking yours," I moan as I fall on top of him letting it run through my body. Holy fuck.

My breathing is uneven and rapid as my chest falls on his. Thomas cups both sides of my head and brings me to hover over him as he stares into my eyes. No words are spoken but I know he feels the change in us, too.

I offer a soft smile and before I know it, he has me flipped on my back, never removing his dick from inside of me. My legs wrap around his waist. He stares deep into my eyes, and I watch as a wave of uncertainty flashes around them.

His head pushes into the crook of my neck and I feel his hot uneven breath on my pounding pulse as he slides in and out of me at a much slower pace. A groan escapes his lips along with a string of curse words.

"Thomas," a moan of pleasure.

"Peyton," he draws out my name in one long breath, almost as if it pains him to say it.

"Thomas," I plead. "Look at me."

He pulls his head from my neck and his eyes are on mine. I use the hands cupping his face to pull him in for a kiss. This time, I kiss him with need. Letting him know that I want this too. More than anything.

I break away from the kiss and smile up at him, "Now fuck me, Thomas. Fuck me like I'm yours."

He thrusts into me hard and deep. I will never recover from this.

"I can't get over how tight you are. This pussy was made for me, baby." He pushes into me harder and faster and that same intense pleasure fucking hits me again. "Come with me this time, Peyton."

"I'm going to—" I pause because I can't say any more words. My hips move on their own, in rhythm with each of his thrusts. My legs tighten around his waist, and it hits me fast.

"You're fucking milking me, baby," he moans as the muscles in his stomach tighten. "Your pussy is squeezing my cock so hard. You're coming. I can feel it."

"Fuck. Oh my God," I scream, pressing my center into him harder as the pleasure shoots right to my pussy. "Thomas."

"Yes, baby!" he screams back right before his own release takes over and he's coming. "Fuuuuck."

His thrusts slow until he comes down from his own release. Our breaths mix together in the space between us. Unspoken words linger in the air. His eyes dance between mine. He removes himself from inside of me and rolls onto the bed next to me. My arms fall to the sides of my head and we both lay spread out on my bed.

"I'm going to get washed up," I cut through the silence.

"Let me," he says.

"No," I cut him off. "I've got it."

He doesn't say anything more as he lays with his eyes closed while he regulates his breathing. Nerves dance around in my stomach as I quickly wash up in the bathroom. I know Thomas would take care of me, but right now I think we both need a minute after that. When I'm done, I throw on a new robe and walk out of the bathroom. My eyes widen in shock as I find Thomas is sitting up in my bed, tucked under my blankets. I don't know what made me think that he would head back to his room.

He lifts the covers next to him and pats the bed. "Come here."

I scurry over to the bed and climb in next to him. He opens his arm for me to snuggle up close to him, and I bury my head in his arm as he settles into the pillow. One leg drapes over his exposed leg and my arm wraps around his waist. Ever so lightly, his fingertips brush the small of my back. Trailing up and down, sending shivers down my spine with each brush.

"Can I ask you something?" I break the silence.

"Of course, baby."

His term of endearment hits me right in my chest. My breath becomes lodged in my throat, and I find it hard to breathe. So instead of asking him the heavy question that I want to ask him, which is what this means between us, I shock myself with the words that come out of my mouth.

"Can you stay here tonight?"

CHAPTER TWENTY-THREE
Thomas

The warm body draped over me wakes me up from sleep before the sun is even up. Her leg is tangled over mine and her head is nestled into my neck, and I feel her breath on my ear as she lays asleep next to me. I lost count of how many orgasms I gave her last night and neither of us had the energy to get up from the bed. That's why I'm now forcing myself to move from the comfort of *her*. It's not the bed and it's not the pillows that make me want to stay here… it's her.

Unfortunately, I have to get to my bed before James wakes up. Every morning when he wakes up, he climbs into my bed, tucks his little feet under my legs and turns on the television to watch whatever cartoon he's in the mood for that day. Honestly, there's no better way to be woken up than that little boy snuggled against me. I know one day he won't climb into my bed anymore, so I live for those little moments.

This moment right here comes in a close second, though. For a moment, I think to myself how much I've missed out on by kicking out one night stands before they fall asleep. Although, I don't think it's the feeling of *any* body next to me. This early morning high I'm feeling is *Peyton's* body next to me and I never want to come down.

I look over at the clock and see that it's four in the morning. Carefully, I pull back the blanket from our legs and slide myself out from under her body. She doesn't wake up but nestles her body into the pillow I was sleeping on.

I take a moment to scan her body from head to toe. We both had a moment of weakness last night where we gave into the temptation that we both have been fighting for far too long. But something shifted between us last night and I want more of that.

Her long, blonde hair is draped over the pillows and is a mess from our hands being all over each other. The thought of last night has my dick waking up to say *hi*.

I leave her room and make the walk to mine, hating the idea of her waking up without me and wondering why I'm not there, but we live in the same house, and I took the day off work today, which she doesn't know yet. I had no meetings scheduled so I said fuck it and decided to work from home since I worked in the office all weekend.

Before climbing into bed, I peek my head into James' room and see that he's sound asleep. I must have been tired enough to doze off the second my head hits the pillow because the next thing I know, James' little feet tuck under my legs the way they always do, and the TV is turned on.

"Good morning, monkey," I manage to get out despite barely being able to keep my eyes open.

"Morning, Daddy," he says before he snuggles deeper into me. "I slepted so great last night. Like a big rock. How did you sleep?"

"I slept like a big rock too." I laugh.

"I wonder if Ms. Peyton slepted like a big rock too!" he says way too excited for this early in the morning. I move my eyes to the nightstand to check the time and see that it's eight in the morning already.

"Shit, bud. You have to get ready for school." I throw the covers off of us and rush to get up. "Daddy must have slept in."

"Shit," he repeats as he climbs out of bed.

"James," I growl. "That's a bad word. You know that."

"Shoot, you're right. I'm sorry, Daddy," he says as he stands there with his head moving down to face the floor.

"Just don't say it again, okay?" I say as I crouch down in front of him to give him a hug.

"You got it, Daddy. I love you the mostest. You know that?"

Fuck. This kid knows just the right strings to pull on my heart.

"I love you the mostest," I say and then kiss his forehead. "Now scoot. You have to get ready for school. I'll make you break—" I'm cut off the second the smell of breakfast food hits my nose.

Peyton.

James is out the door and I throw on a pair of sweatpants and brush my teeth quickly before I head downstairs. When I reach the bottom of the stairs, I yell up to James, "Don't forget to brush your teeth, James."

"Okay, Daddy!" he screams back. "I am doing my morning poopy first. I'm gonna be here for a hot minute."

I shake my head and laugh to myself. That kid has no filter what-so-ever and he talks to Uncle Ollie on the phone way too much. He keeps us on our toes, but he also gives us a reason to smile every day.

I follow the smell of breakfast to the kitchen where I find Peyton standing over the stove scrambling eggs in a skillet and moving her body slightly to the music she is playing on the speaker. She must not hear me come into the kitchen because she doesn't make a move, so I go to her first.

My hands grip her waist from behind, pulling her backside into me and she jumps up with a little startle before giggling into my hold. My mouth finds her bare shoulder to plant a kiss as my hand travels to her stomach to hold her into me. "Good morning, Sunshine," I whisper in her ear.

She spins around in my hold to wrap her hands around my neck with the front of her body pressed into me. Without a doubt, she can feel my growing length on her stomach. I swear I get hard with just the way she looks at me.

"Good morning, Mr. Ford."

A possessive rumble comes from somewhere in my chest and I hoist Peyton up on the kitchen counter and my mouth immediately finds hers. Her hands move from my neck to my hair to pull me closer to her as if she can't get enough of this kiss. Truth of the matter is, that I can't get enough of it either. I feel like I'm living in an alternate universe if I'm being honest with myself. Falling asleep next to her, somewhat waking up next to her, and also getting to wake up next to James just felt so good. Now I find her in my kitchen making breakfast in these damn silk pajama shorts she keeps wearing.

"As much as I want to take you right here and right now, Peyton," I whisper in her neck. "James is going to be down any minute."

"You're the one who put me up on this counter, Mr. Ford," she says with a smirk.

"Are you talking back to me, Peyton?" I raise an eyebrow at her.

She gasps and her hand finds her chest. "Who me? No, I would never do such a thing."

"You're lucky James is going to be here any second," I growl. "Or I would take you over my knee right here, right now."

"Ohh, that sounds interesting." She smiles as she jumps off the counter to finish breakfast. I give her ass a smack and it has the perfect bounce after my hand connects with it. I feel my dick twitch in my sweatpants and the image of my hands gripping her perfectly round ass while she rode my dick last night floods my brain again. She turns her head over her shoulder to give me a smile and a wink.

My thoughts are interrupted when James comes barreling into the kitchen. "I'm ready," he screams. "And I'm starving."

"I made your favorite funfetti pancakes for breakfast," she says to James.

"You're the bestest, Pey!" he shrieks and she returns his excitement with a warm smile. The way she talks to him, cares for him, makes his favorite meals and plays with him, really shows me how much she cares about him and fuck, if that doesn't do something for that organ in my chest.

"Eat quickly, buddy. You have to get ready for school."

"He doesn't have school today, Thomas," Peyton cuts in.

Fuck. I completely forgot. I literally just had this conversation with her last night about him not having school today. Sex with Peyton has thrown my life completely upside down. I don't even know what day of the week it is.

"Shit," I mutter.

"That's a bad word, Daddy," James says as he scolds me, pointing his finger at me like I'm in trouble.

"You're right, JJ," I laugh. "I seem to have forgotten what day of the week it is."

"It's Monday," Peyton says. "Remember, I'm going to take James with me to see Gigi."

"That's right," I say as I run my hands through my hair. "I feel all out of place this morning."

"I bet you do, Mr. Ford." She playfully smiles at me as she starts cleaning up the dishes.

"I'll do the dishes," I tell her with a smirk on my face. "You go get ready for your day."

"Aren't you going to be late for work?"

"I don't have any meetings today. I'm going to work from the home office today and work on some emails."

"Well then," she says as she wipes her hands on the dish towel. "I'm going to take a shower and get ready to head out. James, we're going to visit my Gigi today. Is that okay with you?"

"What's your Gigi?" he asks.

"She's my grandma," she explains. "She's pretty sick and she could use some laughs and cheering up. I think you would be the perfect man for the job. Are you up for it?"

"Yes!" he shrieks, throwing his fist in the air. "I'm sorry your Gigi is sick, Peyton. I will bring my doctor kit with me. I can fix her right up for you."

My eyes move to Peyton as she looks the sweet innocent little boy in the eyes. I can tell by the look on her face that she's holding back tears right now. She says nothing but gives him a tight nod. I don't know what type of cancer her grandmother has, but I know that deep down, right this second, she wishes that a toy doctor kit would be the thing that could fix her. Her gaze moves to me, and I see the sadness in her eyes as she gives me a brief nod before leaving the kitchen to get a shower.

James finishes his breakfast and I finish the dishes.

"Watch some cartoons in your room for a bit while Peyton gets ready. Okay, bud?"

"Okay, Daddy," he says as he skips up the stairs.

I finish the dishes and then find myself walking down the hallway towards her room to make sure she's alright. With a light knock on the door, I hear her say, "Come in." She's not in her room but as I close the door behind me, I hear her from the bathroom, "I'm in here."

I swallow the lump in my throat as I head into her bathroom that's connected to her room. She's in here, alright. My eyes widen as I take in the sight in front of me. She did not in fact take a shower, she's in the bathtub. The same spot I found her the first night she moved into the penthouse. "Peyton," I say through a strangled breath.

You know what she does? She fucking giggles.

"I am not laughing, Peyton."

"I'm just taking a quick bath," she says with a smile. "I'm feeling sore today from the intense hit my body took last night." She winks. "Plus, I'm obsessed with this view."

"Oh, are you?" I raise an eyebrow as I slowly walk over to her. "I wanted to check in on you to make sure you were okay."

"I'm okay, Thomas," she says with a sigh. "James doesn't understand adult stuff like cancer. And I love him for that."

I nod at her statement. Pausing to take in the sight of her in the giant bathtub with the city behind her. It's the most stunning and breathtaking view in the penthouse. And I am not talking about the city behind her. A smile forms on my face without even trying. "How are you feeling now after your bath?"

She pauses for a moment. "Eh, I think I'm feeling better. But you interrupted me."

I raise a questioning brow at her.

"You got me all worked up in the kitchen," she admits, and I feel the corners of my lips turn up. "I wanted a quick release before the day got started."

Holy. Fuck. This woman is truly trying to kill me. Didn't I make her come enough last night? Did she come here to give herself an orgasm before the day gets started? My dream fucking girl.

"You." I swallow another lump in my throat, "You were going to touch yourself, Peyton?"

"Yes," she answers without any hesitation in her voice as her eyes stay laser focused on mine.

My head falls back and my eyes close. *"Fuck me,"* comes out of my mouth, barely above a whisper. My dick is hardening in my pants, and I can't help but bring myself to my knees beside the tub. I want my hands all over her. I want to be the one to make her come. I want to taste her. But right now, I want to watch her.

"Show me," I demand.

Her eyes widen and she shakes her head, "I..." she pauses. "I've never done this in front of anyone before." She tucks a strand of wet hair behind her ear. Which is her signature move when she's nervous.

"Baby," I whisper. "There's nothing to be nervous about with me. Don't you understand by now, that every fucking thing you do turns me on."

"It does?" she asks nervously.

"Yes." I grin. "Now touch yourself. Play with your pretty pussy for me."

She sucks in a sharp breath at my words and her head falls back to the edge of the tub as her hand sinks below the water and her eyes close. I watch as her finger disappears inside of her and fuck, I wish it was my hand. Thankfully, she didn't load the bathtub with a ton of bubbles so I can see as her hand glides in and out of her pussy.

"Thomas," she starts to moan. The water in the tub starts to ripple as her hips begin to buck against her own hand. Sexiest fucking thing I have ever seen.

"You are so sexy, Peyton." I lean in to whisper in her ear. "Make yourself come for me."

"I can't," she pants. "It's not enough."

"Sit on the edge of the tub," I order.

She does as I say. She moves to the edge of the tub with beads of water dripping down her body. Her perfect tits are on display for me. I move my gaze from her body to her eyes and bite my bottom lip. The move causes her to do the same. She's sitting on the edge of the tub with her back facing the floor to ceiling windows. "Show me how you make yourself come, pretty girl."

Her fingers dive into her pussy and it's ten times hotter out of the water than in the water. Her body is still dripping water, and her head is thrown back as her fingers glide in and out of her.

"That's it, baby," I whisper. "Such a perfect pussy."

"Thomas," she groans. I can tell she hasn't reached the point of going over the edge yet and she's definitely frustrated that I haven't touched her yet.

Her head is still tipped back, and her eyes are closed when I reach forward and press my thumb to her clit. I need my hands on her. Her body jolts in surprise and her eyes shoot open to me. Just one small touch and I can already feel I have pushed her close to the edge. She removes her fingers which allows me the chance to dive two of my fingers inside. "Fuck, Peyton," I growl as I dive deep inside of her, hitting her most sensitive spot.

"Don't stop," she moans. Her fingers are rubbing her nipples as I pick up the pace and fuck her harder with my hand. My thumb presses harder on her clit circling it until I feel she's ready to go over the edge.

"The city view behind you has nothing on the view of you when you come," I breathe out. "You perched on the edge of this tub, playing with your tits while I fuck this pretty pussy with my hand." My name rolls off her tongue with my dirty words. She's close. "That's it, baby. Come for me."

"I'm gonna, I'm gonna..." and she doesn't have to say it because her pussy contracts so tight on my fingers I swear I'm about to blow my load in my pants without her even touching me. I keep fucking her with my fingers, harder and harder until her body completely convulses around me. Her head flies back and she's moaning my name over and over again as she rides out her orgasm on my hand.

"Good girl, Peyton," I lean forward to whisper in her ear. My fingers are still deep inside of her. "Such a good fucking girl."

"Thomas." She smirks. "You're such a dirty man."

"I can't help it when you're this fucking sexy, Peyton." I move in and press a kiss to her lips without thinking anything of it. Like we do this every day. I linger longer than I should and a buzz shoots through me. I can tell by her body language that she's confused as well. Does she feel it too? Does she feel the weird electricity I do when she touches me? Or kisses me?

I back away slowly and run my hands through my hair. "Well, I guess you better get ready to head out."

She finally stands in the tub, her eyes locked with mine and her naked body still on full display for me. Her hands move to cup the bulge in my pants. "Let me," she whispers in my ear.

"Peyton," I hiss. "This was about you and your release."

"From the looks of it." Her eyes scan me as she takes in my hard dick in my pants. "You could use a release too."

"Later." I press a kiss to her forehead. Not realizing the act of endearment that I just did but fuck, it just comes so naturally with her. Everything does. "I'll see you when you get home later, right?"

"Of course." She beams and shoots me a seductive wink. "I look forward to it, Mr. Ford."

I shake my head and give her a devious glare. My look warns her that '*you're going to be in trouble, later*' but the words don't come out of my mouth. I shoot her a wink and start to head out the door when I hear a giggle come from her as she gets out of the tub.

"Oh, and Thomas?" I stop in my tracks to turn and look at her. "Thank you for that." Her fingers circle the area where the bathtub is. "Whatever, that was."

"You mean the orgasm, Peyton?"

She softly giggles again and shrugs her shoulders.

"You're welcome, Sunshine."

I'm out the door before she can say anything else. I have to go take care of this hard-on right now and get ready to answer mundane emails all day. My mind is reeling as I walk down the hallway and make my way to the shower. How is everything so easy with her? Is this what a relationship would feel like?

Waking up next to her?

Her making breakfast in the kitchen in her tempting silk pajamas while I kiss her neck?

Orgasms in the bathroom?

Soft kisses to her forehead without thinking about it?

My chest feels tight, and my pulse starts racing at the thought of all of that being a permanent possibility.

She's inadvertently going to make me fall in love with her, isn't she?

That scares the shit out of me because the one thing I won't do is *love*.

CHAPTER TWENTY-FOUR
Peyton

I'm in a dizzy haze driving the expressway to Gigi's house in Thomas' fancy SUV he's been letting me use ever since I accepted this job. The truth is, I haven't used this car at all until today. I've been taking the bus to Gigi's over the last couple of months because I don't want him to feel like I'm using him. Plus, the weather has been entirely too dreary to drive James to the park on the days that we're free. However, it's nice to be in the comfort of a car today.

I continue the drive as my brain goes crazy over the events from the morning. When I woke up early this morning, the other side of my bed was cold when I reached my arm to feel for Thomas. I don't know when he climbed out of bed, but it must have been early this morning before the sun even came up. I allowed myself to feel disappointed for a brief moment, but the reality of it is that we both had a major moment of weakness. It was very clear that it's something we both have been craving and wanting to happen. I straight up asked him to fuck me, and he didn't hesitate when he carried me into bed.

For all I know, this might have been just a one-night thing. I can't allow my heart to get attached because when it does, it's only a matter of time before it's broken.

We didn't plan on falling asleep in each other's arms, but damn, if it didn't feel so good to be wrapped in his embrace. He dozed off before I did with his arm wrapped tightly around my back and his hand resting on my bare stomach. It was the most calm and comfortable I have felt in so long. I've fallen asleep next to plenty of men before, but I felt like I couldn't sleep because I was never made to feel important to someone. I'm not even with this man but he makes me feel more important than anyone ever has.

I can't even explain it.

And what happened this morning in the bathroom? Who am I? I don't do those types of things. Never once has anyone watched me do that to myself. But Thomas wanted to. He wanted to see me fall apart at the thought of him and his words guiding me over the edge.

He makes me feel sexy, bold, and beautiful. I feel like a butterfly coming out of her cocoon since he's come into my life.

Above all that, he just makes me feel seen and he does things from his heart. He notices the small things and makes them big things. I am not a girl who needs a designer bag, a fine dining meal at a five-star restaurant or fancy jewelry to feel loved. A simple text, a phone call or doing something that you know I like is all I need. Like the way Thomas will watch a chick-flick with me, even though it's not his kind of movie. He subjected himself to a total chick movie just to make me happy. Or the way he makes me vegan waffles.

That is what I fall for. The little things.

But I cannot fall for this guy.

I'm pulled from my dream filled daze when James asks for the tenth time if we can get donuts. This kid is seriously obsessed with donuts. I can't fault him for it, honestly. His favorite is glazed with vanilla icing and sprinkles. And I've gotta agree with him. They are the best ones.

"Not this morning, bud," I say to him as I look out the front window. "But we're going to stop for bagels! Gigi loves bagels."

"Oh yes," he squeals in excitement. "I love me some bagels and cheese cream."

I laugh at him and shake my head as I continue to drive the expressway.

We stop and grab a dozen bagels and when we're about five minutes from her house, my phone rings loudly over the fancy car speakers. I didn't realize my phone was automatically connected when I didn't do anything to connect it. Hmm. That's weird.

"Hello?" I ask in a questioning tone.

"Peyton," Thomas says over the speakers with a small laugh in his tone. "I see you figured out how to answer the phone."

"What kind of spaceship is this that the car just automatically connects to my phone?"

"It doesn't."

"What do you mean it doesn't?" I ask. "It rang through the speakers-"

"I connected it to your phone."

"You... what? But when?" I stutter.

He laughs at me stuttering over my words that he did that for me. "The day you started, Peyton. I wanted to make sure you were all settled. I set the car up with a remote start in an app on your phone and connected the Bluetooth so you can be hands free and safe in the car."

"Well," I pause because I'm at a complete loss for words. "Thank you."

"It's no problem at all, Peyton."

"Hi, Daddy!" James screams from the backseat.

"Hey, bud. Are you being a good boy for Ms. Peyton?" he asks James.

"Yes, Daddy. The bestest." He smiles so big at the fact that he has been so good. But honestly, the kid is always the *bestest*. "We got bagels with cheese cream!"

"Oh man," Thomas huffs. "I'm jealous of you, JJ. You know those are my favorite."

James giggles before I speak again, "We're almost to Gigi's house."

"Okay, Peyton," he says to me, changing his tone from three-year-old talk back to adult talk. "Are you alright?"

"I'm fine," is all I manage to get out. I don't know how I am so like every female in the world, we use the four-letter word just to keep the questions and emotions at bay. Between the events last night, the events this morning in the bathtub and now moving my mind the last ten minutes to worrying about Gigi. I'm not sure I'm actually fine, but I hope he believes it.

"Don't sound so convincing," he says. I'm willing to bet he's shaking his head on the other end of the line because he's not dumb. He's the CEO of a billion-dollar investment company, for Christ sake. He can read people like a book. But I allow myself a small smile and I shake my head even though he can't see it. "You know I'm here if you need anything right, Peyton?"

"Thomas," I say through a pleading sigh. I want to say more but James is in the backseat. I want to tell him he doesn't have to be there for me. He shouldn't be there. He's my boss. I'm the nanny. We aren't in that type of relationship.

"I know," he says through his own exhale. "I know," he repeats, as if I said all of that out loud. Did I? Shit. I don't respond back to him, but he breaks the short silence when he says, "I have to get back to work. James, be a good boy when you visit Gigi. And Peyton," he pauses as if he's trying to work through his own thoughts. "I'll see you at home tonight."

"I'll see you at home," I repeat and hang up the phone just as we pull into Gigi's driveway. I'm staring straight ahead, and my mind is running wild with thoughts.

I'm falling for my boss.

———

"Gigi, where do you want me to put these pots?" I shout from the kitchen. I'm helping her clean up her place a little bit because

190

she's having a 'tired' day, as she calls it. This visit was even too much for her. She will never tell me that she's in pain or hurting. Her calling it a tired day tells me all I need to know about the state she's in.

Her and James are in the living room and James is telling her so many stories about school and life while he colors her pictures. He told her all about his love for donuts while we ate the bagels, which those two have in common. He talked about his best friends and the first person on his list was me. I have grown so close to James the last couple of months without a shadow of a doubt. But the problem with that is that if anything backfires with Thomas and I, I'll lose James. I don't want to lose James. I don't want to lose this job and dare I say it... I don't want to lose Thomas.

Gigi walks into the kitchen, and it breaks me out of my trance, and I remember I asked her about the pots. "Gigi, where do you want me to put these?"

"Don't worry about them, sweetheart," she says as she pours herself a cup of water. "Come. Sit and tell me what's bothering you."

"Oh Gigi, nothing is bothering me."

"I've been around this earth for a long time, Pey," she says with a side eye glare and a smirk. "Something is happening in your life and it's time to tell me about it. You're not glowing from the damn sun, sweetheart," she adds with a wink. "Sit down and tell me about him."

"Gigi!" I whisper yell at her so that James doesn't hear. "You are a dirty bird. I am not telling you about my love life."

"Who said shit about love?"

If I was taking a sip of water, I would have spit it out at the words that just came out of her mouth. My eyes go wide. "You really need to stop hanging out with Avery. She's bad for you."

"She's so good for the soul and she keeps me young," she laughs. "Stop avoiding the conversation. Does this have anything to do with that adorable boy's dad?" I don't even answer her because there's no point in lying to her. I turn my head as I grab the kitchen rag and wipe down the counter. "I had a feeling," she adds when I don't give her an answer.

"What do you want me to say, huh?" I throw my hands in the air. "It's so frustrating, Gigi. He's my boss. I'm technically his employee. There're other people to think about." I tip my head towards the living room to indicate that James is the other person. "I live in the same house as him. He does the most perfect things. I can tell he cares deep down. But what do I do? Lose my job because the guy is swoony and perfect and all the things I want in a man? He's straight out of a romance novel, Gigi."

"That's exactly what you do," she says without hesitation.

"That's the worst idea you've ever had."

"Peyton." She moves to stand up. "I haven't seen you in a hot minute. But since the last time I saw you, you're downright glowing. I can see happiness radiating off of you. Sex does that," she adds with a little wiggle of her eyebrow.

"Stop it." I raise my hand to her. "I'm not talking about sex with you."

"Listen to me, you deserve this, Peyton," she pauses as if she's trying to gather her thoughts. "Your grandfather, he was my boss. Did you know that?"

"I had no idea."

"He was." She nods. "We worked in the same bank together and he was the branch owner. We both fought our feelings off for a long time. I was so insanely attracted to him that it was very difficult. I didn't realize his feelings were the same until he asked me out for drinks one night after work. I reluctantly agreed and sparks flew from the first night. We were inseparable and couldn't keep our hands off each other after that."

"But did you lose your job?"

"I didn't." She shakes her head. "But I did leave the job. I know it's a different situation than you because we worked for a bank and you're the nanny working in his house. But I did leave the job and I was the happiest I'd ever been."

"I can't lose this job, Gigi," I sigh. "It's helping me build myself back up from the hole I had to put myself in after Mom and Dad died."

"Your situation is so different, honey," she sounds like she's pleading with me. "You deserve to be happy. You deserve to go after what you want. If he's what you want, then you two need to work together to make it happen. I love you so much, Peyton. I'm so proud of you but you can't let your past relationships dictate your future ones. Not every man out there is the same. From listening to that boy speak, I can already tell his father is different. On so many levels, honey. That boy is being raised right."

My gaze falls to the floor. Deep down, I know she knows what she's saying. I think there's a piece of me that is always going to fear the next step with anyone. I know she's right about Thomas based on her interaction with James alone. He's a direct reflection of who he is being raised by. "Thank you, Gigi."

"Always, sweetheart."

"Are you all settled here?" I ask her to change the subject. "We have to get going before traffic gets too crazy. Kali and Avery are coming to the penthouse today too."

"I'm all good, honey. The groceries and little surprises you had delivered at the crack of dawn today are more than enough. Now you give those girls big hugs and kisses for me." She smiles. "I miss my other granddaughters."

Groceries delivered? I didn't have anything delivered to her today. Maybe it's Avery. I will have to ask her about it later. "They miss you too, Gigi."

I spent the next twenty minutes after that conversation cleaning up the place from the mess that we all made on our visit. James loved coloring with her and seeing her place. His coloring is a typical three-year-old. Messy and perfectly imperfect but Gigi loves that. She even hung all four of them on her fridge.

Grabbing our things, James puts his hand in mine and my heart melts a little more. "You ready to go, bud?"

"I guess." He shrugs. "I had so much fun here today."

"You're welcome here anytime, James," Gigi says to him.

"Thank you so much, Mrs.," he pauses because he's not sure what to call her.

"Gigi," she says. "Just call me Gigi, honey."

"Thank you so much, Gigi," James says. His face lights up that he's able to call her that.

I move to hug my grandma. "See you soon."

"Love you, sweetheart."

"Love you too, Gigi."

"Remember what I said," she continues, pointing her finger at me as if she's scolding me. "You deserve to be happy, Peyton. Follow your heart. Lean into what makes you feel good and take the risks, even if it's scary. Maybe it won't work out. But maybe, it will be the greatest adventure."

I fight back the tears at her wise words and give her a tight nod.

"Your heart is the most beautiful thing about you, Peyton. Let him see that and the rest will work out on its own."

Another nod and I swipe a small tear that threatens to drip down my cheek. "I will see you soon."

"See you soon, honey."

———

We have all the arts and crafts spread out on the massive kitchen table in the penthouse. Thomas doesn't have visitors over often, so it blows my mind that he has a table that seats twelve. It works for James when he has all his arts and crafts out though.

Thomas had to deliver legal documents of some sort to Marc at his office, so Kali and Avery are both here and we're having a craft party with James. They are both so good with James. As much as I have grown to care for him, I can tell they have too. It might be a best friend thing. Whoever I like, they like. Whoever I hate, they hate. You know how it goes. Besties for life.

"I want to use the letter beads to spell my name on this," James says. "We can just glue the beads on the paper."

"What is with three-year-old's and always wanting to play with glue," Avery asks.

"It's so sticky and fun!" James shrieks in excitement while the three of us just laugh at him. "Daddy organimized all my letters in little bags, Ave. Can you help me spell my name and I will glue them on."

Avery chuckles at his mispronounced word and begins to dig into the large bin. It's organized by bags and little bins. He has separate bins for glue and tape. In another bin, there's a set of colored folders that have colored paper in each of them. There's also separate bins for crayons, colored pencils, and markers. She pulls out a large bag that is organized with tiny bags inside of it. Each bag contains multiple beads with the same letter. Like I said, super organized craft bin.

"Look," Avery laughs, and we all look in her direction as she holds up a tiny bag of letters. "It's a bag of D's."

"The letter D," James screams and starts bouncing in his seat. "D is for Daddy!"

"D is for a lot of things." Avery wiggles her brows at James. "It's my favorite letter of the alphabet."

"Stop that." Kali smacks her arm.

"What? It's true," she laughs.

"Back to crafts." I snap my fingers at her. "Oh, I meant to ask you two a question."

"What's up?" They both say in unison.

"Did you have groceries delivered to Gigi this morning?" I ask, continuing the craft of finding letters for James. "Today I was there, and she thanked me for the groceries and care package of goodies."

"I haven't had anything sent there."

"I haven't sent anything either," Kali adds. "I always bring some stuff when I visit but that's about it."

"Hmm…" I hum, trying to figure out what's happening. "Okay."

A few moments of silence pass between us as we organize the letters for James to spell out his name and glue them on the paper. Once he's finished, we're all looking at him from across the table to see what he thinks of his finished masterpiece. He stares down at the paper void of emotion on his face. *Huh?* I think to myself.

It's as if the next series of events happen in slow motion. The world stops spinning on its axis. Time is completely frozen as James places the piece of paper down, his eyes finding mine. I stare at him, my smile turning to a small frown when I see water pooling in the corner of his eyes. My eyes find Kali's next to me and she shrugs her shoulders as if she doesn't know what happened either.

"Are you okay, buddy?" I ask him as I return my gaze back to his.

He pauses for a moment, wiping a tear before it drips down his cheek. "I love you, Pey."

My fucking heart.

I quickly stand up from my seat and move to sit directly next to him on the table. I grab his tiny hand in mine and look him in the eyes. For such a little boy, he has so many emotions. "Why are you crying, buddy?"

"I'm scared," he says.

"You can talk to me, James."

"I don't want you to leave," he admits, as more tears form in his eyes.

"I-I," I stutter and pause to gather my words. "James, who said I was going anywhere? I'm not going anywhere, buddy."

"My mom," he says through sniffles. "She left."

"Oh James," I sigh as I pull him into my embrace for a hug.

For someone so small, he should not be carrying such heavy emotions with him. I never knew he really thought about his mom this way. Other than the time he was sick and asked for her, I haven't ever heard him mention her. There's an ache in my chest at his admission. I care so deeply for him. Honestly, I love this kid. I really do.

Pulling out of the embrace, I use my fingers to delicately wipe away a tear that made its way down his cheek as I look him in the eyes. "I love you too, James. I hope you know that. I'm so happy you're a part of my life and one of my bestest friends."

A smile formed on his tear-filled face. "You're my bestest friend too."

"Let's get this stuff all cleaned up and hang your picture on the refrigerator. Your dad should be home soon for dinner," I say as I start cleaning stuff up. Out of the corner of my eye, I see Kali and Avery moving and I turn my gaze to them. Both are wiping their eyes. "Not you too," I say with a small smile.

"That moment we just witnessed was just so beautiful, Peyton," Avery says.

"James is so lucky to have you in his life," Kali adds as she wipes another tear from her eye.

"Guys." A shy smile forms on my face. "You know how much I love him." I toss my arm around James' shoulders. "He's my best little buddy and I won't be going anywhere anytime soon. Right, dude?"

"Right!" James says as he wraps his arm around me in the same way my arm is around him.

"Alright, James." I clap my hands together to break the big emotion fest happening right now. "Run upstairs and get washed up. Bring your bin upstairs with you. I am going to get dinner started. Okay?"

"You gots it, Pey!" he says halfway out the kitchen with the bin in his hands.

The girls take turns getting cleaned up in the bathroom while I wipe down the kitchen table and move to start getting ready for dinner. When the girls enter the kitchen again, Avery let out a shriek. "It's showtime!" she screams.

The three of us know what that means so my head shoots to the floor to ceiling windows in the kitchen. I don't know how I missed that while I was cleaning up. "Let's go out on the balcony!" I say as we move quickly to get outside so we don't miss it.

We make it out there and stand to admire the most beautiful sunset we have ever seen. No wonder they call this building Sunset Square. We have a perfect view being at the top of the building. It's overlooking Central Park and we can see the sun slowly moving its way to the horizon.

"Every time I see a sunset, I can't help but think of Kate," Kali sighs.

Kate is a fictional character, of course. It's one of our favorite books we have ever read thanks to Kali aggressively pushing us to read it. *Bright Side* by Kim Holden. Our lives changed when we read it, not to be dramatic or anything. But it taught us valuable lessons in life and it's a book that will forever hold a special place in our hearts.

"It's truly unfair you get to experience this epic showtime every night, Peyton," Avery adds.

"Truly one of the greatest perks of living up here," I say.

"You mean greater than getting to fuck Daddy?" Avery scoffs.

"You had to ruin the moment?" I tip my head back and a laugh erupts from deep in my stomach. "That is a really great perk, huh?"

"So, you're finally okay with all of this, Pey?" Kali asks.

I breathe a sigh of relief with them as I turn my gaze to the beautiful sunset and consider her question carefully. I feel their eyes on me as I finally admit, "Yeah, I guess I am."

Avery squeals next to me and does a little dance where she's standing. "Finally! It's about time you settled down a little bit."

"Woah," I throw my hands up in defense. "I didn't say we

were settling down. We are still taking it all in and I guess we will see where it goes. We only fucked the one time. The second time he watched me fuck myself in the bathtub."

"HE WHAT?" Avery screams.

"This is a story for another time," I laugh. "Thomas should be home any minute. Let's figure out dinner."

As we come back in from the balcony, I see Thomas is already standing in the kitchen. I stop dead in my tracks and drink him in. He's wearing dress pants and a simple button-down shirt that is rolled up just enough to expose the veins on his tattooed forearms. His dark hair is done in his classic modern side part. It reminds me of a darker version of *Justin Timberlake* circa 2013. Certainly not his ramen noodle phase, but the hot, sexy phase.

His eyes meet mine and a smile warms his face. Is he as happy to see me as I am him? *Rein it in, girl. You're not a couple. You really aren't anything. Relax.* This is my mind telling my pussy to chill the fuck out.

I am so engrossed in him that I didn't even notice Marc was standing in the kitchen, too. "Hey, you two." I finally managed to get out.

"Hey, Peyton," Marc says from the other side of the kitchen island and my eyes bounce to his.

You can certainly tell they are brothers with how much the two of them look alike. Thomas is slightly taller than Marc with broader shoulders and built like a brick, where Marc is leaner with softer features around the edges. There's no doubt that both of them are built on muscle. They just carry it differently. You can also tell that Marc is the sweeter of the two brothers. He is definitely a mama's boy.

"Hey, you," Thomas says next with a grin spreading across his face. Yes, he's happy to see me. "How was James today?"

Deciding to save the conversation James and I had together for later when no one else is home, I reply, "He was great. We did crafts and he made that picture hanging on the fridge."

He moves to look at the masterpiece. "Wow, he did great."

"I love how organized you are with the crafts, Mr. Ford," I say to him and watch his face morph into a scowl at my use of *Mr. Ford* with a room full of people. I am totally going to pay for that later. *I hope.*

"Totally," Avery chimes in. "Love the bag of D's." His head tilts in confusion at her. "You know, the tiny bags you have for the alphabet crafts. You have a bag of D's in there."

"Get your fucking head out of the gutter, Avery," Kali says with another arm smack.

"Marc," Avery sniffles a laugh. "Don't you dare put in an HR complaint over me. I'm off the clock."

Marc and Thomas both shake their head and laugh before Marc says to Thomas, "What are you making for dinner, fuck face?"

"I was thinking about ordering out," Thomas says to him before he looks back over at us. "Do you girls want to stay for dinner?"

The three of us look at each other in one of our silent conversations where we understand what each other is saying before anything is even said out loud. After confirmation from them, I look back at him. "Yeah, sure. We would love to hang around for dinner."

"Old Jose tacos?" he asks, holding up the menus and a grin on his face. My heart begins beating rapidly because he knows how much I love that place for their vegan options.

"Yes," all three of us say in unison and the biggest smile becomes plastered on my face. I couldn't even hide it if I tried.

"I'll get the tequila," Avery adds.

This is certainly gearing up to be one interesting night in the penthouse.

CHAPTER TWENTY-FIVE
Thomas

My work from home ended up being crazier than expected. We had a mess on our hands with a property in downtown Manhattan that the seller wanted to pull out of. I had to call in Marc to help me fix the mess. I ended up dropping ten grand more than I wanted to, but I know the property will fix up well and in turn, make me much more than I put out when Marc sells it.

With that being said, tacos and good company are exactly what I need after this day. Eddy dropped the food off right after I put James to bed. Avery had poured some tequila and lime for the girls, and I poured some whiskey for Marc and I.

"Marc, what the hell do you have against avocados?" Avery snickers.

"It looks like fucking mashed baby food on a taco, Avery," he scoffs. "How the hell anyone can eat that is beyond me."

Avery proceeds to shove a giant bite of taco loaded with avocados in her mouth. She moans in delight as she overexaggerates her chewing. "Yum, fucking mashed baby food is the best. You're totally missing out, Otis."

"Otis?" He laughs in question.

"Yeah." She laughs back. "You're totally an Otis."

"Whatever the fuck that means," he scoffs.

"It means what it means." She shrugs her shoulders.

"I don't understand how your brain works, Trudy," Marc snaps back.

"Trudy?" A deep laugh erupts from her. "That's actually a good one. I can live with that." Marc just shakes his head and laughs at her. These two are complete opposites and it's hysterical watching them go back and forth with each other. I can only imagine these two in the office. "You know Trudy and Otis get married on that cop show on TV."

"I wouldn't marry you if you were the last person on the face of the earth." Marc laughs at her.

"I take offense to that, Otis," she says defensively. "I'm a good fucking time."

His eyebrows pinch together as he brings the whiskey to his lips. "I bet you are," he says before taking a sip and looking at her over the brim of the glass.

Peyton interrupts their bickering when she rolls her eyes and looks in my direction and says, "Thank you for dinner, Thomas. We really appreciate it." A delicate smile is spread across her lips. What I would give to lean over this table right now and kiss those lips and taste the tequila that's coated on them.

"No need to thank me." I smile at her. I can feel the smile in my eyes as I look at her. "We all have to eat, right?"

A soft chuckle comes from her. "I guess you're right."

"I'm actually glad all three of you are here." I clear my throat, directing my words to all three girls. "I wanted to ask you ladies something."

"Oh boy," Avery says leaning back in her chair, crossing her arms over her chest, and assessing my next move.

"Next weekend, we're taking a trip to my shore house. I know you have the weekends off and I'm not sure what you ladies do on the weekends," I say, waving my finger between the two of them. "But I want to invite all three of you to come down with us."

Peyton's eyes widen and I can tell she's shocked by my question. Kali and Avery both turn their heads to look at Peyton whose eyes don't waver from mine. The corner of her lips tip up in a small smile, "I-I," she starts to say.

"That sounds so fun, Peyton," Kali answers for her.

She turns her head to look at Kali. "I'm not sure Kali." She tips her head down. "I'm not sure I can be far from Gigi right now," she admits.

"Why don't we bring her with us?" I ask.

"Y-you…" she pauses, and shock is plastered on her face as her eyes find mine again. "I…" She can't find the words.

"Peyton." I stop her stuttering thoughts. "I think Gigi would love a trip down to the shore."

Nobody knows this, but I have been sending Gigi groceries weekly to make sure she is taking in the right nutrition. Not that Peyton hasn't been taking care of her, but I wanted to help take a little of the burden from her. My driver delivers them to her door, and I have him make sure that she answers the door so he can get an update for me.

After doing some research when I found out about her grandmother being sick, I learned that while there is no diet to cure her type of cancer, there are certain foods that can help a person cope. This includes plenty of fresh fruits and vegetables. I even saw some information about smoothies to make. I made sure that Eddy included some of those in the grocery bags printed out. I also had a top loading water dispenser delivered to her house last week to ensure she has safe water and drinks plenty of it.

Her grandmother and friends are the most important people in her life, so in an effort to make sure Peyton knows I care for her, I want to show the ones in her life that I care as well.

"Is there enough room for all of us?" Peyton finally asks.

"Yes," I say confidently. "The house is right on the ocean on Long Beach Island. There are twelve bedrooms that each have their own balcony and fifteen bathrooms. There is a private beach entrance, and we have a chef coming in for the weekend."

"Wow," Peyton says in amazement. "That sounds like a dream."

"Say yes, Peyton."

"Despite not wanting to spend any more time with Marcus than necessary," Avery teases. "I'm fucking in. Providing this one is in."

"I'm in too." Kali nods. "I'm free the whole weekend."

"Fuck yeah," Marc adds with a punch in the air. "Peyton, it will be so fun."

After a brief pause, Peyton finally says, "Fine, I'm in."

With that, this trip just got a whole lot better.

———

The last few days have been some of the busiest in the office. I feel like I have barely gotten a chance to see Peyton this week. I've been working later than usual every day as meetings kept running longer than planned. Most of the days, I walked in the door after her and James were both in bed. I appreciate all she's done for me this week.

I want to make a stop at the florist and grab a bouquet of roses for Peyton before we pack and get ready for the shore. My phone rings in my pocket and when I pull it out, I see my mom's name flash on the screen. She must be back from her hiatus in Europe.

"Hey, Mom."

"Oh hello, dear," she says on the other end. "I have missed you so much."

"I missed you too, Mom." I smile into the phone. "How was your trip?"

"It was great!" She beams from the other end of the phone. "It was a much needed two months away. I'm sorry I didn't call you. I decided not to add the international plan for this trip and just wanted to enjoy my hiatus away."

"It's okay, Mom. I'm glad you had a great time. You're back in the states, I'm assuming?" I ask her.

"Yes. I am at the shore house," she admits. "Are you and Marc coming here for your birthday weekend?"

Dammit. I was hoping to have the space just to myself since I didn't want to have to introduce Peyton to her. She's very protective of me as her 'first baby,' she says often. In fact, she still pushes me to reach out to Sheila to try and make it work. I don't think she will ever understand that it will never work out.

Her being so protective comes with faults. She isn't the nicest to people we introduce her to at first. Hell, even Logan got the brunt of it when we first became friends years ago. The first time I brought him home, she grilled him for hours. I'm pretty sure he wanted to run out of the house. She was downright nasty. But Logan grew on her, and she started seeing him like another son because he wasn't going anywhere as my friend.

I certainly don't need her grilling Peyton this weekend and scaring her away from me.

What is Peyton to me, though? I don't even know. I am starting to want her more than just as my nanny. But what if she doesn't feel the same about me? She has to. There is no way the chemistry between us is one sided.

"Honey? Are you there?" My mom asks.

"Yes, sorry," I say forgetting I was on the phone. "We're coming down. Oliver is in Australia this week on his trip around the globe, so he won't be there. I am bringing a couple friends with us."

"Oh dear, you know Logan is always welcome down here."

"Logan is coming." I clear my throat with a small cough. "But we have three ladies coming with us, as well."

"Ohh," she says, less than amused.

"Well," I pause. I'm trying to find the right words for now. I am not about to admit this to her over the phone. "One of them is James' nanny, Peyton. I asked her to come and told her she can bring her two friends along for the weekend."

"You got a nanny?"

"Yes," I admit. "She's amazing with James. Her two friends are great too. Oh, and her grandmother is coming down too."

"Oh, wow," My mom pauses as she takes in everything that I just threw at her. "Is there something you want to tell me, Tommy?"

"No," I snap. "Her grandmother is sick, and I think it would be nice for her to get away with Peyton and spend some time on the beach."

"Oh," she says with a sympathetic sigh. "That sounds… interesting. Peyton is her name?"

"Yes," that's all I say. I don't want to admit too much to her right now before I speak with Peyton. I also don't want to get into a full-blown conversation where she asks me if I have spoken to Sheila. I am not doing this today. Quickly I add, "Mom, I have to get going. I have to stop at the store before I head home."

"Okay, honey. We can finish this conversation later," she adds. "Love you, Tommy."

I sigh into the phone because that's not fucking happening, "Love you too, Mom."

I end the call and pick out a bouquet of multicolor roses. White, red, orange, pink, and yellow all wrapped in one bouquet. I know roses symbolize romance, but they also symbolize beauty and courage. They are nature's most beautiful flower and as corny as this may sound, Peyton is the most beautiful person I have met in my life. Besides, I will never forget the aroma of roses I smell when I am near her. All those years ago, that is the scent that stuck with me, quickly becoming my favorite flower.

On the drive back to the penthouse, my phone buzzes again in my pocket. I can't help but think, *'Leave me the fuck alone.'* When I look down, I notice it's a three-way call between Marc and Oliver.

"Hey," I answer in an aggravated tone.

"Don't even start with the attitude, fuck face," Oliver says through the phone.

"You're annoying me on my peaceful drive home," I snap. "What do you two want?"

"Marc says you invited the nanny and her friends to the shore house for your birthday." He laughs.

"I did."

"Well," he draws out the word. "What's going on with you two?"

"Nothing."

"Tommy," Marc cuts in. "Don't lie. We know you better than that. I witnessed you firsthand with her the other night. You two have feelings. I could tell just from watching the way you two looked at each other."

"Yes, so you also know I don't do relationships."

"But you can," Marc adds.

"Have you ever seen Tommy with a girlfriend?" Oliver scoffs.

"Exactly," I answer Oliver's question before Marc could. "I am insanely attracted to her. But I don't know the first thing about relationships."

"It's not rocket science." Marc chuckles on the other end. "You're already doing half of what most people in a relationship do. You spend time together. You buy her shit. You feed her. You fuck. Women are not complicated creatures."

I don't respond to that. He's got a point and I fucking hate telling him that he's right when he is.

"You don't have to tell me that I'm right," Marc laughs. "You're an open book and I've learned that growing up with you. You show people you love them in your own unique way and that's what we love about you as your brothers." Fuck, he's getting all sappy on me. "You're falling for your nanny. Head over heels."

"I…" I pause, running my hands through my hair. "Fuck, I think I am."

"It's about fucking time someone got to you, Tommy." Oliver beams through the phone. I can tell he's got a shit eating grin plastered on his face.

"Listen guys," I stop them, having to end this phone call before I get hives. "I have to go, I'm pulling up to the penthouse now."

"We love you, bro," Marc says first before Oliver says, "Love you, my dude."

I pause on the phone before I finally admit, "I love you guys, too." Just as I pull the phone from my ear to hit the end call button, I can hear them both cheering and screaming things on the other end. *Have I really never said it to them?* Damn, Peyton is changing me.

Jim greets me in the lobby a few moments later as I enter the building. "Good evening, Mr. Ford. You're off early today."

"Yes," I sigh. "It's been a long week, Jim."

"I bet it has." He nods as his eyes take note of the bouquet of flowers. "Those are some beautiful flowers, Mr. Ford."

My eyes travel to the flowers in my hand and then back to him. I don't have to say anything for him to know that they are for Peyton. "You think so?" I ask him.

"Yes, sir." His smile is a hundred miles long. "She's a special one. Her chocolate chip cookies are out of this world. You would never be able to tell she uses a vegan recipe to make them."

My eyebrows pinch together and my head tilts to the side in confusion.

"I'm sorry, sir," he says quickly as if he's trying to hide what he just said. "She brings down a batch of chocolate chip cookies for me whenever she makes them. I don't mean to get her in trouble if she's not allowed."

I shake my head and let out a small laugh, "Oh no, Jim. I am so happy she's bringing you some cookies. We appreciate everything you do here in the building."

"Thank you, Mr. Ford." He smiles. "I don't mean to overstep with what I am about to say, but if those beautiful roses are for who I think they are for, she truly deserves them. And if those flowers mean what I hope they mean, then I am so happy for you and James. James loves her so much. I can tell from their brief visits down here." He pauses for a moment. "Don't let her go, sir."

I feel a lump in my throat as I smile and nod at his statement. "Thank you, Jim. Have a good night."

With that, I am in the elevator and nerves build up in my stomach. This day has already been too much for me. First my mom, then my brothers and now Jim. I need to talk to Peyton and find out where we stand.

It's confirmed she's home when the elevator doors open, and the aroma of chocolate chip cookies hits my nose. *She's home.*

When I enter the kitchen, I notice she's wearing a simple pair of black leggings and a shirt that's three sizes too big for her. She's covered in baking batter with her hair in a messy bun on the top of her head. I've never seen anything more beautiful.

She doesn't realize I'm in the room until I clear my throat. Her head turns to look at me quickly as if I startled her and a soft smile forms across her face as she takes in the flowers I'm holding and the smile I am wearing to match hers.

"Hello, Sunshine," I finally say to her.

She doesn't reply. She picks up the tea towel to dry her hands and walks over to me standing in the entrance of the kitchen. She's inches from me, the smile never wavering from her face. Her arms wrap around my neck as she presses her body flush with mine and buries her face into my neck. Warmth floods my body as my arms wrap themselves around her waist to hold her tight to me.

"You're home early," she whispers into my neck as I make no move to let her go.

I feel my heart rate pick up and I know, without a doubt, she can feel it pounding in my chest. "We have to get ready for the weekend," I reply. I can feel her arms loosen around my neck as if she's ready to let go. But I'm not.

Tightening my grip on her, I drop the flowers to the kitchen counter and lift her in my arms. Her legs wrap tight around my waist and a giggle comes out of her as I walk over to the counter and place her on it.

I stand pressed against her as her thighs grip my waist like she doesn't want to let go. Her arms release from around my neck and our eyes find each other. My hand reaches her face to brush the loose strands of her messy bun out of her face. "Excited to see me, huh?" I say with a smirk.

"Incredibly," she says, throwing her head back and laughing.

"Is that sarcasm, Ms. Kelly?"

She scoffs as she places a hand on her chest, "I would never, Mr. Ford."

I growl as my lips move to her ear. "If James wasn't home, I would take you over my knee. You know what it does to me when you call me that." I press a kiss to the hollow of her neck. "Right here." Another kiss to a small spot of exposed skin on her shoulder. "Right now, Ms. Kelly."

"Lucky for me," she pauses as tilts her head to the side, allowing me better access to her neck. "James is with Emiline. He's going to drive down with her."

"Tell me, Sunshine." I cup her breast with a kiss to her collar bone. "Do you have a batch of cookies in the oven right now?"

"No, Sir," she says, and I feel my dick twitch at her use of 'Sir' with me. "I was just cleaning up."

I move faster than I have ever moved before when I lift her off the counter and throw her over my shoulder. A squeal combined with laughter erupts from her. "Thomas," she laughs. I don't reply as I am practically running up the stairs with her over my shoulder to my bedroom. I have never taken her in my bed yet and I'm about to change that, right fucking now.

I kick the door to my bedroom open and gently place her on the ground. I expect her to take in the room and her surroundings since she's never been in here before that I know of, but her eyes never leave mine.

Her arms move from around my neck to her sides as she takes one delicate step away from me. Cold air hits me from her lack of touch and closeness. My eyes stay fixed on hers, but I can see the small grin on her face as she takes another small step back and pulls her bottom lip between her teeth with the most seductive look on her face.

Her hands move quickly to pull the oversized t-shirt over her head, and I swear, I could pass out right here and right now. How the fuck did I not notice she had no bra on under that shirt? My eyes trail down her body as I take in the most perfect sight in front of me.

Her tits are the perfect size. Enough that I can cup them in my large hands. I move to take a step towards her because I can't keep my hands off her, but she stops me. Holding up a finger and shaking it with a smirk on her face. "No, no, Mr. Ford."

I breathe a heavy sigh and take a step back. I need to touch her. I need to taste her. I fucking need her. I continue to watch as she hooks her thumb in the waistband of her leggings and pushes them to the floor. Standing completely naked in front of me. My cock is hard as steel at the sight of her.

She doesn't even have to use words to confirm my every thought of the day.

She wants me too.

My eyes trail her up and down before I snap, "On the bed, Peyton," I demand. "On your knees and lean down on your elbows. I want to see this perfect ass on display for me."

"Yes, Sir." She giggles.

"What did I say about the sarcasm, Ms. Kelly?" I say to her as

I walk up behind her. She's already in position on the bed eager for my cock.

Pressing the bulge in my pants to her backside, I hear her breath get lodged in her throat as I lean down over her to whisper in her ear, "Let me remind you, Peyton." My right hand connects with her ass and the sound of the slap echoes in the room as I hear a moan escape from her lips. My hand grips the same cheek that I just slapped. "You like that, don't you?" I whisper. Both of my hands are now gripping her ass. "You like being spanked like a dirty girl."

"Yes," her voice filled with desperation.

"Tell me what you want, Peyton."

"I-I want…" she pauses. "I want you."

"You have me, baby. Tell me what you want."

"I want your mouth on me," she says through a long-drawn-out breath.

"Where, Peyton?"

She pauses, unsure of her words. "I want your mouth on my pussy."

I give her a playful smack on the ass and my hand finds her upper back to push her head down more forcefully than I want too. I want her ass higher in the air for me, exposing her pussy to me because I need to fucking taste her.

I can already see her arousal glistening before my tongue finds her pussy and I moan into her as I taste her coating my tongue. "I'm fucking starving," I whisper into her. "And you taste so fucking sweet."

She widens her legs for me as she arches her back more to give me the best angle as my tongue laps her clit over and over. Her hips rock into my face like she's craving more. I'm fully fucking planning to give her everything she wants.

"Thomas," she moans as her back arches. "More."

I suck her clit hard and insert a finger into her tight pussy. I will never get enough of her. So tight. So soft. So wet. *So fucking mine*. My tongue works on her clit as my finger slides in and out of her pussy. She rocks her hips harder into me.

"That's it, baby," I say as I remove my mouth and insert a second finger and move my fingers even harder into her. "Come for me now. Then you can have my cock."

"Thomas, Thomas," she repeats. "I'm going to come."

I remove my mouth from her and lift my body to hover over her back, never removing my fingers from her. She scoots herself up in the bed to allow me room to be on top of her. My fingers move faster and faster while her hips buck hard into my hand. I can feel her pulsing around me. I lean down to whisper in her ear, "Come. Now." I demand.

With that, I watch her shatter around my fingers. A string of moans come from her mouth. "Fuck," she curses in a moan. "I'm coming," she screams.

I slow my fingers as the orgasm takes over her body. She's moaning into the bed sheets and her slickness covers my fingers. I remove them just after I feel she has come down from her high. Her head turns over her shoulder to look at me and I can see her rapidly breathing. I lick her cum from each digit and she pulls her bottom lip between her teeth as she watches me.

I walk to the nightstand and pull out a condom when I hear her whisper, "Leave it." It was so quiet, I almost missed it.

My head snaps in her direction. "What?"

"I'm on the pill and I'm clean, Thomas. I haven't been with anyone in longer than I care to admit," she says with a small smile.

Fuck. *Is this for real*? The thought of feeling her with nothing between us for the first time has my cock standing higher in salute. At the same time, it's hard for me to fully trust anyone after what happened with my last one-night stand. But Peyton is nothing like Sheila.

"Are you sure, Peyton?" I ask. "I—"

"I trust you," she cuts me off.

"I haven't been with anyone else in…" I pause trying to figure out how to say that it's been years. "A long time."

"Thomas." She moves off the bed to stand directly in front of me. She lifts her hands to run them through my hair before repeating the words, "I trust you."

"Peyton," I whisper as I bury my head into the crook of her neck before I say what I haven't told another woman in so long. "I trust you too."

She pushes me off of her and grips my shoulders to push me down on the bed. I feel myself losing control and I have never let anyone take control of me before. But I give in, just this once as I sit on the edge of the bed and lean back, using my hands to hold me up.

She surprises me when she moves to sit on my lap. Both of her thighs straddling mine. I sit up taller, and my hands grip her rib cage. My hands are large compared to her body. She sinks into my lap, my cock pressed into her pussy, and I can feel her wetness through my work pants, and she begins to slowly move her hips back and forth on top of me. Her body craves the friction.

My hands cup her breasts and I take one in my mouth. Sucking the nipple hard and pinching it between my teeth. Her head falls back, and she arches more into me, her hips grinding into me more. She will not fucking come again like this. My hands move to her hips, gripping her tight to slow her movements and I swear a small whimper comes out of her.

"You're not coming like this," I whisper in her ear. "The next time you come, it will be with my cock buried deep inside of you while you're screaming my name." She bites her bottom lip and smiles at me as she moves and allows me to pull my pants down. Her eyes widen when my cock springs free, as if it's the first time she's seen it.

"Turn around," I order. "Hands on the edge of the bed."

She turns around and does as I said. Spreading her legs, arching her back and giving me those sultry eyes over her shoulder. I give her a smack on her right cheek and a small squeal comes out of her.

"You like that don't you, baby?" I say through gritted teeth as I lay another smack on her ass. "You like it when I fuck you rough. You like my hands on your ass."

"Yes," she moans. "Fuck, yes."

"My dirty fucking girl," I growl as I press my dick against her ass, and I feel her press harder into me. I grip the base of my cock as I bring it to her entrance and tease her just a little bit before I thrust deep inside of her. I can't remember the last time I was bare inside of a woman, but fuck, she feels like a dream. I'm already minutes away from coming and she hasn't even moved yet.

"Holy fuck," she moans into the sheets, and she begins to press her hips into me with my cock deep inside of her. "I never knew it could feel this good."

"You've never been fucked raw before?" I ask her.

"No," she shakes her head.

"Good." I smirk. "Because I'm about to ruin you for anyone else."

My hands cup her breasts from behind as she starts to bounce her ass into me while I drive in and out of her. A stream of curse words coming out of her mouth over and over again.

She spreads her legs just an inch wider and her back arches more as her face presses against the mattress. The small change in movements has me unhinged and ready to explode. "Fuuuuck, baby," I hiss. "You're going to make me come already."

"I'm almost there," she screams. "I just need… I just need—"

I reach around her as my thumb finds her clit and I begin to rub circles around it, giving her the more she needs. The more she craves.

"Thomas," she yells out again. "Oh God, Thomas."

"That's it, baby. Scream for me," I tell her, pressing harder on her clit and working my finger in quicker circles and I thrust faster from behind. "I want you screaming my name when you come all over my cock."

"Come with me, Thomas."

I swear to God, hearing her say that I almost blow my load right then and there. I want her with every fiber of my being. I want her. More than just now and this sex, I fucking want all of her.

I press my hips into her deeper as I give her more to tip her over the edge, closer to her orgasm. "You're mine, Peyton," I groan. Moving my body to hover over her so my mouth is closer to her ear. "You're fucking mine."

"I'm coming," she begins to scream.

"Yes, you fucking are," I say into her neck. "Your pussy is milking my cock, baby. You are squeezing me so tight." I continue bucking my hips harder until my own release crashes over me. "Fuck, Peyton. I'm coming."

"Yes," she screams as I fill her with my cum. "Yes, Thomas! Fuck."

As we finally come down from our highs, we both fall onto the bed as we try to regulate our breathing. Her messy bun is practically off her head and sprawls out over my chest as she moves to lay her head down on me.

Slowly she lifts her head. "Holy shit, Thomas."

I don't reply to what she just said, because I feel the same way. Holy shit. Instead, I tell her, "I meant what I said."

"Y-you…" she cocks her head to the side. "What do you mean?"

"You're mine."

"I am?" She asks as if she doesn't already know it.

"Yes, Sunshine," I whisper as I move to where she's now sitting on the edge of the bed. I bring myself eye level with her and give her a smile. "You're mine, baby. Your smile is mine. Your kisses are mine. Your pussy is mine. Everything about you, is mine."

Her mouth parts with a shocked look on her face as her eyes

bounce between mine. "But..." she stutters. "What are you saying, Thomas?"

"I'm saying I want you," I admit. "I've wanted you since the moment I saw you across the ballroom. Then I wanted you again when I saw your beautiful hair blowing in the wind at the park. And I've wanted you again every single fucking day I come home from work."

"B-but—"

"You drive me absolutely insane, Peyton," I cut her off with a grin on my face. I brush a strand of hair away from her face as I look deep into her blue eyes. "But I want you. I want this."

She pauses before the corner of her lip curls up the slightest. "What is *this*, Mr. Ford?"

"Listen." I smile at her use of *Mr. Ford*. "I don't know what the fuck I'm doing here. I don't know the first thing about dating. I don't know how to do relationships. But I want this with you, Peyton. I want to figure it out along the way. I want more than just this random sex in the kitchen or living room. I want us," I admit.

She hooks her arms around my neck and in a low whisper she says, "I want that too."

I lean down to press a hard, passionate kiss to her lips. I grab her and pull her to me to deepen the kiss. I forgot how perfect her lips feel against mine. Soft and seductive. I kiss her with need as my tongue sweeps inside of her mouth and tangles with her tongue. Her hands cup my face as she holds her kiss there, pressing hard into me. Reluctantly, I pull away. "Now get this sweet ass up, baby," I tell her with a small smack to her ass after she stands. "Let's go get washed up. We have to finish packing."

"I got all packed up this afternoon. I've been ready to go for *hours*," she rolls her eyes as she draws out the word hours.

"You're asking for another spanking, Sunshine."

"Oh no..." she says with a shocked look on her face and sarcasm dripping from her words. "Whatever will I do?"

I growl and move quickly in my attempt to give her a smack

on the ass, but she scurries into the bathroom. She's laughing wildly when I reach her in the bathroom. She spins around to circle her arms around my neck and surprises me when she kisses me hard.

All I can think of right now, is how natural it feels to be around her.

How happy she makes me.

I'm pretty sure I'm falling in love with her.

CHAPTER TWENTY-SIX
Peyton

After the greatest sex of my entire life, Thomas joined me in the shower for another round. I'm almost positive he gave me six orgasms before we even left. We got to the shore house late and that's why I ended up sleeping most of the drive last night.

Something shifted between us the second he got home from work. *He wants me.* He finally admitted to me. I won't lie and say that I don't want him, but there's a lot we have to talk about when this weekend is over. I keep thinking, what am I going to do about work? I can't continue to be his son's nanny with this insane wage. I would feel like he's paying me to be his girlfriend. It's just weird, so I need to discuss what we're doing here with him when we get back to the city.

Earlier today, Gigi arrived with Kali and Avery. A few hours later, his brother Marc and best friend Logan showed up with Emiline and James not too far behind them. Gigi was introduced to everyone. Her and Thomas hit it off right away, just like I knew they would. He spent most of the day close to her. Almost like he was afraid to leave her alone for two minutes. Made my heart swoon how much he loves her already.

Thomas warned me that his mom would be here this weekend, but she wasn't here when we arrived. I'm not sure I am ready to meet his mom. Because, you know… I'm still the nanny.

"What's on your mind over there, Sunshine?" Thomas breaks me from my trance. I'm sitting on the screened in porch with a view of the ocean, next to the heater, while reading one of my smutty romance novels. Considering it's late November, it's the perfect temperature to curl under a blanket with a gorgeous view of the sun setting around me.

"Nothing," I admit with a small smile.

Thomas just nods and takes a seat next to me. He lifts the blanket, and our legs connect as he sits so close to me. He wraps an arm around me and presses the most delicate kiss to the side of my head before whispering, "Get out of your head, baby." My head tilts up so that our eyes meet. "I meant what I said last night. I want to give this a shot with you. I have no idea what I'm doing but I know that I'm crazy about you, Peyton."

A soft smile forms on my face as his stare burns deep into me. "I'm crazy about you too," I admit. Because I am. I'm falling so hard for him. "I just think we have a lot to talk about."

"I know, Sunshine. I know." He places another soft kiss to the side of my head and shivers run down my spine. "When we get back to the city, we will talk everything through. But for now, Gigi has whipped out a deck of *Cards Against Humanity* and wants us all to play now that dinner is cleaned up." He laughs.

"She did not bring that with her!" I exclaim as shock takes over my face. "She's such a dirty bird."

"Oh, she did." He laughs. "Everyone is already in the kitchen getting ready to play. Let's go, baby."

Once we're in the kitchen, we each pour our favorite drinks. The boys are drinking whiskey and the girls are drinking tequila and lime. Gigi opted to not drink tonight despite her love for wine. She says it makes her extra tired with her medication.

"Okay, do we all know how to play?" Gigi announces as she shuffles the cards and begins to pass everyone their starting hand.

"Yes, Ma'am," Logan answers for all of us as he rubs his hands together like he's ready to dominate this game.

"Relax, Logy," Emiline says as she rolls her eyes. "It's not that serious and you're going to lose anyway."

"I never lose, Em," he says, facing her with a wink and she rolls her eyes again.

"Peyton," Gigi announces. "You're up first to pick from the deck. Read it out loud and then we will all look at our cards and put them in the center. Then you can pick your favorite and whoever played that card is the winner of that round."

I pull a card from the deck in the middle of the table and begin to read it out loud, "A successful job interview begins with a firm handshake and ends with *blank*."

"Oh fuck." Avery laughs as she picks through her cards. "I have a good one."

"You can't beat mine, Princess." Marc chuckles in his seat.

"I'm blowing all you bitches away." Gigi laughs and everyone's eyes shoot to her with shocked looks on their face. "What?" She laughs. "I'm a pro at this game. You're all going down." With that, we all let out a full belly laugh, tipping our heads back.

You see, this is the Gigi I already know. Half of the people at this table don't understand her sense of humor yet, but they are about to find out that she's the funniest lady in my life. She has her mind stuck in the gutter ninety percent of the time and she lives like she's still in her twenties.

I shake my head as everyone comes down from their laughter. "That's Gigi for you."

"Well, Gigi," Logan begins, but pauses his thoughts. "I can call you that, right?"

"Of course, sweetheart." She chuckles and winks at him. "A fine young man like yourself can call me whatever you want. Just don't call me late for dinner."

"Well, well." Logan sits up straighter in his seat, and he

smirks. "I will have you know that my card will be a favorite of yours."

"I bet it will, Logy," she mocks the nickname Emiline has for him and I hear Emiline chuckle under her palm that covers her face.

"Wrong," Kali chimes in. "Gigi is going to get the biggest kick out of mine. I know her dirty personality."

"Hey," I interrupt defensively. "I'm the one voting here. Give me your cards, let me read them." I grab the stack from the table and begin a small shuffle.

"Alright." I clear my throat. "I'll read the card again and then the answers. "A successful job interview begins with a firm handshake and ends with." I pick up the first white card to read, "*A plunger to the face.*"

The table begins to laugh, and I swear Emiline almost spits out her drink. "That was even funnier when you read it all together," Emiline says. "I gave myself away, but that one is mine. It's what I would like to do to Logan."

"First of all," Logan adds. "You're not supposed to tell her it's your card. Second of all, you fucking love me."

"Never in this lifetime, Logan," Emiline scoffs.

"Shush you two." I grab the next card. "A successful job interview begins with a firm handshake and ends with *Fuck Mountain*," I read. I already know that this is Avery's card without even looking her in the eye. "That's a good one, guys."

"The fucking best one," Avery adds with a laugh.

I begin to read the next card, "A successful job interview begins with a firm handshake and ends with *blowing some dudes in an alley.*" I shake my head.

"Oh, fuck yeah!" Logan claps his hands together. "But that wasn't mine. It was a good one though." I see Gigi laughing in her seat next to me. It was definitely hers.

"Next," I say before I repeat the sentence again and add another card option, "*Just the tip.*" My eyes glance over to

Thomas because I wonder if that was his. He shakes his head and laughs but Logan chimes in.

"That's all you need," he laughs.

"I beg to differ," Avery adds. "Just the tip is a tease. You want to get a girl off, you have to give her all the meat, Logy." I can't help but laugh at everyone calling him that now.

"I second that," Kali adds.

"I know how to get a girl off," he defends himself. "And multiple times. Thank you very much."

"In your fucking dreams," Marc adds.

"I have to agree with them," Emiline adds. "Just the tip does nothing."

"My ears are bleeding, Em," Thomas adds. "Please don't talk about your sex life. I'm begging you."

"She doesn't have a sex life," Logan adds. "She's just a baby."

"I'm fucking 21, you Lincoln Log," Emiline defends herself.

"Since when?" Logan begins to shout. "Good gracious. How have you two not tied her up and locked her in the basement to protect her?"

"Because the last two people I want to be tied up by are my brothers."

"Emiline, I'm begging you," Marc groans, covering his ears. "We don't need to know this stuff."

"Can I go back to reading the last three cards?" I interrupt and go back to the game. "A successful job interview begins with a firm handshake and ends with *tongue*." My gaze falls on Thomas who has a smirk on his face and I watch him slowly as he drags his tongue along his bottom lip. That card was definitely him. Thankfully, no one picked up on his subtle move he just did because I'm not ready to answer questions. I haven't told Avery and Kali about us yet.

I repeat the sentence again with the last two cards. "*Fisting*," I read out loud. "And lastly, *masturbating in a robe like a rich person*."

"That one is Marc," Avery says confidently. "I can picture that."

"Can you?" Marc questions with a grin plastered on his face. "You think about me fucking my fist wearing nothing but a robe, Princess?"

"In *your* dreams, Marc." She rolls her eyes. "Calm down with your big dick energy and watch your language around Gigi."

"I'm sorry, Gigi." Marc says sympathetically as he turns to face her.

"Oh, please." She waves her hands in the air. "Don't stop being horn dogs on my account. You all are keeping me young."

"Well, who wins?" Avery says, clapping her hands together.

"I'm not picking anyone," I admit, crossing my arms over my chest and leaning back in my chair. "You all told me who laid down what cards. It's not fair for me to choose now."

"Come on." Logan stands, throwing his hands in the air. "I totally won that shit. Just the tip is the perfect fill in the blank."

"Would you give it up already," Emiline huffs. "Just the tip is never perfect. In any aspect of life."

"I swear to God, if you don't lock her up." Logan turns to Marc and Thomas. "How the fuck did you allow her to grow up?"

"I'm allowed to do whatever I want," Emiline snaps back. "I'm a grown adult, whether you like it or not."

"I don't like it," he snaps at her. Closing the gap on the two of them and coming face to face with her. "I. Don't. Fucking. Like. It."

"We've accepted it." Thomas shrugs his shoulders. "You can too."

"She's even legal drinking age," Avery adds with a laugh. "Best night of my life that night we went out." Emiline has gotten close to us over the last couple of months and her and Avery have really hit it off. They are practically the same person and Avery needs someone just as wild as her in her life.

"I love a wild girl," Gigi adds.

"My head can't take all of this in one night," Logan says as his hands come up to his temples and rub them with his pointer finger.

The group continues their bickering back and forth when I feel Thomas' large hand splayed across my thigh under the table. A chill runs down my spine the same way it always does when he touches me or is in close proximity. My body instinctively leans into him.

He leans into me just enough that no one else could notice it. "You want to take a walk and get away from this mess for a bit?"

"Yes, please."

"You head out first," he tells me with a head tilt towards the back door. "I'll meet you outside in a couple minutes so that they don't start asking questions."

I nod, understanding what he's saying, because I'm not ready to answer questions yet. Especially since I haven't told Kali or Avery what's going on.

I slowly move to get up while the table continues to argue. I look to Gigi who is so engrossed in their conversation and laughing at them as if it's a comedy show happening. I don't say anything as I exit the kitchen and head out the back door to the open deck. The cold air hits me like a brick wall. I wrap my arms around myself and rub my exposed arms to cause some friction to warm me up. I didn't expect to come outside again tonight, so I left my sweatshirt in the bedroom on the other side of the house.

The cold doesn't last long when I feel warmth wrap around me like a sweater. Thomas stands behind me with his front pressed to my back and I feel his solid muscles against me as his arms circle me. His body is larger than mine and made of steel, but I melt into him.

"Hey, you," I smile, even though he can't see my face. "Long time no see."

Our height difference allows him to rest his chin on the top of my head. "Too long if you ask me."

"It's been all of two minutes, Thomas."

"Like I said," he presses a kiss to the top of my head. "Too long, if you ask me."

My body spins around and he doesn't move from where he's standing. Our bodies melt back together as my arms wrap around his waist and my chin tips up so I can look him in the eyes. His large arms wrap around my neck as he tips his head down to meet my gaze and I can't help the smile that forms on my lips.

"Well, aren't you the sweetest?"

"No, baby." His smile meets mine. "I think we both know, you're the sweet one."

I don't reply to him as I continue to stare into his eyes. Deep ocean blue that glistens from the reflection of the moonlight outside. Slowly, he tips his head down and his lips are on mine. It's a soft kiss. It's a kiss that tells me this could be more or that this *is* more. I've wanted this for so long too. Despite both of us not wanting to do relationships, I know deep down that Thomas is different. I know he would protect my heart.

I melt into his body as his hands cup the side of my face. He tilts my head up just slightly to deepen our kiss and I part my lips just the smallest amount to welcome him as his tongue sweeps my mouth in one move. My hands grip his back, craving more from him.

He releases my lips. "Peyton," he whispers through a broken breath. "What is it about you?"

As I look into his eyes, trying to figure out how to answer that question, I notice darkness taking over them. "I could ask you the same question, Mr. Ford." The corners of my lips tip up to a small smirk. I love playing this game with him.

He growls and his lips are back on me. This kiss is filled with want and primal need. His hands are now exploring my body until they find my hips where he grips them hard pulling my body even closer as if we weren't already melded together.

But then he breaks the kiss. "Not now," he hisses. "We have a house full of guests. But fuck, Peyton. I have never wanted anyone as bad as I want you," he says before pressing his forehead to mine as his eyes close. "What the fuck are you doing to me?"

"Thomas," I whisper back. His eyes don't open, and he doesn't remove his head from resting on mine. But I gently pull back my head so he can look me in the eyes. "Look at me," I demand through a low voice. He opens his eyes and I feel the heat of his stare. "You know I want you too, right?"

"Tell me you do, Peyton. Please."

"I do," I say without any sign of hesitation. "I want this. I want you. I want more."

He responds with a deeply passionate kiss and his hands gripping each side of my face. That's all the confirmation that I need right now.

Our kiss is interrupted when I hear a throat clear behind me. Thomas releases my lips, and his gaze moves to look over my shoulder. A soft smile forms on his lips and I release my grip from around his waist as I turn my head in the direction he's looking.

"Hey, Mom." Thomas says.

I smile at the woman standing behind us with a smirk on her face. She looks so much like Emiline. She's gorgeous with short blonde hair and a petite frame body. "Is this Peyton?" She asks as she starts to walk closer to us. The smirk still plastered on, and I can't quite read what she's thinking right now after she caught her son basically making out with me at, what I assume, is her house.

"Hi, Mrs. Ford." I extend my hand out to greet her. "It's nice to meet you."

She doesn't take my hand in return. Her eyes trail down to my hand and back up to my face. I feel Thomas lay a protective hand on the small of my back as he moves forward to stand next to me.

"Mother," he hisses at her.

"Is this the nanny?" she asks him.

"Yes," he pauses. "She's James' nanny."

"Well," she says as her eyes find mine again. "Since when do we make out with the hired help?"

CHAPTER TWENTY-SEVEN
Thomas

"Mother," I hiss at her. I can't believe her right now. I know she has a soft spot for Sheila since she's James' mom, but she has no right to disrespect Peyton like this.

"Just asking." My mom shrugs.

"I…uh," Peyton pauses as her eyes bounce between me and my mom. "I'm going to go inside to check on Gigi."

Reluctantly, I nod. I don't need Peyton to be a witness to the argument I'm about to have with my mom right now. This isn't how I wanted to introduce Peyton to her. I press a soft kiss to the side of her head, and I feel her shy away. She begins to walk away but my hand grips the crook of her elbow, and she stops to give me a sympathetic look. "Peyton," I whisper as my look matches hers. "Please."

"Thomas, it's ok." She nods and a soft smile appears on her face. "We'll talk later." She reaches up on her toes and presses a quick kiss to the corner of my lips. It's so quick that I barely have time to react and kiss her back.

Peyton retreats into the house without a glance back and then my eyes find my mom's. "Mom, why?"

"I'm just saying, honey." She shrugs her shoulders. "Since when do we sleep with hired help?"

"It's not like that with her," I snap back. I'm furious with her for acting this way. I should have known she would. "Peyton is different. I knew her before she became James' nanny."

"So, you hired your girlfriend to be your son's nanny?" Her eyes widen. "That doesn't sound like the smartest move on your part, honey."

"Listen," I sigh. "I'm not going to get into it with you right now. But she means a lot to me, and you need to apologize to her for how you just treated her."

She crosses her arm over her chest as if she will do no such thing. "Have you spoken to Sheila?"

Here the fuck we go.

"No, Mother. And I have no plans to speak to her, either. She signed her rights over to me," I add in a much angrier tone than I have ever spoken to my mom with before. "She wants no part in James' life and I, frankly, don't want her a part of ours, either."

"I don't understand why, Tommy!" She throws her arms in the air and adds in an eye roll for more dramatics. "Why are you so against making it work with her?"

"Do you speak to her?"

"No," she admits. "I haven't spoken to her since you two have been together."

"You know nothing about what happened between us then," I tell her as I bring my voice back down to a normal speaking level. "She left us, Mom. I tried to make it work with her for the sake of James. I *fucking tried.* Do you know that she resented James? Did you know she blamed him for messing with her body when she *'had a whole career ahead of her?'* Did you know that there was never a point in our entire relationship where I loved her?"

"I-I—" she stutters and the color drains from her face.

"I've never admitted this to you because I've never had anyone that I care about in my life," I say as my chin falls to my chest and I avoid eye contact with her. "You know I don't do relationships, Mom." My eyes find hers again. "I have never been in one in my life, besides with Sheila. I wouldn't even consider that a relationship. No one does if they are outsiders looking in."

"But..." she attempts to continue. I hold up a hand to stop her from continuing the thought.

"I never loved her, Mom. I tried to make it work. I tried so fucking hard to fall in love with her," I finally admit out loud. "James was never supposed to happen, but I will never fucking regret that time because he's the greatest thing to ever happen to me." I look her deep in the eyes and I can see sympathy fill them as she takes in everything. "Sheila was simply the product of me trying to forget someone. The truth is, I met someone about a year before I met Sheila. We had only just met and talked briefly but I knew there was something about her and I wanted to know more," I pause, collecting my thoughts. "But I lost her when the building was evacuated and never saw her again. Sheila was just there for me to forget someone I couldn't fucking get out of my head."

"I had no idea," she admits.

"Yeah, well." I cross my arms over my chest. "Now you know."

"Was it," she pauses. "The girl you met before Sheila... was it Peyton?"

"Yes." I nod. "When Emiline found someone to be a nanny for James, I had no idea who it was because Emiline didn't tell me. I didn't know until I showed up at the park to meet with Emiline, and Peyton was standing there."

"Wow," my mom says with a smile.

"You can say that again," I let out a small laugh. "I'm sorry for yelling, Mom. I need you to know that Peyton may be James' nanny right now, but I don't plan on her being the nanny for much longer. I—" I cut myself off as I find myself on the verge of saying three words that I have never said to anyone other than James. "I care about her a lot."

"Oh, honey." My mom smiles back at me. "It sounds like it's much more than that. I'm sorry for the way I acted. I wish you told me all this years ago. I fought so hard for you to make it work with Sheila for James. Every little boy needs their mother growing up."

"You're right." I nod. "Now bring it in," I say as I hold out my arms to bring her in for a hug. "I'm sorry I didn't tell you all of this sooner. This isn't how I wanted to see you for the first time since you left for Europe but I'm glad it's out there."

She nods into my chest as she returns my hug. "I'm happy for you, Tommy."

"I'm happy too, Mom."

As soon as the words leave my mouth, I see a figure out of the corner of my eye coming out of the house. It's Gigi. Both my mom and I look at her and for the first time, I can see how frail she truly is. She doesn't notice us, and my eyes move back to my mom's, and I can see a questioning look on her face because she doesn't know who this is.

"That's Gigi," I say in a low voice, so she doesn't hear us. "Peyton's grandmother." My mom nods at my statement before I continue. "She's very sick. She has stage four Non-Hodgkin's Lymphoma."

"Oh, honey." Her hands land on her chest.

Gigi approaches us and gives us a soft smile. "Hey there, handsome." Gigi says to me.

I return her smile. "Hi, Gigi. How are you?"

"Oh, you know me." She swats her arms in the air and laughs. "I get younger as I get older."

"My name is Ann Marie," my mom says as she reaches out her hand to Gigi. "It's so nice to meet you and have you here for the weekend."

"You can call me Gigi or Esther," she says. "Thank you so much for having me. The shore has a special place in my heart, and I was so ecstatic when I was invited down here. You raised a good set of boys, Ann Marie. And Emiline too. She reminds me a lot of myself when I was younger."

My mom looks at me with a proud smile on her face. "They sure are special." She returns her look back to Gigi. "I'm heading inside to make a cup of tea, would you care for some?"

"That would be so nice." She smiles at my mom. "I can't drink the bottle of wine I would love to drink right now. So tea will have to do."

My mom nods and retreats back into the house at the same time Gigi goes to stand by the porch railing and leans on it.

"How are you feeling, Gigi?" I meet her at the railing and lean on it next to her.

She doesn't answer my question and remains silent for a moment. Looking at the ocean and taking in the moonlight reflecting on the water. She breaks the silence as she stares out at the water and says, "I know it's been you."

"I..." I stutter as confusion takes over. "What do you mean?"

"I know it's been you." She turns her head to look at me, finally. "You've been having groceries, care packages and my medical stuff delivered to my house."

Fuck. How did she know?

"I'm sorry if I overstepped." I turn to look out into the ocean. "I care about anyone who Peyton cares about."

"You care about her, huh?"

"I do, Gigi. More than I've ever cared for another woman that isn't a family member," I admit. I pause as I continue to stare at the ocean. A weird sinking feeling hits my gut and my heart rate starts to pick up. My chest aches as I admit out loud, "I think I'm falling in love with her."

"Tommy boy." She laughs. "You're already there."

My head snaps to her. "Huh?"

"You don't *think* you're falling in love with her." She laughs. "You're already head over heels in love with her."

I shake my head and let out a small laugh with her.

"Don't try to deny it, sweetheart. Listen." She places her

hand on mine that's resting on the railing. I feel her cold frail hand on mine and it sends an uneasy feeling down my spine. "I have known Peyton her entire life. She might not say it to you, but I know she loves you too."

"How can you be so sure?"

"I see the way she looks at you. I see the way you look at her." She lifts a brow. "Did you think I didn't notice you staring at only her during our little card game back in there? I've had my eyes on you, Tommy boy."

"She's beautiful, Gigi." I smile in her direction. "How can I not stare at her?"

"Oh, I know." She laughs. "She's the most beautiful person I know. Inside and out. It's what makes me so nervous about the future. She doesn't deserve it."

My stomach drops at her admission. "What do you mean?"

"Don't play dumb, Tommy boy. I'm not doing well. I put on a really good front, and I hide my pain well so that I don't let on to the fact that I've been having some really bad days. Today was one of my worst, lately. Your family welcoming me here and being surrounded by laughter has brought me so much joy though. I can't thank you enough for putting a permanent smile on my face."

"Does she know?" I swallow the lump in my throat. "Does Peyton know how sick you really are?"

"She knows that I'm sick, but I leave out the rest. She's been through a lot the last year and a half."

"What do you mean?"

"You know, with her parents dying last year."

My heart drops to the deep parts of my stomach and I feel a horrible queasiness take over. She never told me the reason she moved or that her parents died. "I…" I feel a lump in my throat and tears pool in the corners of my eye. "I had no idea, Gigi."

"Wait," she pauses as shock takes over her face. "She never told you?"

"She didn't." I shake my head. "I just assumed she moved here to be closer to Kali and Avery."

"She did." She nods. "She lost everything, Tommy. When they passed, she fought so hard to keep their house. For almost a year. Finally, she had to sell the house, the car, and everything. She moved in with the girls with nothing to her name but those naughty books she reads. You've helped her in more ways than one," she adds.

"How?"

"Listen," she pauses as she lets out a small cough and catches her breath. "I shouldn't be telling you any of this. I feel bad enough because it's her business. But when you gave her a chance on this job, it helped her get her feet on the ground. Before you..." She wipes a small tear from her eye. "So many people have walked all over her, men included." Anger boils in my blood at her admission. "They treated her like shit, used her and tossed her to the curb." Now I'm ready to murder anyone who's ever been with her. I clench my teeth together as she continues. "You, Tommy boy, are nothing like them. I've been blessed to watch Peyton come into her own person since you. Her confidence is blossoming. She's found herself. I can tell she's the happiest she's ever been. You did that." She pokes my chest and laughs. "You brought her back to life."

I swallow another lump that's lodged in my throat. "She's changed me, Gigi."

"I bet she has, boy."

"Gigi, I'm pretty confident that I lo—" my words are cut short when a small voice cuts me off from the sliding glass doors and my head turns to see James standing there with tears in his eyes.

"Daddy," James cries in the doorway.

My eyes snap back to Gigi. "Go." She waves her hands to swat me away. "I'm going to get that tea your mom said she was making. It sounds so good right about now." She walks towards the door and before crossing the doors, she reaches down to plant a kiss to the top of James' head and my heart skips a beat.

"What's wrong, JJ?" I open my arms for him to come and sit on the patio chair with me.

"I had a bad dream, Daddy."

"Talk to me."

He sniffles as tears come out of his little eyes and I feel my heart cracking. "What if Peyton leaves, Daddy?"

"Oh, James," I say with a sympathetic sigh. For someone so little, he holds so much emotion in his tiny body. "What makes you think that?" My arms wrap around him as I embrace him in a tight hug.

"My m-mom," he sobs into my shirt. "S-she left me. I-I don't want P-Peyton to l-leave us too. I love her so much, Daddy."

"James, look at me." I lift his chin as tears form in my eyes too. "I don't think Peyton is going anywhere."

"Are you sure?" He sniffles.

"Because…" I wipe a tear from his eye before I wipe the tear from my eye. "Because I feel the same way, JJ. I don't want to lose her either. I want her around for a very long time."

"You do?" A mix of shock and excitement crosses his face.

"I do, bud," I admit with a soft smile. Looking him in the eyes, I run my hands through his messy blonde hair. "I love her, James. A whole lot."

"So, can we keep her?" he asks with a smile on his face and tears still staining his cheeks. "She does the best crafts. She's the best dinosaur buddy. She takes care of me when I'm sick. She loves to close the blinds and watch movies with me," he spits out at a rapid speed. "And she makes the best waffles ever, Daddy. She does the funtetti like I like a whole lot."

"Woah, slow down, JJ." I laugh. "She really is a keeper, huh?"

"We *need* to keep her, Daddy!" he screams.

"Then I say, we keep her."

———

The past hour has been running on repeat in my head. The heavy conversation with my mother, the even heavier conversation with Gigi, and James breaking my heart into a million pieces over his fear of losing Peyton. I admit, I have similar fears.

I lost her once, and I just can't fathom losing her again.

After I put James back to bed, I came downstairs to find Avery, Kali and Emiline drunk off tequila singing *Breakfast at Tiffany's*. Marc and Logan were sitting off to the side, fully engrossed in them as they laughed into their glass of whiskey. Marc can't keep his eyes off Avery and honestly, he's got to rein that in because she works for him and she doesn't seem like the type to settle down. She's a fucking wildcard.

Peyton wasn't there with the group, so I assumed she had gone up to bed. When I finally make my way back upstairs, I discover I am right when I find her sitting on the balcony of her room with a book in her hand.

As I slide the glass door open, she startles in the lounge chair and smiles. "Hey, you."

I return the smile as I walk to her. The smile remains on her face as I bend down at the foot of the lounge chair. She drops her book to the side as I spread her legs to lay between them. The side of my head resting on her stomach and my arms wrapping around her as I snuggle into her as far as I can get. She lets out a small chuckle and her hands comb through my hair.

"I missed you," I whisper. "I'm sorry about my mom."

"Don't be," she says as she runs her fingernails down my back. *Fuck that feels good.*

"She shouldn't have said what she said," I admit. "I'm sorry she said it."

She reaches for my face to move it off of her stomach so that I'm looking up at her from my position. "Stop," she says. "I know the truth, Thomas. I know we're more than what she said we are."

I push myself up from the lounge chair and my body moves quickly to hover over her. Her head tips up so she can maintain eye contact with me. Her hands cup my face and my lips hover over hers as my eyes bounce between hers. I can feel her breath on my lips and my breath catches as I feel the urge to say those three little words.

"Thomas," she whispers against my lips.

"Yes, Sunshine." My voice breaks as it comes out.

"I—" she stutters, eyes burning a fire through me. "I want you."

My lips move so close to hers that not even a grain of rice can fit between them. "What do you want, baby?" I whisper against them.

"All of you."

My lips crash to hers. My tongue rips through her lips, parting them so I can taste her. The faintest taste of tequila touches my lips. She moans into me as her arms wrap quickly around my neck, pulling me closer to her. My body lowers down until we're fused together, and I melt into her kiss. I take her bottom lip between my teeth as the air gets trapped in her lungs.

I pull my head back slightly so I can take her all in. She has the sexiest smile plastered on her face. It's a look that says she wants me and *fuck,* if that doesn't make my dick rock hard.

"How soaked are your panties right now, Sunshine?"

"I'm not wearing any panties, Mr. Ford."

FUCK. ME.

"You're going to be the death of me, baby," I groan as I lower my body, so my head rests between her thighs. She's wearing nothing but an oversized t-shirt. Ready for me. She adjusts herself as she opens her legs wider for me and I lower my mouth to her exposed pussy. "Fuck me, Sunshine. I can even see how wet you are. You're fucking dripping for my cock. Can you be a good girl and stay quiet, so the entire house doesn't hear you?"

She nods and bites her bottom lip.

"Thomas," she moans. "Please."

"You're going to get my cock, baby. I promise," I whisper

against her wet pussy. "But I didn't get any cake tonight. And I am craving something sweet right now."

She nods and bites her bottom lip.

Immediately, my tongue swipes through her and finds her swollen clit. She moans and arches her back, which forces her legs to open even wider as her hips buck into my face. My tongue continues to work through her as I build her up closer and closer to her release.

I can feel she's on the verge of coming from just my mouth so I pull my head away and her head snaps down to me while I look up at her with my mouth still hovering close to her pussy. "Thomas," she groans in frustration.

"Don't worry, baby." I smirk up at her. "I've got you. But you're not coming yet."

"What?" she pants. "Why not?"

"Because the only place I want you coming is on my cock." I pull myself out from between her legs and move my body on top of hers. My mouth crashes to hers and she opens her mouth for me to swipe my tongue on hers to taste herself on my lips. I pull back. "How good do you taste on my lips?" Her eyes close as she moans against my lips again.

Her hands pull at my shirt telling me she wants it off. With one hand, I reach the collar behind me and pull it off. My thumb hooks into the waistband of my pants and with one swift move, they are off.

Excitement covers her face as I grip the base of my cock and line it up with her entrance. She's already soaked for me, so it slides in effortlessly. I slowly press my cock to the hilt until it completely disappears inside of her pussy.

"Thomas," she breathes out as her head falls back and her back arches off the lounge chair.

"You're so fucking tight. Fucking so perfect," I say as I throw my head back. Hands gripping her hips as I slowly move in and out of her. "You take my cock so well, baby."

"More," she moans. "I need more."

I pick up my speed, pounding her with my grip tight on her hips. I can sense she's getting closer and closer to her orgasm because I hear a string of curses coming out of her mouth between her moans. The walls of her pussy are squeezing my dick and I'm on the verge of my release.

"This pussy was made for me. This is mine, baby," I hiss. "Fucking mine."

"It's yours, Thomas," she moans. "I'm all yours."

Her words send me over the edge, I lean down over top of her. She tips her head to the side to allow my lips to find her neck while my cock stays buried deep inside of her. "Come for me, baby," I say against the pounding rhythm of her heartbeat against my lips.

"Fuckkkkk," she moans. "I'm coming!"

"Fuck yes, you are." I pump harder as an orgasm hits her. Her pussy milking me right into my own release. "I'm coming too, baby."

"Yes!" she screams over and over again.

I release everything I have into her right before I fall on top of her. Our breaths are wild and uneven as we come down from the high. She lets out a small giggle under my body as I pick up my weight from on top of her. "I'm sorry." I laugh back. "I got a little carried away."

"That was fucking hot," she says as she brushes her hair away from her face. "I wonder if anyone heard us out here."

"I doubt it." I laugh. "The girls are drunk and singing *Breakfast at Tiffany's* downstairs."

"Of course they are," she rolls her eyes.

I laugh with her as I pull up my sweatpants. "Come on." I wave my hand to bring her inside the room with me. "Let me get you washed up."

"Such a gentleman." She smiles before she reaches up to press a quick kiss to my lips before both of us retreat for the bathroom.

When we enter the bathroom, I turn on the water for the

bathtub. It's not as big as the one in the penthouse but it does the trick. She throws in some lavender bubbles and sinks into the tub. I kneel beside the tub and pick up the sponge to wash her back.

"Aren't you going to join me?"

I don't respond, I just stand to pull my sweatpants off, and she leans forward to allow me to step in behind her. I sink into the hot water, and she nestles herself between my legs causing my dick to stir again.

"Peyton," I hiss into her ear. "You're going to make me hard again."

"Oops." She giggles. "Did I do that?"

I wrap my arms around her to pull her back to my chest. She tips her head back to rest her head on my shoulder. I press a delicate kiss to her temple, and she breathes a relaxing sigh as she settles perfectly between my legs.

I pick up the sponge and begin to wash her arms and her chest. "Mmm," she sighs. "That feels so good. We should do this in my bathtub when we get back. It's bigger and has the best views."

"The view is nice," I reply to her. Except I don't mean out the windows. I know what the city looks like, but nothing compares to the beauty of her soaking in the bubbles in that tub.

We spend a few more minutes in silence as I continue to wash her. "Can I ask you something?" I say, breaking the silence.

"Of course," she says.

"In two weeks, I have a holiday charity event I need to attend on behalf of Ford Investments," I pause and swallow the lump in my throat. "And I need a date."

"Oh," she says. It comes out as a disappointed sigh.

"Sunshine," I say as I bring my lips to the hollow of her neck. "I want you to be my date."

She pulls away from me in the tub and does a weird spin move so that she's now facing me in the tub. "Are you sure? I won't be mad if you have to bring—"

"Stop." I hold up a finger to her lips to stop the nonsense coming out of her mouth. I can't help but smile at how fucking cute she is. "If it's not obvious by now, you're the only one I want, Peyton."

Her cheeks turn pink at the admission, and she tucks a strand of hair behind her ear. "I don't know, Thomas. I don't own any fancy dresses anymore."

"I'll buy you one."

"I can't ask you—"

"I want to," I say, cutting her off. "Don't worry about the dress or any of those details. The dress, the shoes, the hair, and makeup. I'll take care of all of it." I can sense her starting to deny me again when she begins to shake her head, so I beat her to it. "Don't tell me I can't, Peyton. I want to do this for you because there's no one else in the world I want on my arm as I walk into that event, but you."

She's deep in thought for a brief moment before she sits up in the tub and moves to straddle me. Both of her legs on each side of my hips and she lowers herself so she's now sitting directly on my dick.

"Peyton—" I growl.

"Yes, Thomas," she finally says. "I'll go with you as your date."

I wrap my arms around her waist and my lips crash into hers at the same time a thought crosses my mind.

I guess I have to fire the nanny.

Which means I need a new plan in place.

Because I'm so fucking in love with Peyton.

CHAPTER TWENTY-EIGHT
Peyton

The past week has been nothing short of a fairytale. Ever since we got home from the beach house, there has been a change in Thomas. I mean, don't get me wrong, the guy is swoony as fuck. He has been since the day I met him. He *knows* how to sweep a woman off her feet. But we've gotten… closer? I'm not even sure how to classify what this is.

Are we dating? Officially?

Are we just sleeping together?

He's been deep inside me a minimum of twice a day since being home, and never going a day without *having dessert*. That's what he calls it. He's constantly telling me that he's got a sweet tooth and the taste of me is the only thing that can satisfy it.

However, we haven't spoken about what *this* is between us. I'm anxious to ask. This weekend is the gala, though. And I made the decision a couple of days ago that I would see what happens this weekend and then finally bring up the elephant in the room.

"Margaritas?" Kali asks, cutting my thoughts and forgetting we're at Old Jose for our taco Tuesday dinner meet up.

"Yes," Avery and I say in unison.

We spend the next half hour making small talk. We chat

about how nice it was to get away for the weekend and how great it was to see Gigi so happy. Kali tells us about her job and how it's stressing her out and she might consider a change in careers. To what? She has no idea. It's finally my turn to tell them what's going on, despite not having a damn clue what's going on myself.

"Soo," I draw out with a sigh. "I have an event this weekend." I bounce my eyes between my two friends sitting across the table from me. Their faces are masked with confusion. "A charity event," I add. Avery's eyebrows pinch together, and Kali tips her head to the side. Both remain silent as they wait for me to continue. "With Thomas." I pinch my lips together after his name leaves my mouth. I reach for my margarita to take a long sip.

"Okay?" Kali questions.

"Spill, bitch," Avery says as she sits back in her chair and crosses her arms over her chest.

"Well," I start, but pause because I'm unsure of how to proceed. "Thomas asked me to go with him," I say over the brim of my drink glass. My eyes bounce between both of them. "As his date."

They both look from me to each other. Silence stretches over the table and I'm not sure how to take it.

"Can you two say something?" I plea.

"What do you expect us to say?" Kali says with a small chuckle.

"We were waiting for this," Avery adds.

"What?" I stammer.

"Girl, we saw how Daddy was looking at you at the beach house." Avery laughs. "Like he couldn't wait to get you upstairs and fuck you into next year."

"He… no… I mean." My words fumble as I try to defend myself.

"Don't bother trying to hide it," Kali says. "The man is crazy about you. That much is obvious." She rolls her eyes.

"And we've noticed a change in you," Avery cuts in. "You have been straight up glowing the last couple of weeks. Only one thing can make you glow the way you have been glowing." She wiggles her eyebrows and I roll my eyes.

"You're annoying." I laugh at her.

"But I'm not wrong." She shrugs her shoulders. "So, tell us more."

"I am not going into details about my sex life," I snort.

"At least there's a sex life for you to even get into," Kali laughs. "We don't want to know the details, but we want to know the details. If you're picking up what I'm putting down."

"No, I want allllll the dirty details." Avery laughs loudly.

"Guys, I don't know." I tuck a small strand of hair behind my ear, all of sudden feeling shy. "I don't know what we are. We haven't discussed anything. I want to believe that we're more. I *feel* like we're more. But am I just someone that's convenient for him since I live there?"

"Girl," Kali stops me. "He asked you to this event, didn't he?"

"Yeah," I draw out.

"Well." She opens her arms as if to be like *duh*. "He must see this as something more."

"There's more to factor into this, Kali. He's a dad. He has a son," I let out a long sigh. "And he doesn't do relationships. He made that very clear."

"Neither do you," Avery snaps. "And now here we are, on taco Tuesday, talking about how head over heels you are for your boss."

"I am not," I defend myself.

"Stop playing, girl." Kali rolls her eyes. "You have feelings for him. Strong ones. You can't hide them from me, from us. I can see it. I see how you two interact. I see your cheeks flush when he's near you. I see the smile he puts on your face. I see how much you love and care about James. I also see..." she pauses and takes a deep breath. Releasing the breath before she continues, "You've never been like this with a man before. You're so confident and bold. When I say you're glowing, Pey, I mean it. You've always been a ray of sunshine in our eyes. But Thomas brought out an even brighter you. One for the whole world to finally fucking see. How can't you see that?"

My chest aches at her words. She's not wrong. Thomas *has* brought out a new side of me that I have never known before. Confidence in every aspect of my life. From the bedroom, to walking down the street.

There's no doubt in my mind that I am in love with Thomas Ford.

Fuck.

"I-I," I stutter. "I'm in love with him."

Kali chuckles in her seat, "The first step is always admitting it, babe."

"What do I do?" My questioning eyes bounce between the two of them.

"You know what you have to do," Kali says. "You have to tell him."

"You can't continue to be his nanny if you guys are in a relationship," Avery adds.

"I think that's what's making my brain go haywire." I shake my head and my head falls to my hands. "I won't have a job. What the fuck will I do? And then the next question, do I continue to just live there? Like… that's pretty fast."

"These are all valid questions," my responsible friend, Kali, adds. "I think you need to have a sit down and have a talk with him, honestly."

"But I think you should wait until after the gala," Avery cuts her off.

"Why?" My head tips to the side in question. In my head, isn't it better to get this conversation done and over with sooner, rather than later?

"Because we have to get you ready for a gala," Avery gleams.

"I don't understand," I say as confusion crosses my features.

"Ohhhh," Kali giggles. "I see where this is going." She takes a sip of her margarita with a devious smile plastered on her face. These fucking two. I can't. "Yup, we have to get you ready for a gala."

"Someone, please fucking explain," I snap.

"Listen," Avery continues her laughing fit. "You need to use this event to your advantage. Let's show him how irresistible you are."

"So irresistible," Kali chirps.

"Let's show him your best fucking features," Avery continues.

"The best," Kali echoes again.

"Let's make him beg you to stay in his life."

"Beg."

"Kali," I snap. "I get it. I get it."

"I just wanted to add to the dramatics," Kali laughs.

"So dramatic," I mock her the way she echoed Avery's words before.

Avery and Kali both laugh and pull their phones from their purses. Typing away as I continue to stare at them. "This good?" Kali asks Avery. "Yeah, that's the one. How's this?" Avery adds. They are having a conversation with themselves. Showing each other things on their phones and scheming away.

"Hello." I wave my hands in their faces. "I'm still sitting here."

"Okay, we're all set." Kali smiles at me.

"And what are we all set with?"

"You're getting beautified for this, babe," Avery adds.

Nerves run through me at what these two just planned in the span of three minutes sitting here on their phones. But excitement also mixes with that feeling.

I want Thomas. I really do.

After this weekend, I fully plan to hand in my resignation papers and terminate myself as James' nanny.

Because the truth is, I will always want more.

CHAPTER TWENTY-NINE
Thomas

I'm sitting at my desk at work, trying my hardest to focus on my work today. However, the only thoughts that consume my mind lately are those of Peyton. This week has been nothing short of amazing. I was inside her no less than two times a day because I can't seem to stay away from her.

I have become an addict. I am addicted to everything about her.

Not just sex but being around her. Just wanting her somewhere near me. I want her in my bed every night and I want to wake up to her hair splaying across my chest with her body pressed up against my side. I want her arms wrapped around my body every morning when I kiss her forehead goodbye before I leave for the office. I want to see her launching off the couch into my arms when I step through the elevators coming home from work.

Fuck.

Is this what being in love feels like?

If it is, I can confidently say that I never want to be without it.

I can also confidently say that Peyton has changed me. I like who I am these days. I'm a different man, inside and out. I walk around with a smile on my face, and I notice I'm less aggravated than normal.

There's a soft knock on the door, pulling from my constant thoughts about Peyton. "Come in," I shout at the same time my eyes travel to the door.

"Hi, Tommy." Emiline smiles.

"Hey, Em." I smile back. "To what do I owe this visit?"

"Can't a girl just come and bring her brother some lunch?" she scoffs as she places her hands on her hips.

"I mean," I say as I shrug my shoulders. "I guess you can. Come sit." See? The old me would have been so annoyed that she showed up unannounced. Is my family seeing the change too?

"How's everything going?" she asks as she takes the seat across from my desk. She pulls out two small takeout containers and I can tell its sushi.

"It's going," I say as I take the container that she's offering me. "How about you? How are classes going?"

"Ugh," she groans. "Don't get me started or I will start crying. I have never been so stressed in my life. I thought college was hard, but nothing in the world could prepare you for nursing school. I want to die."

"That bad, huh?" I ask, taking a bite of sushi.

"Tommy," she huffs. "Pretend you have a question that asks, 'What color is the fruit?' and it's a picture of an orange. The choices are A. Orange. B. Orange. C. Purple. D. Do not resuscitate."

"Ouch," I chuckle.

"Yeah, ouch my fucking head." She laughs. "The correct answer is B. Because I'm supposed to know that *that* orange is the color, not the fruit."

"Double ouch." I laugh.

"Plus, I ran into fucking Lincoln Log earlier today when I was leaving from my overnight shift in the Emergency Room when he was bringing in some early morning drunk."

"Logan?"

"Yes," she sighs. "He's been so fucking annoying since the beach house trip. I don't understand how he's so shocked that I've grown up. It's like he can't accept that I'm a 21-year-old now."

"You will always be a baby in our eyes, Em."

"I don't want to be a baby anymore," she huffs. "I hate that I took this new job as an aide in the Emergency room too. Because now I am constantly seeing him when he brings wackjobs in from the streets. Isn't he up for a promotion soon to get off the streets?"

"I think so." I shrug my shoulders. "But you're not a baby, Em. I'm proud of the woman you have grown up to be. I'm proud of you for advancing your career and taking a step in the right direction to achieve your dream of becoming a nurse."

"Thank you, Tommy." She smiles at me. "Please tell Logan that. If I have to see him one more time at work with a scowl on his face and a look like he hates me, I might scream."

"I'll talk to him and ask him to back off."

"Thank you. So now you understand why I needed some sushi and a quick visit to see you," she huffs as she sinks into the chair.

"I can see that," I say in response.

"How's Peyton?" she asks with wiggled eyebrows.

"What do you mean by that?"

"Listen," she chuckles. "I might not know the difference between orange the fruit and orange the color spelled on paper, but I am not dumb enough to not see that you're in love with her."

"I…" I pause as I rake my hand through my hair. "What do you mean?"

"I know this is probably a new feeling for you, big bro." She laughs. "But that pounding in your chest, the sweaty palms, the constant thoughts of her and always wanting to be near her," she pauses and gives me a soft smile. "And the smile that reaches your eyes when you see her. That's love, Tommy."

I return her smile as silence stretches between us. I already had a feeling I was in love with Peyton. Despite not having a clue what it is. I mean, don't get me wrong, I know what love is. I love James more than life itself. I would jump in front of a bullet for him and do whatever I needed to do to protect and care for him. I would do the same for my family. I love them and I have for my entire life.

But Peyton is a whole new kind of love I have never known or felt before. It's crazy how someone who was once a stranger to me, is now someone I can't picture my life without.

"Thanks, Em." I smile at her.

"That's what I'm here for." She perks up. "Have you told her?"

"No," I admit. "I'm taking her to the charity event this weekend, though, as my date."

"Ohhh, totally swoon," she says as she bats her eyelashes.

"Oh stop," I laugh. "I have my assistant, Ruth, picking out a dress for her."

"No," she stops me.

"No?"

"No, you have to let her pick it out." She sighs in her seat. "From a woman's point of view here, it's easier to go to an event where you won't know anyone if you feel comfortable in what you're wearing. I mean, Peyton seems confident. Much more confident than the first day I met her, might I add. But something tells me, she's the type who would want to pick out a nice dress to feel comfortable in."

"You think?"

"I know, Tommy. It would be romantic if you were picking it out, but Ruth… it loses the sentiment."

I run my hand through my hair again. She's got a good point. I want Peyton to feel comfortable. I think back to that first night I met her all those years ago. She was shy and timid and might have even mentioned that she doesn't go to those types of events often.

I'm *asking* her to this event, after all. It's only right we go all out.

I quickly pull my phone from my pocket to shoot her a text.

> I need you to do me a favor.

Yes, sir.

I swear to God, I am going to take her over my knee for using that tone via text message with me.

> Are you being sassy, Ms. Kelly?

Me? Never. *wink face emoji*

What favor do you need?

> Go into my office. Top drawer on the right. There's a small box that looks like a safe. I need you to go in and grab a card out for me. It's all black. Matte black.

> Code to the safe is 0932.

There's a pause in her texting. I could have just called her, but I'm having lunch with my sister. Nerves dance in my belly as I continue to take a bite of the sushi that she brought me. Emiline is texting away on her phone.

Ok. Got it.

> Great. I need you to go buy yourself a dress for the charity event.

A bubble pops up as if she's texting but then it disappears. Seconds later, my phone rings and I see her name across the screen. "It's Peyton," I tell Emiline.

"I have to get back home to study anyway," she says. "Tell

Peyton I say hi." And then she's out the door, knowing I need this privacy.

"Hello?"

"Thomas," she hoarsely whispers in my ear.

"Peyton," I sigh back. The way she fucking says my name like that can bring me to my knees.

"I can't ask you to buy me a dress," she continues. "I can do it myself."

"I won't take no for an answer, Sunshine." I smile through the phone even though she can't see it. "I asked you to this event. I want you to find something you like."

"I-I," she pauses. "Thank you. I don't know what to say."

"Just tell me..." I pause. I don't know what I want her to tell me. I was just on the verge of asking her to tell me she loves me. I can't do that right now over the phone. I need to see her face and look into her eyes when I say it for the first time to her.

"I know, Thomas." She sighs. "I know."

Fuck, she knows. She has to know that I am head over heels in love with her. She has to know I would do anything for her. I would give her everything I fucking own to make her happy. I hope she knows that.

"Just tell me you won't settle on the dress," I continue. "That card has no limit. Head to Sacks Fifth, if you need to."

I hear an audible gasp on the other end as if she is shocked to hear that.

"And Peyton?"

"Yes?"

"If the shoes aren't red on the bottom, then I don't want to see them on your feet."

———

"You're fucking chipper today." Logan smirks my way.

"And you're fucking annoying," I snap back.

I decided to meet Marc and Logan at Moores for our

Wednesday drinks for the first time in a few weeks. Admittedly, I haven't had the desire to go out for drinks. I would rather be home with my face between Peyton's legs. Tastes way better than whiskey ever will.

"Leave him alone, Logan. He's getting pussy regularly now." Marc laughs.

"No shit." Logan smirks. "That a boy. Let me guess, hot nanny?"

"Call her a hot nanny one more time," I snap my gaze to him as I give him a warning glare.

"Ohh, sensitive subject." He throws his hands up defensively. "So, there's more there than her being just a nanny, I presume?"

"I, uhh…" I stutter as I swipe my hands down my face. I have to tell them about her. How I feel and how she's now going to come to this event with me as more than just a nanny. "She's coming to the charity event with me," I pause. "As my date."

Marc's eyes go wide, but then quickly morph into a smile.

"Bout time," Marc says over the brim of his glass.

"Yea," I reply, doing the same with my glass of whiskey.

"So, this is a thing with her?" Logan laughs.

"I don't know what we are," I admit. "But if this is going to be a *thing*, then I am going to need to fire her."

"Fuck," Marc sighs from his seat.

"But…" I pause. My eyes darting between the two of them. "I have a plan."

"Can't wait to hear this," Logan scoffs.

"You know that vacant building on the corner of 67th and Columbus? That has been empty for a hot minute?"

"Yeah," Marc says. "The one we can't sell for shit. I don't understand why. It's a great location."

"Yeah, agreed. Well." I clear my throat. "I'm buying it."

"What the fuck are you going to do with that hole in the wall?" Logan asks.

"I'm going to turn it into a daycare center for Peyton to run."

"Oh." Marc's eyes widen. "Wow. That's uh…"

"She's going to need a job," I cut off his thoughts. "I'm probably going to have to fire her. She can't be James' nanny when I'm in a relationship with her. I can't pay her to live with me if I'm in love with her. I have to at least offer a backup plan for—"

Their stares cut off my train of thought. Marc's eyes are wide, and I hear Logan choke on his whiskey.

"Wipe those fucking looks off your faces."

"You, uh…" Marc fumbles over his words. "You love her?"

That makes sense as to why they have the look of shock on their face. You would think I just told two young children that Santa isn't real. I mean he is. Everyone knows that. Wink wink.

"Never thought I would see the day, Tommy boy." Logan smiles ear to ear. "Tommy finally found the one."

"I think I did."

"I know you did," Marc adds. "Have you told her?"

"No."

Marc sighs and runs his hands down his face, rubbing the scruff on his beard a second longer, as if he's deep in thought. "Listen, I'm going to tell you something and you have to listen."

"Oh boy," Logan sits back in his seat and crosses his arms over his chest.

"And you will shut the fuck up," Marc snaps at him. "Don't you have to go to the bar for your next pick up?"

"You know I don't pick up here, ass hat."

"Anyway." Marc shakes his head. "Listen, I love you, Tommy. You don't have to say it back and I know you never will because you're you. With that being said, you're excellent at *showing* those you love that you love them. I have no doubt that you have shown Peyton that and she has an idea of how you feel. But women need to hear it, too. Have you thought about telling her?"

"Yeah," I admit softly. Tilting my head towards the table and swirling the ice in my glass around. "I just don't know how."

"It goes like this," Logan chimes in. "I. Love. You. It's easy."

"I haven't heard you ever tell someone you love them before," I snap back. "I think you're incapable of it, too."

"It's not that I'm incapable." He laughs. "It's just that I have no desire for that life. You will never catch me tied down. Plus, my line of work is dangerous. I worry about protecting myself enough and I don't need to worry about not coming home to a family because some bastard shot me square in the chest."

"Logan," I pause. "I'll tell you. There is no greater feeling in the world than loving someone the way I love Peyton. She's flipped my world around for the better," I run my hands down my dress slacks as I feel sweaty palms coming on. "I can't imagine my life without her anymore."

"That." Marc snaps his fingers together and then points it at me. "Make sure you tell her that. We're making progress, big bro."

I smile up at him over the brim of my whiskey, "Thank you, Marc."

"No problem," he sits up straighter in his seat. "Now that we have figured out your problem... help me with mine."

"What do you need?"

"I need a date for the charity event this weekend," he says as he rolls his eyes. "The owner of the agency, Bill, is going to be there. He wants to retire, and I am in the running to take over the entire agency."

"Wow, that's awesome, Marc."

"It is." He nods. "Except it's between me and some fuck twit from another office across town named Todd. Fucking Todd."

"Ooof," Logan adds. "Fucking Todds."

"Exactly." Marc laughs. "Bill says I have it in the bag. His only hesitation is that he wants a family man to take over ownership of the agency. I don't exactly have a wife. Or a girlfriend, for that matter."

"That does sound like a problem." I nod.

"It is. I guess I need someone to come with me as my date

and I..." he pauses, cringing at his own words. "Be my fake fiancé, maybe?"

"Shut up." I laugh harder than I have laughed in so long. "What the fuck did you tell Bill?"

He shakes his head in disgust. "I might have told him that I have a fiancé. At the time, I didn't realize I would have such a hard time finding someone to play the role with me."

"Hey," Logan sits up straight in his chair and claps his hands together. "What if you asked one of Peyton's friends?"

"That's a great idea." I clap my hands together. "You and Avery seem to get along nicely?"

"That's a joke, right?" he scoffs. "She's a fucking wrecking ball. You've seen her drunk. Plus, she fucking works for me now. That's a fucking disaster waiting to happen."

"It might be." I shrug my shoulders. "But do you have any better ideas?"

Marc runs his hands through his hair and then immediately pounds his glass of whiskey, drinking it in one big gulp. "Fuck."

CHAPTER THIRTY
Peyton

It's the day before the charity event and I have successfully found the perfect dress and shoes to go with it. Every part of me hated buying both items because I am almost positive that it costs more than I have made in the last few months, even with my ridiculous wage working for Thomas.

Guilt creeps up as I stare down at my bags in the coffee shop with the girls.

The dress is perfect, though. I went with a long sleeve, floor length black gown. The dress has an A-line frame with a plunging V-neckline. It's so deep that I can't wear a bra with it, but the dress has built-ins. Avery insisted I get this one because she loved the look of my long legs with the high slit up the side of the dress.

Everything about this dress made me feel so incredibly sexy when I had it on in the dressing room. At the next store we went to, I was able to find the most perfect red bottom, black strapless heels. Surprisingly comfortable and very easy to walk in.

The girls treated me to a spa day to prepare myself for tomorrow. We got facials, manicures, and pedicures. Then we went to a salon, and we all got our hair done. I didn't change anything to the color because I love my golden locks and I feel like they make me, me. But I did get a little trim and added some layers to it. It was probably the best blow out I have ever had in my life too. I truly feel like a new woman.

"One last stop," Kali says, clicking away on her phone.

"What else could we possibly do?" I ask. "We got facials, manicures and our hair done. That seems like everything on our checklist."

"That's just the checklist we gave you." Avery smirks, also clicking away on her phone.

"What the fuck else is there?"

"We're going for a vajacial," Avery smiles from her phone.

"A vaj—" I stutter. "A what?"

"A vajacial." Avery laughs. "You know, like a facial for your vajayjay."

"This cannot fucking be a thing."

"It is," Kali adds. "It feels fucking amazing."

"You've had one of these vagina facials too?" I ask in straight horror. The thought of all of this sounds like a lot. The fact that both of them seem to have had it done before and I have never even heard of it, blows my mind.

"We both have," Avery cuts in. "It's a quick fifteen-minute thing. In and out like trout. They put on some great lotion and a little steam—"

"Steam?" I ask, horrified. "On my pussy?"

"Oh, yes. Girl, yes." Avery continues laughing. "It turns you into a whole new woman down there. Little rip rip and you have the softest kitty in the city for like a month."

"This can't be a real thing."

"You're gonna become addicted." Kali chuckles.

"I don't see how I ever will. This sounds absolutely horrible."

"You will," Avery affirms. "First is the worst, but after a few, you're basically a professional. You will look at yourself differently down there."

My fingertips find my temples as I begin to rub small circles. "I think I'm in an alternate universe."

"Come on," Kali says, standing from her seat. "The Uber is here to take us there."

Words don't come out of my mouth as I get up to follow them, hoping that maybe I just fell asleep and am dreaming that these two are taking me to get my pussy waxed right now. No, not waxing. A fucking vajacial.

An hour later, we walked out of the tiny salon feeling slightly embarrassed but also rejuvenated. I have never, in my life, even had a simple waxing done. I have gotten my eyebrows done here and there, but that is a luxury for me. However, this… feels incredible. I sort of want to do this often.

"Well," Avery asks.

"It wasn't terrible." I shrug with a smirk.

"Get the fuck out," Avery laughs loudly. "You know you have the softest kitty right now and are absolutely loving it. Thomas is going to die when he sees it."

That thought didn't even cross my mind. Of course he's going to see it. He's going to see it up close and personal. The thought sends shivers down my spine and butterflies swarm in my belly with anticipation. God, just the thought of him drives me absolutely wild.

Avery's phone ringing interrupts all the dirty thoughts I have of seeing Thomas later today.

"Hello?" she says into the phone. "Marc?" All of us look around to each other wondering why Marc is calling her on her day off. She takes a few steps away from us to have a conversation with him. She's deep in conversation with him when a few minutes later we hear her curse under her breath. "No, I will not be your fake fucking fiancé. Are you drunk?" Kali and I gasp as she takes a long pause to listen to what he's saying. "You fucking owe me the biggest raise of my life, Marcus." And she hangs up on him abruptly before she glances at Kali and me. We stand there still as a board, eyes wide and jaws probably on the concrete.

"Looks like I'm coming to this shindig."

———

A knock on my door wakes me up from a deep sleep. I pull the covers off of my head and begin to rub my eyes as I try to adjust them to the light shining through the windows. I reach over the nightstand to light up my phone and see the time says 7:10 in the morning. I panic for a split second, thinking that I am late for work with James, but then I remember that he's with Emiline. Thomas worked late last night trying to finalize some project that he and Marc are working on. I ended up falling asleep in my own bed reading a book. I groan as my head falls back to the pillow. "It's fucking Saturday," I mumble under my breath.

Another knock sounds at the door and I groan again in frustration as I throw the blankets off me, walk over to the door and swing it open.

My breath gets trapped in my lungs as I stare at Thomas leaning against the door. One hand rests on the top door frame and the other is tucked into the pocket of his blue suit pants. His gaze travels from the floor, up my body to my eyes.

I quickly run my fingers through my hair that probably looks like a bird's nest sitting on top of my head and I realize I'm only wearing a thin white tank top and a pair of panties.

"Well." Thomas eyes me up and down while the corner of his lips pull up into a grin. "Can't say I expected you to answer the door like this."

"Can't say I expected to be woken up before 8am on a Saturday."

Thomas quickly pushes off the door frame and steps into my room, swinging the door shut behind him loud enough to rattle the walls. He spins me around quickly and my back crashes to the door and his arms cage me in. He leans in close and trails his nose from my collar bone up my neck before he lands on my ear. "What did I say about the back talk, Sunshine?"

"I can't quite remember." I smirk. "Remind me?"

A rumble erupts from deep in his chest at the same time his

fingers find the hem of my panties. "I missed you last night. You looked comfortable when I got home and didn't want to wake you up." I feel his breath on the pulse pounding in my neck and my head instinctively tilts up for him. In one quick pull, he rips my panties off. The delicate fabric falls to the floor and his hand comes back to my center.

"What's this?" He smirks. His eyes are now fixed on mine as his fingers explore the new soft landing of my pussy.

"I got a..." I stutter. "Kali and Avery took me for a waxing."

"So. Fucking. Sexy." He rasps as his fingers dip into my pussy in one swift move. "Already wet for me, baby?"

"Always," I pant. "Always ready for you."

His hands leave my pussy, and he unbuttons his work pants to push them to the ground. "I have to go to the office for a few hours today to finish this deal." He pushes his boxer briefs down just as quickly as the words leave his mouth. "But I can't go another minute without my cock being inside your tight, wet pussy." His hand fists his cock and gives it a few strokes. It's hard as steel within minutes of being this close to me. I was soaked the second I opened the door and saw him standing there, so I can't judge the man.

My hand reaches down to take over and stroke him a few times.

"Then we better make it quick, Mr. Ford," I add. I push myself off the wall to lean into him and press a kiss to his lips. It's quick, but when I begin to pull away, he pushes me backwards with urgency. My back is up against the wall again as his one hand finds the back of my head and lifts it just the right amount to deepen our kiss while his other hand reaches behind my lower back. My hands grip his hard biceps and pull him closer to me. We couldn't get any closer if we tried as our bodies melt together.

My legs instinctively lift to wrap around his waist, and he lifts me up like a feather. I reach down to line his hard cock up to my center and with one plunge, he's deep inside of me.

"Fuck, I love when you call me that," he growls as he begins to thrust in and out of me. "I can never get enough of this pussy, Peyton."

My hands are wrapped around his neck as I tighten my legs around him and he thrusts harder and harder. "Thomas," I choke out as he fucks me hard against the wall. "Oh my God."

"I'm not going to work until you come on my dick a minimum of two times, baby."

"Fuckkk," I draw out as he picks up the pace. My hands claw at his back still covered by his suit jacket. His words are causing me to inch closer and closer to my orgasm. I never knew I was someone who likes the dirty talk, but coming from Thomas, I fucking love it. "I'm going to come."

"Yes, you fucking are," he growls. "Now."

At his words, my orgasm courses through my body. My legs begin to shake uncontrollably and I'm thankful that he's holding me up right now, because if he wasn't, I would, without a doubt, melt into a puddle on the floor. A string of curse words comes out of me, and I scream his name over and over again.

Once I come down from that, he places me on the ground. "Turn around. Hands on the wall." I do as he demands. I place my hands on the wall and spread my legs to allow him access from behind. "That's my girl," he praises before he drives into me quickly from behind.

His hands grip my shoulders as his hips pick up the pace, fucking me hard and raw from behind. There's something so animalistic about this right now. It's not a *want* to fuck me, it's a *need* to be inside of me. A need to feel me. To feel the closeness.

Giving him what he wants, I press my hips into him without warning and I hear him gasp before letting out a '*fuck*' under his breath. He stills his movements with his cock buried deep into my pussy. He's giving himself a minute, but I am using this time to drive him wild. I slowly grind my ass against him, not allowing him the time to regroup. "Baby," he hisses through gritted teeth. "You like my cock deep inside of you, huh?"

"Yes," I breathe out.

"Your pussy was fucking made for my cock, Peyton," he groans. "So soft. Velvet smooth. Perfect pink. Soaked, just for me."

"Thomas," I scream out. "Fuck me, please."

He grips my hips harder as he continues pounding me against the door. I scream out his name and a string of curse words as a second orgasm takes over every part of my body.

"Fuck, baby. I'm coming."

"Yes. Yes." I moan over and over again as his thrusts begin to slow while he pours himself into me. He slowly pulls himself out of me and I can feel our tangled mix of cum drip on my thigh. With a swipe of his finger, he brings it back up to swipe the wetness back over my clit. So fucking hot.

Our fast breaths are mingled together, and he doesn't hesitate to crash his lips into mine, not putting me down and not removing himself from deep inside of me as we both come down from our orgasms.

His kiss is deep and passionate, nothing like the quickie was. His kiss feels like a promise of more. Of him giving all of himself to me.

"Thomas," I murmur as I pull out of the kiss.

"I-I lo—" His words are cut off by the phone ringing in his pocket. "Fuck," he says under his breath as his forehead rests on my shoulder. Slowly he leans in to press another kiss to my lips and he brings me down so my feet meet the floor.

The phone stops ringing but he grabs it and checks the call. "Fuck," he grunts in annoyance. "I have to go, baby. I'm going to be late."

"But it's Saturday…"

"I know," he says. "I'm so sorry, but this deal I'm working on with Marc is blowing up in our face right now. I have to take care of it to make sure we get the property."

"O-okay," I say in a hoarse whisper, wrapping my arms around my waist.

"Baby." He smiles at me as he uses his pointer finger to delicately bring my chin up, which forces my gaze to be locked on his. "I will be home after we take care of this so we can go to the gala tonight." He pauses as his eyes bounce between mine. "And one more thing."

"Yeah?"

"A team is coming over for you around 10am."

"For what?"

"For you." He smiles.

"What do you mean?"

"Whatever you want, whatever you need, they are here for *you*," he replies as he pulls his pants up and begins to fix his belt. "Hair, makeup, and dressing. All of it. There will also be a jeweler coming over around 3pm for you to pick your accessories to go with your outfit," he continues as he adjusts his cufflinks. "I couldn't pick because I don't know what your dress looks like. So, pick whatever you'd like."

"Thomas," I gasp. "That's too much."

He fixes his last cufflink and smiles up at me before he walks over to me to tuck a strand of hair behind my ear and then landing on my neck to rub a thumb on my cheek. "You look thoroughly fucked, baby. I like this look on you."

"Thomas," I groan as I playfully swat at his arm. "Don't ignore my comment. It's too much and I can get ready myself. It's really okay."

"It's never too much for you, Sunshine."

CHAPTER THIRTY-ONE
Thomas

The meeting today left me in such a sour mood that I ended up staying at the office longer than planned. They fought us hard in negotiations because they wanted a deal that was almost half a million dollars less than what it's listed for. Marc knocked it out of the park with his fight back, though. In the end, we ended up getting it for what it was listed for, which made both Marc and I millions of dollars.

"Did you hear anything back about the deal on 67th and Columbus?" I ask Marc.

He nods as he takes a sip of whiskey from my office stash. "It's yours. We can even sign the papers today."

"That would be great." I smile. "I have to fire her when I get home. It's time to lock this down and make it official."

"You're really doing this, huh?"

I nod. "How can I not? I mean, come on, you're the relation-ship guru of the family. If it feels this good, then I shouldn't let it go right?"

"You're learning." He laughs. "Have you told her you love her yet?"

"No." I shake my head. "I almost did this morning, but my fucking phone interrupted us."

"Probably for the best. Don't tell her you love her after you unload inside of her, bro."

"How do you know I was even inside of her today?"

"I saw how you looked when you walked in this morning," he scoffs. "Practically fucking skipping in here."

"Touché." I nod and smile. "So is Avery coming with you tonight?"

He groans as he leans back on the couch. "Don't get me started. This is a fucking disaster waiting to happen."

"I'm sure it will all work out. Hopefully in your favor."

"Speak it into existence for me, bro." He rolls his eyes before he checks his watch. "I have to bounce. I have to stop at the jeweler."

"For what?"

"A ring." He shrugs his shoulders. "If she's going to play the role of my fake fiancé, I kind of have to buy her a ring."

I shake my head and laugh. "You're so fucked."

"You fucking think?" he curses as he walks out of my office.

The next few hours, I make myself busy getting caught up on emails. The last order of business was signing the deal for 67th and Columbus. I want to do this for Peyton because she deserves it. From the moment I first saw her with James at the park, I knew she was special and patient with kids. As time went on, I realized she is the perfect fit for a nanny role. I can't exactly fire her and let her go get another nanny job, though.

That's selfish of me, right?

But… another nannying job would mean her moving to live with another family and a job as a nanny provides very little time off. It's a job for a single woman, that's for sure. And after tonight, Peyton won't be a single woman.

This morning *I love you* almost slipped from my lips. Not that I'm second guessing myself, but I just want it to be the right time. She deserves the grand gesture, a room full of roses and everything life has to offer when those three little words escape my lips.

The contract for the deal was left untitled, something I was able to work my way around. I want this to fully be Peyton's project and help her fulfill her dream of owning a daycare center with whatever name she chooses for it.

After I signed the contract, I packed up to head to the florist to grab a bouquet of roses and head home. When I arrived at the penthouse, the team was scattered everywhere but Peyton was nowhere to be found. Asking one of the women who was messing with a steamer in the living room, it's confirmed she's in her room having her hair done. So I take that time to put the roses in a vase before I head to my room to get myself ready.

An hour later, I'm back downstairs and the team looks like they are packed up to head out.

"We're heading out, Mr. Ford," one of the men says.

I give him a tight nod. "Thank you."

"My pleasure." He nods back. "She's simply stunning. Her beautiful features made our jobs so easy to do."

"She really is," I reply.

"She's just putting her dress and shoes on," another woman comments. "She said she will be out soon, Mr. Ford."

"Thank you again. I will have my assistant take care of the bill."

"Thank you, Mr. Ford." They all say in unison.

They grab their belongings and scurry into the elevator, leaving me standing in the living room alone in silence. James has been at Emiline's since yesterday morning and is spending the whole weekend with her. I take another minute to adjust my cufflinks. I traded in my navy-blue suit for a black tuxedo. I had this custom made seven years ago and it's my go to suit for events like this.

I move to the bar cart sitting right outside of the kitchen and pour myself a glass of whiskey. I take a long sip of the brown liquid and then swirl it around the ice in the cup. Nerves are getting the best of me as I wait for her. As I wait for her to come out so I can fire her... and tell her I fucking love her.

At that moment, I feel her presence before I hear the faint sound of heels against the hardwood floor. I take one more sip of whiskey before I place it on the cart. I turn around and the second I do, my heart stops.

She's breathtaking.

Air is trapped in my lungs as I stand where my feet are planted. My mouth parts as I take her in. My eyes begin to scan her from top to bottom. She's wearing the most beautiful black gown with a neckline that dips well below her breasts, exposing the perfect cleavage line of her tits, which also shows me that she is not wearing a bra. *Fuck. Me.* My eyes continue to scan down her body and they land on the slit of her dress that exposes her long, slender legs. My tongue instinctively runs over my bottom lip as my eyes graze down to her heels. She's wearing black open toe shoes and I can see a mark of red on the edge of one of them.

Fucking red bottoms.

A grin forms on my face as my gaze travels back up her body until our eyes meet and I can see the smile on her face, too. Her hair is pulled up in a bun on top of her head. This isn't one of her usual messy buns, but a perfectly placed elegant bun with small wisps of hair to frame her face.

She's simply stunning.

I finally move my feet to walk towards her, my eyes never leaving hers. The closer I get, the more she has to tip her head up to keep eye contact with me. I take a closer look at her features, and I take note that she is barely wearing any makeup. She doesn't need it, honestly, because she is flawless without it. However, the makeup she is wearing is the perfect amount to bring out her long lashes and brighten her pink lips.

"Is this okay?" she asks as she breaks the silence.

"This is more than okay." I smile down at her. "Peyton, you are so fucking beautiful. You've taken my breath away."

She takes a small step back and gives a little twirl. "So, you like it?" She beams up at me as she finds her footing again and her hands land on my chest.

"This dress was made for you, baby."

"Thank you," she says as her cheeks turn the lightest shade of pink.

My hand finds the side of her face and my thumb lightly strokes her cheek bone. I can't take my eyes off of her. "Listen," I sigh. "I have to tell you something."

The smile vanishes from her face, only forcing my smile to grow.

I don't wait for her reply before I continue. "You're fired."

"What?" She gasps as she takes a step away from me and begins to shake her head. "What do you mean? Why? I can't be fired, Thomas. Did I do—"

I cut her off by stepping back into her space, wrapping my hands around the sides of her face, thumb resting on her jaw line and silencing her when my lips crash against hers. At first, she doesn't kiss me back but as I kiss her harder, she melts into me. There is no better feeling than kissing Peyton and feeling her body relax into me. Her arms wrap around my head, and she kisses me back with as much desire as I kiss her with.

After our moment, I pull away and she looks perfectly sated. Her lips are swollen from our kiss, and I am sure I am wearing some of her pink lipstick. I run my thumb across her bottom lip. "I can't date my son's nanny, Sunshine."

"So," she pauses to gather her thoughts. "Because I'm your date tonight? Do I get my job back tomorrow?"

She's so fucking cute when she's delusional.

"No." I shake my head.

"But, Thomas... I need this job."

"And I need you." She doesn't respond to my comment but her eyes snap back up to mine. "I need you, Peyton. I need you as more than just James' nanny. I want to make *us* official." She shivers. "I want you in my bed every fucking night with your legs tangled in mine and the heat of your body pressed against me. I want to wake up with my head between your legs for breakfast before breakfast," I chuckle. "And I..." Fuck, saying those words are hard.

"I know." She silences me with her finger pressed to my lips as if she can sense my nerves. "You don't have to say it, Thomas."

"Peyton," I drag her name out, and I'm sure she can now sense the desperation in my voice.

"I want all of those things too, Thomas."

"Tell me you mean that."

"I do." she nods her head. "I really do. I want you. I want it all with you." I answer her with a kiss, but she pulls away. "What am I going to do about work now?"

"About that." I run my hand through my hair. "I got you a parting gift."

"A parting gift?" She laughs. "Is this a '*hey, you're fired*' gift?"

"You could call it that." I laugh back. "I got you a building."

Her eyes widen at my admission. "What do you mean you got me a *building*?"

"Down the street is a vacant building. It's small, nothing crazy. But when I realized I had to fire you, I wanted to have a backup plan for you. So I bought you a building that you can convert into a daycare center, here in the city."

"W-wh—" she shakes her head. "No, you didn't."

"I did. You should know by now that I would give you the world if you asked for it, baby."

She steps closer to me and wraps her arms around my head, looking deep into my eyes and I finally see a smile form on her lips. I wrap my arms around her waist to hold her body close to mine. "Just you," she whispers. "I just want you."

"I'm all yours, baby." I press a kiss to her temple and step away. "Let's get out of here. We're going to be late."

"Are Marc and Avery riding with us?" she asks as she gathers her phone to tuck it into her small purse and the elegant floor length jacket she bought.

"Hell no. Can you imagine riding in the car with those two?"

I raise a questioning brow at her. "That's a fucking disaster waiting to happen."

"You're not wrong." She laughs. "I can't believe Avery even agreed to the deal. She's the least eligible person as a fake fiancé."

"Clearly Marc is desperate here." I laugh as we ride the elevator downstairs.

When we enter the lobby, Jim is standing there with a smile on his face. "Good evening, Mr. Ford." He nods his head to me, then turns his gaze to Peyton. He reaches out his hand and she places hers in his. "Good evening, Ms. Kelly. You look absolutely stunning tonight," he says before placing a light kiss to the back of her hand.

"Thank you, Jim," Peyton replies shyly.

"Jim," I say in a stern voice. "Did you just kiss my girlfriend's hand?"

His eyes widen as Peyton begins to chuckle.

"Oh stop it, Thomas."

I smile at Jim to reassure him that I am only joking, and he returns a soft grin back to me. "Thank you, Jim. For all you do."

"My pleasure, Mr. Ford." He nods. "It's a beautiful evening for this event."

"It is, isn't it?" I reply but my eyes are on her.

Only ever on her.

"Have a good night, Jim," Peyton says as we begin to walk outside.

Eddy is already parked there with the car, waiting for us. He opens the door and lets Peyton in first and then I round the car to get in next to her.

Once we are on the road, my eyes turn to Peyton sitting next to me. Her hands are in her lap and she's staring at the city lights. She's truly the most beautiful person I have ever met in my life. I briefly think back to what life was like before her. I can't imagine life without her anymore because this right here, right now, is all I ever want to know for the rest of my life.

My hand lands on her thigh and she snaps her head to look at me as if I startled her. Every single touch I have ever felt with her has been pure electric. From day one, until right now. I wonder if she feels it too.

"Are you excited for this?" she asks.

I shrug my shoulders. "These events are fun, but it usually ends up with a lot of crowd mingling. Many of my business associates will be there. Unfortunately, it ends up feeling like work."

"Well." She smiles. "When you need an escape from work, I will be there."

"Thank you again for coming tonight." My hand finds her bare leg as the slit opens when she makes the smallest move in her seat. "This dress." A low guttural growl leaves my chest.

"You like it?"

"I fucking love it," I reply as my hand slides higher up her thigh, brushing her skin. "Is this why you picked a dress with a slit like this, Sunshine? Did you want me to have easy access to you?"

"I might have."

"Eddy," I growl. "Privacy screen."

"You got it, boss."

The screen between the front and back seat goes up and my hand immediately travels higher up her thigh as Peyton's head falls back against the seat. When my hand reaches for her panties, I find nothing. "Peyton," I tease. "Are you not wearing panties?"

"No," she says as she shakes her head. "The lines showed through the dress."

"Fuck." I move quickly to kneel on the floor of the car. I twist her body so that one leg is propped on the seat and the other is on the floor. I spread her legs open in front of me. "I'm starving, baby."

I waste no time before my head dips under her dress and my tongue finds her clit. I lap her pussy hard and fast with my tongue before plunging a finger inside of her. I want this orgasm from her before we get there. There is nothing sexier than her falling apart in my hands.

"Oh my god," she murmurs under her breath.

"You don't have to be quiet, Sunshine."

"But…"

"Soundproof." I cut her off, my hot breath on her bare pussy. "Now fucking scream for me while I fuck you with my fingers. I want your cum on my tongue when we walk into this event."

"Thomas," she cries out. "Fuck."

I pump her hard with three fingers inside of her until she explodes and comes all over my tongue. Just the taste of her on my tongue has me ready to explode in my pants. I wasn't planning on fucking her back here, but I fucking need to be inside of her.

"That was so incredibly hot," she says, coming down from her orgasm.

"I'm not done," I hiss as I unbutton my pants and push them down.

Shock stretches across her face. "We can't do it here."

"Turn around," I demand. "I don't want to mess up your hair. I'm going to fuck you hard and fast, baby. You okay with that?"

"Oh my god," she pants. "Yes."

"I'm going to spend the whole night thinking about my cum dripping down your gorgeous legs as you walk around on my arm all night."

She turns around and lifts her dress until her entire ass is exposed to me. I give it a small slap and I hear a squeal come out of her. I line up my pulsing cock with her entrance and plunge deep inside of her until I'm lost in her.

I begin to move in and out of her and within seconds I feel like I'm going to come. She feels like heaven when I'm inside of her. Everything I have ever said before about having the same pussy for the rest of my life being stupid, has gone out the window. Because this, right here, I could never get enough of this.

"Thomas," she whimpers.

"Am I hurting you?"

"No. Fuck me, Thomas." Urgency laced in her words. "I want you to fuck me hard."

This fucking woman. With that, I thrust harder and deeper. My hands grip her hips hard as I drive myself into her over and over again.

"I'm going to come again," she gasps.

"That's it, baby. Squeeze my cock with this tight pussy," I hiss. "Fuck, you feel so damn good, baby. This pussy was fucking made for me. I can't get enough of it."

"You feel so good, Thomas," she screams. "Come with me, please."

A few more thrusts and we both crash together with our orgasms. I pour into her, and I can feel a mix of our cum dripping down my balls. Our breaths are fast and uneven as I fall over her back. She tips her head to the side, allowing me to press my lips to her pounding heart rate in her neck. I pepper kisses along the pulse and down to her shoulder before I pull myself out of her. I reach into the console to grab some paper towels to clean us up before we sit back down just in time to pull into the event.

I glance at her direction again and notice her fixing her dress again. "You look incredible tonight, baby."

She smirks back at me. "So do you, handsome."

There's no doubt in my mind that I've made the right decision with her.

Tonight, is going to be the best fucking night.

CHAPTER THIRTY-TWO
Peyton

"I am not cut out for this shit, Avery," I murmur into her ear as I scan the room and realize we are surrounded by very powerful people.

This is a holiday charity event and Thomas is here to represent his company. The event happens to be at the same place I came all those years ago, the Edison Ballroom. But tonight, is to raise money to purchase toys for the families who can't afford to give much this holiday season. When I used to live in New Jersey, I helped organize a much smaller fundraiser every year that was similar to this. Working in daycare, I've seen a lot of children go without for the holidays and I always wanted a way to help give back to that.

"Oh, would you relax?" Avery scoffs. "You're made for these events now. You're not the same shy and timid girl you were the last time you were at an event like this."

I don't reply, instead just simply nod and smile. Because she's not wrong. The last time I was ever at an event this fancy was the night I met Thomas. I feared social environments and the last thing I wanted to do was to be seen in an evening gown. Over the last several months, I feel like I have grown into my own person. The truth of the matter is, Thomas has a lot to do with that.

I know the whole, *you don't need a man to make you feel like that* bullshit. Trust me, I get that. But when you have someone in your life that makes you feel comfortable, confident, sexy and loved, you learn to feel it yourself.

For the first time in my life, I don't feel scared, either. My last few relationships, I was constantly worrying. I was always waiting for the nail in the coffin of the relationship and to be cheated on. I truly dated some pieces of shit. But Thomas has erased all those fears, though. There isn't a doubt in my mind that would lead me to believe that he would ever cheat on me. I don't feel like I'm waiting for a ball to drop and be led straight to heartache.

I've never felt more confident that he's it for me.

"Let's grab a drink," I say to her.

"You read my mind, sister." Avery chuckles.

We make our way over to the bar together. Thomas and Marc are mingling, with whom I can only assume are some powerful people in their line of business. I grab a tequila and lime and Avery gets a glass of champagne. I feel my phone buzz in my purse and when I pull it out I see an unknown number and silence it because it's probably a telemarketer trying to sell me on lowering my cable bill or some shit.

"This is really some event, huh?" I say as I scan the room and take everything in.

"It is." She nods. "And probably the dumbest fucking thing I have ever done in my life."

"How's being a fake fiancé going?" I wiggle my eyebrows as I lean my head in, so no one overhears what I say.

"Marcus is a pain in my ass, Peyton." She groans in annoyance before taking a sip of champagne. I can't help but notice the giant rock on her finger. That ring had to have been insanely expensive. "He's lucky he's so fucking hot, otherwise I wouldn't be doing this."

"Are there benefits to this arrangement?" I raise a single eyebrow.

"Doubt it," she scoffs. "But I'll do whatever I can to get a chance to ride that hot bologna pony."

"You're incorrigible."

"I'm horny as fuck, Pey."

"I can see that." I laugh at her.

"I have to go to the bathroom," she announces. "I'll be right back."

Avery leaves and I take a sip of my drink while scanning the room again. My eyes find Thomas on the other side of the room where he's listening to a man speak. As if he can feel my eyes on his, his gaze turns to meet mine. I feel a heat pool in my center and a shiver run down my spine. A small smirk forms on his face as he lifts his glass of whiskey to take a sip while maintaining eye contact with me. I feel myself shift just the slightest in my seat, rubbing my thighs together. When he notices my slight movement, he shoots me a wink and runs his tongue along his bottom lip.

He's eye fucking me from across the room and *fuck me,* if that doesn't turn me on.

He turns his gaze back to the man quickly as if it's his turn to speak so I twist my chair around to lean on the bar to wait for the bartender to come back around. To my side, I feel the presence of someone sitting next to me. I tilt my head the slightest to take note of who it is. I already know it's not Thomas because my body knows when he's close and this wasn't that. However, my body shifts into high alert mode as if it knows something is off.

The woman next to me orders a gin and tonic. I turn my head a bit more to get a good look at her. She is stunning. Long blonde hair that cascades down her back with loose curls that reach her ass. She looks like a model or an actress of some sort wearing a long black gown that hugs every curve of her body. She has the type of body that women would kill for.

When she catches me staring, her gaze shifts to mine. I simply smile and turn my head back to my drink to avoid social interaction with this beautiful woman. But she speaks anyway.

"You must be the new woman that Thomas is fucking," she announces.

My eyes widen in horror as they snap her way, "Excuse me?"

"Don't play coy," she chuckles. "I saw the way he was looking at you a few moments ago."

I remain silent, unsure of what to say.

"You don't have to tell me." She waves me off. "I already know the answer because there was once a time, he looked at me the same way."

My mouth parts the slightest bit as I continue to stare at this woman. Who is she? Did she used to date Thomas? He said he's never been in a relationship before.

My thoughts are interrupted when the buzz of my phone vibrates in my purse again. Pulling it out, I see another unknown caller flash across the screen, and I silence it again before stuffing it back into my purse.

"Boyfriend calling?" She smirks.

This bitch. Who does she think she is? And where the fuck is Avery when I need her messy self to come pull me out of this?

"Actually," I say as I straighten my spine and take my almost empty glass in my hand. "My boyfriend is over there." I turn and point to where Thomas is standing and notice he's not looking in my direction anymore. "And you're right. I just so happen to be fucking *and* dating him."

"That's impossible," she shoots me a sinister laugh. "Tommy doesn't do relationships."

"People change," I mutter before taking a sip of my drink.

"Tommy doesn't," she scoffs.

"Who are you?" I finally ask, turning my body to face.

"I'm Sheila." She smirks. "James' mom."

This is the moment all the color drains from my face and my jaw hits the floor. My heart is beating rapidly behind my ribcage, and I can't help but feel so small compared to her. My feet are telling me to run and get out of here, but my mind is telling me to stay.

This. Is. James'. Mom.

"Cat got your tongue?" The grin on her face is as ugly as her attitude.

I feel rage creeping up on me. Not only is this James' mom, but this is the woman that abandoned her child. For what? To pursue her career? How could she do that to the greatest little boy I have ever met.

"Where have you been, *Sheila*?" My tone is harsh and protective of both Thomas and James. Her name slips off my tongue as if it's laced with acid.

"Oh sweetie," she says in a condescending tone. "You act like you know it all. You think you can jump in and play mommy dearest?"

"No," I snap back. "But at least James has someone there for him." I stand from my seat as anger courses through my veins. "Where were you when he was sick? Where were you when I held him in my arms while he cried for his mom? You weren't there. That's for damn sure."

"I have a life." She stands up to meet my stance. "I have a career to pursue, and James didn't fit the bill." She shrugs her shoulders. *She. Shrugs. Her. Fucking. Shoulders.* As if leaving your child is no big deal.

"You don't deserve him," I say, my voice growing louder. "You don't deserve either of them. I have never met anyone more selfish in my entire life and I have only known you for a couple of minutes. You do know that's not how being a parent works, right?" I pause and she just sits there with that ugly smirk on her face. "When you become a parent, you put your children before your own selfish needs. Then, you figure out a way to make it work and pursue your goals. You could have had it all, Sheila." I feel tears prickle behind my eyes. "Those two deserve the fucking world."

"You think you can give that to them? You don't even belong here. This isn't your crowd, and these aren't your people. I could tell that before I even sat here next to you," she scoffs.

"If it makes me anything like you, then I'll *fucking pass*."

I begin to walk away, and my blood is boiling. I swear you can see smoke coming off the top of my head if you looked close enough.

"He's never going to love you," she says to my back. My steps falter as I stand there and slowly turn to face her again. "He doesn't know how to love, and he will never love you."

"What makes you believe that?"

"He never loved me." Her smile falters. "He never once showed me or told me, at least. He will always be hung up on a girl he met before me. She was the '*one that got away*,'" she says with air quotes and an eye roll. "No one in his life will ever measure up to that woman. Not even you."

I swallow the lump in my throat and realization hits me like a ton of bricks. The girl before her, the one that got away, the one no one will ever measure up to…

Is it me?

"From the look on your face." She smiles up at me. "You understand exactly what I'm referring to. You're so stupid to think you can measure up to that girl."

"I know exactly what you're referring to, Sheila."

"Good. I'm happy I could warn you so you can walk away from him before he walks away from you."

"He won't," I tell her, the grin on my face growing.

"Again." She laughs and shakes her head. "Delusional."

"I may be," I say as I take a couple of steps closer to her, closing the space between us so I can make sure she hears what I really have to say. "But fate has a funny way of working out, you know?"

She tips her head to the side in confusion while my grin spreads from ear to ear. I watch as the color drains from her face and the realization hits her right in that smug face of hers.

"I…" she starts.

"From the look on your face," I throw her words back at her. "You understand where I'm going with this. That girl you're referring to…" I pause and let it boil in her brain for a minute. "It's me."

"H-how? What? How did—"

"Fate, baby." I smile down at her in her seat before I straighten my spine and take a step back again. "And I must say, you are missing out, Sheila. Thomas and James deserve the world that you couldn't give them."

"You can't just play mommy dearest," she scoffs.

"No, I can't." I shake my head. "But I will be there for him. Whatever he needs, he will have me. Both of them."

"What aren't you understanding?" She laughs. "Thomas is not capable of love."

"Oh, but he is," I smile. "And that man standing over there, I love him with every fiber of my being. You fucking missed out on the chance to have him. So, thank you."

"Thank you?" she asks.

"Thank you for being the fucking bitch that you are and walking away from them."

With my final words lingering in the air, I grab my purse and turn to walk away. My body is shaking because I can't believe I just stood up to her like that. But no one talks about Thomas like that. No one talks about James like that. Fuck, no one talks to *me* like that.

I feel my head beginning to pound from the adrenaline rush and I know that I need to go find Avery and tell her what just happened. Then I need to go find Thomas.

I head toward the hallway leading to the restrooms to find Avery. As soon as I enter the hallway, I find Avery coming through a supply closet door while fixing her dress with her hands as if to flatten it back down.

"What the—" I start to say but stop myself when I see Marc following behind her, adjusting his cuff links.

My anger from before has turned into laughter because Avery, one hundred percent, just fucked Marc in the supply closet. Or he fucked her? I feel like Avery is the type to take control in that situation, but then again, it's always the quiet, soft ones you have to watch out for.

"Don't say a word," Avery growls.

"I don't have to say a word." I laugh. "You smell like sex and champagne."

"Smells hot, doesn't it?" She laughs and turns her gaze to Marc. "Nice doing business with you, big man."

"Told you it was big, Princess," Marc leans in to whisper but it's loud enough for me to hear. Then his gaze meets mine. "Hello, Peyton."

"Hey Marc." I laugh. "Having a good night, I see?"

"You could say that." He smiles down at Avery.

"Listen," I say to stop this weird post-sex moment that these two are having. "I'm going to the bathroom and then I need to find Thomas." My smile fades as I think about telling him she's here.

"What's wrong?" Avery asks as if she can sense the look on my face.

"I-I," I stutter, playing with the loose strands of hair hanging around my ear. "Just had a run in with an ex of Thomas'."

I watch as Marc pinches his eyebrows together with a questioning look, "Tommy doesn't have an ex. He's never been in a relationship."

"He never dated James' mom?"

Realization hits him as he figures out what I am saying. The color drains from his face as he quickly pulls out his phone and starts typing away on it before looking back at me. "They never dated. Tommy wanted to make it work with her and try a relationship for James' sake. But there was never anything there."

"Oh," is all I manage to get out.

"Trust me, Pey." He puts a hand on my shoulder. "You're end game for him."

I give a tight nod as I feel tears prickle behind my eyes again. I blink rapidly to make sure they don't fall. Thomas loves me. I know he does, despite him not telling me, I know that he loves me.

"I'm going to freshen up in the bathroom," I announce. "Marc, please don't tell Thomas. I will find him after and tell him."

He gives me a tight nod. Avery gives me a look. You know, the *bestie look,* where she doesn't have to say the words for me to know that she's asking if I'm okay. "I'm good, Ave. Go," I tell her as she nods her head and takes off with Marc.

After doing my business, I step out and stand in front of the mirror. My hands rest on the sink as I stare at myself in the mirror. I'm giving myself a mental pep talk before I head back out there. Will he be mad at me for standing up to her? Will he be mad at me for saying the things I said?

I know I don't believe a word of what she told me. The Thomas that I know, he knows how to love. Despite him not telling me those three little words yet, I know he does. It's in everything he does for me. *The little things.*

I know I am, without a doubt, in love with this man. I am in love with Thomas Ford, and I have to tell him. *Tonight.*

As I exit the bathroom, I feel the vibration of my phone again. I groan in frustration and pull it out to see an unknown number calling again. "These telemarketers are ruthless," I mutter to myself as I swipe right to answer the call.

"Hello," I say in frustration.

"Ms. Kelly?" The woman on the other end replies.

"This is she."

I don't think I register anything other than her name and where she's calling from before everything goes black. My head started spinning, my lungs stopped taking in air and my pulse pounded harder with every second that passed. A silent scream erupted from my chest before I ran as fast as I could, grabbed Avery and we were out of the Edison Ballroom in minutes.

My world will never be the same again.

CHAPTER THIRTY-THREE
Thomas

Normally, I would eat this shit up at these events. The free food and whiskey would have me buzzing with excitement. However, tonight, all I want is to be doing it with Peyton. She's here with me, but she's not here with me. I have spent the last hour mingling with business associates and discussing future investment properties.

I donate a lot of money to these events, especially since becoming a dad. I can't imagine a little boy the same age as James, waking up Christmas morning without presents under his tree. It makes my stomach churn, and it makes me want to give more than I already have. Ford Investments donated one million dollars tonight and I still feel like it's not enough.

"How's little James doing?" Bob asks. I sold Bob a property last year that I invested in and fixed up. He bought it for triple what I paid for it. He holds a lot of power in this city. He's one of the richest men in this room. While my name is tied to most of the city high rises with my investments, he owns double that.

"He's doing good." I nod. "Getting big already. He's three going on thirteen."

Bob laughs. "Time sure does fly."

"That it does." I smile and nod back to him.

He continues talking, but I don't register what he's saying because my eyes are scanning the room looking for a glimpse of her golden blonde hair. I don't see her at the bar where she was sitting before and I feel a twitch in my chest, wondering where she is.

She must have gone to the ladies room.

Logan interrupts my thoughts when he places a hand on my shoulder. "Hey, Tommy," he says before turning to Bob. "Hi, Bob. How are you doing?"

"I'm good, Logan." He nods. "How's New York City's finest doing? Are they treating you right there, boy?"

"Yes, sir." Logan replies. "I'm up for a promotion soon. Trying to get off the streets."

"That a boy." Bob grips his shoulder the way a dad would. "Your dad would be very proud of you, son."

I watch as Logan swallows a lump in his throat and nods. His dad passed away when he was a teenager after being caught in the crossfires of a robbery gone wrong. He was the Chief of Police and Logan has always wanted to follow in his father's footsteps.

"Thank you, Sir."

"How many times do I have to tell you, son. You can call me Bob. And if you ever need a reference, you know my number and where to find me. I will happily put in a good word for you."

Logan smiles and nods again. "I appreciate that."

"I have to get back to my wife," Bob announces. "It was a pleasure talking to you both. Logan, you let me know. And Thomas, I will be in touch with you next week about that place downtown."

"You got it, Sir." I smile and nod.

Bob walks away leaving Logan and I standing there. "He's fucking awesome," Logan laughs.

"He is. How's the night going so far?"

"Good," Logan says, scanning the room. "Trying to figure out who I'm taking home tonight."

"Is that the only reason you come to these things?"

"Duh." He rolls his eyes. "That and free whiskey, my friend."

I take a moment to scan the room again, hoping for a glimpse of Peyton's hair to flash my way. She's still nowhere to be found. There is no way she's been in the bathroom this long.

"Hey, have you seen Peyton?" I ask Logan.

"No," he says before taking a sip of whiskey. "I saw Avery going down the hall towards the bathrooms earlier."

Now that I look more closely, I don't see Marc or Avery either.

Where the fuck is everyone?

As I scan the room once more, my eyes lock on long light blonde hair and a wave of nausea hits me with more force than it should. I'd know that blonde hair anywhere. There was a time, one fucking single time, that I had that hair wrapped around my hand while I fucked the thought of Peyton out of my head years ago.

Bile rises in my throat, and I feel my head start to spin with waves of dizziness.

It's fucking Sheila.

As if she can sense me staring at her, she turns, and her eyes meet mine. A smug grin appears on her face, and I can taste bile sitting in my throat.

"You look like you've seen a ghost." Logan laughs.

"I have," I reply to Logan, but my gaze is fixed on Sheila. Logan's eyes travel to where my furious eyes are stuck.

"Oh fuck," he mutters under his breath. "What the fuck is that bitch doing here?"

"Your guess is as good as mine."

"You don't think she found out who Peyton is and approached her, do you?"

I turn to face Logan and I can feel the color draining from my face. Did she? I don't know, but the thought of it makes me sick.

Sheila is vindictive and will make up any story to make sure I'm forever unhappy.

I don't say another word to Logan and my feet begin to move on their own towards Sheila. I need to find out why the fuck she is here, back in the city and not in California pursuing the fucking career she was so hell-bent on achieving.

My body feels stiff and cold as ice as I approach her. She has never had an effect on me. Yeah, one night I was attracted to a pretty face at the bar, but the more I got to know her, the more I realized how ugly she is on the inside. She's not warm, she's not caring, and she only gives a shit about one person. Herself.

"Sheila." I taste the acid when her name passes my lips.

"Tommy," she says. Her voice filled with fake excitement as she starts a show for the world to see. She moves to wrap her arms around me for an embrace and I take a step back. "Long time no see."

"Yeah, you can fucking say that again. What are you doing here?"

"I was invited by a brand company that I model for. They flew me in for the weekend from Los Angeles to attend this. I'm here to support the children, sweetheart."

"Don't you dare call me that," I snap. "I am not your sweetheart. Never have been, never will be. And since when do you *support* any children?"

"Don't be like that." She gives me a stupid pouty face, ignoring my question. This is why it never worked. She's fake as fuck. "We had a really good thing going. We could always try again."

"Are you drunk, Sheila?"

"No," she giggles. "I'm just happy to see you. Why don't we get a drink?"

"I'm here with someone," I snap. Rage is flowing through my blood, and I want nothing more than for her to be out of my hair.

"The pretty little thing I met at the bar not long ago?"

The questions floating around my mind are answered with

her one single question right there. She did run into Peyton. An array of new questions come crashing into my head and worry hits my gut.

"What. Did. You. Say. To. Her?" I hiss through gritted teeth.

"Oh, would you relax? I just told her what she needs to know," she says with a small laugh and a shrug of the shoulders.

"You have no right to tell her anything."

"I don't? Because last I checked, *I* am that little boy's mom."

"You may have birthed *James*," I emphasize his name because she can't even say it for herself. "But you are far from being a mother. As far as I'm concerned, you're nothing more than the person who carried him *for me*."

She sucks in a small gasp and her hand lands on her chest. "You don't mean that."

"Oh, but I do," I say as I can feel the anger rising in me. "You do remember that *you* left us? It was *your* decision to leave. I tried hard to make it work when that isn't something I fucking do."

"But you can do it with *her*?" she says, like poison is coming out of her mouth.

I pause and feel my jaw clench even tighter. "She's different, Sheila."

Her eyes bounce between mine as if she's trying to assess my demeanor. I stand there still, ready to run and find Peyton. Ready to make this right because I can't lose her. I fucking lost her once and after the last couple of months, I know, without a doubt, it will ruin me if I lose her again.

"Wow," she says at the same time her lips part open. "She really is that girl."

"What girl?"

"The one that got away." She shakes her head and moves her gaze away from mine. "She's the girl from before me that you never got over."

"How—" I start to say before she cuts me off.

"I will right my wrong here," she starts to say. "I did talk to her after I saw you two eye fucking from across the room. I tried to warn her that you are not the relationship type and that you will never love anyone," she pauses, and I feel the rage creeping back up with each word that comes out of her mouth. "I told her that no girl will ever measure up to the one who got away. She realized that the girl was her."

I don't say anything but just simply nod. Sheila knew I was hung up on someone. I met her and the deal was I needed to fuck the other girl out of my system. We had a mutual agreement, but mistakes were made and a few weeks later, she called to tell me that she was pregnant.

"I can tell…" she pauses, and her features soften. "I can tell she loves you. I can tell she loves James."

"Sheila," I start, but tread lightly with my tone. "She cares for James a lot. You're right, she is the girl that got away all those years ago. I care for her as much as she cares for us. I can't let that go. I might not be able to do relationships, but I damn well plan to try to and keep her in our lives. I deserve it, for once. James deserves it." I swallow the lump in my throat. "She deserves it."

She gives me a tight nod. "She's a fireball that one." She lets out a low chuckle before she continues, "I want you to know, I'm not back in the city for James. I know that still makes me a piece of shit, but kids are not for me. I hope you understand that. After meeting her and having this talk with you, I know that me leaving was the best decision for everyone. I'm so sorry I hurt you. I'm even more sorry I hurt James."

"Don't, Sheila." I snap. I don't have time for this with her. Yes, I might be blowing her off. But she blew us off three years ago when she voluntarily walked out of our lives. I am being such a dick, but I only care about one thing right now, and that is to find Peyton. "It's in the past. We have moved on. James is happy and safe and lives a great life. But where the fuck did Peyton go after you fed her with your bullshit?"

"After she stood up for you and James? After she told me

that she loves you with every fiber of her being?" She smirks up at me and all the air in my lungs is now trapped.

"She told you that?"

She nods her head as the smirk grows wider. "That girl is hopelessly in love with you, Tommy."

"The feeling is mutual." I nod.

"She ran off towards the bathroom," Sheila finally says. "Her phone was ringing like crazy the whole time I sat here with her, but she refused to pick it up. I was being the nosey body that I am and peaked over her shoulder one of the times she took it out to silence it. It was an unknown number, but I recognized it coming from a New Jersey area code. North Jersey to be exact. Probably somewhere right outside of the city."

New Jersey area code.

Right outside of the city.

Realization dawns on me and my stomach churns with nausea as I think the worst possible thing I can think of. Walking away from Sheila without another word, I reach into my pocket for my phone to call Eddy to see if he picked Peyton up.

"Mr. Ford," he answers on the first ring.

"Eddy, did you pick up Peyton from here a little bit ago?"

"No, Sir. She hasn't called me. I have been on the side of the building all night waiting for a call."

"Shit," I mutter under my breath. "Bring the car around front. I think she might have gone home, and I need to get there now."

I hang up the phone and begin walking towards the exit. Logan spots me and stops me in my tracks. "Hey, what's the 9-1-1?" He laughs.

"Logan," I manage to get out in a hoarse whisper. My throat is dry from panic, and I can't find anything to say. Logan knows me, and sensing my panic, he begins to scan the room.

"She's gone, isn't she?" He places a hand on my shoulder.

"She is." I nod. "But I don't think it was on purpose. Can you call me in a favor?"

"Yes," he says quickly as he pulls his phone out of his pocket. "Tell me what you need."

"I need you to get me an escort home." I place my hand on his shoulder. "As fast as you fucking can."

"Let's go, brother."

We're out the door in a matter of minutes. The world around me is just a blur. I spend the short drive to the penthouse shaking my leg and staring at the city lights. I hope she's there and I hope she's alright. We come to an abrupt stop in front of the building, and I am out of the car before Eddy can even put it in park. When I enter the lobby, I barely register Jim sitting there. When I blow past him, his words stop me in my tracks.

"She's not here," Jim says in a sympathetic tone.

"What do you mean?" Panic sets in, yet again.

He comes out from behind his desk, his face never once forming a greeting smile like he normally would. In fact, his eyes look sad and sympathetic. Something is wrong and I feel my pulse beating faster and faster with every second that passes before he speaks.

"When they couldn't get a hold of Peyton," he starts, shaking his head as if he's trying to avoid tears forming in his eyes.

"Tell me, Jim." I plea. "Please tell me."

"They called here to look for her. The hospital." He wipes a tear from his eye and shakes his head again. "It's her grandmother."

CHAPTER THIRTY-FOUR
Peyton

It was around five in the morning when Gigi took her final breath.

When the hospital called last night, I was forced to leave the charity event abruptly. I couldn't think straight, and I couldn't find Thomas. My only thought was getting to the hospital as soon as I could.

Avery was with Marc when I found her and told her the news. I barely remember being able to get my words out while telling her about the calls. Marc was quick to have his personal driver meet us out front and take us to the hospital. Avery wanted us to stop at the penthouse for me to change but I didn't want to waste any more time than I already had when I was ignoring the calls, not realizing it was the hospital calling. Kali said she would meet us there when she spoke to Avery and ended up beating us. They are just as affected by this loss as I am because they adopted her as their grandmother too.

She had taken a turn for the worse and the decision was made to place her on hospice care almost as soon as I got there.

It wasn't a decision that was made lightly because Gigi is my world. She's my rock. She's my everything. But she wasn't herself. She was disoriented and kept calling for my parents. Her heart and kidneys were failing her. Cancer had taken over every part of her body.

My phone had died so I couldn't even get in touch with Thomas. Admittedly, it was the last thing on my mind when we arrived close to midnight. I laid in the hospital chair next to her bed, in my gown, while I listened to her snore all night long. She did that in her sleep all the time, so it didn't bother me. I was woken up in the early morning hours from my half-sleep state to silence.

That's when I knew she was gone.

Gigi passed peacefully in her sleep, feeling no pain.

The way she always said she wanted to go.

She remained silent in her hospital bed as the nurses assessed her to confirm she had passed. I'll never forget the nurse lowering the stethoscope from her ears, turning to look me in the eyes and saying, "I am so sorry, honey."

Next thing I knew, my knees and hands were the only things holding me off the ground as I fell and let out the most gut-wrenching cry that has ever left my body. My dress splayed over the cold hospital floors, and I screamed a plea to whoever was listening to let her come back to me. To let her stay with me longer. "Please, don't take her from me," I cried over and over again in the nurse's arms until I had no voice left to cry.

She's no longer in pain and for that, I'm thankful. However, I can't imagine this pain becoming anything less than what I feel right now. It feels like a dagger straight to my heart. I feel like my heart has been ripped out of my chest and left with her spirit.

I call Kali and Avery back to the hospital as soon as I have the strength and courage once I pull myself off the floor. I barely said anything over the phone, but the sobs in my throat were enough to send them running to me. When they show up minutes later with clothes and a toiletry bag of things for me, I am still sitting in the chair, staring at Gigi as she lay peacefully in the bed.

"Babe," Kali says as she crouches down next to my chair. "We have to get you out of these clothes."

I don't move.

My eyes don't move to Kali's.

I have never felt numb like this in my life. When I lost my parents, I was shocked and heartbroken, but losing Gigi, being here in this hospital room as she took her final breaths, feels like someone took a knife and stabbed me in the chest. Not once, not twice, but over and over again until there's nothing left of me.

"Pey." Avery moves to now crouch in front of me. Tears fill her eyes. "Let's get you home. I can't begin to imagine how hard this is on you." She sniffles. "Gigi," she can't say the words without breaking down. My eyes finally move to hers and tears I didn't know I still had come rolling down my cheeks as I look my best friend in the eyes. "Pey, I am so sorry."

"Ave," I cry out and move into her arms and sob harder. "I don't know how to do this. I don't know how to live without her. I need her here. I fucking need her."

She says nothing but holds me tight. She lets me sob into her shirt, my makeup from last night smearing her white t-shirt. I'm sure black streaks run down my cheeks and the world around me is blurry from tears.

"I fucking hate cancer," I cry out.

"I know, babe," Avery cries with me. "Me too."

She doesn't have to say anything. Neither of them has to. They may not know my pain, but they know what I need right now and it's to be able to cry into their arms and feel their comfort. I know nothing will be able to take this pain away.

I allow myself to catch my breath as tears stain my cheeks. The nurse walks in and begins to speak but I don't register a thing she's saying. I hear words such as funeral and contact so and so. My eyes shift to Kali who is speaking for me. She maintains composure as she helps me handle what needs to be handled. I've mentioned it before, but it feels right saying it again, I would be lost without these two.

"Thank you," a hoarse whisper comes out of me.

"Pey," Kali sighs. "You do not need to thank me. This is what friends are for. This is what *sisters* are for. You know we are always here for you, babe."

I nod my head and wipe another tear from my eye. "I guess we have to go."

"We will give you a few minutes with her," Kali says. "We will be right outside this door."

I nod and the girls give me soft smiles, but don't say anything else before they leave me here to say goodbye. I stand up from the chair with my gown still clinging to me. I look over to Gigi where she lays and place my hand in her cold hand. I lean down and give her one last kiss on the forehead, lingering a second longer as I cherish this last moment I am physically in her presence.

"I'm going to miss you so much. I know you're no longer in pain, and that makes me so happy for you. The selfish part of me wishes you could live forever. I love you so much, Gigi," I silently sob. "To the moon, stars, Jupiter, and back."

Sobs racking my body harder, I take a seat in the chair closest to her bed. I take her hand in mine, and the other hand circles my legs as I bring them to my chest. I rest my head on my knees and cry for the loss of my best friend, my rock, and my angel. I allow myself to think about all the amazing memories I have with her.

I remember trips to the grocery store with her and the cashier would complement her and say, "You have a beautiful daughter." Gigi would smile from ear to ear, taking it as a compliment that she was young enough to have a daughter my age. She would hit them with a simple 'thank you' and we would be on our way. She would never correct them, and I loved that for her.

I remember all the wild and crazy stories she would tell me. There was this one story she would always tell us about how she left my mom in a grocery store when she was a baby so she could beat the shit out of a woman who was hitting a dog with a whip. The way she tells the story is ingrained in my memory, knowing exactly how she would hold her hand up to show us the scar when the crazy woman tried to whip her, but Gigi caught the whip.

To this day, I still don't know if any of these stories are true because they were so wild and out there. But that is who she was. As crazy as the stories seemed, she always managed to make people laugh with them.

I remember growing up with her because my parents worked so much, and if I had a bad day after school, she would always be there to offer up snacks. She loved her food, but she loved offering food to others even more. She was the type of person who would make a tray of lasagna for the dentist when she went for her cleanings. And don't get me started on the pharmacist. She always came bearing some form of food, whether it was lasagna, eggplant parmesan, or her famous pepperoni bread.

The tears don't stop running as the memories continue to flood me. I don't know how long I sit in this position, but in my dizzy haze of grief I feel strong arms lift me off the chair, and wrap me in a tight embrace.

"Shhh, baby," he whispers. "I'm here."

CHAPTER THIRTY-FIVE
Thomas

My head is pounding and it's not from the whiskey I had the night before, or the fact that it's six in the morning. Last night when I got back to the penthouse, I learned from Jim that Peyton had gone to the hospital because her grandmother had taken a turn for the worse. She wasn't answering her phone which was justifiable as I am sure she was a mess. Marc wasn't answering his phone all night and eventually it was shut off. Fucker probably forgot to charge it.

I spent an hour pacing my living room trying to figure out what the fuck I should be doing. Do I find out what hospital and show up? Do I give her some space and wait for her to call me? Those questions circled my brain on repeat. Until I finally made the decision to find her.

At first, it was me calling a few hospitals around the area. But because I wasn't family they couldn't give me information over the phone. I finally said fuck it, got in my car and started going hospital to hospital until I found her.

There aren't many hospitals in the area, but it still took me all night. I exhausted all the hospitals in the city before I started hitting the ones in North Jersey where Gigi actually lived. For whatever fucking reason, traffic was a mess everywhere, even in the middle of the night. My GPS was on a mission to sabotage me left and right.

It wasn't until around five in the morning when I finally walked into a small private hospital in New Jersey where I saw Marc sitting in the waiting room.

"Thomas." He stands from his chair and quickly walks to where I stand in the waiting room. "I'm sorry we couldn't get in touch with you," he says quickly as if he can read my thoughts. "All of our phones died. Avery ran home to grab clothes and stuff for Peyton, but she wasn't even thinking straight to grab phone chargers. Both girls fell asleep in the waiting room because only one person was allowed in the room overnight. I don't have your number memorized. I'm so fucking sor—"

"Don't," I cut him off from rambling. I know he's beating himself up right now. "Where… is she," I say with a hoarse whisper, nerves replacing the adrenaline of rushing around the city trying to find her. Tears prickle in the back of my eyes, and I attempt to blink them away.

Before he can answer me, Avery and Kali come around the corner.

"Thomas," Kali breathes out. Almost like she was holding the breath and waiting for me. Was Peyton waiting for me too? *Fuck.*

"How is she?" I ask.

I watch as Kali shakes her head. A tear escapes her eye, and she quickly wipes it away. "Gigi passed."

I don't say anything. My feet want to run, but my immediate reaction has my feet cemented to where I stand like a concrete wall as I let the news soak in. My first thought is that I fucking hate myself for not finding her quicker and being there for her. I should have been there. I should have been holding her hand and given her a shoulder to cry on.

Gigi was an angel on earth. I may have only known her a short time, but she impacted my life in so many ways. I saw the way she cared for Peyton and the way she loved her. The laughs we shared at the beach house are some of the best memories I am sure I will cherish for a long time. The thoughts of her with James are enough to send the tears spilling out of my eyes. She loved that little boy, and he loved her. He loved his visits they took to see her and never stopped talking about her famous spaghetti that she served while coloring pictures with her.

Marc pulls me out of my thoughts of Gigi. "I'm so sorry, bro," he says as he holds me tight. It's as if he knows I am about to fall apart any second.

My gaze drifts to Avery who gives me a soft smile and greets me with the same warm embrace that Marc did. "She's in room 309," Avery says with a tip of her head.

"How is she?" I hesitantly ask despite knowing the answer already.

"She's not good," Avery says, shaking her head. "She's numb. She refused to leave her side and she's been curled up in a ball in the chair next to her."

"Thank you for staying here with her," I tell Avery and turn my gaze to Marc. "You too. Thank you for taking care of the girls."

"Always." He nods.

I don't say anything else as I move to Gigi's hospital room. My knuckles tap lightly three times on the door. But I don't hear a sound coming from the other side. Slowly I push the door open, and I see Peyton curled in a ball with her knees to her chest on the chair closest to the hospital bed. She's sound asleep so she doesn't notice me entering the room.

I don't waste another minute before my arms wrap around her body as I pick her up and place her on my lap. I slowly brush the strand of hair out of her face as I take in her pale features and swollen eyes. My movements cause her to stir.

"Baby," I whisper. Her eyes snap open as if she's shocked to see me. A sob erupts from her as she moves to cover her face with her hands. "Shh, baby. I'm here," I say as I lean in to brush more hair from her face and press a kiss to her forehead. "I'm here."

"Thomas," she shudders. I plant a kiss in the hollow of her neck as I hold her close to me.

After a few moments, she lets out the tears she needs to cry. My heart continues to break as I hear gut wrenching sobs coming from her. I want to take away her pain. I want to make this better for her. But I know nothing will.

When the tears slow down, she wiggles free of my hold to turn her body to face mine while not leaving my lap.

I stare up at her and delicately run my hand down the side of her face as tears fill my eyes for the first time since being here. Looking at Peyton in this state just shatters me right down to my core. My thumb swipes a tear that escapes from her eye.

"Baby."

"You're here," she says. Her voice sounds so small and broken.

"I will always be here for you," I say as I take her chin in my hands and lean in to press a soft kiss to her lips. "There's nowhere else I would rather be than right here with you. Tell me what you need."

"I just need you to hold me."

"I've got you," I say just as I pull her head to my chest and hold her tight once again. My hand strokes the back of her hair. "I've always got you."

"Thomas?"

"Yes, baby?"

"Take me home."

———

Peyton has her arms draped around my neck and her face buried in my neck as I carry her into the bathroom in the penthouse. I gently place her down in the middle of the bathroom and move to turn on the bathtub. She doesn't move from where she is standing, and I see her gaze looking out the windows behind the tub.

She's numb. She's completely and utterly numb.

Slowly, I move to stand in front of her. Her gaze shifts to me as I see her watery eyes looking back at me. My hands find the hem of her oversized tee and she doesn't move to stop me. Slowly, I remove the shirt, my eyes never leaving hers. There is nothing sexual about this and that's not my intention. She needs me in so many ways right now, and I plan to take care of her in any way she needs for the time being.

She doesn't stop me as I hook my fingers into the waistband of her sweatpants and push them to the floor. Her hands rest on my shoulders as I bend down for her to step out of them.

"Thank you," she says hoarsely.

"I got you, baby."

I slowly remove her bra and panties before I place her in the warm bathtub. I remove my jeans and t-shirt before I climb in behind her. She scoots forward to allow me to sit behind her. Her head tips back to rest on my shoulder as she lays there allowing me to wash her body with the sponge.

"She's really gone, Thomas."

"I'm so sorry, Peyton." I continue to wash her arms with the sponge and press a kiss to the side of her head. Tears spring my eyes, but I blind them back knowing she needs a strong pillar to lean on right now. "I know how much she meant to you. She was an incredible woman."

"She was." She nods. "I know she's no longer in pain, though. She deserves that and that is what I am choosing to hold onto." I don't answer but continue to wash her and plant kisses on the side of her head. I know that nothing I say will take away the pain she's feeling. "Tell me how the rest of last night went," she continues. "I'm really sorry I bolted out of there without finding you."

"Hey," I say as I move so she can turn her head to look at me. My hand cups her chin to hold her there. "You have nothing to be sorry for. I will say that I was very nervous when I couldn't find you. I may have had a minor panic attack."

"What?" A half grin forms on her face as if she's making an attempt to let out a giggle. "Why would you have a panic attack?"

"I thought," I pause as my eyes bounce between hers. "I thought I lost you again."

"You could never lose me, Thomas." She turns her body which allows her hands to cup both sides of my face. "You won't lose me, okay?"

"Peyton." I melt as my arms wrap around her small waist. "The way that I felt that night, all those years ago when I lost you. I never want to feel that again." She starts to speak, but I cut her off. "I know that I knew nothing about you other than your first name, but I felt something when you were near me. This wild electricity shot through my body that night. When I saw you again in the park five years later, I felt it again."

"I felt it too," she murmurs. "I still do."

"Sunshine." I lean in close, so my lips are hovering close to hers.

"I love you, Thomas." She cuts me off and I swear the air in my lungs can't escape as I hold my breath and pray this isn't a dream. My pulse begins to pound wildly in my chest as I continue to stare in her eyes.

"Say it again."

A soft giggle comes from her, "I love you, Thomas Ford. So much. You have no idea."

My hands cup her face as my lips crash to hers. I have never felt so whole and complete in my life. This is everything I could ever want and then some. All these years, I have never told anyone those three little words. But I know I can now say them without hesitation to her because I feel it in every part of me.

"I love you, Peyton."

She moves her entire body to straddle my legs so she's able to wrap her arms around my neck and she crashes her lips to mine again. I can feel a smile on her lips as she kisses me fiercely.

"You love me, huh?"

"Always have, Sunshine." I give her my biggest smile. "I have never dreamed of having a family or a fucking white picket fence, until you. I have never said those words to another woman before, until you. I wasn't looking for anything until you walked back into my life. You have always been mine, baby," I pause. "Ever since that first night, all those years ago. You have always been mine."

"That first night." She smirks back at me.

"I'm pretty sure I fell in love with you, that first night."

CHAPTER THIRTY-SIX
Peyton

It's been a long two weeks since Gigi has been gone. The numbness has worn off and I have resumed some normalcy in my life again. The pain still sits there and every so often, a tear escapes that I can't stop. I miss her so much.

James didn't handle the news very well after Thomas sat him down and told him. He was devastated and didn't understand why we couldn't just go pick her up from heaven. Every day he asks about her and says, "Gigi is an angel now," as he looks out his window and up into the night sky. His new bedtime routine is looking out the window to say goodnight to her and it breaks my heart every time.

Thomas didn't leave my side for the first couple of days. He worked from home, and I use the term 'worked' very loosely. He basically canceled all his meetings and calls to take care of me, even after I insisted that he didn't need to do that. Being with him at night, curled up next to him in his bed, was more than enough for me.

I no longer sleep in the room that was mine when I first moved in. I've permanently moved into Thomas' room. Are we doing things a little backwards? Maybe. But we already lived together when I was working for him, and now that I've been fired, I spend my nights in his bed, tangled in the sheets and his arms. And Thomas never misses an opportunity to tell me he loves me.

It's Christmas morning and I lay here in Thomas' bed, *our* bed, as he sleeps peacefully next to me. It's really early, but I couldn't sleep. I glance over to the clock and see that it's just after 4am. Damn, I didn't realize it was this early. I guess I am more excited than James to watch him open up his gifts.

I scoot my body closer to Thomas to feel his warmth. I truly can never get close enough to him. He stirs slightly in his sleep, and he turns his body to wrap over mine. I know he's half-awake even though he hasn't opened his eyes because his arm pulls me closer to him. I move just the smallest bit to get myself comfortable in his hold.

"Peyton," he grunts. "You keep pressing your ass into me like that and you're going to end up with my cock in your ass."

I chuckle at the thought and tease him a little while I wiggle my ass a little more. His hand grips my hip to hold me still as he presses his erection right between my legs, grazing my center. I am sure he can feel how wet I already am since I never put panties back on before we fell asleep.

I moan at the feel of him already pressed into me as I wiggle my body some more, craving the friction of him between my legs. His hand moves from my hips and wraps around where he immediately finds my clit with his index finger. His head props up on one elbow as he leans over to press a kiss in the hollow of my neck. "Is this what you want, baby?" He teases into my ear. My head tilts to the side to allow him better access. "You want my cock this early in the morning?"

"I always want your cock," I mock him back.

"You're a greedy little thing, aren't you?" he says into my neck again as his finger works faster circles on my clit. My hips bucking into him as my orgasm builds. "You're always so ready for me, baby."

"I want you." Desire drips from my tongue. "So badly, Thomas."

"You have me, baby. Be more specific."

"I want your cock," I groan. "Please."

"Where would you like my cock, Sunshine?" His lips skim my neck and pleasure runs down my spine. "Here?" he asks as his fingers continue to play with my pussy.

"Yes," I moan and arch into him.

In seconds, his hands leave my center and he's lifting one of my legs and scooting himself in just the right position to allow him access to plunge deep inside of me from where he's lying. Both of us laying on our sides, he thrusts deep into me, and I scream out in pleasure.

"I can never get enough of this pussy, Peyton."

"Fuck," I drag out as I press my ass into him allowing him to press deeper into me. "This feels so good."

"Right now, I'm going to fuck you." He thrusts into me, harder and faster with each movement. I can feel him shift on his elbows, as my body twists the slightest bit while he stays deep inside of me and lifts my one leg over his shoulder. "Later, I'm going to make love to you."

"Yes," I shudder in his hold.

"I'm already close, baby. Do you feel what you do to me? Do you feel how fucking hard my cock is buried deep inside of this pretty little pussy." He leans over me more so he can take a breast in his hand. He circles my nipple with his finger, pushing me closer to the edge.

"You're close. I can feel it, baby," he murmurs. "Come with me."

His words send me over the edge. "I'm coming," I scream out. "I'm coming."

"Fuck." He picks up the pace and within seconds, our orgasms crash together. He falls on top of me as all the strength leaves his body. Our breaths are rapid and mixed together as we lay there in a pile of sweat together.

He lifts his head, and his eyes find mine. "Merry Christmas, Sunshine."

"Merry Christmas, Mr. Ford," I say lustily.

"I need to know," he starts saying before he pauses. "What the fuck are you doing up so early?"

We both laugh together as my head falls back on the pillow. "I don't know. I couldn't sleep. I am excited for James to wake up."

"And this is how you get your excitement out, huh?" he asks, pressing kisses along my collar bone. "Getting fucked before the sun is even up?"

"Are you complaining, Mr. Ford?"

"Are you getting smart with me, Ms. Kelly?" he mocks back.

"Me?" I bring my hand to my chest in mock horror. "Never, Sir."

"Call me sir again and I will take you over my knee." He plants a kiss on my neck. "Right here." Another kiss on my breast. "Right now." He sucks my nipple hard.

"Thomas," I giggle in his hold. "I need to get up and shower."

He throws himself off the bed and yanks me to the edge by my feet. I can't help but laugh at his animalistic behaviors. He picks me up and throws me over his shoulder as he begins to walk in the bathroom.

"You animal." I writhe in his hold.

"I'll show you an animal, baby."

"Get in the shower, Thomas," I say, playfully swatting his arm. "You're a dirty man."

"But I'm your dirty man." He kisses my lips.

"That you are." I wrap my arms around his neck as he picks me up, my legs wrap around his strong naked body as he steps into the shower. "All mine."

"I love you so much, baby," he whispers into my ear.

"I'll never get tired of hearing you say that." I melt into his hold.

After another two orgasms in the shower, we make our way downstairs to get started on breakfast before James wakes up. Thomas insists on making waffles. He calls it our special breakfast now. Both Thomas and James have learned to love the vegan waffles that he learned how to make for me. James always gets the one with extra sprinkles.

Before we know it, James is running at the speed of lightning down the stairs screaming, "Santa came!" It takes James less than an hour after that to tear open all of his Christmas presents, and he loved each and every one of them.

I'm getting ready to stuff the wrapping paper in the garbage bag when Thomas clears his throat behind me. I look up and am immediately confused as he and James stand next to the Christmas tree. Both of them look like they are up to something with shit eating grins plastered on their faces and hands behind their backs. My eyes bounce between the two boys.

"What's wrong?"

"Sit down," Thomas orders.

Hesitantly, I take a seat on the edge of the couch and my curious eyes continue to bounce between them. James is so cute as he looks up at his dad as if he's waiting for him to give him the next orders on what they are doing.

"We have something for you," Thomas says.

"I thought we agreed on no gifts," I reply. Placing my hands on my hips as if I'm frustrated that he did this when I didn't get him anything. "I didn't get you anything."

"You gave me plenty this morning." Thomas smirks.

"And Santa gave me plenty this morning," James mocks the smirk that Thomas just did.

"James," he says looking down at his son. "Go ahead and give her your gift."

"Okay, Daddy." He beams from ear to ear as he skips over to me and sits right next to me on the couch handing me a small square box.

Nervously, I open it up to find the most beautiful rose gold necklace with a diamond rose hanging from the chain. On the stem of the rose in script writing is 'Sunshine' and my heart melts into a puddle.

"Thank you so much, James." I pull him into me with a tight hug. "This is so beautiful."

"I picked it out myself." He looks at me with a pleased look in his eyes. "I hear Daddy call you Sunshine all the time and that's what I wanted it to say."

"You are so special to me, James." I press a kiss to his forehead.

"I love you, Pey." His tiny arms wrap around my waist, and I feel a tear break free from my eyes as I tighten my hold on him.

"I love you too, James."

I truly have grown to love James as if he was my own child. I don't know if the name 'Stepmom' is anywhere in my future, but if it comes down to it, I would without a doubt accept the role and love him endlessly for the rest of my life. No one deserves that more than he does.

A throat clearing breaks me from my thoughts as I look up to see Thomas standing closer to me. "Sunshine." He uses his term of endearment and my heart swoons. But quickly, that swoon turns into a frantic beating in my chest as I watch him drop to his knee in front of me at the couch.

"Thomas," I gasp.

"This might seem like I'm rushing things. But I believe when you know, you know. Some years may be missing from our time-line, but from the moment your eyes first locked with mine across that ballroom, I knew I would never love another woman the way that I would love you. That first night you walked into my life like a ray of sunshine in a dimly lit world and you took my breath away. You continue to do so every single day. I love you so much, Peyton. And I want to spend the rest of my life loving you more than I did the day before."

"I love you too, Thomas," I say through blurry eyes as I wipe tears from my cheeks.

"Make me the luckiest guy in the world and be my wife, Peyton." He pops open a teal blue ring box and my eyes widen. It has the most beautiful diamond platinum band with an elongated cushion cut diamond. "Will you marry me?"

"Yes." I don't hesitate as I nod. "Yes, I will marry you."

We both laugh as he takes my hand to place the ring on my finger before he pulls me into his arms and crashes his lips to mine.

"Ew gross," James says as he covers his eyes. "Mommy kissing Daddy."

We break apart and both of our eyes widen as we look down at James and the words that just came out of his mouth. Thomas crouches down next to him, "What did you just say, buddy?"

"Mommy kissing Daddy." He laughs uncontrollably.

"But Peyton isn't your Mommy, bud." Thomas says to him with a hand on his shoulder.

"But she can be." He shrugs his shoulders. "Right?"

I crouch down beside him and place a hand on each of his shoulders as I turn him to face me. "I will be whatever you want me to be, James. You know I love you more than anything in this world. If you want to call me Mommy, you can. But don't feel like you need to since your dad and I are going to be getting married now."

"I want to," he says without an ounce of hesitation. "I love you so much, Pey. You're always there for me." He sniffles the smallest bit. "I love when you take care of me when I'm sick and how you pull the curtains down for movies and how you play dinosaurs with me. You're my best friend and the bestest Mommy I ever had."

Thomas wipes a tear from his eye as I do the same thing.

"I love doing all of those things with you too, James." I give him a hug. "Now we have a lifetime to do hundreds more fun things too."

"I can't wait!" he screams as he jumps up and down. "I'm going to go upstairs to play with my new toys," he says as he begins to run off. He's halfway up the stairs when he screams, "Love you Mommy and Daddy."

We both smile at each other before Thomas pulls me in for a kiss.

EPILOGUE

Thomas

Six Months Later

"Babe, your waffles are ready," I yell out to the living room where Peyton is playing with James while they watch cartoons.

It's been six months since I proposed to Peyton, and it still feels like a dream that I am going to make her mine for eternity. Right after New Year's, she went into full blown wedding mode with her friends. We agreed we would have a fall wedding because New Jersey during fall has the perfect backdrop and weather for an outdoor wedding. If that's what she wants, that's what she gets.

New Jersey.

I never thought I would be a suburbs kind of guy, but here I am. Last month, we officially moved out of the city. Peyton's dream was to own a house out here with a yard, a white picket fence and no neighbors up our ass. Of course, I gave her just that. We live right outside the city on eight acres of property. You can't even see the neighbors and she now has what feels like miles of white picket fence.

The commute to work for me is obviously a little bit longer but Eddy still drives me, which allows me plenty of time to work through emails on the thirty-minute drive. However, I only travel into the office three days a week now. We set up a perfect home office for me which allows me to take calls virtually and has plenty of space for me to get work done from here.

James turned four in March and he's even smarter, if possible, and is really enjoying his new school. He has made so many new friends in the last couple of months. He goes there full time now instead of half days and he claims to love it even more because he gets more play time with his friends. So far, this move is working well for all of us.

As far as Peyton starting her daycare center, she opted to wait until the move and the wedding was over to get it up and running. We had the place completely gutted a couple months ago for renovations, and they have been working every day to make it exactly as she pictures it in her head. It will double as a day-care center and preschool for kids that are just a little too young for the bigger school. I'm so damn proud of her for what she's doing with it.

"Ahh, you made my favorite?" Peyton asks as she enters the kitchen.

One thing Peyton would not settle for, in a new place, is the kitchen. She still makes a batch of chocolate chip cookies at least two times a week. She says that the kitchen is the heart of a home. It's the space friends gather when they come over. She fell in love with this house because of the kitchen alone. It's nearly identical to our kitchen in the penthouse. The windows allow the right amount of natural light and overlook our property in the backyard.

"Of course." I lean in and press a kiss to her forehead. "You know I will be making you these for the rest of our lives."

"You're too good to me, Mr. Ford."

I groan as I wrap my arms around her and bury my face in the crook of her neck. "You know what it does to me when you call me that."

"Do I?" she asks seductively as she wraps her arms around

me and claws at my back. Her body melts into mine as she presses herself into my groin.

"You're insatiable, woman," I say as I push her off of me before my dick gets hard with James in the next room. "James is right out there, and you have to eat your breakfast."

"Fine," she rolls her eyes. "But you should know that as much as I love these waffles, I would much rather have something else in my mouth for breakfast."

I don't reply but give her a kiss before I turn her around to give her a smack on the ass as she saunters away to the kitchen table to eat her waffles.

"Are you heading into the city today for work?" she asks between bites.

"Not for work," I tell her as I clean up the dishes. "But I am meeting Marc in the city for lunch to go over a couple things that we have meetings for next week. There's a big property we're trying to lock a deal in with. He's also got some shit going on with his predicament that he got himself into back in December. You know, the whole fake fiancé thing with Avery."

"What kind of shit?"

"They didn't lock in the deal at the charity event in December." I shake my head and laugh. "Apparently the owner hasn't made up his mind yet. He was supposed to decide by the end of May. Now, he claims he needs the summer to make up his mind. Which means he and Avery have to go back to playing house for show."

"You're joking!" Her eyes widen.

"I wish I was," I scoff. "Why the shocked look?"

"Well." She shakes her head and pauses. "I know she doesn't bring much of her personal life into work. She's been really good about keeping it professional at work with Marc, but she started seeing someone casually a couple of weeks ago."

"This…" I laugh. "This is a disaster waiting to happen."

"Don't tell him when you see him today," she pleads. "Let her tell him and let them figure out their own shit."

"Absolutely will not be breaking that news to him," I shake my head. "He's going to fucking lose it, you know."

"Big time." She laughs. "What time will you be back?"

"I'm not sure." I tilt my head to the side in question. "Why? What do you have planned today?"

"I..." she pauses as she swipes the last piece of waffle through some syrup on her plate. "Nothing. I will probably just hang out here and clean."

I raise a questioning brow at her. "Why would you be doing that when Rosie takes care of that for us?"

"Good point. Although I don't mind helping her." She rises from the kitchen table to put her dish in the sink. "I think I will... watch a movie. Yes, that's it. I will watch a movie."

What the fuck? She is acting very strange right now. She knows we still have the housekeeper from the penthouse. She even still makes us some amazing grab and go lunches. That makes this whole encounter pretty weird.

"Uh... Okay?" I say in confusion.

She moves to stand in front of me where I lean on the kitchen counter and wraps her arms around my waist. She's going to be my wife soon. We have lived with each other since she first moved into the apartment. Yet, every time she touches me, it sends a wave of electricity through my body. Her touch still lights me on fire, and I feel that will never stop.

What's that country song that I never really paid attention to until Peyton waltzed into my life? '*I thought I loved you then.*' I know that a year from now I am only going to love her more than I do at this moment.

"What's the questioning look for?"

"You're acting weird," I tell her. Because that's exactly what's on my mind.

"I'm not." She clears her throat. "I'm due for a relaxing movie day."

"Alright," James breaks our thoughts. "I'm heading out."

"Excuse me?" I laugh. "Who do you think you are? You're four, not fourteen, little dude."

"Hey!" He sounds offended. "I am a big four-year-old."

"You're the biggest. But you still need us to walk you to the car buddy."

Eddy still drives James to and from school despite there being a bus where we live. Both James and Eddy love the little bit of time together. Peyton had offered to drive him multiple times, but he refuses every time she offers. The two of them exchange jokes on their short seven-minute car ride. Eddy even takes the time to look up jokes to tell him and we always hear about it later in the day over dinner when he gets home.

After walking James to the car, I head back into the house to find Peyton sitting on the couch. She's in the same corner she always is. The sight brings me back to the early penthouse days when I would come home and find her curled up in the corner of the couch with every pillow surrounding her. She fits there. She fits here. She fits in my life perfectly.

"Well." My gaze travels down her body. "This brings me back."

"Oh does it, Mr. Ford?" She shoots me her favorite seductive eyes.

"You're lucky I have to get ready… Future Mrs. Ford," I say as I make my way to stand in front of her on the couch. "Otherwise, I would take you over my knee right now."

"That doesn't sound very lucky for me at all," she quips.

"Baby, you're getting smart with me again."

"I am doing it on purpose," she pauses as she licks her lips. "The waffles were good, but I want your cock in my mouth."

This woman is a goddamn dream. Her words send blood straight to my cock and within seconds it's hard for her. I swear she wants to suck me off just as much as I want my mouth on her pussy. Our relationship is so far from being all about sex, but our attraction to one another is insane. There's no denying she was made for me.

I cup her chin and force her eyes to meet mine. "Take it out, baby."

She does as I say and scoots herself so she's on her knees for me. She shoots me a smirk before she grips the base of my cock and licks the precum already dripping from the tip. "Fuckkk," I groan out as my head falls back. She strokes the base as she takes my full length in her mouth in one fast movement. "Your mouth feels so good, Sunshine. I never get tired of seeing you on your knees for me. Feeling my cock reaching the back of your throat."

She lets out a moan as she sucks harder. Her head bobbing faster and faster while her grip tightens around the base. Her other hand reaches my balls to cup them, and I fucking lose it.

"Peyton," I hiss. "Fuck. I..." I stagger as I feel my cock throb in her mouth. I look down and see a smile spread across her face while she still bobs in and out. "I'm coming down your throat, baby. I want you to drink every last drop."

The second the words leave my mouth, she quickly pulls her mouth and hands off of me.

"What are you doing?" I growl.

"As much as I love when you cum in my mouth," she grins as she pushes me down on the couch beside her. Cock still fully erect and pulsing for a release. "I want you to fill me up."

She doesn't allow me to say another word before she's straddling my thighs and lining my cock up with her center. She doesn't need me to warm her up, clearly. She is *soaked* already.

"Dammit, Pey." I let out a low, guttural moan of pleasure. "You're dripping on my cock and I'm not even inside of you yet. You love sucking me off, don't you?"

"Yes," she cries out as she slides down until I completely disappear inside of her. "Fuck, yes."

She begins to rock back and forth on top of me. I know how she works when she does this. She rocks back and forth to take the pleasure for herself. I allow it because watching her come undone for me is the sexiest thing I have ever seen. Then when she begins to bounce, that's when she's giving me the pleasure.

Allowing me to release inside of her. They think we don't know this little move, but we do.

"That's it, baby." She rocks harder and faster, clawing at my shoulders, while my hands tightly grip her waist. "Ride my cock like a good fucking girl." She screams out my name and a string of curse words, sending her closer to the brink of her orgasm within seconds. "Yes, baby. That's it. You're squeezing my cock," I growl in her ear.

"Thomas," she whimpers. "I'm gonna come."

"Yes." I wrap my arms around her to bring my body as close to hers as I can get, and she begins to bounce up and down as she fucks me senseless. I thrust my hips into her to meet her movements and I swear I am already seeing stars. "I'm close."

"Come with me, Thomas," she murmurs between ragged breaths.

"Always, baby." I press a kiss to the hollow of our neck before we both fall apart. Her orgasm causing her body to convulse around me as I pour my release into her. Her head falls down to my shoulder, and she wraps her arms tight around me as both of our movements begin to slow.

Peyton lifts her head off my shoulder, arms still tight around my neck as she meets my gaze. I'm silent as my eyes bounce between hers and I brush the loose strands of hair away from her face. My lips curve into a smile, and I'm reminded again how fucking lucky I am to have found this connection and this kind of love with someone.

I spent my whole life swearing off relationships and wanting nothing to do with love, and then Peyton walked into my life and flipped my world upside down.

"I love you so much, Sunshine."

"I love you too, Mr. Ford."

Peyton

"I'm fucking late," I roar into the phone.

"First of all," Kali screams back. "Relax, you psycho."

"Don't tell me to relax," I huff back. "You can't tell someone freaking out to relax. Don't you know this already? Besides… I AM LATE."

As much as I love… hell, even crave… sex with Thomas, this morning was just so he didn't sense me acting weird on him. I could tell he was going to question what I was doing today. Over breakfast, I told him I was going to clean the house. I have *never* cleaned the house aside from just tidying up James' toys or dishes. Then to make it worse, I told him I was going to have a lazy day watching a movie. I can't help but laugh at myself for that. The only time I ever have a lazy day is when I am sick. There is always something to do.

We're officially getting married in a few months. Listen, it might seem fast to some but when you know, you know. I knew he was the one, from that first night. I was a complete goner for him. I often wonder what life would be like if the kitchen fire never started. Would I have really gone home with him? Would we have dated?

I stop my own thoughts most of the time because I can't

focus on what if. I was an entirely different person back then. I was shy, reserved and broken from past relationships. Thomas was probably a total playboy. If I went home with him, I could have easily been just another notch on his bedpost. Who the hell knows.

Not for nothing, James wouldn't be in the picture. While I despise the thought of Thomas with another woman, it brought him that amazing little boy. Without James, I wouldn't have been hired to be his nanny and Thomas wouldn't be back in my life.

Fate works in wild ways.

"Did you call her and tell her you were at least on your way?" Kali cuts through my thoughts.

"No. FUCK!" I scream as I drive south on the Parkway.

"I just texted her," Kali says in a calming tone. It doesn't matter how irrational I am when I am angry or upset. This girl grounds me. Fucking love her for that. "She said you're not late. I'm going to say it again, relax, you psycho. Because otherwise your fancy spaceship of a car will end up in a ditch on the side of the Parkway."

"I know, okay?" I sigh. "I just don't want anyone to take him."

"No one is going to take him." I can feel a smile through her words. "He's yours and was meant for you."

I let out a long breath as I relax into my seat a little more. I've spent months searching high and low for the perfect puppy. James once told me that he would love a fluffy puppy that he can dress up as a dinosaur. I knew I would surprise him with this when we got settled into the house with more property. You know, something a little more pet friendly.

I've talked to Thomas about a puppy before and he's not opposed to it. However, he's always pushing it off. Saying next month, next year or after the wedding. I don't think there will ever be a *perfect* time to get a puppy.

I *really* wanted to surprise James for his birthday back in February, but we took him to Florida instead. We met up with his brother Oliver, who I met for the first time. He is nothing like his siblings. Oliver is certainly the party animal of the family. Single and ready to fucking mingle. That's putting it mildly.

Needless to say, today is the day I surprise my boys with the cutest puppy I found online. It's the cutest little cavapoo, or cavoodle. The internet has so many different names for them. He is a crossbreed of a Cavalier King Charles and a miniature toy poodle. Everything I read online says they are easy to train, hypoallergenic and the perfect family dog. Everything I could have only dreamed of in a dog.

The best part? I am not getting him from a breeder. I wanted to adopt and change the life of a dog, not shop from a storefront or a mill. This little guy is just a puppy but was placed in foster care when he was just a few months old because the owners changed their mind just after Christmas. You know, the family that gets the dog as an extravagant Christmas gift but forgets how much work is involved in caring for an animal? Their loss is my gain because this puppy is checking off all my boxes.

Small and fluffy? Check.

Family dog? Check.

Up for adoption and not from a chain store? Check.

"I just can't wait to pick him up, Kali," I say into the phone.

"I can't wait to come over and cuddle up on the little man," she coos. "Did you pick out a name yet? Or are you going with a name the foster parents picked?"

"I don't know if I like the name *Matty* for a little puppy."

"Yeah, you got a point." She laughs.

"Besides, I think I am going to let James pick."

"Do not let him name that dog Dooky-West, Peyton! I swear to God."

"Oh my god," I cry out in laughter. "I forgot about that."

"I can never forget that," she scoffs.

"Listen, I'm getting off the exit in a couple minutes. I will call you later."

"Okay, love you, bitch."

"Love you too, bitch."

———

"Honey, I'm home," Thomas yells as he walks through the front door.

"Honey, I'm home," James repeats as he steps in after him.

I jump off the couch with a little too much excitement. I take a mental note to bring it down a notch because I was supposed to be watching movies all day.

"Hi, you two," I squeak out before I wrap my arms around Thomas.

"Hi?" He pulls his head back to take in my features as if he's trying to figure me out.

"Can you two sit down? I have something to tell you."

"Peyton." His eyebrows furrow. "What's going on?"

"Am I in trouble for something?" James frowns.

"Absolutely not, buddy." I give him a reassuring smile. "As you know, I was supposed to be sitting home today and watching movies…" I pause as I assess their body language.

"Oh, no." James starts fidgeting in his seat. "I hope you didn't go through a playroom clean up. I don't want to get rid of my toys."

"What?" I shake my head. "What makes you think that?"

"Robbie at school. His mom went through his toys and threw a whole bunch out."

"I did not throw your toys out." I chuckle. "But I did go out and get you a new toy."

"A new toy?" Thomas raises a brow.

"Stay here," I tell both of them.

I shuffle down the hall into the spare room to take the little puppy out of his crate. Thankfully he's crate trained already and he also doesn't bark. The foster parents told me that the only time he barks is when you are playing with him. Another box that was checked off for me.

I snuggle him in my arms as I nervously make my way down the hall. As soon as I turn the corner and make eye contact with both of them, all the nerves I felt before disappear.

"IS THAT MY NEW TOY?" James jumps from the couch and runs to where I stand at the end of the hallway. "A PUPPY?"

"Yes." I smile down at him, and then move my gaze to Thomas still sitting on the couch with a questioning look on his face. "I have been looking for a certain dog for months to surprise you with. I found this little guy and I knew he would be the perfect addition to our family."

"You got James a puppy?" Thomas asks. He has no emotion on his face and the nerves come back.

"I... yeah," I frown. "I hope that's okay."

He rises from the couch and shakes his head. His face is still void of emotion. Panic ensues as my eyes lock with his before he's standing directly in front of me. My arms feel like they are holding the puppy even tighter, but not too tight to hurt him.

"I..." I start to say.

"Stop," he cuts me off. "I'm not mad at you."

"Then why do you look like you're going to kick me and this cute ball of fur to the curb?"

"I don't look like that." He smiles. "But you got James a puppy."

"James. Us," I correct myself. "I got us a puppy."

Thomas takes his eyes off of me and drops them to the puppy in my arms. He smiles as he reaches for him. I hesitantly let go, afraid of what is going on inside of his mind right now. To my surprise, he wraps the dog into an embrace. The puppy looks so much smaller in his giant arms. I watch as the puppy looks up to him. Thomas dips his head down to kiss the top of his head and the dog begins to lick him aggressively.

"Daddy." James chuckles. "He's giving you puppy kisses."

"He is, isn't he?" Thomas says, returning his gaze to mine.

"Can I hold him?" James jumps up and down in his spot with his hands in praying position, as if his dad can ever say no to him. Thomas places the puppy on the floor and James brings himself to lay on the floor next to him. The two of them roll around each other while James laughs uncontrollably. "What's his name?"

"Right now, his name is Matty," I tell him. "But… if you want to help me come up with a new name, we can always give him a name that you pick out. Since he's your dog."

"I get to name him?" James gasps.

"Whatever you want, buddy."

James thinks long and hard for a couple of minutes while he pets the cute puppy and lets him jump all over his lap. The internet was right about something for once, I can already tell that he will be a family friendly dog.

"I want to name him Cooper!" He beams.

Cooper? I didn't see that coming considering he named Jim's goldfish Dooky-west. Thomas and I look at each other and back to James.

"Cooper it is. I'll go get his toys for you," I say, before I turn around quickly to head for the space room to get them.

After I enter the room, I start sorting through the bag of things I got and find the toys. I feel Thomas before I see or hear him enter the room.

Slowly, I turn around to meet his gaze and frown. "Listen, I'm sorry. I wanted to do this for James. I wanted-"

Thomas cuts me off when he stalks across the room and circles me in his arms and shuts me up with a mind blowing kiss. I relax into him and wrap my arms around his center. His hand circles the back of my head, holding me in place as he devours me with his lips. His tongue dances with my lips, silently asking to slip in for a tango.

I pull away and raise a questioning brow at him.

"Peyton," he sighs. "I am so fucking far from mad at you."

"You're not mad?"

"No." He shakes his head. "You bought my son a puppy. Did you know that his dream was to own a fluffy puppy so he can dress it as a dinosaur one day? It's what he has asked for the last two Christmas' and the last two birthdays. It just never made sense in the penthouse."

I step away from him and make my way to another bag I got for the puppy that has a perfect fit dinosaur outfit that is made for dogs. It was hard to find because it's not Halloween season, but I knew it's everything James wanted.

I lift it up to show Thomas. "Yes, I knew that. That's why I went crazy looking for this outfit for the little guy."

The smile on his face practically reaches his eyes and it causes me to match the smile. He shakes his head as he walks back over to me. "You're something else."

"I hope that's a good thing," I joke.

"I don't know what I did to deserve you, Peyton." He tells me as he wraps his arms around my waist and relaxes his head in the crook of my neck. "You're like a dream come true."

"I could say the same for you."

"I'm like a dream?" He chuckles.

"You are." I nod. "You know I read a lot of romance books. And when I say a lot, I mean *a lot*."

"Trust me," he scoffs. "I know. The library downstairs is packed full of porn on paper."

"Hey." I playfully slap his arm. "It's not porn. *'There's nothing wrong with a woman enjoying a little... erotica,'* as Rachel Green would say."

"And as Joey Tribiani would say... *'You got porn.'*"

"Like I was saying." I brush off his comment. "I read a lot of romance novels. Most of them have these happy endings. You know, with the most perfect man who swoons the shit out of the girl and does all the right things?"

"What are you telling me?" He raises a brow.

"I'm saying you are *that* dream man. It's like you stepped out of a romance novel. You are all my fantasies about fictional men come to life. I don't know what I did to deserve you. I don't know how you can be so perfect, swoony, sexy, and everything a girl could dream of. But you are. You're here. Standing right in front of me. You're my happy ending, Thomas."

"But… I'm not." He shakes his head.

"What…" I'm taken back by his comment. "What do you mean by that?"

"It means that I am not your happy ending." He smirks. "Because that would mean that there will be an ending. Baby, you're stuck with me for life. I put a ring on your finger because I want you for the rest of my life. I want to grow old with you. I want to put babies inside of you. Yes, plural." I chuckle at him. "I don't ever want to live another minute of my life without you."

His arms tighten around my waist, and he lifts me up, so my legs wrap around him. Instinctively, my arms circle his neck and I smile down at him.

"You're my forever, baby." He plants a kiss on my lifts. "There will be no happy ending in this book. This is a forever kind of thing. You're my happy forever."

"That doesn't make sense." I giggle in his arms.

"Make it make sense." He kisses me again. "Because I'm making it our thing."

"I love you, Thomas. And I always will."

"I love you too, Sunshine."

Vegan Chocolate Chip Cookie Recipe

Try this Vegan Chocolate Chip Cookie recipe the next time you need to bake when you're feeling stressed and overwhelmed like our bestie, Peyton.

Cook time: 11 minutes   Serving: 11-14 cookies

Ingredients

1 cup white, oat, or spelt flour
1/2 tsp baking soda
1/4 tsp salt
1/4 cup sugar, unrefined if desired
1/4 cup brown sugar or coconut sugar

1/3 cup chocolate chips
2 tbsp milk of choice, plus more if needed
2 tbsp oil or melted vegan butter
1/4 tsp pure vanilla extract

Directions

1. Combine all dry ingredients in a bowl, then stir in wet to form a dough – it will be dry at first, so keep stirring until a cookie-dough texture is achieved. If needed, add 1-2 tbsp extra milk of choice.
2. Form into one big ball, then either refrigerate for at least 2 hours or freeze until the dough is cold.
3. Once dough is chilled, preheat the oven to 325 F.
4. Form dough balls, and place on a greased baking tray, leaving enough room between cookies for them to spread.
5. Bake 11 minutes on the center rack. They'll look underdone when you take them out. Let them cool on the baking tray 10 minutes before touching, during which time they will firm up.
6. If for whatever reason the cookies don't spread enough (climate can play a huge role), just press down with a spoon after baking. You can also choose to make extra cookie dough balls and freeze them to bake at a later date.

Recipe from: https://chocolatecoveredkatie.com/vegan-chocolate-chip-cookies-recipe/

Vegan Waffle Recipe

How to make the vegan waffles that Thomas taught himself how to make for Peyton.

Prep time: 15 minutes
Cook time: 15 minutes
Total: 30 minutes
Servings: 6 servings

Ingredients

1 ½ cups unsweetened soy or coconut milk, or any vegan milk
2 teaspoons apple cider vinegar
2 cups all-purpose flour
1 tablespoon baking powder

1 tablespoon brown sugar or maple syrup
¼ cup melted coconut oil or melted vegan butter
½ teaspoon sea salt
½ teaspoon vanilla extract

Directions

1. Mix the nut milk, vanilla extract and the apple cider vinegar together in a small bowl/measuring cup. Set aside for about 5 minutes - this will make the vegan buttermilk.
2. In a large bowl, sift the flour, baking powder and salt. The sifting really helps to make the waffles fluffy.
3. Add the sugar, melted butter/oil, buttermilk mixture into the dry ingredients and using a spatula, gently mix the batter until JUST combined. It's okay (and normal) to have some lumps. The batter should be thick and scoopable.
4. Turn on and preheat your waffle maker according to which done level that you want. I set mine to about medium because I like mine crisp and golden but also very fluffy.
5. Using a ½ cup (125mL) measuring cup, scoop out some batter and pour/spread into the middle of the greased waffle maker. You don't need to push it to the edges. Close and let cook until the steam has COMPLETELY stopped from the waffle maker. Don't open it before the steam is finished!
6. Remove each waffle and place on a baking sheet in your oven or toaster oven on "warm" or 200F/95C to keep warm and crispy until finished with the entire batter. Continue with the rest of the batter.
7. Serve with your favorite toppings and enjoy!

Recipe from: https://jessicainthekitchen.com/vegan-waffles/

ACKNOWLEDGMENTS

I DID IT FRIENDS. I wrote my very first book. This would not have been possible without the help of so many people.

First, my husband. Thank you for sticking by me during this process. You may have thought I was nuts at first for this endeavor, but you never stopped believing in me, supporting me and cheering me on. Thank you for listening to me go on and on about my fictional characters as if they are real.

My boys, I hope you don't read this until you're 35 years old. But I love you to the moon, stars and Jupiter and back.

The powerpuff girls, Kelse and Briel. This book wouldn't even be possible if it wasn't for both of you. That one day I pitched a random book in our group chat and you both went nuts. Your encouragement is the reason this book happened. You never thought I was nuts and you never stopped hyping me up. You were always there for talking with me through scenes, reading as I wrote and never blowing smoke up my ass. You inspired Kali and Avery and made them who they are. Thank you will never be enough.

My editor, Caroline. You put up with the most amateur writing that ever existed. It was straight trash before you came in and fixed all my late-night writing errors and my lack of periods and commas. Thank you for taking on the tedious project of editing this for me. Because I am *sure*, this was a tedious task.

My local best friend, Paige M. I remember the day I texted you about this idea and you were all about it. Thank you for encouraging me, supporting me and being just as excited as I was every step of the way. I can't wait to attend future bookish events with you, but you will be my sidekick behind a table some day!

Melissa, you… I don't even have the words. I have never been so grateful for a social media website to bring someone into my life. I just know that the world needs more people like you, and everyone needs a friend like you in their life. Thank you for always being a phone call away to listen to me stress cry and talk through scenes. Your positivity and encouragement helped me in more ways than you know.

Trilina Pucci, I owe you so much more than I can write here in words. It was one of our many phone calls where you said the words to me, '*The beautiful thing about writing, is that you can write whatever the fuck you want.*' That was the moment my writing changed, I found my author voice and I blew through the writing process. You will never know what your small words of encouragement did to me. You were always a phone call away for advice and you believed in me as an amateur author. I hope you know how much that meant to me and how much *you* mean to me.

Cathryn Carter, I don't even know where to start. You're the best cheerleader a girl could ask for. Thank you for always being there to answer my questions and cheering me on with every post or message. Most of all, thank you for making this book as perfect as it is and formatting it so beautifully for me.

My incredibly talented cover designer, Emily Wittig. I vividly remember telling Kelse and Briel that I will not write a book unless you designed the cover. You came through and took a chance on me as a brand-new author and it became everything, I have ever dreamed it would be. Your talent is unmatched. Thank you endlessly for doing this, and mostly, for your friendship.

My alpha and beta readers. You have no idea how much it means to me that you took a chance on a draft and loved it as much as you did. The ideas you presented as you read, and little changes, made this book what it is. Thank you all for the time you spent reading this for me.

Bookstagram: I started as a book blogger. I started here reading an insane amount of spicy romance books and then randomly decided to write a book. From the outside looking in, that might sound absolutely absurd. But you welcomed me with open arms. Your excitement brought me to life. Your support as I transitioned from blogger to author was nothing less than amazing. It was the most nerve-wracking thing I have ever done, and you made me feel at ease.

Thank you everyone for taking a chance on my debut novel. You truly have no idea how much it means to me. Someone needs to wake me up because I can't believe that I WROTE A BOOK.

ABOUT THE AUTHOR

Jenn McMahon resides along the shore in New Jersey with her husband, Daniel, two children, Zachary and Owen, and two dogs, Cooper and Piper. She has spent the last couple of years engrossed in romance books and finding the best book boyfriends out there, to now writing her own and sharing them with the world. When Jenn is not writing, she can be found reading, watching reruns of her favorite TV shows (Scandal, Grey's Anatomy and Friends—just to name a few), or petting her dog. She also loves taking trips to the beach with the kids, Atlantic City date nights with her husband, and thunderstorms in the spring.

COMING SOON

Are you itching for more from this amazing friend's group? The second book in the series will feature our sweet Marc, and wild child Avery. Marc needs a fake fiancé to help him lock in the deal of a lifetime. Avery wants nothing to do with a relationship, she's only here for a good time.

Coming August, 2023 is a spicy, fake dating, opposites attract romance —*That First Date*, which is now available for preorder.

Printed in Great Britain
by Amazon

21112508R00203